YUKON JUSTICE

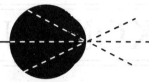

**This Large Print Book carries the
Seal of Approval of N.A.V.H.**

THE HOLTS: AN AMERICAN DYNASTY VOLUME SEVEN

YUKON JUSTICE

DANA FULLER ROSS

G.K.HALL &CO.
Boston, Massachusetts
1992

Published in large Print by arrangement with Book Creations, Inc.

G.K. Hall Large Print Book Series.

Printed on acid free paper in the United States of America.

Set in 16 pt Plantin.

Library of Congress Cataloging-in-Publication Data

Ross, Dana Fuller.
    Yukon justice / Dana Fuller Ross.
       p.   cm.—(The Holts—an American dynasty ; v. 7)
(G.K. Hall large print series)
    ISBN 0-8161-5487-2 (lg. print).—ISBN 0-8161-5488-0
(pbk. : lg. print)
    1. Large type books.   I. Title.   II. Series; Ross,
Dana Fuller. Holts—an American dynasty : v. 7.
[PS3513.E8679Y8 1992]
813'.54—dc20   92-15296

Oklahoma!

The Holts: An American Dynasty
Oregon Legacy
Oklahoma Pride
Carolina Glory
Hawaii Heritage
Sierra Triumph

Wagons West The Frontier Trilogy

Westward!

I

Monterey, California, March 1897

Frank Blake got up out of the raccoon-style nest
he had built for himself in the hollowed-out trunk
of an old redwood. He stretched, arms out flung,
and let the salt wind blow the sleep out of his head.
On the rocks below the point, the sea lions were
barking, arfing like a pen full of spaniels. Mating
season, Frank thought with a grin.

The breeze ruffled his sandy hair and whispered
through the stubble of beard he was beginning to
grow. He was tall and broad shouldered, muscular
with youth and a winter spent working at whatever
he could come by. Not quite nineteen, Frank was
also good-looking enough that chophouse
waitresses often slipped an extra biscuit onto his
plate.

Frank poked up the embers of his fire, which
was shielded against the constant wind by the hollow of the tree, and put his coffeepot on it. He
stretched once more, then cracked his knuckles
and wriggled his neck and backbone into line. It
felt good to be alive this first morning on the road
again.

Frank had spent the winter in the agricultural
country around Point Sur, far enough north from

the town of Sierra to be fairly certain that whatever might have been sicced on him from there wasn't going to find him. On the farm where he had stayed, he built a pig trough, learned to cane a chair, helped to raise a barn, replaced a rotted stoop, and in the process became a fairly decent jackleg carpenter. He could have stayed on longer—the farm was too much for the widow who owned it—but Frank had known uneasily that his relationship with her was moving toward more than carpentry, and it was time to go.

Besides, rumors were still coming down from the north, the reports flickering through the invisible wires of the railroad boomers' telegraph and the hoboes' grapevine. The words were just bits in the wind, like melting ice, but with a flake of something substantial at the core: gold, they said, in the Yukon Territory. It had been as good a reason as any to go, with spring coming.

Lately Frank hadn't been able to shake loose the feeling that he was the target for something out of Sierra. He doubted that Sanford Rutledge was looking for him. Although the old man had blown up his own oil refinery just to close it down, he hadn't been jailed for it— Frank read the papers—so Rutledge had gotten away with it. Frank didn't suppose his brother, Peter, or his father gave a flying damn where he was. His mother might be a different case, Frank thought, feeling guilty. Now that he was moving on, he would send her a note to let her know that he was all right. He'd be long gone from Point Sur before she could hire anybody to come out and find him.

While the coffee boiled and the remains of the previous night's stew heated in a tin pie plate, Frank shrugged out of his greatcoat—except for his boots, it was the last relic of the Hargreaves Academy, a promising career, and some other life. He buttoned up one of the wool shirts that the widow had pulled out of a clothespress for him. After he drank the scalding-hot coffee and polished off the stew, he picked up his bindle—his bedroll of coat and blanket, with pots inside—and looked up the coast. Monterey was only a few miles away. The canneries and the fishing boats promised work, and there was a rail yard for transportation. Whistling, he started off. At the tip of the point, he stopped to bark back at the sea lions, then headed toward the main road.

For a Tuesday morning in March, the road seemed unusually congested with foot and horse traffic. Frank tried to think if it was some holiday, some sacred family event he had overlooked, the way he had forgotten Thanksgiving the previous autumn. He had knocked on a door to ask for work and seen past the housewife into a farm kitchen. Scrubbed children sat gathered around a table laden with turkey, steaming corn, and sweet potatoes. The startled woman had handed him a plate and left him to eat it, mortified, on the back stoop.

No celebration of the sort came to mind now as he neared the town. And it was too early in the year for the politicians to be gearing up again. Enlightenment dawned as two small boys darted by with their older sister in pursuit.

"Come on, Angela!" the younger boy piped. "We'll miss the elephants!"

"You wait up, Harry!" She irritably made a grab at his overalls. "You aren't going to miss any elephants. How're you going to miss something the size of a house?"

The older boy turned in the road and stuck out his tongue at her. "Maybe they'll give me a job. Then I won't have to listen to you no more!"

His sister gave him a look of scorn. "Oh, sure. You're going to run away with the circus and tame lions. More likely, you'll end up like him." She jerked her thumb in Frank's direction.

Frank chuckled. "That's right, bud. It gets mighty cold at night. You listen to your sis."

The girl stared at him as if a piece of the scenery had spoken. She swooped down on the boys and hustled them away.

Frank found the circus workers setting up tents in a meadow on the inland side of town, where a row of eucalyptus trees blunted the cold Pacific wind. A canvas banner snapped between two poles. It read: Pierce Brothers and Gryphon Circus. The horses and big cats were still being paraded through town from their cars in the rail yard, but the elephants were already at work. Huge and purposeful, they pulled bundles of tent poles as heavy as ships' masts. Nearby, the menagerie, dressing tents, and the sideshow canvas were going up. The sideshow unfurled a banner listing its inducements: the bearded woman and the tattooed lady, the fattest man, and the blood-sweating hippopotamus. A canvas mural depicted the hippopotamus, its mouth agape.

Frank stared, enthralled. A red-haired fellow who looked to be Frank's age and wore a python around his neck stepped out of the tent opposite the sideshow.

On impulse, Frank called to him, "I'm looking for work."

"See the manager." The boy pointed at an unmarked wagon. He looked Frank up and down, his fingers caressing the python's head. "He don't hire hoboes."

"I've been doing carpentry around Point Sur," Frank told the manager before he, too, could say he didn't hire hoboes. "I can build pretty much anything you're likely to need."

"I don't need a carpenter," the manager said. He had brilliantined hair, as sleek as if it had been painted on his skull. He reminded Frank of the sea lions. "But I hire locals to clean up after the elephants. If you want to shovel your way to fame, you can tell Steele I said to put you on."

"Who's Steele?"

"Ask anybody." The manager turned back to his desk.

Steele proved to be a wiry little man, slightly bent over and completely bald, with ears like a leprechaun's. He handed Frank a shovel. "Once

5

an hour," he instructed. "In between, you do whatever I need you for."

"Sure," Frank agreed.

"A dollar a day for two days, and we give you meals. You eat with the roustabouts."

"Fine," Frank said.

"Accommodating, ain't you?"

Frank laughed. "I'm fulfilling a long-standing dream. Who wouldn't want to say he had worked the circus?" He shouldered his shovel and went off, whistling, to the elephants. He stopped to watch the big top shake itself outward, and begin to rise.

When Frank came back, Steele was mending a red leather bridle with a harnessmaker's kit. Frank leaned on his shovel. "I see why you hire locals. Nobody would shovel this much shit on a regular basis. You ever figure it out in cubic yards?"

"Why in hell would I want to?" Steele inquired.

"Scientific curiosity."

Steele snorted. "Hand me them scissors." He snipped off the waxed thread. "Here, take this to Gilda. And don't give her any backchat—she'd bite your head off."

Gilda, Frank knew from the posters plastered on every fence, was the equestrienne, the star of the bareback act. He found her in the pad room, a rectangular tent that held dressing space and the performing horses.

"And who the hell are you?" Gilda had im-probably bronze-colored hair piled high and secured with three egret feathers. She wore a blue-and red-spangled basque and blue tights on shapely legs.

"I work for Steele," Frank said. He supposed he did. "That's an awfully pretty outfit."

Gilda shut the canvas flap in his face, but Frank heard her giggling.

He started back to Steele, taking the long way so that he could look around. The big top was up, and the calliope outside it was playing "Camptown Races." The midway was crowded with people waiting for the show and trying to catch a glimpse of the clowns and the tightrope walkers. Frank liked how it felt to be a part of it, to be on the inside looking out. He set his cap on the back of his head and stopped by the pit show to look at large glass tanks full of snakes, lizards, and a small, depressed-looking alligator. A woman in black and green tights was climbing into the biggest of the tanks while the red-haired boy set up his ticket booth at the tent door. The python was still draped around his shoulders.

"She's mighty beautiful," Frank said. The snake woman pretended not to have heard, but she simpered. Frank stroked the python's head. "How long is she?" The snake woman shot him a scathing look.

"Near ten feet," the red-haired boy answered, thawing a little. "You get a job?"

"Sort of," Frank said. "I'm the shovel man." The snake woman sniffed derisively. Frank looked across the road at the sideshow. "What in tarnation is a blood-sweating hippopotamus?"

"A plain old regular hippo," the boy replied. "They all give off some kind of gunk that looks like blood, out of their hide. It's pretty cold today, though. They don't do it if they're cold. Then all the marks get mad and want their money back." He climbed onto the ticket wagon and settled the python more dramatically around his shoulders.

The snake lady picked up a pair of smallish king snakes.

"If you're waiting for the big circus to open, you need wait no more!" The boy adjusted his panama hat to a rakish angle. "The reptile show, the monster show, is now open for your entertainment, education, and edification. You'll see creatures gathered from swamps, deserts, and jungle lands from every corner of the globe! Wilhelmina Serpentina walks among them! How does she live? How can she live, in the pit with these deadly reptiles—hissing, twisting, creeping, crawling, coiling, crushing reptiles! You'll see snakes so long, so strong, they could swallow whole the largest creature alive just as easily as you or I could swallow a pea! The largest and most complete exhibit of reptiles ever taken on tour by any exposition in the history of the world—"

People began to file in, handing over a nickel for a ticket. Frank watched, impressed, as the boy made change and tore tickets without pausing for breath.

"Hey! Kid! First of May! Get your tail over

here!" Steele popped around the side of the reptile tent and glared at Frank. "If I have to come looking for you again, you're out!"

"I'm sorry," Frank said contritely. "I got interested. It's a whole world of its own here, all self-contained. It's fascinating."

"You ain't gonna be in it long if you keep lollygagging."

"Sorry." Frank picked up his shovel. "What does First of May mean?"

"New hire. Out here we hit the circuit in March, but it don't matter. And you ain't even that, strictly speaking."

"I could be," Frank said. "I need the work. I can do pretty much anything you need." By now it had dawned on him that Steele was a power in this circus, a central point around which its inner workings revolved.

Once again Frank went down the line of tethered elephants. Seen close up, they were amazing beasts, huge and wrinkled. A trainer on a ladder was renewing the painted designs across a ponderous head. Something nuzzled Frank's ears, and his cap sailed off. The trainer guffawed as the elephant presented it to him. "Got me a new hat."

Frank grinned. "How do you get him to do that?"

"Like this." The trainer made some motion, and the elephant took the cap back and dropped it in the muck.

Frank picked it up gingerly. "Nice trick." He swished it out in a water tub, then emptied the tub under the trainer's ladder so he would have to climb down in the mud. If this was a form of initiation, it was probably better to fight fire with fire. While keeping a good grip on the cap, Frank rubbed the elephant's surprisingly soft trunk.

After he had finished with the elephants and wheeled his barrow away, the other trainers began to dress their beasts. Frank sneaked away from Steele long enough to watch. The elephants were more bespangled than their riders, with jeweled headdresses and velvet howdahs. Silk tassels bobbed from their trappings, and their bright eyes looked out from concentric circles of lime green, fuchsia, and scarlet.

The first show was at one o'clock. Frank watched it from the inside out and as he was able, between running errands for Steele: finding more oil for the burners that warmed the reptile tanks, conveying an order to the roustabouts to tighten the ropes on the menagerie tent, carrying a sandwich and a glass of milk to the youngest of the aerialists.

Frank watched the high-wire performers bending and stretching like ballet dancers at the bar, heard the applause and the fanfare as they pranced, bowing, to the center of the ring. He folded his arms and closed his eyes, imagining what it would be like to soar through the air, like the daring young man on the flying trapeze. The tune of that song came back to him, and he whistled it until Steele grabbed his arm and informed

10

him that it wasn't any better luck to whistle back-stage at a circus than it was in a theater.

"Lord God, you're green!"

"I can learn," Frank said. "No whistling. I've got that down."

"I don't need anybody," Steele retorted. Suddenly a furious squabble erupted from in front of the reptile tent. "Unless you think you might grow breasts," he added.

"I'm an artist! You try to treat me like some cooch dancer!" Wilhelmina Serpentina, the lady whom Frank had seen writhing sinuously among the boas in the pit show, stomped in a rage from the tent.

"You are a cooch dancer," the red-haired boy said. "What do you think this is, the opera?"

Nearly all the customers were under the big top now, and the front people, the popcorn sellers and sideshow crews, took a break to listen.

"You treat me this way, and I'll just take my talent somewhere else!" Wilhelmina shrieked.

"You haven't got any talent!"

"I'll tell management how you've treated me!"

Steele sighed. "I knew we shouldn't have hired that one. All she's supposed to do is walk around with a bunch of snakes, for God's sake. But she's had elocution lessons and theatrical training, and she thinks she's Ada Rehan." He stalked over. "Willie, shut up and get back in with them snakes, or I'll fire you."

"My name ain't Willie."

"It is while you got this job."

11

"And that's another thing. I want my own billing."

Steele jammed his cap down over his bald head. "I'll mention it to management." He glared across the way at the tattooed lady of the sideshow, who was watching from a deck chair. "And you put some clothes on or get inside. This ain't supposed to be free."

The tattooed lady uncoiled her resplendent limbs and pulled a wrapper on.

"They're like a bunch of kids," Steele muttered. "They're as bad as the performers. Worse maybe. They all want to be performers, and they start with the temperament."

Frank was puzzled. "Aren't they performers?"

"Naw, these folks are just plain carny. The performers are the main-tent show, the big acts. They don't talk to the front people. They won't talk to you, either, so don't try it."

"Gilda talked to me," Frank said. "Sort of."

Steele chuckled. "I'll bet. Gilda's about as sweet as a wolverine."

"That little aerialist talked to me. She thanked me for the sandwich."

"She's only twelve. She don't know better yet," Steele said. "She's a nice little kid. Her folks have been flyers for over fifty years. The Flying Le-Vitas."

"How do you get a job? How do you get to be an act? Is there some school?"

"You're born to it," Steele said, "if you're in one of the real acts. Or you devil somebody long

12

enough. If they think you got promise, they'll train you." He looked Frank up and down. "You don't want to be a circus brat. You got folks somewhere. Here in town, I reckon."

"I'm too old to be a circus brat," Frank said. "And I've got folks on the other side of the country. I've been on the road for over a year."

"Hoo! Big time. What've you done?"

"Carpentry. Cow punching. Jackline tender in the oil fields. Horse breaking. Canning fish. Picking lettuce. Riding the rods."

"Don't stick with much, do you?" Steele said, but he looked impressed.

Frank chuckled. "The circus being such a stick-in-the-mud job."

"Aw, go get your dinner," Steele said. "Show's out. You got half an hour."

Dinner was served in a chow tent set up at the rear of the lot. The tables were unmarked, but a clearly defined hierarchy existed. At the central table were the office people, ticket takers, ringmaster, and manager with his brilliantined hair. Around them in concentric rings were the star performers—Gilda and the Flying LeVitas and the lion tamer—and then the lesser lights, followed by the front people from the sideshow and the "butchers" from the food booths. Finally, at the outer tables sat the roustabouts and the locals hired for a dollar a day and a chance to gawk before the circus moved on. There were two local hirelings besides Frank—boys of maybe fifteen, still in short pants, staring avidly at the other tables.

Because the food was eaten by management as well as by the others, it was tolerable; but Frank barely noticed. Like the younger boys, he was staring at everyone else, especially at the Vespaccis, a family of Italian bicyclists with muscular legs and peaked sequined caps. Nearby, the little aerialist of the Flying LeVitas saw him from across the tent and waved. She wore tights and leotard and a fringed sash. She had the same ring of milk around her mouth that Frank's sister, Midge, always managed to get. I've got to write to Midge, he thought.

The second show was at eight in the evening, and after the tent and grounds had been cleaned up, Steele showed Frank the bunk tent where the roustabouts slept. "I ain't supposed to do this. Locals go home and sleep, but since you ain't got a home—"

"You're the soul of kindness," Frank said. "Allow me to kiss your ring."

"Shut up and go to sleep," Steele growled. "Four poles is at five A.M."

"I hear and obey."

Steele snorted. He went away without telling Frank what four poles meant.

Frank grinned. He already knew; the red-haired kid had warned him. All those who didn't have their own acts—the butchers, the roustabouts, the local hirelings—were expected to help set up the main tent every morning before breakfast. After the people who knew what they were doing had the center poles in place, everyone else hauled up the baled canvas and helped to drive five-foot-long tent stakes. On the second day all they did was check for blow downs and tighten rigging; but still it was a miserable, nasty job in the pitch dark and mud. That was why it was the peons' responsibility.

Four poles also served as the wake-up call for the whole encamped show, as Frank learned the next morning. At the call of "Four poles!" Frank stumbled out into darkness, pulling on his trousers as he went. An elephant trumpeted. Another and another answered with the stentorian sound of an orchestra's horn section run amok. Next the big cats began to roar, and the twelve trained poodles who jumped through hoops for the dog act began to yip. Finally the horses neighed, and the donkey act brayed.

In the darkness Frank fell over a dog and cursed. Ahead of him in the thinning blackness he could see the outline of the tent. It loomed like a ghostly whale, humping itself up into the sky. Half of it had come loose in a blow down during the night. Frank ran up and steadied poles where people told him to, swung a sledge on the stakes as instructed, and tried to figure out what exactly everyone else was doing. With canvas folds flapping everywhere, it was difficult to see more than his own end. By the time the big top was up, he still wasn't quite sure how it had been accomplished, but it was impressive.

Frank stood inside, his head tipped back, and

turned slowly to watch the dawn sun come through the canvas high above his head. The light slid over the rigging and spilled a rosy wash down the far wall.

"Not a bad job, kid," Steele said. "I watched you."

Frank, surprised, smiled at him.

"Don't let it go to your head. It just means you know how to take orders."

Frank chuckled. "I've had a fair amount of practice. My dad's in the army."

If Steele had been going to answer, he was forestalled by the snake lady. Wilhelmina Serpentina, wrapped in a kimono, tore up to Steele in the semidarkness. "Where is he? Where is that little brat? If he thinks I'm going to feed all them snakes for him and clean their cages, he's got another think coming!"

"Simmer down," Steele said. "He probably overslept. If you're too delicate to pry him out of bed, I'll send someone over."

"I already went to chase him out of there!" Wilhelmina shrieked. The snake wagon included a small sleeping compartment for its attendant. The reptiles were tricky to keep alive and didn't take well to cold weather. "He let the oil burner go out, too," she said triumphantly.

"Goddamn it, if Tommy's gone on another bender—" Steele glared at Frank. "You were getting to be pals with him. Where's he gone?"

Frank threw up his hands. "No idea."

"Well, go find him. I got to go warm up them

16

snakes. Nobody else in the whole dang show knows a iguana from the back end of a boa." Steele gave Wilhelmina a scathing look.

Wilhelmina sniffed. "I'm an artist."

"And I'm a blue-bottomed baboon. Get on over to the ticket wagon and keep the rubes from robbing us blind. I reckon you can handle that."

Frank watched him stomp off. Steele's nominal title was troupe manager for the Pierce Brothers and Gryphon Circus, and what that amounted to was being able to draw on a lifetime of experience to spot what was wrong before anyone else did, then fix it before management even worried about it.

Where was Tommy? Frank wondered. Wasn't he worried about his snakes? Frank recalled that at dinner Tommy had sat as far away from the seething Wilhelmina as he could get and muttered about women. Combining that with Steele's remark about "another" bender, Frank concluded that Tommy had gone to town and was probably asleep in a ditch.

Frank strolled past the sideshow, waved at the tattooed lady, who was having her morning coffee in her deck chair, and headed for town. All the roadhouses were between the circus's meadow and Monterey. There wasn't anything in the other direction but farms, and he didn't think Tommy had had time yet to get in hot water with a farmer's daughter.

Frank peered in the darkened window of the first roadhouse he came to—Monterey was a hard-drinking town and had plenty—and saw nothing but upended chairs. He peered into the unmowed grass around the back, the most likely place to dump a drunk. Tommy wasn't there. The grass was wreathed with the shiny leaves of poison oak, so Frank backed away carefully. If Tommy was lying in the midst of that, he could get himself out.

Frank set out again toward town and in a quarter mile came upon a beer wagon up on the shoulder. The four-horse team appeared slightly puzzled but mouthed grass through their bits. A thunderous snore erupted periodically from the driver's seat. Frank climbed the steps and found Tommy sprawled, mouth open, on the seat. Resisting the urge to drop a beetle in Tommy's mouth, Frank shook him instead.

Tommy opened his eyes and said, "Are we home?" then closed them again.

Frank looked at him in disgust. He supposed he could carry Tommy a mile back to the circus if he had to, but he was darned if he would. And where had Tommy gotten the beer wagon? Frank poked him. "Whose wagon?"

"Dunno." Tommy rolled over. His red hair stuck up in spikes.

Frank poked him again. "Then why'd you take it?"

"Didn't know the way back," Tommy mumbled. "Too drunk."

"So you figured somebody else's horses would know?" Frank threw up his hands. "Never mind."

He looked at the beer wagon. The back was loaded with kegs, and the driver's seat was shaded by a canvas umbrella painted with the brewer's name. Conspicuous was an understatement. On the other hand, it was only six in the morning. No one was around to see them.

Frank shook out the reins, and the Percherons plodded obediently to the road. Frank, trying to look like the authorized driver, tipped his cap to a passing farmer whose wagon was loaded with piglets.

A little while later, Frank was tethering the team across the road from the circus. He slung an empty water bucket over one arm, to get water for the horses. Then he threw Tommy over the other shoulder and hauled him back toward the reptile show. Pressed for any better idea, he threw Tommy into the hippo's tank, then waited until he surfaced.

The tattooed lady appeared at Frank's shoulder, and they watched Tommy clamber out.

"I don't know what to do with the beer wagon," Frank said.

"What beer wagon?" Tommy asked.

"Don't worry, boys—they'll find it," the tattooed lady assured them. She pulled the morning newspaper from under her arm.

Frank looked at the headline: "Brewery Wagon Stolen. Daring Midnight Theft. Statewide Search."

Tommy groaned. He turned and fled, dripping, into the reptile tent. Frank and the woman heard

19

him wailing to Steele. His voice dropped abruptly and was followed by the unsavory sounds of someone being sick.

"Tommy's got a problem," the tattooed lady said placidly. "When he gets on one of these jags, nothing breaks it off but some jail time. He's been working up to it for a couple of weeks. He'll tell you it's all Wilhelmina fault, but no woman ever drove a man to drink if he didn't want to go."

"Somebody's not going to be happy about that beer wagon," Frank said.

"Anyone know you have it?"

"We passed a farmer on the road."

Tommy evidently shared Frank's opinion. When the hippo pool, a pot of the tattooed lady's coffee, and Steele's tirade—arguably the most effective of the three—had sobered him up enough to resume his responsibilities outside the pit show, he did so with his panama hat pulled as low over his eyes as it would go. Anxiously he scanned the crowd for helmets and badges. To cover the lower half of his face, he kept attempting to persuade the python to abandon its usual place around his shoulders in favor of coiling about his chin instead. The constant motion of pulling the hat down and the snake up persuaded the townspeople that he had some kind of twitch, and they began to edge away.

Finally, in disgust, Steele sent him to shovel manure with Frank and took over the pit show himself.

"Steele started out with three blacksnakes and

a half-starved boa in a carny when he was thirteen," Tommy complained. "Never shuts up about it, either. It makes me crazy. Where's that wagon?"

"Right where I left it," Frank answered. "I went back and gave the horses some grain and water, though."

"You idiot!" Tommy cast a hunted look over his shoulder. "Why didn't you leave it where you found it?"

"I might ask you the same thing," Frank said. "If I'd left it, I'd have had to leave you."

"Statewide search." Tommy groaned. "Oh, God."

Frank laughed. "Doesn't give you much faith in the Monterey police, does it? I expect they'll come through eventually."

Tommy pulled the hat farther down over his ears.

The Monterey police apparently believed that the daring midnight hijacker would be far into the next county by now, not hiding under his hat behind an elephant. The lawmen finally found the wagon, although it took them awhile. Eventually the farmer who had passed Frank and Tommy on the road got around to mentioning it, and the police arrived across from the circus. They had brought the brewery driver, who duly identified his wagon. When the police demanded that all red-haired members of the troupe present themselves, the driver pointed at Tommy as the man who had staggered out of Aunt Lilah's Roadhouse half an hour before the brewery driver had noticed his wagon was missing.

"He didn't have any business leaving the wagon unattended out there while he got soused," Tommy protested.

But the policemen were unmoved by that defense and took Tommy away. At dinner that night, Frank, concerned about when Tommy would be released, talked to the tattooed lady.

"He'll catch up to the show in a month or two, after they turn him loose," she predicted. "It's happened before, which is why Steele's so riled. Most of us enjoy a nip now and then, but we're supposed to keep quiet about it." She cocked her head at him and flexed the Oriental landscape that adorned her throat. "You want to have a little shot with me? You got a few minutes before Steele'll be looking for you, and I like to have a nip to warm me up before I go on."

"Sure."

Frank followed her to the sideshow tent, where she produced two bottles—one of liquor, the other containing skin oil—from the painted wooden chest upon which she posed for the public.

The woman took a sip from the bottle, then passed it to Frank. "That's better. It takes more than oil heaters to warm all this skin." She slipped out of her kimono and stretched kaleidoscopic arms and legs. A mane of brown hair pinned into a knot on her head was the only solid-colored area on her body. Her costume below consisted of a short, draped bathing skirt that grazed the tops of her thighs above a fire-breathing dragon (left thigh) and a representation of the Tower of Babel (right thigh). Above, she wore a modified harem jacket with no sleeves or back. It stopped short just below her voluptuous breasts and above the sailing ship that cut through turquoise waters across her midriff. Oddly enough, she looked fully dressed. Frank thought it must be all the tattoos. They seemed like clothes—sleeves of flowers, stockings of tigers. He took a sip from the bottle and passed it back.

She took another swallow. "They call me Illuminata," she said, "but that's really just a stage moniker for the show. My name's Lil."

"I'm Frank." He sat next to her on the wooden chest. "How'd you get to be a tattooed lady?"

"I like the colors. You know?" She flexed her fingers, multihued and splendid. "All my folks were carny people, and there aren't too many tattooed ladies. Tattooed men are a dime a dozen." She sniffed her disdain for tattooed men. "But ladies—we're a rarity. I've been working on my show for ten years now, and I've pretty much used up all my canvas, you know? There're some pieces under my costume that are still blank, but they won't let me show them."

"Oh."

"I'd like to get them done anyway. I feel kind of naked with bare skin." She passed him the bottle again, and he stared, fascinated by the blooming garden on her right forearm, which grew out of the city of white-domed buildings that circled her wrist.

"That's the skyline of Jerusalem," she said, following his gaze. "My art's real educational. Over here on my back I got Columbus discovering America." She turned and displayed a man in doublet and hose standing upon the rocky promontory of a shoulder blade. The colors rippled as she moved. She poured a palmful of oil from the other bottle and began to rub it in.

The tent flap opened, and the bearded lady came in, twirling her handlebar mustache. She nodded politely to Frank and settled herself in her chair to groom her beard with a comb. The world's fattest man heaved himself through the door, behind the genuine giant from Borneo. The two-headed calf, dead and pickled in a large vat, was already in place.

"Here we go," Illuminata said, standing. "Better scram. Steele will be after you." She tucked her bottles in the chest, then stood on top of it.

The barker outside had begun his spiel. "See the living, breathing, human wonders of the world! The only show of its kind ever to be taken on tour—"

Frank paused at the back door to wave. The oil lamps reflected off Illuminata's glowing lubricated skin. She looked like a stained-glass window.

A hand emerged from the darkness and yanked Frank the rest of the way through the tent door.

"For God's sake, don't you get tangled up with her."

"I was just looking for you," Frank told Steele.

"Well, you ain't gonna find me coiled around that hussy's belly button. You want work or not?"

Frank sighed. "I hear, obey, and shovel."

Steele studied him. "We're pulling up tonight. You still want to run off and join the circus?"

"I already ran off," Frank pointed out.

"Don't get smart. The local police ain't about to let Tommy out on bail; they know he'll skip with the show. And he ain't any use to me till he's been in jail long enough to get repentant. That generally takes a couple months, minimum."

"Does he get religion, or just sick of jail?" Frank asked.

Steele chuckled. "A little of both. His dad was a preacher. One of them weird sects that used to handle rattlers during services. You know anything about snakes?"

"Not like that," Frank said. "I went to a pretty tame church. I'm a quick study, though."

"I may be nuts," Steele said, considering Frank's handsome profile, "but maybe you could handle Wilhelmina. You're good looking enough to put in the ticket wagon—probably draw the ladies better'n Tommy did. If you can learn the spiel and keep your hand out of the till, you got a job."

"Thanks!" Frank grinned happily. "What do I do?"

"Clean out the snake cages before we strike camp," Steele said.

"A lot of this business is shoveling up after critters, isn't it?"

"Yeah, but I'll help you till you got the hang of it." Steele chuckled. "We got six hundred horses with this outfit. Be grateful you got snakes."

"Oh, I am," Frank muttered.

Within the hour he was finished with the last cage under Steele's instruction. Its inhabitant, a rosy boa, twined affectionately around his arm. He scratched the boa's head before he put it back. Frank felt considerably friendlier toward the boa than he had toward the cobra, which had coiled itself into a corner, sullenly raising its hood now and then for effect while Frank reached in with a gloved hand. Now he and Steele began packing the heavy glass cages into the reptile wagon. The last show was over, and the roustabouts were pulling the canvas down.

"Remember to keep the heaters going," Steele warned. "That's why your sleeping box is in the reptile wagon."

Wilhelmina had her own bed in a foldout corner of the ticket wagon, where she was now, presumably doing her nails or reading great literature.

"I'll remember." Frank had discovered that circus workers spent much of their time trying to keep the exhibits warm. Many of the menagerie animals were tropical beasts.

"Practice that spiel, too," Steele said. "You get tongue-tied in the middle tomorrow, you're out."

Frank, having heard both Steele's and Tommy's

26

patter, thought he had it pretty well down. Then the man's last sentence registered on Frank. "Tomorrow?"

"You don't think we waste a day on the road, do you?" Steele shook his head despairingly.

Frank, closing the gates of the reptile wagon, looked around to discover that the entire circus was dismantled and ready to move. Canvas, animals, and performers all were stowed in the red and gilt wagons. The work teams were hitched, and hostlers were settling into their boxes.

Frank, unwilling to miss anything, climbed up beside the reptile-wagon driver. The darkened town receded behind them.

At the railroad yard, the teams were unhitched, and the wagons rolled up ramps onto the circus's flatcars. The elephants, marching nose to tail, lumbered aboard their own cars. The performers climbed into the passenger coaches. Then the engine whistle shrieked, and steam puffed up around its drive wheels. Frank climbed into his sleeping box but left the door open so he could see what was going on. The rail yard was lit by the dim globes of signal lights—blue, red, and green.

Steele trotted by, bent on some last-minute errand. He glanced up at Frank. "You okay, kid?" he yelled.

"Sure!" Frank shouted. "Okay!"

Wilhelmina pained voice came from her sleeping box. "Some of us would like to get some sleep."

Frank rolled on his back, hands clasped under his head. It felt odd to be on a train again, not stretched out flat and holding on for dear life or sprawled in some boxcar, but traveling on the plush. A bed in a circus wagon certainly counted as on the plush. It was cozy, like being in a shoe box, and he could see the night slide by outside his window. The wagons had dutch doors that opened top and bottom, like Gypsy caravans. The train lurched and began to move, depot lights rolling by. This was the way to go, Frank thought, just rolling north on the plush. . . .

He was half-asleep when it occurred to him that he had no particular reason to assume that they were going north, other than that it was the way he wanted to go. He got up, balancing on the swaying flatcar with the ease of one who has ridden the roofs, and pounded on Wilhelmina's door.

"Hey, Wilhelmina! Where are we going?" His words fell away into the rush and the roar of the night, so he shouted again, louder.

Wilhelmina opened the top of her door. "You're going straight to perdition if you don't shut up and let me sleep!"

"Where's the train going, Wilhelmina?" Frank balanced himself with a hand on her wagon wheel.

She glared at him. Her hair was pinned up in curlpapers, and her skin was smeared with green night cream. "Where do you want to go?"

"North," Frank said. "Come on, be a sport. Are we going north?"

Wilhelmina smiled. "We're headed for Seattle." She shut the door.

Frank woke with a jolt when his wagon rolled down from the flatcar. He peered out. It was still pitch dark, but the hostlers were hitching up the teams. This couldn't be Seattle, he thought, not already. He rubbed his eyes, combed his hair back with his fingers, then stuck his head out the wagon door. "Hey! Where are we?"

The hostler hitching up the wagon looked over his shoulder. "Bakersfield, First of May. Better get ready to roll."

"Bakersfield!" Frank yelped. "I thought we were going to Seattle. Isn't the show going to Seattle?"

The hostler chortled. "Sure it is, kid. Ain't you got no patience?"

Suspicion began to dawn on Frank. He looked balefully at Wilhelmina's wagon. "When is it going to Seattle?"

"Round about July," the hostler said. "It's our midseason stop."

II

The Pierce Brothers and Gryphon Circus was a "railroad show," an emblem of modernity and big-city allure. It differed from the "mud shows" that traveled by wagon only in that it could be slightly choosier in its stops. Towns too small to draw a good crowd could be bypassed. The advance men, working two weeks ahead of the troupe, knew it all—the prevailing weather, the crops and harvest dates, even the paydays, and booked the circus into each town accordingly: two shows a day and one on Sunday, clear through the season. Each town was plastered with posters by the billboarders two weeks in advance.

"When do you sleep?" Frank asked Steele.

"In the winter," the man replied.

Bakersfield was flat and dusty until the laborers were striking the canvas after the second show. Then the skies opened and rain poured down, rendering the town flat and muddy. So were Visalia and Fresno. The San Joaquin Valley was an agricultural belt. Sprawling farms coalesced around towns that appeared to have been plunked down at random in the middle of the land, one settlement per so many square miles to supply feed and dry goods and entertainment—traveling preachers, theater stock companies, and the circus. To the circus people, these villages were insubstantial, temporary illusions, coming to life only for the day the show stopped there, fading to mist again as soon as the show pulled out. The circus people carried the real world wrapped around them. It moved as they moved, and they saw very little beyond it.

The circus issued route cards for only two weeks at a time, and the current one stopped with Sacramento. In Fresno Frank had finally achieved the same latitude at which he had joined the show in Monterey. By what arcane formula the advance men had chosen a route that dropped south of Bakersfield, he had never found out. It certainly had no basis in linear geographical logic.

In Fresno the men set up their canvas in a strong wind, uneasily eyeing a funnel cloud that lurked on the horizon. The advance men, walking encyclopedias of geographical knowledge, said that these funnels never amounted to anything out there in the valley. But the sky seemed shaky, like something half-jelled and quivering. The animals hated it. The big cats, their fur electrified, roared and fussed. The horses laid their ears back, and even the hippo was moody, rolling her small, frightened eyes at the sky. Uneasy, Frank watched the swaying canvas of the big top and wondered how long it would take to get to Seattle.

The wind snatched Frank's panama hat and sailed it over the heads of the crowd gathering around his ticket wagon. "If you're waiting for the big show to open, wait no more! The reptile show, the monster show is open!" He let his hat go, and the wind lifted his hair and whispered in his ears. "Alive and deadly! Wilhelmina Serpentina walks among them! Thank you, go right in." Frank took nickels, tore tickets, let the patter flow, and smiled at the girls. The crowd stepped right up, eager to be amazed and educated, to see the deadly reptiles from six continents. He was getting good at this.

Frank glanced over at the big top, its seven flags snapping in the wind. The structure looked solid, too stable for a blow down. Presumably the advance men were right, and the funnel cloud would fizzle. The townies didn't seem worried. Frank peered at the horizon. For a tornado, it was pretty halfhearted. Oh, beat it, he thought. You're just a dust devil.

"Hey, Blake!"

Frank peered into the crowd and saw a man pushing forward, toward him. The fellow had a beer belly draped over his blue jeans and a felt hat wedged down over his ears against the wind. After a second his identity clicked into Frank's mind: Rafferty. He had been another jackline tender for Sierra Oil.

"What are you doing here, Blake?"

"Just working for a living," Frank said. "What brings you here?"

Rafferty presented the woman on his arm. She had a round face and an elaborate fringe of frizzed curls under a straw bonnet. "I got hitched up with Milly here—"

"You're married? Congratulations!"

"Well, not yet—"

"But we're gonna be," Milly said firmly. "Ain't we, love?"

Rafferty said he supposed they were. "Milly runs a boardinghouse out on Fulton Street. Sierra laid off a lot of folks, so I thought I'd try my luck hauling ice down out of the Sierras. Where'd you go after the fire? Word was you'd been burned up, but I never could get a straight story."

"I darn near was." Frank tore tickets as he

talked. "Step right in, madam. See the wonders of the tropics, the denizens of the Amazon's farthest reaches. I just saw the writing on the wall, to tell you the truth. With the refinery up in smoke, Rutledge was bound to lay off hands. And I was good and sick of oil fields by then, anyway. Seemed like a fine time to head out."

Rafferty looked at him curiously. "I heard you didn't even get your pay envelope."

Frank laughed. "I've never been in that much of a hurry in my life. Of course I got my pay." He pointed at the reptile-show door. "Go on in. Show's on me. Step up and see the reptile show, the monster show, open for your education, entertainment, and edification—"

He checked quickly over one shoulder to see that Rafferty and Milly had gone inside. He didn't like running into Rafferty like this. And he didn't like it that the man knew he hadn't gotten his pay. That made Frank Blake an interesting subject of speculation and argued a guilty conscience into the bargain. Frank felt much too noticeable up on the ticket wagon. He didn't see Rafferty again, though, after the crowd filed out of the tent.

The sky seemed to lower a little more, stooping down over the field, but the funnel cloud had disappeared. Eventually the storm that had been alternately threatening and backing off all day hit. Just before the evening show, rain pelted down in sheets, sometimes blowing nearly horizontal curtains of water flapping in the wind. Lightning crackled, splitting the darkness and sending the animals into hysterics. The elephants lumbered, trumpeting, at the ends of their chains. The performing-poodles' trainer huddled in her wagon counting wet dogs, then burst forth screaming, "Trixie!"

Frank, trying to get the reptiles stowed away, discovered Trixie cowering under the warming lamps while the python eyed her with interest. Wondering if Steele would have fired him if one of his charges had eaten one of the other acts, Frank stumbled through the storm to return the poodle.

"Baby!" The trainer gratefully clutched Trixie to her bosom. She wore jodhpurs and a pith helmet, and a long flame-colored scarf wound around her throat. "How can we thank you?" her voice boomed deeply, rolling out on a wave of wet dog and chamomile tea.

"It's all right, ma'am," Frank said, shouting against the wind. "Glad to be of help."

He pushed his way back through the deluge. The tents were a sodden mass of flapping canvas and snaking lines. The ropes whipped out in the wind, and the tent walls billowed and bulged. The roustabouts were busy pulling the canvas down.

"Hump it, First of May! Get out here and help!" The crew that was pulling the stakes from the reptile tent shouted at him, and Frank ran through the mud to lift the poles into the wagon. The roustabouts knelt on the ground and rolled the canvas up as they moved forward. Opposite them the sideshow performers were assisting with their own tent. The field was so drenched that in another few minutes the ground might be too muddy to get the vehicles out. The sideshow wagon was already listing dangerously and might have tipped over altogether had not the world's fattest man been leaning against the other side. Through the driving rain, Frank could see another wagon that had crashed onto its side being hauled upright by a team of elephants.

The last of the canvas was stowed, and the circus began to head out for the rail yard while the wagons could still get there. The sky was as black as pitch, and lightning crackled through it. The hair on the back of Frank's neck began to crawl. He wanted to be out of there, out of that open field. The wagons and their drivers were tableaux lit for a frozen instant by the lightning and then plunged again into darkness. The reptile wagon became stuck in the mud, and Frank and another man heaved against its rear until the wheels moved.

"We're rolling, First of May. Jump up!" a hostler yelled.

Frank ran for the wagon box. As he leaped to the seat, another clap of thunder exploded, and the horses jerked their heads around. Frank sat down and clung to the seat. The hostler, his slouch hat pulled low over his eyebrows, shook out the reins. He looked at Frank through the rain. "How do you like the circus now, First of May?"

"I like it fine," Frank answered. "About as much as you do right now."

The hostler laughed. "You might make a trouper. Lord God, it's wet. I don't remember anything like this since ninety-two. We got flooded out of Sacramento. Floated a lion cage and the ringmaster's horse clear to Freeport."

"How long have you been with the show?" Frank asked.

"Eight, nine years now," the hostler said. "I was with Sells Brothers before that. It's not a bad life if you don't mind staying single. There's about ten men for every woman, and that counts the performers who wouldn't have anything to do with the crew anyway. 'Course there's winter quarters, but not too many females are willing to hitch up to a fellow who's going to be off down the road come spring."

They reached the rail yard and loaded the wagons in the downpour. The train wasn't due to leave for hours, so Frank went visiting his friends in the sideshow car and recounted the hostler's complaints to Illuminata.

"Hmmph," she said. "Nobody wants to hitch up with a man who smells like a horse, either, and doesn't bathe but on Saturday nights."

"The gentlemen on the crew, they do just fine," the bearded lady said. She smiled at Frank. "Oh, I get offers, honey. Plenty of them. Don't you worry about me."

Frank wondered what it would be like to snuggle up to that beard. It was downy—she had let him feel it—not as wiry as a man's. She wore it neatly plaited into two braids, rather like an Egyp-

36

tian king. The bearded lady seemed to divine his thoughts and giggled. Frank blushed.

"You let him alone," Illuminata, otherwise known as Lil, scolded.

Frank thought she sounded proprietary and slid his eyes back to her. It was not difficult to envision cuddling up to those decorated limbs, imagine kissing the domes and towers of Jerusalem or the dragon's opalescent scales.

A whistling switch engine bumped its way down the siding.

"Sounds as if we're ready to roll," the fat man said.

Frank stood. "I'd better go check the kids. I don't like the way Rosalie's been looking." He let himself out the car door and picked his way down the steps in the dark. The stock cars and then the flatcars that carried the wagons were strung beyond the coaches. Bundled forms were already snoring under some of the wagons. Animal handlers, like Frank, had to ride with their charges. Everyone else was allotted sleeping space in the coaches; but the roustabouts' accommodations were the least comfortable—bunks stacked three high in a hot car. Nearly half the roustabouts chose to sit up all night in the pie car, where food was available, or to spread their bedding under the wagons on the flatcars. The next tier up in the hierarchy, the sideshow acts and the candy butchers, had slightly better arrangements. But a number of them who had a wagon available and liked their privacy chose to bunk there instead of in a coach. Wilhelmina was already asleep in the pit-show ticket wagon. Frank could hear her snoring. He chuckled, thinking that he would tease her about that the next time she put on airs.

He climbed into the reptile wagon and turned the lamp up to look at Rosalie. The boa seemed sluggish to him, and her skin wasn't clear. Maybe she was just going to shed? He didn't know much about snakes, although Steele was pounding information into his head daily. He adjusted the warming lamp, then crawled into his sleeping box. He stretched, wriggled his toes, and cracked his knuckles. He listened drowsily to the slow roll of barely moving wheels and the quick fall of steps along the flatcar bed. The wagon door opened and closed; he wasn't altogether surprised to see a faint splash of moonlight along multicolored skin or to have a guest in his bed.

"I heard you last night, carrying on." Wilhelmina glared at him over the python she was settling about her midriff. "It was just so disgusting."

"I don't know what you think you heard," Frank said blandly, "but you couldn't have heard much. You were snoring when I went to bed."

"I was not! I don't snore!"

"Of course you don't," Frank said. He went off whistling and then remembered not to. He was beginning to fit into the circus.

Over the course of the next few weeks, the fit seemed closer, more natural. As he had predicted, Rosalie shed her skin and perked up. Frank, having learned the spiel by heart, began to vary it. Now he reeled it off with infinite complexities. He fixed the ladies with a dashing glance, his hat set at a rakish tilt, and lured them in.

He spent some nights with Lil, twining himself around her variegated torso with the sinuous affection of the boas. Lil was utterly unself-conscious about her body, possibly because she could never be truly naked, but she made it plain that these nocturnal rendezvous were for amusement only. "Don't you go all crazy on me," she warned him.

The show moved north through Merced and Stockton and Sacramento. It crossed to the coast to play San Francisco, where Frank developed a convincing case of food poisoning when he suddenly recollected that his cousin Tim Holt lived in that city.

Steele, grumbling and suspicious, was forced to cover for him and didn't like it. "What have you been up to?" the man demanded. "So help me, if you pull one of Tommy's tricks on me—"

"I haven't been up to anything." Frank groaned and buried his face in the pillow. "I ate something."

"You ate what everybody else ate," Steele said. "None of them is carrying on."

"They must be used to it. I had a sandwich in the pie car. Maybe that was it."

Steele inspected him. "I got to admit, you look sick."

"I am sick." Frank moaned. "Go away."

"I still think you're up to something." Steele left, and Frank took the bottle of syrup of ipecac out from under his pillow and hid it more thoroughly in his clothes box. Then he crawled back into bed. The ipecac was unpleasantly effective.

Miraculously recovered the following day, Frank emerged from his bed to entice the crowds in Santa Rosa, then in Redding, and northward through Oregon.

"Step right up and see the reptile show, the monster show, alive and deadly, twisting, hissing—"

"Them snakes ain't alive!"

Frank stopped in midspiel and bent a mock-horrified eye on a large woman in a pink felt hat. "Madam, I assure you—they are alive and deadly."

She waddled forward. "Them snakes is stuffed by a taxidermatrist. Or else they's celluloid. I want my nickel back."

"Madam, all our reptiles are alive and kicking—or alive and coiling, rather. Step right up, folks, and see for yourselves." Frank pushed his panama hat onto the back of his head and spread his arms, waving them forward. "Coiling, hissing, twisting, snakes so long, so strong—"

"Them snakes is stuffed!"

"So long, so strong, they could swallow whole the largest animal alive as easily as you or I could—"

"Them snakes is stuffed by a taxidermatrist. I want my nickel back."

Frank glared at her. "The word, madam, is taxidermist, and they are not. Kindly take yourself away. Only a nickel, folks, to see the greatest collection of reptiles ever assembled from the deserts, from the jungles, from the darkest depths of the African continent. Wilhelmina Serpentina walks among them. How does she live? How can she live, among these coiling, deadly reptiles? The reptile show, the monster show——"

"Them snakes is stuffed."

Frank bent down, eye to eye with the woman. "My snakes, madam, are the genuine article. They are neither stuffed nor celluloid, neither fake nor false. And you can't have your nickel back because you have already been through the show."

"Them is taxidermatrist's snakes, and I want my nickel back."

Frank reached into the reptile tent and pulled a young blacksnake from its tank. It undulated friskily about his wrist. Holding the snake out in front of him, Frank stepped down from the platform. "Madam, this is a deadly African black mamba, and I am going to stuff it right down your bodice!"

She screamed, backing away with exceptional speed for so large a woman, and plunged through the crowd with Frank in pursuit.

"Come back!" he shouted. "It's just stuffed!"

He chased her halfway down the midway, then returned triumphantly, holding the snake aloft. Wilhelmina had stuck her head out of the tent to see what was going on, and with a flourish Frank presented the snake to her. "My assistant will now return the deadly creature to its habitat. Just a nickel, the twentieth part of a dollar, to see the monster show—alive and unstuffed—man-eaters, bone crushers alive!"

The crowd surged forward, laughing, elbowing one another, wide-eyed at what else might be concealed within the tent. The outer canvas was painted with the wonders it promised—jungle pythons, hooded cobras, and crocodiles with hapless natives in their jaws.

It was all hucksterism, all in the pitch, as Lil said, all ballyhoo from the bally stand. Frank loved it. He learned to work the crowd as the troupe traveled north from Grants Pass through Roseburg and Eugene. Steele had heard about the incident with the heckler and liked the outcome so well that he sometimes hired a shill to repeat it.

By Portland, Frank had nearly decided to stay on with the circus rather than move to the Yukon. Who knew whether there was really any gold in the Klondike or just in a few wanderers' heads? And he hadn't seen any sign of Rafferty. The notion that he was an agent dispatched by Rutledge and had pursued Frank from Sierra seemed more insane with every mile. Rutledge wasn't a professional thug; he was just a ruthless bastard like every other business owner Frank had encountered. He went to church on Sunday, cheated his employees, and blew up his own refinery because it won him his argument with the other directors. Nope, nothing unusual about

Rutledge—business as usual. Plutocratus Americanus.

Frank was feeling so cocky that he declined to get out the syrup of ipecac and have food poisoning again in Portland. There was a small chance that his uncle Toby might be at home on the Madrona Ranch, but it was far more likely that he was in Washington. Frank supposed that his uncle must be out of a job in the State Department since the Democrats had lost the election; but Toby Holt was a hugely admired man, and someone would want to capitalize on the famous Holt name and hire him. Toby liked Washington, and as far as Frank could tell, so did his aunt, Alexandra. They liked being in the thick of things, up close, Frank thought, where they could watch the common man getting handed the short end of the stick with their naked eyes. They wouldn't leave Washington any more than Frank's parents would. Frank's father, Henry Blake, was a career army man with a history of special assignments, and his mother, Cindy, had her art gallery. Portland was too much a hick town for Cindy, even if she had grown up there.

Very likely there wouldn't be anybody at the Madrona but his grandmother, Eulalia Blake. And she was seventy-eight or seventy-nine. Frank had to stop and think back to her seventy-fifth birthday celebration. She was not likely to come out to see the circus, he thought. Not that he wouldn't have liked to see her. She was about the only one of them he did want to see—his one and only surviving grandparent, through one of those complicated Holt/Blake genealogical snarls. But he couldn't risk a visit to her.

That afternoon, he kept half an eye out for any face he might know, but none from the Madrona appeared. He doubted that even Toby's foreman, White Elk, or any of the old-time hands would recognize him. It had been nearly four years since Frank had been to the Madrona, and he had changed mightily.

Following the magical lure, the crowd began to arrive at the same time as the first cage wagons from the street parade. The circus was ready for them. The big-top show wouldn't start for two hours, but the sideshow, the pit show, the candy butchers, and the novelty men were ready to relieve the locals of their money.

With some amusement Frank saw a couple of hoboes, their bindles on their backs, trying to scare up some work. They looked dispirited, so his amusement turned to sympathy. He had been in their spot often enough, and they were going to get management's stock answer: "Beat it. We don't hire 'bos." One of them looked younger than Frank—another "road kid" out on the loose, on the run from who knew what. Frank narrowed his eyes. Something about the boy's face was familiar.

"Step in at this end of the tent, folks, to peruse the wonders of six continents—"

The hobo boy turned to look at the painted wonders on the canvas of the reptile tent. His eyes caught Frank's for an instant, and they both stiffened. Then the kid deliberately turned his back and shouldered through the crowd, leaving memories splattered over Frank like a bucket of cold water:

Digger Bill was as cold as a stone, and Frank was bending over him while the other 'bos watched and muttered. The assumption of his guilt was forming across their faces. He knew it wouldn't matter that he hadn't killed Bill. Frank had run before they jumped him and meted out their own form of justice. The road kid's voice had spoken into the space behind him. "You're marked, fellow. You've cut yourself off."

Frank shook the memory off and found the boy's name beneath it. Doc. His speech had been like Frank's, schooled, from a real family somewhere, not just spun out of the maelstrom on the margins of society. Frank felt a fleeting stab of anger that Doc still believed he was a killer.

The circus played for two days in Portland, a city eager to be entertained. Frank didn't see Doc again and relegated him to the back of his mind, where he stored the memories of his months as a hobo, Digger Bill, and the gold ring that had been Frank's military school senior ring. Bill had stolen it from Frank, and the last time Frank saw it, it had been on the finger of the man he was reasonably sure had killed Bill. Frank didn't want to dwell on any of it for too long; these memories were saved for nights when he was alone and had the leisure to try to figure out life.

Portland sat in tall timber country at the confluence of two rivers, and its overpowering smells
were of sawdust and fish. They overcame even the
rich tang of the circus animals. In the cold pre-
dawn of the second morning, Frank stumbled out
for four poles and took a deep breath. It had
rained in the night, and the riverine smell hung
in the air, reminiscent of old fishing holes and
pleasant afternoons spent in boats. He trotted
over to the big top to see what damage the rain
had done.

The field was muck, slithery mud that sucked
at his boots. The center poles were upright, but
two of the quarter poles were askew, dragging the
canvas down with them. The boss canvas man was
swearing energetically and shouting instructions
to his subordinates. They, in turn, snarled at the
hapless flunkies on their crews until everyone except the lowest echelon had someone to yell at.

"Heave! Move your asses!"

Frank hauled on the ropes, and the canvas
lifted. The rain started up again, driven on a contrary little wind and causing the folds to flap vi-
ciously. The canvas bellied sideways, and the men
hauled it taut again. Outside, the roustabouts
were trying to pound the stakes deeper into the
sopping ground. The canvas surged and buckled,
and the wet ropes stuck in their rings.

"Get it up, goddamn it!" The boss canvas man's
furious bellow boomed over the rain.

Suddenly the whole end collapsed. The canvas
sank with a flat smack, and a quarter pole crashed

down, hurtling free of its tether. Frank heard the whoosh of its falling and fueled only by instinct, dived for safety, not even knowing if it was in the right direction. He hit the dirt, his face in the sod border of the right ring, and jerked himself into a ball as the pole smashed the first ten rows of seats to kindling.

There was a tight, stunned silence, and then everyone under the tent began to talk.

"What the devil happened?"

"It nearly got him."

"Shush! Don't talk that way."

Frank uncurled and stared at the quarter pole lying six inches from his ear. Its bottom end had dug a furrow in the dirt of the ring, and its top end lay embedded in the seats. If he hadn't moved so quickly, he would have been crushed beneath it. He stood up slowly, making sure that he hadn't been hurt, that everything worked, that this wasn't some delirious dream born of the shock of a mangled body.

The boss canvas man shook himself into action. "You all right, kid?"

Frank nodded. "I seem to be."

"Then get out of here and let us get this canvas up."

"I'm all right. I can—"

"I said get out."

Frank found Steele at his elbow, dragging him away. "Just shut up and walk, will you?"

"I didn't drop the blasted pole!" Frank spluttered indignantly.

"You nearly got squashed by it," Steele said. "You almost got killed, and they don't want you around right now, reminding them of it. Makes them edgy."

"But—"

Steele looked exasperated. "Circus people are just about the most ignorant, superstitious bunch of morons it's ever been my pleasure to know, and I been one for forty years," he said, pushing Frank along. "Accidents make everybody crazy. They start thinkin' there's a hoodoo on the show."

"Oh." Frank stopped short, and Steele bumped into him.

"Quarter poles don't just hop up and drop on people of their own accord." Steele snorted. "Not as a rule. Or nobody thinks they do. So when one does, everybody looks around for the jinx."

Or human help, Frank thought, suddenly uncomfortable. He thought of Doc. You're marked, fellow. Doc had said that. How far would the hobo fraternity go to gain vengeance? Were they capable of banding together long enough? Frank doubted it. But the sensation of that pole falling through space stayed with him.

It stayed with everyone else, too. Prevailing wisdom said that accidents occurred in threes and thus created a self-fulfilling prophecy—riders, fearful of bad luck, conducted their nervousness to their horses and turned them skittish. Aerialists checked and rechecked their rigging until they were so tense they fumbled. Every near miss caused apprehension to grow. The big cats felt it, like electricity in their fur. Well-fed, they stared hungrily at animals that they usually ignored. A terrified hyena bit its keeper.

"It'll settle down in a while," Lil soothed him that night. She was propped on her bejeweled elbow in Frank's narrow bed, apparently unconcerned with a possible jinx. "But then," she added, grinning, "I don't have to hang by my toes a hundred feet up or get in a cage with those cats."

"It's not me," Frank insisted. "Really."

"These things get blamed on people," Lil said. "It doesn't matter if it's their fault or not."

"Well, it's not." Frank was outraged. "I nearly get killed by the damn tent pole, and all of a sudden everybody turns around and points their finger at me, as if it was my fault. Wilhelmina acts as if I've got leprosy."

In the morning, pulling into Tacoma, Washington, the flatcar carrying the reptile show came uncoupled from the one ahead. It drew away, but then as the engines ahead slowed for the depot, it picked up speed on a slight downgrade and smacked into the forward car, forcing the glass tanks in the reptile wagon out of their brackets.

Frank, thrown out of his sleeping box, took frantic stock of his charges. The boa's cage was cracked, and Frank lifted Rosalie from a nest of glass shards. The cobra cage mercifully was in one piece, but he checked it three times, anyway. The warming lamps had spilled oil, and as Frank carefully mopped it up, he wondered what he would do if the car caught fire. Outside, he could hear the monkey trainer attempting to coax one of his charges down from the depot water tank. Obviously the monkey cage had toppled during the collision. The trainer spoke soothingly, albeit between clenched teeth, while the monkey flung back furious and unintelligible imprecations.

Brakemen came running down the length of the train. Restored order was followed by a shouting match between the circus baggage team and the railroad crew. The cars were checked for damage, then recoupled. The show limped into Tacoma an hour late. It was too late for breakfast, which meant no one got a decent meal until dinner—lunch consisted of sandwiches, boxed the night before.

Everyone ate jumpily, flicking uneasy glances over their shoulders as if something lurked at the door. The first show had gone badly, the timing off, the spectators unreceptive. No one could identify precisely what was wrong, but the more they tried to put things right, the wronger they got.

"It was his car."

"It all started since he came on."

"Any fool knows it's bad luck to hire townies."

Frank could hear the whispers eddying around him. He ate placidly, ignoring them, but he felt like the cursed Jonah.

"Just give it time," Lil said again.

But Frank began to wonder if he had any time. He came back one night to the reptile wagon and found the cobra out of its tank and a terrified Wilhelmina gibbering in the corner.

Frank's eyes widened. "Be still," he whispered.

Wilhelmina moaned. She waved her hands as if to shoo off the snake.

"Stop it." Frank gritted his teeth. He reached slowly for the snake pole, the forked stick Steele expertly used to twirl the reptiles like spaghetti. Frank was a beginner. He took a step toward the cobra, and it raised its hood at him while swaying. Wilhelmina, whimpering, stared at it. Frank got a good grip on the stick, prayed, and lunged with it at the cobra.

Got you! Frank let his breath out in a sigh. He grabbed the pinned snake behind the head and dropped it quickly into its box.

He glared at Wilhelmina. "How did it get out?" he demanded.

Her teeth chattered. "I came in, and it was—it was—"

Even when he felt sorry for her, Wilhelmina managed to irritate him. "Don't be such a rabbit," he said.

She caught her breath and glared back. "I didn't let it out. Do you think I'm crazy? It got out. They ought to get rid of you before somebody gets killed!" She ran out of the wagon.

"I'm sorry to do it, kid, but things are out of hand," Steele said. "They all think there's some kind of curse on you." He scratched his chin. "Hell, maybe I do, too. I don't like what's been going on. Even if it's all in their head, I got to humor them after it gets to a certain point."

"I understand." Frank held out his hand. "At least I made it to Seattle. That's where I started off heading." Before I got suckered in. He scratched his chin, grinning. He could smell salt water. It took some of the sting out of getting fired. He had been crazy to think he wanted to spend his life ballyhooing a bunch of snakes for a pit show. He would probably have figured that out somewhere around Minnesota, when it was too late to get to the Yukon.

"Good luck, kid," Steele said. "Go see the ghost for your pay."

The ghost was the paymaster; there seemed to a circus taboo against calling anything by its correct name. Frank picked up his envelope, then went to say good-bye to Lil.

"Aw, I was afraid of that," she said. "I kept telling you it would blow over, but if wishes was horses . . . Well, you remember me now, you hear?"

Frank smiled. "I'm not likely to forget you." He shouldered his bedroll and slipped away with the feeling that if he lingered, the rest of them might drive him off the lot with rocks. He couldn't say he blamed them. It might be closer to the truth than they knew to call him a jinx. Steele and Lil could talk about superstition all they wanted, but Frank wondered if he really had had someone after him. He couldn't shake the memory of Doc staring at him out of the crowd and turning his back on him. That was assuming, of course, that Rutledge wasn't hunting him down. Yeah, sure. Frank snorted in amusement at his own jumpiness. Rutledge in disguise, masquerading as a candy butcher. Rutledge in a dress, sneaking into the bearded lady's place. Right.

Having chased away his fears with self-derision, Frank turned his steps into town and looked for the docks. Seattle curled like an octopus around and through the waters of Puget Sound. There would be ships aplenty heading north.

III

Sierra, California, March 1897

At about the time that Frank was first cadging a job with the circus, his father, Henry, was arriving by train in Sierra. A spur line from San Buenaventura on the coast had just been completed, allowing Henry to ride inland in comfort and descend unrumpled on the Sierra depot platform. Henry wore civilian clothes but looked like a colonel, anyway. In fact, he looked like a colonel when wearing a bathing suit. His older son, Peter, took due note of the erect carriage, military starchiness, and parade-ground walk and thought moodily that it boded no good for somebody—probably himself, since no other offspring was handy.

"I hope you had a pleasant journey, sir." Peter held out his hand.

"Spare me the formalities," Henry said, shaking his son's hand briskly. "Why in the blue blazes did you wait so long before telling me you'd found Frank?"

"I wired you last fall," Peter said indignantly. "Mother's Pinkerton men have been crawling all over the place ever since. It's embarrassing. People are beginning to wonder if I've robbed a train or embezzled company funds."

"I am given to understand," Henry said dryly, "that by the time the lawsuits stemming from the fire have been settled, there may not be any company funds. In any case, I am well aware that Frank was here all summer before you wired me. Don't try to evade the issue with references to my arrival. I've been out of the country."

"I see." Peter raised an eyebrow. "Would it be indiscreet to ask where?"

"Not at all," Henry said. "But it would be indiscreet of me to tell you."

Peter decided to humor his father, since he looked like a wasp captured in a bottle. "Maybe you'd like some dinner," he suggested. "And a bath. And a drink."

"All three," Henry grunted. "I hate trains." He looked around for Peter's carriage. When he saw that the vehicle in which Peter was ordering the luggage stowed had no horse attached, Henry gritted his teeth. On the hood of the motorcar a little silver Diana pranced jauntily, bow drawn, and the front grillwork said Blake in silver script. The fact that his son's company produced these monstrosities did nothing to reconcile Henry to their existence.

Peter was a modernist, as was his late mother, who had been the terror of her German village. Gisela, who had died when Peter was two, would have loved automobiles. Henry, on the other hand, was too much a traditionalist—not to mention a cavalryman—to have any fondness for machines that rattled, banged, stank, and frightened horses.

Henry had sandy hair and green eyes and the broad-shouldered build that Frank had inherited. A faded scar down his left cheek did nothing to detract from his good looks. Peter was shorter and slighter, with his mother's build and ears that stuck out just a little too much under his chestnut hair. Gisela had been beautiful, but much of that beauty had been owed to the imperious electricity that radiated from her. Peter, without that aura, was pleasant but plain.

Father and son surveyed each other with affection tempered with bafflement. Peter trotted around to the front of the motor car and turned the crank. The engine sputtered to life with no fuss.

"Runs like a top," Peter said, beaming. "Rufus and Calvin made some adjustments that we think will take the market by storm."

"I'm not to be sidetracked," Henry said, climbing onto a padded leather seat. "Why did you wait for months to tell us about Frank? Your mother is sick with worry."

Cindy Blake was the only mother Peter remembered. They had all long since ceased to make the distinction of her being Peter's stepmother. Peter did happen to know her condition because she wrote him regularly. She laid the blame for Frank's disappearance at Henry's door. A little more than a year before, Frank and Henry had had a furious argument, after Frank had transformed from a dutiful son eager to follow in his father's footsteps into a rebellious loner eager to follow any other path. It was Peter's opinion that Henry had kept Frank too dutiful for too long, and now Frank was trying to use up all his rebellion at once.

"He asked me to give him a month to go home on his own," Peter said now. "It wasn't months; it was weeks. He said he didn't want to be dragged back like a truant schoolboy by Mother's detectives."

"He is a truant schoolboy," Henry muttered.

"Not now," Peter said gently. "Give it up, Dad. Frank got away from you and grew up on his own before you could stop him. I saw him. I was mad as hell at him, too, for not letting you know he was all right. But the genie's gotten out of the bottle, and you aren't going to be able to stuff it back in."

Grim-faced, Henry folded his arms and regarded the passing scenery. The motorcar proceeded in a cloud of fumes down Sierra's main street, but no horses reared or bolted.

"See, Dad?" Peter pointed out. "They've gotten used to it. I've had it here over six months now, and nobody pays it any attention—except to ask where to buy one. Don't you ever drive yours?"

"Reluctantly," Henry admitted. "Your mother enjoys it," he added. "I have been persuaded to take it to church on Sundays for the edification and astonishment of the parish."

Peter chuckled. "Ha! You do drive it."

"All right! I drive it, I drive it! But not voluntarily. Now, what are you going to do about these lawsuits?"

"I understand your not wanting to waste time on small talk," Peter said, drawing the motorcar to a stop in front of his rented house. "But could we at least get inside first?" He climbed out and hefted his father's bag from the rear seat.

The rental was small, with a meticulously tended garden of flowers and orange trees and a gardener whose fee was part of the rent. Inside, it was high polish and clean smells. The parlor furniture was plain but serviceable. A housekeeper was included with the rent, too. Peter poured his father a glass of whiskey and sniffed the air appreciatively. The housekeeper had left a goose roasting in the oven for them.

Peter drew a hot bath in the ornate claw-foot tub and hung a towel by the radiator. Henry, moodily sipping his whiskey, disappeared into the bathroom, closed the door, and emerged fifteen minutes later with his glass empty and his hair slicked back.

57

Peter had put dinner on the table, and Henry sat down to it. He inspected the goose as if it had been an unpromising cadet.

"Have some peas," Peter offered.

"Tell me about Frank."

Peter sighed. "He looked good, Dad. Healthy, I mean. He was working for Sierra as a jackline tender, and he'd put on some muscle. I swear he was taller. His hair looked like he'd cut it himself with the nail scissors, until he got—" Peter had been about to say until Frank had got Peggy Delaney to trim it for him, but Henry was already in a bad mood. He probably wouldn't appreciate the humor in Peter's having caught Frank in bed with the local laundress. Actually, Peter hadn't appreciated it much himself at the time. But Peggy had left town right after the refinery blew up, killing her brother, so it was a moot point. Peter knew he shouldn't have been courting Peggy—the differences between them, which appeared not to bother Frank, had made Peter uncomfortable. He had been slumming, and he knew it; and it embarrassed him to recognize that fact.

"Go on," Henry urged, eyeing him suspiciously. "What is a jackline tender?"

Peter swallowed the food in his mouth to buy time. "A jackline is an eccentric wheel that runs a lot of pumps simultaneously. It's powered by a steam boiler and an engine. It takes some skill to run it. They don't just let any puttyhead mess around with it."

58

"Reassuring," Henry said. "And how did he come to relinquish this promising career?"

"Oh, boy." Peter took another bite of goose and chewed it. "It was my fault, Dad, for not listening to him. Sierra's board of directors had been fighting over whether to close the refinery here and move the whole operation to the new facility at Oleum, near San Francisco. Rutledge wanted it moved, and Kemp wanted the refinery to stay here, with necessary repairs made. I was the swing vote. I agreed to the move—the facility here was falling down, and the repairs would have been prohibitively expensive—but only if some provision was made to move our refinery workers and their families to Oleum. The refinery was the whole economy of this town. It's suffered terribly the last few months since the fire."

"Commendable of you," Henry said impatiently.

"Well, Rutledge agreed, but Kemp wouldn't. Kemp just wanted to block the move. So there it sat. That's when Frank came to me. We'd already had one argument, so I wasn't very receptive."

"Argument over what?"

"Over his running off," Peter said uncomfortably. "Over his not going home." Over Peggy Delaney. "So when he came to me with some story he'd overheard in the Wellhead Saloon, I wasn't receptive." Peter stared at his plate. "The Wellhead is pretty disreputable. Frank shouldn't have been there in the first place. When he said he'd heard Sid Delaney and his drunken pa shooting their mouths off about a plan to blow something up, I figured they were just drunk and disgruntled. There was plenty of bad feeling in town over moving the refinery to Oleum. Besides, we had a plant security force that should have prevented any trouble."

"I gather it didn't," Henry said, and looked thoughtful. "You didn't tell me sabotage was involved."

"It wasn't something I wanted to put in a letter," Peter explained. "Frank also said that Rutledge was behind it. I wasn't willing to believe Rutledge would go that far just to make sure the plant closed."

"The plant's employees certainly wouldn't blow it up to protest its closing," Henry commented.

"I know." Peter looked morose. "Although people have done stupider things. But I couldn't believe Rutledge was a criminal. He was wrong —headed, yes, but not insane. I told Frank to keep his mouth shut. I warned him that if he spread any more slander about Rutledge, I'd have him fired."

"What do you think about Rutledge now?" Henry asked.

"Oh, I think he did it," Peter said. "Set it up, I mean. I can't prove it, of course. Sid Delaney got killed in the fire—handy, huh? And his pa left town and hasn't been heard from since. And Sid's sister, who didn't have anything to do with it, left, too, for fear Rutledge was going to start trying to shut people up."

Henry laid his fork down. "Including yourself?" he inquired.

"Of course not," Peter said irritably. "Not even Rutledge would go that far. He knows I couldn't prove anything."

"Then why did Frank leave town so suddenly?"

"So Mother's Pinkertons and you wouldn't catch up to him," Peter said. "No offense intended, but he hasn't any intention of going home."

"I am aware of that," Henry said stiffly. "And you had a row with him over more than the refinery, am I correct?"

"Yeah," Peter admitted. "I feel bad about it now, too. Before he took off he wrote me a note that was nicer than I deserved. He said Rutledge's men were after him, and I suppose maybe they were, but Rutledge wouldn't pursue it once Frank took off."

Henry studied Peter's unhappy face. "Consider yourself on my territory now, professionally speaking. I spend most of my time unearthing what other people don't want me to know and what they are capable of doing—usually things that no one in his right mind would dream of. I don't like the sound of this."

"I didn't think you would," Peter said. "But you can understand why I felt reluctant to write this in a letter."

"Thank goodness," Henry said. "The things

that people are willing to commit to paper would stun you." He picked up his fork again and, deep in thought, disposed of goose and peas.

Peter watched his father. The waspish look had been replaced with a kind of thoughtful concentration. When Henry looked up, a small fire blazed behind his eyes. "Why are you still here?" he demanded.

Peter blinked. "In the room or in Sierra?"

"In Sierra. Don't play games with me."

"I can't leave," Peter said. "There are too many loose ends."

"What is the status of the lawsuits?" Henry said.

"The chemist who was killed had relatives who knew what to tell a lawyer," Peter said. "The other victims were roughnecks, and their survivors hadn't a clue. Then the ambulance chasers came around."

"I'd feel better if you were elsewhere," Henry said. "Would you consider visiting your mother in Washington?"

"No. If I were to go anywhere, it would be San Francisco." Peter's chin jutted out. "That's where I live, Dad. My house is there. My company is there."

"Not San Francisco," Henry said. "If that's the alternative, then stay here."

"Well, I intend to. I'm planning to sell my stock in Sierra—I refuse to be associated with Rutledge—but not until these suits are settled. It'll take my vote on the board to stop the rest of them from fighting about paying out anything at all. If

Sierra drags out the settlement negotiations, the plaintiffs will still win; but they won't have anything left after they pay the lawyers' fees. I can't allow that."

"Very ethical, but that's not why I want you here." Henry looked at Peter with the air of someone attempting to explain purple to the blind. "If you are in Washington, I doubt that Rutledge would bother you or have the resources to do so, even if he wanted to. San Francisco is another matter. It's too close to Oleum."

"I've been right under his nose all winter," Peter protested. "And nothing's happened to me. I think I'd notice if someone was trying to kill me!"

"I think you've been safe precisely because you have been here under his nose. You didn't make a stink right after the fire, so Rutledge probably safely assumes you aren't going to."

"I would have if I'd had any evidence," Peter said. "I wouldn't have dragged Frank into it even if he'd been around. Or Peggy, either."

Henry's eyes narrowed. "Who's Peggy?"

"Peggy Delaney. Sid's sister. She ran the laundry down the street. She didn't have anything to do with it."

"How do you know?"

"Because she's not that kind of a girl!" Peter said indignantly.

Henry's brows rose just a trifle. "You knew her well?"

"She was a friend."

The brows rose a shade higher. "And you say she was a, er, a laundress?"

"Yes." Peter declined to elaborate.

"I see." Henry looked as if he thought he did. "Well, I won't pry, son, but I do wish you'd leave town. Your mother would like to see you."

"She'll see me next month at Tim's wedding. Why does she need to see me now?"

"Because I am going to make a stink," Henry answered. "A quiet one, but eventually Mr. Rutledge will notice."

Peter rose from the table and began to clear the dishes. "I can take care of myself." He shouldered his way through the swinging door between dining room and kitchen.

"Certainly you can," Henry muttered. He got up and followed Peter into the kitchen. "Six months in this town, and you've managed a threat on your life and an unsuitable affair with a laundress."

Peter was running hot water from the kitchen boiler into a dishpan.

"Doesn't the housekeeper do that?" Henry inquired.

"Well, she would, I suppose." Peter rolled up his sleeves. "But she doesn't come back till morning. Am I supposed to leave them on the table for her, with the food still on the plates?"

"I would," Henry answered seriously. He poured himself another whiskey, then leaned his shoulder against the kitchen cabinets while Peter washed dishes.

"Then you'd have a lot of flies," Peter said, grinning. "As well as an inconsiderate nature."

"Nothing of the sort," Henry denied. "If I'm paying a housekeeper to do a job, then I expect her to do the job. She can't expect me to do part of it. The laborer is worthy of her hire."

"Was this how you got into it with Frank?" Peter asked mildly. Washing dishes here in his own kitchen, he somehow felt more willing to butt heads with his father. Until now he had in his way been as rebellious as Frank. But it had been a respectful rebellion, consisting of a polite and steady determination to go his own way with his mother's inherited fortune and his own motorcar company. There had been no shouting across dinner tables, no political or ideological arguments.

"I did not 'get into it' with Frank." Henry, still holding the glass, crossed his arms. "Your brother proposed dropping out of school to help the anarchists stage a revolution." Henry's tone was sardonic. "I felt this to be ill-advised."

"I don't suppose there's any point in my telling you that socialists aren't anarchists," Peter remarked, "if Frank didn't manage to."

"I am not mentally deficient or uneducated," Henry said. "I've even read Karl Marx, as you have, but I very much doubt that Frank has. Marx has dangerous notions, badly thought through. And those people Mike Holt introduced Frank to in New York are radicals of the worst sort. No matter what they call themselves, they propose anarchy. After they have taken over the country, where do they expect to find the trained and educated people to run it?"

"You have a point," Peter admitted. "I don't suppose you managed to put it to Frank quite so calmly."

"When you have children of your own," Henry retorted, "you may second-guess the way in which I've raised mine."

"I'll make a note of it." Peter handed his father a dish towel. "Here, you dry."

Henry regarded the towel with the air of a man who had not dried dishes since his teens and had no intention of starting again. But he picked up a plate and began to dry.

Despite its unpromising beginning, the evening ended as possibly the most satisfactory one Peter had ever spent with his father. Somehow they had undergone a shift in the kitchen. Although in Henry's eyes, Frank remained a truant child, Peter had been promoted over the dishpan to the status of fellow adult. Peter was aware of two things: First, Henry's concern for his son's safety was undiminished, and second, Henry was convinced that anybody who had not proved in some two-fisted fashion that he knew how to take care of himself probably couldn't.

In the morning Father and son went out together. Peter took Henry in the Blake motorcar to the Sierra Oil headquarters on Main Street and presented him to Sanford Rutledge as "My father,

Colonel Blake, who will be staying with me for a while."

Rutledge, the only board member to be found in the offices, shook Henry's hand and regarded him from beneath bushy brows. "How do you do," he said. "Delighted to meet you."

"Yes, indeed," Henry murmured, looking around him at the framed photographs of oil wells. "Delighted."

"Troubled times," Rutledge said. He shook his impressive set of biblical whiskers mournfully. "Troubled times. Hope you enjoy yourself anyway."

"I'm sure I shall," Henry said. "It's a charming town."

"Not like San Francisco, though," Rutledge said. "Lawsuits. Saboteurs." He peered intently at Henry.

"Yes," Henry replied. "I did hear of your misfortune."

"Still a danger," Rutledge said. "Still a danger." He looked at Peter. "Kemp's a blockhead."

Peter grinned. "Perhaps we should save that for the board meeting. I'm about to take my father sightseeing."

Peter looked at his father as they made their way down the burgundy plush runner that cushioned the stairs. "Now really, Dad, how much danger can I be in from that old bird? He couldn't lift anything heavy enough to hit me with."

"But he could hire someone who could—and already has, if the body count you gave me was correct. Besides the people who were killed in that fire he had set, there are Sid Delaney and Frank's belief that thugs were after him."

They pushed their way through the front doors and onto the sidewalk.

"I know that," Peter said. "I have been cautious. But I'm beginning to think that Rutledge isn't capable of that kind of thing anymore. Maybe he scared himself with what he started with the fire. There's a good chance that the directors may be held personally responsible for negligence."

"All the more reason for Rutledge to dispose of anyone who might prove that only one director was responsible. He'd lose his shirt if he had to pay it all."

"You have a knack for making me feel insecure," Peter said. He motioned Henry into the buggy he had rented from the livery stable. "A treat for you. Where we're going, the roads won't accommodate the motorcar."

"Delightful," Henry said.

They clip-clopped down Alvarez Street, past the Fine French Laundry, where Peggy Delaney had labored. After her departure it was bought by the owner of the Chinese laundry on the next block, and one of his numerous sons was running it.

Henry and Peter turned up the road toward Avenal Canyon. Its sides were already green with the spring rains and yellow with a profusion of mustard flower.

"Up here was the last place Frank worked," Peter said.

Henry roused himself from whatever he had been contemplating. "Did Rutledge know Frank?"

"I don't know." Peter thought about it. "He must have, or he wouldn't have set his dogs on him. But I don't know how. After he came to me and I wouldn't listen, I wouldn't put it past Frank to have confronted Rutledge himself."

"He seemed very interested in my face," Henry said, "so I assume he saw the resemblance. That makes me think that he knew Frank and knew he was your brother."

"I'll go along with that, just to be on the safe side," Peter agreed. "But I honestly can't get too worked up about old Rutledge. He's a jerk. I wouldn't give him the time of day. Anyway, since the fire he hasn't seemed interested in anything but hurrying up the move to Oleum and worrying about John D. Rockefeller."

"What about Rockefeller?" Henry inquired. "Is his health declining? Or is he preparing to gobble down Sierra Oil for breakfast?"

"I find it fascinating," Peter mused, "that you always know so much about everything. He's concerned about the latter. Standard Oil has an appetite for smaller companies, and their attorneys have made overtures before. Rutledge is so convinced the rest of the board will vote for a fire sale and let Standard grab us that he doesn't seem to be capable of concentrating on much else."

69

"Monomania, you think?" Henry asked.

"I do. You saw him." Peter drew the buggy to a stop at the foot of a tramway, which appeared to Henry to run straight up the mountain. There was a car at the bottom, and after a brief conversation with an oil-smeared workman, Peter motioned Henry into it.

"Here's where the scenery gets exciting." Peter started the tram up its cable. The yellow flowers faded to dispirited sagebrush and dust. At the top of the track, a well-worn path led still farther up-hill to a bunkhouse, a cook shed, and a well house from which a dozen cables fanned out to the derricks of as many pumps. The dusty hills were studded with the twisting red branches of manzanita. A flight of crows sailed over them, cawing furiously, and in the air hung the overwhelming smell of sulfur.

"My God," Henry said. "This place is right out of a nightmare."

"It's pretty bad, isn't it? The men who work here say they get used to it. I've never been willing to stay long enough to try."

Peter drew Henry down the path and showed him the cook house and the bunks, above one of which Frank had idly carved his name. Henry stiffened, then wilted at that.

"Come on, Dad. I'll show you the jackline wheel. It's interesting."

As they walked across the dusty yard, Henry was still deep in thought. At first Peter thought he was mourning Frank, but he had forgotten his father's capacity for gnawing relentlessly at whatever matter seemed to him to be the most immediate.

"Rutledge," Henry said as Peter pulled open the sagging door of the jackline shed. "Stay away from him as much as possible. And don't vote for a fire sale. You can sell your stock later."

"Why?" Peter asked.

"There's something very wrong with Rutledge."

"You mean besides being a murderer?"

"Yes. He makes the skin on the back of my neck prickle."

"Maybe you just have sensitive skin."

"I have trained skin. There's something else wrong with him, and until I find out what it is, I don't want you to stumble upon it—particularly unexpectedly, if you get my drift."

"Certainly, sir." Peter was offended. "And I will always wear my galoshes in the rain, and flannel next to my skin in the winter."

Henry glared at him. "Show me your damned machinery," he growled.

IV

San Francisco, April 1897

The wedding of Elizabeth Emory and Timothy Holt took place in the bride's Unitarian church on a suitably balmy day, which provided just enough of a breeze to flutter the ribbons on the carriage horses' harness. A fair wind, it brought with it the scent of flowers but refrained from snatching bridesmaids' hats. Because the day before had poured buckets, Tim viewed the fine weather as a personal blessing conferred on his union. His confidence did not, however, prevent him from asking his brother, Michael, six times within thirty minutes, if he still had the ring. And the arrival of Elizabeth's carriage eliminated the imagined disaster about her being killed on the way to the church by a runaway cable car.

The entire Holt/Blake/Brentwood clan had turned out for the nuptials, coming from as far away as Hawaii in one direction and Washington, D.C., in the other. With the rowdier addition of the reporters from Tim Holt's Clarion, they packed the groom's side of the church. The bride's family and friends filled the other side, with the respective parents allotted the front rows, thus allowing the Holts and the Emorys to pursue their study of each other while pretending to admire the altar arrangements.

Due to the distances involved, the two families had met for the first time at the previous night's rehearsal dinner. Toby and Alexandra Holt had hosted this extravagant and stiffly starched event in the dining room of the Palace Hotel. Afterward, Rafe Murray and Hugo Ware from the Clarion and Michael Holt had spirited the groom away for a bachelor party at the Poodle Dog Restaurant.

Tim, who was prepared, had encouraged them to drink their champagne while he poured his own into a potted palm and thus spent the small hours of the morning sobering them up in a Turkish bath. They still looked wan, but at least he could congratulate himself on not being in the same condition.

Michael, waiting beside him, was the best man. The others, whom Tim would always think of as the Hungover Ushers Union, were palely escorting guests to their seats: Rafe Murray and Hugo Ware; Michael's brother-in-law, Sam Brentwood; Elizabeth's brother, Tom; and Jack London, a friend of Elizabeth's. London was a devil-may-care young man with curly hair, restless feet, and a wonderful gift with a pen. As he escorted Tim's brother-in-law, Charley Lawrence, to his seat, London walked very deliberately, as if he was carefully balancing his head.

Madeleine Emory inspected her older sister in the antiquated gaslight of the choir robing room. "I must say, when you finally make up your mind to do a thing, you go the whole hog. You look like a picture out of Harper's Bazaar. No dress reform at this wedding."

"You look very nice, dear," Mrs. Emory said. "And entirely suitable." Elizabeth's dress was of white satin, cut princess style, with leg-of-mutton sleeves, a wide lace fichu, and a high gauze collar.

"Bloomers would have been better," Maddy

said. "Make a statement." She was still sulking over her sister's refusal to let her wear them.

"I am making a statement," Elizabeth said crossly. "I'm letting Tim's family know that I am not going to be a public curiosity on all occasions." She smiled at Tim's older sister, Janessa Lawrence, and his younger sister, Sally, to indicate that that was partly a joke, partly true, but said with the best intentions. It was all very complicated.

They looked back at her with the frozen smiles reserved for brides picked out by brothers who have not first consulted their sisters. Theoretically, of course, they approved of Elizabeth's commitment to the movement for women's rights. Sally found it quite exciting that Elizabeth had actually been arrested while trying to cast a ballot. But bloomers? Sally shuddered.

Janessa's expression was warier. At thirty-six, she was several years older than Elizabeth. She had seen what she wanted, gone through medical school, and achieved her life's ambition—but now felt herself losing it, mired in the responsibility of raising twins. Beyond being irked by Elizabeth's freedom, Janessa had concluded without any particular evidence that Elizabeth judged her to have shirked her duty in not joining the movement.

"You look very nice," Sally and Janessa said together in haste.

"Are you ready, dear?" Aurelia Emory smoothed the folds of Elizabeth's skirt. "Your father is pacing in the hallway."

"Yes, Mother." Elizabeth clenched her hands into fists so they wouldn't shake. It irked her that despite her age and her unusually liberal, bordering on radical, upbringing, she was behaving like any twittering bride. She led the way through the doors and into the hallway, with Madeleine holding her train straight, to find not only her father but Tim in the corridor, sharing the contents of a flask.

"Go away!" Maddy said indignantly. "You aren't supposed to see the bride before the wedding."

"He's trying to develop the same disability as the ushers," Sidney Emory said. "He was just leaving."

Tim ducked through the cloud of bridesmaids and kissed Elizabeth. "That's for courage."

"Whose?" Elizabeth asked faintly.

"Yours," he said, and vanished.

An usher appeared, to escort Mrs. Emory to her seat. Maddy, staying behind with Elizabeth, peered through the door. "Goodness, what a crowd! Did they all send you presents?"

"You're a disgrace," Elizabeth said.

The organist shifted into the strains of " 'Tis a Gift to be Simple," a Quaker tune that Tim and Elizabeth preferred to the Wagnerian thunder of "Lohengrin."

"Go on, Maddy. There's the music."

"Charming," Elizabeth heard someone say with disapproval. "How unusual."

Maddy, as maid of honor, made her grand entrance on the fourth bar. Clutching a bouquet of lilies of the valley and tea roses, she took her place at the left of the altar, then turned to watch Sally, Janessa, and three of Elizabeth's closest friends walk down the aisle. The guests craned their necks and made suitable exclamations as the bride appeared on her father's arm.

"If I ever get married," Maddy whispered to Sally, who stood next to her, "I'm going to walk down the aisle by myself."

"Eden did that when she married Mike," Sally whispered back. "Everybody talked about it for weeks. Of course her father was dead and her brother was in jail, so they couldn't do it with her."

"Sam was unfortunate enough to be caught up in the revolution in Hawaii," Janessa hissed from her sister's other side. "You're making him sound like a burglar. Now be quiet."

The friend on Janessa's other side giggled, and then everyone put on their most solemn faces as the bride and groom approached the altar.

Tim, who had never been able to concentrate totally on anything, even the things that were most important to him, without some piece of his mind wandering off to watch the parade, stood beside Elizabeth and wondered how the two families in the front pews were taking to each other. Everyone looked odd to him today, but that might only be because he was odd.

Alexandra had thrown herself into planning the rehearsal dinner with an enthusiasm he hadn't seen since Janessa's wedding. Alexandra liked to throw parties. She was still annoyed that Mike and Eden had planned their own wedding. She had had a fine time arguing with the chef at the Palace Hotel and choosing the flowers, the china, and several new gowns for herself, for Sally, and—on an impromptu shopping trip—for Janessa, who since choosing the role of a working mother, had no time to buy clothes until her old ones actually disintegrated. Now that all the planning was over, Tim thought she looked lost.

He had sneaked a look at his father, too, who had talked politics with Dr. Emory all evening at the rehearsal dinner. Now he looked merely preoccupied. Neither Alexandra nor Toby was looking at the other.

His aunt and uncle, Cindy and Henry Blake, had seemed peculiar, too. They sat side by side, but they looked like the positive ends of two magnets trying to repel each other. Only the fact that they were wedged in at either side by Peter and their daughter, Midge, kept them from sliding to opposite ends of the pew.

All the older generation in his family, the stable couples who had once been so solid, seemed ready to break apart. Tim squeezed Elizabeth's hand, tucked into his while the minister recited the service that would tie them together forever. Forever was a terrifying step. No wonder Elizabeth had been afraid of it. Many of the women in her movement believed in divorce, but only as an extreme measure—to free a woman from a husband who was a drunkard or beat her. Divorce did not extend to those who had merely grown apart and angry, or worse, disinterested. Those couples were stuck with each other forever.

Tim looked sideways at Elizabeth, almost his wife, and tried to see through the veil. It was made of some wispy stuff, but it blurred the outline of her features until she was only watercolor under a wash of silver.

What would stop them from experiencing the anger that he saw between his uncle and aunt? Tim and Elizabeth had been bitterly angry with each other already but had come to terms with their differences by shifting, adjusting, compromising, and fiddling with the pattern until they fit together. Had they gotten the anger out of the way already or only forestalled it? And what would spare them from suffering the indifference he saw growing between his father and Alexandra? That was more difficult yet. Did time simply numb people? Tim knew it did not; he had seen an alive marriage between the Emorys. In fact, he had seen it between his own parents only a year before. Or maybe two years, while his father had still been in the Senate. His fingers tightened on Elizabeth's again, seeking the charm, the magic formula that would save them from that dispassion.

The reception was held at the Emorys' yellow clapboard house on Van Ness. The windows of its cupola had been draped with white bows, and its flower beds were bright with red geraniums, purple

78

heliotrope, and yellow marguerites. The pennant at the top of the cupola snapped jauntily, welcoming the guests whose carriages labored up the hill.

An enormous yellow dog, almost the same butter color as the house, barked hysterically at each arrival. Fortunately, she had been prudently attached to a chain anchored in the yard. Her back end supported a frantically waving tail. "Be quiet, Alice," everyone said ineffectually.

The two families and the bridal couple, jammed shoulder to shoulder in the receiving line, presented themselves for inspection by friends and relatives.

"I understand you're a journalist," said an elderly gentleman with an ear trumpet aimed at the bridegroom. He said it in tones of deepest disapproval.

"True, but I don't actually have a prison record," said Tim.

"You ought to have." Tim's grandmother Eulalia kissed his cheek. "You behave." She beamed at Elizabeth. "You are very lovely."

"You look so tired, dear," said an old lady with less tact. "You be, well, careful, on your honeymoon." She glared at Tim as if he were a would-be assailant.

Hugo Ware escorted his wife, Rosebay. They had known Tim for a long time.

"Such a lovely wedding, and a perfect day for it." The tips of Rosebay's gloves rested on the tips of Elizabeth's. Rosebay looked searchingly at Tim. "I hope you will always be happy. . . ." There might have been just a shade too much emphasis on the word hope.

"Congratulations, old man," said Charley. He had resorted to putting his and Janessa's twins, who had just turned two, in a pram; Janessa was in the receiving line, and the nursemaid, Kathleen, had disappeared for the moment. "Remember, Tim"—he lowered his voice solemnly—"we have found what causes this."

A seemingly endless stream of guests made the proper pleasantries. Charming wedding . . . lovely bride . . . charming wedding . . . so delightful . . .

"How do you do? We're Zachary Taylor," Rafe Murray and Jack London announced in unison as they went down the line. No one seemed to notice.

After the last guest had been greeted, the bridal party faded gratefully toward the punch, and Janessa retrieved the twins from Charley. Brandon Tobias and Mary Lavinia, known as Lally, were enticed by the sight of cake and trying to climb out of their pram. "I might as well let them get good and sticky right away," Janessa said, resigned, "and then I won't have to worry about how soon they'll soil their clothes."

"You could let Alice lick them off," Charley suggested. Alice had slipped her collar and, hoping no one would notice, was lurking under the table on which the wedding cake was displayed. Charley bent to scratch her ears.

Tim and Elizabeth cut the first slice of cake,

then froze, knife in hand, while the photographer peered at them from beneath his black cloth. There was a bright light and a bang of flash powder, and the twins squealed in delight. Like most two-year-olds, they could produce a credible imitation of a steam whistle. Charley still wasn't used to it. At least the sound had brought their nursemaid, Kathleen, back into the room.

Elizabeth dutifully admired the twins. "They're darling. I wish we could recruit you for the movement," she said to Janessa. "You set a wonderful example of women's capabilities."

"They're very time-consuming," Janessa said stiffly. "I'm afraid that between the children and my medical practice, I don't have the leisure for other activities."

"You don't consider women's suffrage important?" Elizabeth stopped cutting cake and turned to Janessa, sidetracked by the issue. Tim and Charley looked at each other dubiously.

"Being able to vote would be desirable," Janessa said coldly, "but I have managed to get where I wanted to without it. I am afraid I don't fit in well with clubs."

"There's Eden over in the corner," Charley said, taking his wife by the elbow. "We haven't said hello yet." He signaled to Kathleen to come and collect the twins.

"We saw Eden at breakfast," Janessa reminded Charley as he towed her toward Mike and his wife.

"I thought it would be useful if you didn't get in a brawl with the bride," Charley said.

"I wasn't going to. But I don't have time for their precious movement, and I won't be sneered at because I haven't joined the tea party. I have work to do."

"Aren't you overreacting just a tad?" Charley inquired.

"I went through my girls' club phase in college," Janessa said. "I have no intention of repeating the experience."

"Oh." Charley looked as if understanding had dawned. Janessa, conceived in a hospital tent in the early days of the Civil War, was the daughter of Toby Holt and Mary White Owl, a Cherokee nurse. Toby hadn't known of her existence until Mary, dying, had brought her to him when Janessa was nine. It hadn't taken long for that background to become known at her college and for the clubs that she had optimistically joined to let her know that she was not welcome. Since that time, Janessa had been a loner as far as her own gender was concerned. Now that Charley thought about it, he realized Janessa's only close female friends were his sister, Nan, and Mike's wife, Eden. "I doubt that you would find the same reaction today," he said tentatively.

"I don't have time to find out." Janessa hugged Eden, then kissed Mike on the cheek. "You look near death," she told her brother.

"I had hopes of it this morning," Mike said solemnly, rubbing his temples, "but I'm beginning to feel a little better."

"Tim cheated," Eden said. "He got them drunk

82

instead." She looked over her shoulder. "We're trying to avoid Uncle Henry."

Charlie was incredulous. "He still thinks it's your fault that Frank took off?"

"It's ridiculous," Mike fumed. "He's decided I'm some sort of fiery-eyed anarchist who introduced his baby to all of my lowlife pals." In his morning coat, boutonniere, and hangover, he looked anything but, although his drooping copper-colored mustache gave him a slightly raffish air.

"We bumped smack into them in the hotel lobby yesterday," Eden said. "Aunt Cindy was perfectly nice, but Uncle Henry looked right through me, then glared at Mike as if he were a toad."

"That's an improvement on the last time," Mike said. "He chewed me out for a solid half hour and accused me and all my 'free-thinking socialist friends' of sending the country down the drain. I tried to point out that I make entertainment—moving pictures—and if he wanted to talk to the man in charge of the revolution he'd have to go elsewhere. But it didn't do any good."

"Can Peter talk some sense into him?" Charley asked.

"Peter says he's tried," Eden answered. "Besides, Peter has enough trouble without alienating his father. These lawsuits are worrying him . . . although he did tell me that the oil company proposed a settlement that is reasonable to both sides."

Mike chuckled. "That alone ought to doom it. How do you know all this?"

"I talked to Peter yesterday afternoon, while you were at the rehearsal. I wanted to ask about Frank. Peter doesn't hold us to blame, and he says Aunt Cindy doesn't, either."

"What a mess," Mike grumbled.

"Gunboat on the horizon," Charley murmured.

They turned to see Henry Blake shouldering his way purposefully through the parlorful of guests, a plate of cake in his hand and a scowl on his face. Cindy was half a step behind him, apparently trying to talk to him. She kept looking over her shoulder at her brother, Toby, as she trailed after her husband.

"It looks as if he got into it with Dad," Mike said. "Oh, no." Across the room they could see Toby with an expression that boded no one any good. The four in the corner tried to flee, but the parlor was too crowded. Mike, attempting to dodge an aged woman in an unwieldy hat, bumped smack into his uncle.

"Excuse me," Michael said.

"I have nothing to say to you!" Henry snapped. His voice rang out above the polite conversation in the room. Silence descended, and all eyes turned toward the source.

"Uncle Henry—" Janessa laid a hand on his arm and instantly regretted it when she saw his green eyes flare up.

"I consider your behavior only marginally bet-

84

ter than your brother's," Henry said, still too loud. "I gave my son into your care for a two-week visit, and he returned as an utterly corrupted stranger."

"Now see here, sir—" Charley started to protest.

Cindy, mortified, put her hand on Henry's wrist and dug her nails in. "Henry, I wish to speak with you."

"Fine!" Henry said, finally getting a grip on his temper. He turned his back on the others and allowed her to lead him away, past the wide-eyed guests.

"Just one of those pleasant family get-togethers," Mike said shakily. "I'm sure the Emorys find us delightful."

Cindy dragged Henry through the parlor door and into the foyer. Her expression was furious. "Henry, how could you? You had no business speaking to Mike like that, far less Janessa! And to pick a fight with Toby at his son's wedding reception—"

"I didn't pick the fight," Henry said. "I expressed an opinion of Michael's culpability, and Toby chose to differ with me."

"The whole family differs with you," Cindy said. "Accept the fact that you drove our son away."

Henry ran his hands through his hair in exasperation. "That is absolutely untrue!"

Cindy eyed him icily. "You want to blame Michael so you won't have to take any responsibility. —That's why you started an argument where a roomful of people could hear you. Would you like to stand up on a chair and make another speech? Many of the Emorys' friends happen to be socialists. With a little effort you could insult everyone here."

"That wasn't my intention," Henry said.

"Daddy!" Midge galloped into the foyer and threw her arms around him. Midge was twelve, with a smattering of freckles across her well-scrubbed face and a broad straw sailor hat on her head. Her brown hair was in braids. "Guess what! We're going to the Madrona to stay with Gran! She says White Elk has a horse he's trained just for me."

The color drained from Henry's face as he turned slowly to look at Cindy. His expression was grim. "I don't believe we've discussed this."

"I've been trying to," Cindy said. "But you've been too busy picking fights to listen to me. If I have your full attention now, I will spell it out."

"Daddy?" Midge looked from one to the other of them apprehensively. "Mommy?"

"Just a minute, darling."

Midge's face took on an expression of resignation. She had learned to recognize when her parents were going to fight. "Daddy, don't you want us to go see Gran?"

"Midge dear, this is a grown-up talk," Cindy said. "Would you go and play with Sally for just a little?"

"I'm almost thirteen," Midge muttered rebelliously. "I'm not a baby." Tears ran down her face. "And I want to see Gran!" She turned and ran out the front door.

"I hope you're satisfied," Cindy said.

"I didn't do that," Henry protested. "Now what the devil is going on?"

"I'm taking Midge and staying with Mother for a while."

"That seems like a good idea, since I'll be in Sierra for some time," Henry said carefully. "How long do you plan to stay?"

"Possibly indefinitely."

Henry's face tightened. "What am I to infer from that?"

"Anything you please." Her chin, very like her father's, jutted out at him. "I've decided to make an extended visit to Mother. There is a possibility that Frank might contact her before anyone else."

"I won't have her serving as an intermediary," Henry seethed. "Frank will contact me directly and make an apology, or he won't be allowed to return."

"You cannot order us around or treat us like mutinous soldiers! I hope you realize that, before no one in the family is speaking to you." She picked up her skirts and turned away.

"Cindy, wait!"

"I'll see you at the hotel tonight. Please book yourself a separate room." She strode past him, out the front door and onto the lawn.

Outside, the younger adults had congregated around a croquet set, leaving the parlor settees to the aged and infirm. The children had been encouraged to expend their energy outdoors, and they ran shrieking across the lawn. Starched nursemaids pursued them.

Fourteen-year-old Sally, with Midge at her side, watched the activities with aloof superiority. Sally had recently been allowed to lower her skirts to a length that crossed the middle of her shin, and Midge enviously eyed the velveteen folds. Sally's rose-gold curls were pulled into a single braid at the back of her neck, and the braid was doubled under and pinned with a velvet bow, in contrast to Midge's plain brown plaits.

The girls watched as Cindy Blake strode past the croquet game.

"Your mother's had another fight with Uncle Henry, hasn't she?" Sally said knowledgeably.

Midge sighed and looked uncomfortable. "They don't fight, exactly."

"Yes, they do," Sally told her. "Everybody in the family knows about it. It's not your fault."

"Well, I don't like it!" Midge said. "It's not their business."

"Uncle Henry's mad at Mike," Sally said. "That makes it our business. And Aunt Cindy is Dad's sister. And Gran's everybody's mother."

Eulalia Blake and her first husband had had two children, Toby and Cindy. After Eulalia's first husband, Whip, had died, she married Leland

Blake and, with him, adopted Henry. The result was a closely entwined family nearly incapable of staying out of one another's affairs.

"How long are you staying at the Madrona?" Sally inquired, proving it.

"I don't know," Midge answered. "They won't tell me." She sighed again. "What do you do when your parents have a fight? Sometimes I just don't know where to go."

"They don't fight," Sally said. "They don't talk enough to have fights. Dad's always downtown. Mother has all her clubs."

"Oh."

They stared at the croquet players again.

"It's all right," Sally said airily. "I like Washington. There are lots of parties. Not like boring old Portland."

Midge flicked a glance at Sally's profile, her turned-up nose and Cupid's bow mouth. Maybe if I looked like Sally, she thought, I'd like parties better. Or know what to do at them. If Frank had still been here to take me . . . "I like Portland," Midge said. "Gran has a horse for me. I hope we stay a long time."

"I'd die if I had to go back there," Sally said dramatically. She took note of a boy of about fifteen who was drinking lemonade on the lawn and pretending not to look at them. She smiled at him, and he smiled back. "Portland's just such a backwater, you know. Not like San Francisco."

"That child's a menace," Charley said, observing

Sally from the far side of the croquet game. "In about three years, poor old Toby's going to be knee-deep in her beaux. He won't be able to go into his own parlor without falling over some idiot with a mandolin."

"That's an outrageous frock for a fourteen-year-old," Janessa said. "Much too old for her. Her hairstyle, too. I don't know what Alexandra's thinking of."

"I expect Sally just mows her down," Eden said. She bent to take careful aim with her mallet. They had slunk out the back door while Cindy was upbraiding Henry beside the front. Eden, just twenty, was closer in age to Sally than any of them and had a certain appreciation for her tactics. Her marriage to Mike Holt had been accomplished by the direct route: While her brother, Sam, was in jail in Hawaii for trying to put the deposed queen Liliuokalani back on her throne, Eden had, without permission, taken a ship for the United States. It had been an outrageous, risky thing for her to have done, and Mike and Eden had been afraid that Sam and his wife, Annie, were going to greet them at Tim's prenuptials in less than friendly terms. But to everyone's relief, all had been forgiven. It was the family consensus that Henry and Cindy offered the family more than enough volatility without complications from anyone else.

Now Eden tapped her croquet ball, and it sailed through the first two wickets to roll tauntingly near to Charley's.

"Aha!" said Charley, laughing.

"Oh, you beast." Eden watched as he put his foot on the ball he had tapped into hers and smacked it with his mallet. Eden's ball disappeared into the shrubbery. With a hysterical bark, Alice appeared from nowhere and dived after it. For a moment all that was in view was her back end buried in the ivy. Then she emerged triumphantly and dropped the ball at Eden's feet.

"How can I get anywhere if that blasted dog keeps bringing the balls back?" Charley complained.

"She brings them all back," Janessa said. "Consider it a handicap of the course. Oh, look, there they are!"

The bridal couple emerged from the front of the house. Elizabeth had changed from her wedding gown into a berry-colored going-away suit. She stood beaming at the guests. Tim's arm was around her waist, and her bouquet was in her hand. The unmarried bridesmaids and younger guests gathered around, and Elizabeth, with a wicked grin, tossed the bouquet to Eulalia.

"Not on your life!" Eulalia called out, laughing. She tossed the bouquet again, over her shoulder, and it spiraled down so that all that Sally had to do was hold up her hand for it.

"Oh, no," Janessa groaned, covering her eyes.

The bride and groom, pelted with rice, ran down the steps and to their carriage. The driver, who had been standing guard over it, held the door open for them.

"Did you check the luggage?" Tim asked him. "No fish in the smallclothes?"

"I took the liberty of removing a rubber snake from the lady's dressing case. I didn't find anything else."

"Good man," Tim said.

"We'll send you a postcard from Paris," Elizabeth called out. She and Tim waved. "Good-bye! Good-bye!"

Janessa looked at her husband. "Well, he's done it," she said. "Charley, do you think he'll be happy?"

"How do I know? What makes anyone happy?" He slipped his arm around her, and they went to make their farewells to the Emorys.

"I don't know," Janessa said softly.

Later, Janessa picked up the conversation as she and Charley were walking to their carriage, followed by Kathleen with the twins. "I'm happy with you, but—"

"But, not with much else, huh?" Charley said, having been married long enough to pick up the thread with her. "I know."

They rode in thoughtful silence, out of deference to the twins' nursemaid, who heard enough of their private business as it was. Kathleen didn't eavesdrop precisely, but she was what one might call interested.

At the hotel, after the twins had been bathed and put to bed in the adjoining room with Kathleen, Charley continued their brooding conversation.

"I am happy with you, you know," he observed.

"You aren't happy with your work," Janessa said. She was in her nightgown and brushing out her hair.

"I loathe it," Charley conceded. "But you hate yours, too."

"It doesn't seem right for you to be stuck just because I am," Janessa said. "I appreciate your willingness to suffer with me, but you'll drive yourself over the edge."

The Lawrences were both commissioned officers in the Hospital Service, and they had traveled to wherever there was an epidemic. Then the twins came. Motherhood had made traveling and exposure to disease impractical for Janessa, and she had been reassigned to the Immigration Service on Ellis Island. There she screened shipload after shipload of steerage passengers. As they went by, she marked on their coats with chalk: E for bad eyes, K for a possible hernia, X for the mentally defective. Charley, ever loyal, had taken reassignment with her.

"What about your yellow-fever research? You can't keep doing that at night." Janessa looked at him, brush in hand, over her shoulder. "Some nights you don't come to bed until four."

"We've been all through this," Charley muttered. "I won't go back in the field and leave you alone at home. You have a right to a husband you see once in a while."

"I don't see you now," Janessa said. "I hear you

grumbling while I try to go to sleep at night. Very soothing. Sort of like the sound of rain."

"Janessa—"

"I can't bear having you be a martyr for my sake! Every time I look at Henry and Cindy—and now, God help me, I don't like what I'm seeing between Dad and Alex—I can't stand the thought of our ending up that way!"

"If I understand your rather convoluted logic," Charley said, unbuttoning his shirt, "you're afraid that if I go on working for Immigration, I will get so bored that I'll blame it on you?"

"No, of course not," Janessa said. "You're not like that. Well, you wouldn't mean to be. . . ."

"But I might anyway?" Charley pulled off his shirt. "Well, I suppose I might, human nature being what it is. But I'd try like hell not to. And what about you? You can't tell me you're in clover."

"No, I'm not. But I'm not missing out on anything specific. If I'm fed up with Immigration, it's up to me to find something to replace it with. I don't have that yet. I'm thinking about it."

"And what have you come up with?"

Janessa smiled. "Nothing yet. And we're talking about you, Charley. I want you out of there and back doing what you ought to be."

Charley hung his suspenders on the wardrobe door, then he came and stood behind her, resting his hands lightly on her shoulders. "If I returned to the field, I'd be gone for months at a time."

Janessa leaned her head back against his bare chest. "Then you'd be happy when you were back home," she pointed out. She smiled at him, tilting her head farther, looking at him upside down. "You'd probably be a lot more fun when you were around, too."

"Am I that bad?" Charley looked contrite.

"You mutter," Janessa said gently. "You sit at your desk and write letters and mutter."

"Israel Richardson in London says he has a line on a man in Baltimore who's actually given it to guinea pigs," Charley mused.

"It" was yellow fever. Charley had had it himself four years before, while Janessa and he had been treating an epidemic. The disease had become his passion, his research project, his bête noire, his virulent mistress, ever since.

"I thought it couldn't be transfused to guinea pigs," Janessa said.

"Well, I couldn't do it," Charley admitted. "And neither has anybody else who's tried— except apparently this fellow in Baltimore. Richardson's insane to get his hands on some of this man's guinea pigs." He gave her shoulders a squeeze, then pulled a nightshirt from his suitcase. "The fellow in Baltimore's too frail to travel. Richardson wants me to bring him some guinea pigs," he said through its folds.

"And work with him? Charley, how long have you known about this?" Janessa demanded.

He looked sheepish. "A week or so. Maybe three."

"Three weeks! And you didn't tell me?"

"I didn't want you to feel—"

Janessa put her hairbrush down. She stood up and stared at him in exasperation. "You're going to London," she said emphatically. "If you don't go to London, I'll lock you out of the house. So you might as well go to London."

V

Janessa nearly made good on her threat. Consumed with guilt at the notion of abandoning her to the twins, a nursemaid, an empty house, and a loathsome job, Charley got cold feet and tried to wire the aged professor in Baltimore that he couldn't make it after all. Janessa, whose patience was wearing thin with Charley as well as everything else, packed his suitcase and dumped it on the porch steps.

Consequently, Charley found himself on board the Campania with a parting box of his favorite chocolates from Janessa and a ticket for a stateroom, in which he found awaiting him the professor's shipment: six guinea pigs in wire cages inside a large, custom-made wicker hamper, together with several bales of leaves and a sack of cabbages. The ship was crowded, and there were no empty berths. Charley would have a cabin companion, assigned by the purser. At the opposite end of the cabin were a steamer trunk and an imposing mound of luggage, belonging, Charley supposed, to that gentleman. He wondered if the man would complain; the cabin smelled like guinea pigs and cabbages.

Charley watered the guinea pigs and gave them each a cabbage leaf, then inspected them for signs of illness. Two had been inoculated in Baltimore the day before, and in addition there were four healthy ones to carry the strain. It was quite simple, the professor in Baltimore had explained: "You just take a batch of them with you on the steamer. Every eight days you inoculate a fresh one from one that's dying or has just died. No problem, really."

The professor hadn't had any suggestions as to what to do with the dead ones. Burial at sea, Charley guessed. He looked suspiciously at the brown and white guinea pigs, supposedly infected with yellow fever. Nobody else had been able to give yellow fever to guinea pigs, but he had seen the old man's notes, and the infected humans from whom he had drawn the serum almost certainly had had yellow fever. And the dead guinea pigs in the professor's laboratory had just as certainly died of their inoculations with symptoms comparable to yellow fever's. If it wasn't yellow fever, Charley hadn't the foggiest notion what it could be.

He settled down in an armchair to peruse his notes. Passengers were still boarding, and in ten minutes the steward appeared with a white-bearded gentleman who was apparently Charley's traveling companion.

"Here you are, Colonel Epperly. You'll find your luggage waiting for you."

Colonel Epperly sniffed the air. "What's that awful smell?"

The steward sniffed, too. "This gentleman's luggage, I believe," he said apologetically.

Charley buried his own nose in his notes, hoping the colonel would give up.

The colonel, however, was made of sterner stuff. "See here, sir! What are you traveling with? The place smells like a damned mouse nest."

Charley gave up and put his notebook down. "I'm a doctor, sir," he said, holding out his hand. "My name's Lawrence."

The colonel shook it as if it might be the source of the odor. "And what the devil's in that hamper?" he demanded.

"Guinea pigs," Charley said mildly. "They're being taken to London for some especially crucial research in yellow fever. They're extremely valuable."

"Yellow fever? You'll start an epidemic! This is an outrage!"

"We can't have contagious animals on board," the steward said. "You'll have to put them back on shore."

"They aren't contagious," Charley explained. "They have to be inoculated one from the other to transmit the strain. You can't possibly catch anything from them, Colonel, I assure you."

"I could catch my death from the smell," the colonel said.

98

"We can't allow infected guinea pigs on board," the steward insisted. "It's the rules of the line."

"Where?" Charley demanded. He could hear the "All Visitors Ashore" being sounded for the last time. "Where in the rules does it say that?"

"It says no passengers with infectious diseases," the steward responded.

"These aren't passengers," Charley said.

"No infected animal cargo."

"They aren't cargo. They're my luggage. Is there anything anywhere in your rules that specifically mentions guinea pigs? By name?" He could feel the throb of the engines through the floor. The Campania sounded her whistle.

"I refuse to stay in a cabin with those vermin!" the colonel protested. "I'll bring suit against the Cunard Line, sir!"

Charley made a placating gesture. "If you'll just put up with it until morning, sir, I'll try to make other arrangements." The cabin was, admittedly, no rose garden. It was hot and smelled more like a mouse hole all the time. "They're not dangerous." He reached into the hamper and extracted a squirming guinea pig. "They're quite friendly fellows, really."

The colonel was not beguiled. "I'll have it thrown overboard," he threatened.

Charley looked around. The steward had vanished, presumably for reinforcements. The cabin mates glared at each other for several minutes, Charley in his chair with the guinea pig, the colonel in another chair at the far end of the cabin.

The accommodations did not afford much distance between the men, but the colonel took all he could get.

"Where did you get your medical degree?" he demanded.

"From the University of Southern California," Charley said. "I assure you I am quite bona fide. In fact, I work for the U.S. government."

"Country's going to hell. Breeding infected vermin, letting them escape into the populace."

Charley was wondering if there might be a single cabin, with an occupant willing to trade. The smell seemed to be lessening—or maybe he was getting used to it. Maybe the colonel would.

In five minutes the captain, the purser, and the ship's doctor appeared in solemn procession—an official visit. Among them they had enough gold braid for a South American general and the certain knowledge that the captain of the Cunard liner was God upon the high seas.

The captain, wrinkling his nose, inspected the hamper and the bales of leaves. "You'll have to get rid of it all," he informed Charley. "We can't risk our passengers being infected."

"It's not possible to infect humans from them," Charley protested again. "They would have to be inoculated."

The captain regarded the guinea pigs with distaste. They made a funny little noise, like someone with a scratchy throat, and that seemed to irritate the captain. The colonel had already commented on it. Epperly was now engaged in lighting a cigar and waving the smoke about the cabin. It did not eradicate the smell of the guinea pigs but merely gave passing nostrils the impression that the critters were on fire.

The captain coughed. "I won't have them on my ship. It all has to go—all your fodder and everything. The whole business."

"Now wait just a minute." Charley prepared to defend his mission. If the captain threw the guinea pigs overboard, he would arrive in London with both his time and his ticket wasted. "I understand the colonel's unwillingness to travel with them. If you like, I'll keep them in the ship's morgue. There'll be no risk of contact with any of your passengers. Your own doctor here will tell you that's quite safe." Charley looked with hope at the Cunard Line doctor.

The doctor hooked the hamper open again with the tip of his forefinger and stared undecidedly down at the guinea pigs.

"It's extraordinarily important research," Charley said quickly. "I've been working on it for four years now, and Dr. Richardson in London is waiting for these fellows. Perhaps you know him? He has offices in Harley Street." Charley dropped London's most impressive medical address with ease and was gratified to see it register on his peer. "I assure you, they won't set foot out of the morgue."

The ship's doctor scratched his chin. "This gentleman is on government service," he murmured to the captain. "It wouldn't be good relations to tip his research samples overboard. I daresay they'd do very well in the morgue."

"I'll check on them three times a day and take complete responsibility," Charley said.

"You will indeed," the captain growled. "Very well. Get them out of the cabin immediately."

They all marched out again. Charley, with hamper and fodder, followed the Cunard Line doctor to the morgue, while the colonel continued to fumigate the cabin with cigar smoke.

On the first eight days of their voyage, it rained hard, and the wind blew incessantly, pitching the ship. Nearly all the passengers were seasick. The colonel retired to his berth and refused any offers of assistance from Charley, whom he continued to regard with grave suspicion.

Charley, who possessed a maddening immunity to seasickness, strolled on the deck in the howling rain and tended his guinea pigs. Unaffected by the weather, they scampered about their cages and squealed. On the eighth afternoon, Charley inoculated a black-eared guinea pig with the blood of one of the brown-and-white ones, who were beginning to be ill. The sick guinea pig died that evening, and Charley scuttled onto the deck with the corpse in his pocket and furtively dropped it overboard. He hadn't mentioned to the captain that the guinea pigs were actually going to die of their ailment on the voyage, martyrs to science. If all went well, Charley would arrive in London bringing two pigs who carried an active strain of yellow fever, with two healthy ones left as backup in case of delays.

He fed and watered the remaining guinea pigs, then returned to the cabin, noting with some satisfaction that the colonel was now sick enough to have given up cigars. Even the dining-room stewards had looked green as they staggered about with trays of sliding china. They had had very few diners to tend, however. Most passengers were afraid to ingest anything that might immediately come back up. Charley had ordered a rare steak and a plate of oysters and horrified even the chefs.

When Charley returned to his cabin, he had observed that the sky was still leaden and the rain still sheeting sideways on a raging wind. Now, he undressed and crawled under the blankets and tried to block out the sound of the colonel's mournful snores. The Campania rolled and pitched with the vicious determination of a bucking horse. Really quite restful, Charley thought as he drifted to sleep with the ease of those to whom a rolling ship is a cradle and not an invitation to nausea.

In the morning when he cheerfully whistled "Fifteen Men on a Dead Man's Chest" while pulling up his socks, the colonel furiously requested that he be quiet.

After a breakfast of bacon and eggs in the second-class dining room—a meal shared with a handful of stalwarts who had become a sort of intimate club during the prolonged rough seas—Charley ambled below to the morgue. An attendant was stationed on a stool outside the door and doing something that looked suspiciously like a crossword puzzle. Charley opened the door, whistling again, dreaming of discovering the cause of yellow fever, of tracing its transmission to the source. Researcher Carlos Finlay said it was mosquitoes; but why, Charley pondered, hadn't anyone been able to give it to experimental animals —or people rash enough to volunteer—with infected blood? Of course, now these guinea pigs

Charley stopped short. An overwhelming smell of formalin hit his nose. Even the smell of the guinea pigs and the by now staggering smell of overripe cabbage paled and vanished against this new odor. Charley choked and put his hat in front of his face as his eyes lit on the source of the odor—the embalmed body of a middle-aged Chinese man was stretched on a rubber mat on the morgue table.

Charley pulled the door wider and fanned the air with his hat.

"Don't do that!" The attendant got up from his stool. "You'll stink up the whole passage with formalin, and the smell will travel. The passengers won't like it! No one likes to know there's a corpse on board."

"Well, why the devil is there?" Charley asked irritably. He looked at the guinea pigs in their cages. They didn't look as if they liked the formalin, either.

"Well, in the usual way we just keep them long enough to be sure they're good and dead," the attendant said chattily. "No offense to the profession, but mistakes have been made. Then the sailmaker stitches them up in canvas, and whoops-a-daisy, over they go." The attendant winked. "Gives the poor bloke something to do—we hardly ever haul up sail these days; it's just for emergencies."

"The formalin's making my guinea pigs sick," Charley said.

"Sorry, guv'nor, but we're stuck with the fellow. These Chinese don't like being buried at sea. They always pay a deposit so if they die en route, we'll send them on to wherever they've specified. Otherwise, their descendants can't say the proper prayers, and they don't get into heaven—or wherever it is a Chinaman thinks he goes."

Charley looked resignedly at the corpse, cold and rubbery as the mat it lay on, clad only in its underclothes. "How long has he been dead?"

"Died last night. Doc had him brought up here and shot him full of formalin."

And left him here as a little surprise for me, Charley thought. "I should think ice would have been preferable," Charley said.

"I think ice is nicer myself," the attendant agreed. "But we haven't got a cold room. We can't have him in the larder with the fish and the pork chops, now, can we? He's no nosegay, of course, but frankly, guv'nor, begging your pardon, neither are those guinea pigs of yours."

Charley sighed. "Very well. For goodness sake, try to air the place out now and again, won't you?"

Being a practical man, he extracted a five-dollar bill from his pocket and pressed it into the fellow's palm. "I can't believe a little formalin will creep all the way up to the promenade deck and assault some debutante's sensibilities."

"I'll give it a try, guv'nor."

Charley fed the guinea pigs, who looked as nauseated as a guinea pig could. Then he strolled back to his cabin. The colonel had just risen, moaning, from his bed and was tying his dressing gown around his middle.

The colonel sniffed the cabin air suspiciously. "What's that smell? You haven't got those animals on you?"

"It's formalin," Charley said. "There's a dead Chinaman in the morgue. Due to religious beliefs, they can't bury him at sea. He's embalmed in formalin."

"I don't want to hear about it!" The colonel staggered out the cabin door to the gentlemen's lavatory down the passage.

At lunchtime the storm reached gale proportions. Passengers bundled like pupating moths in swathes of blankets huddled in the lounge or simply took to their beds and stayed there. The cabin stewards bore trays of light broth and coddled eggs to the sufferers and listened to their complaints about the voyage.

After lunch, Charley went to see his charges and discovered that the second of the Baltimore-inoculated pigs had died—from the effects of the

106

formalin as much as the fever, Charley thought, grumbling and opening a cage. He hadn't inoculated a healthy pig from this one yet, and now he was going to have to do it the unpleasant way.

The ship was pitching violently, so Charley sat on the floor, scrunched down, and braced his feet against the wall and his back against a cross rail of the high morgue table with its unlovely burden. He took out a healthy brown pig with white ears and shaved its belly while the morgue attendant watched him interestedly.

The guinea pig didn't like the cold water or the shaving soap, but the razor appeared to tickle its belly. It wriggled and squealed while Charley held it determinedly upside down with one hand and shaved it with the other. When its lower half was denuded, Charley put it back in its cage and gingerly picked up the dead pig. He shaved it, too, and then selected a small, sharp scalpel from his kit. Very carefully he made an incision in its belly and began to cut out the liver.

The morgue attendant squatted beside him, fascinated, falling over every time the ship pitched. "What are you doing, guv'nor?"

"Excising the liver," Charley said between his teeth. "It's very difficult in this sea, and quite full of dangerous microbes. I would advise you to stand back."

The morgue attendant moved off. "Yes, sir. I'll just wait outside the door."

"Do that," Charley muttered. Carefully he cut deeper into the dead guinea pig's abdomen. Theoretically, he was immune, of course, having already recovered from yellow fever; but the liver was highly infectious. And there was always the possibility that these guinea pigs didn't have yellow fever after all but something unpleasantly like it, to which he might not be immune.

The ship lurched again. A pallid hand from the table above flopped past his peripheral vision and dangled beside his ear. Charley ignored it and worked on. He had checked with the Cunard Line doctor and found that the man had died of heart disease. And if there had been anything infectious about the corpse, the condition surely would have been neutralized in all that formalin.

Charley cut carefully, trying not to let himself look sideways at the fingers just beyond his field of vision. Every so often one would brush his ear as the ship rolled. Charley finally scooted around the table and sat on the floor with the back of his head between the deceased's feet. Suddenly the vessel pitched again, a tremendous heave and wallow. The corpse slid back, away from Charley's face, and then, as the ship rolled again, it shot forward and came to rest on Charley's shoulders, with its legs about his neck.

Charley froze. In the trickiest stage of the excision, he had a scalpel in one hand, tweezers in the other, and the guinea pig in his lap. A gelid kneecap pressed against his cheek. He didn't dare move except to continue his work with the guinea pig. A bare foot swung slowly in front of him, then back again. Charley gritted his teeth and ignored it. The ship rolled in the opposite direction, and the other leg brushed his elbow with its toes. Doggedly, Charley finished the excision, abraded the denuded belly of the healthy guinea pig, and rubbed the liver on its skin, while the corpse swung its legs back and forth like a petulant child at the dinner table.

After he had the inoculated pig stowed away and the dead one and its liver wrapped in paper, he heaved the corpse off his shoulders and kicked the morgue door open.

"Where the hell are you when I need you?" he bellowed.

The morgue attendant looked up from his puzzle. "You told me to clear out."

"Well, clear back in," Charley growled, "and strap that fellow down." As he spoke, the ship heaved again, and the corpse slid entirely off the table.

"Whoopsie," the morgue attendant said unnecessarily. "Give me a hand here, guv'nor."

"I don't know why I should. I had the blasted fellow sitting on my neck the whole time I was taking out that guinea pig's liver. I've had all the acquaintance with him I could possibly want."

The morgue attendant heaved the body at the table and got it halfway up. The ship was still rolling.

Charley relented. "Here, that's no way to treat him. He's somebody's dad, I suppose." Years of dissections in medical school had given Charley a somewhat casual attitude toward corpses, but

he had also been a doctor long enough to understand that people didn't feel that way about their
nearest and dearest.

Between them, Charley and the attendant got
the body suitably laid out on the table and
strapped down lest he wander again.

Charley beat a grateful retreat into open air,
pushing his way through the raging storm on the
promenade deck to drop his paper parcel over the
rail. He staggered quickly back before the storm
dropped him over, too. He stood for a moment,
just letting the rain wash the formalin smell off
him—if that was possible—and taking deep
breaths of the wild salt air.

Dear Janessa, he thought, composing a letter
in his mind. I can't tell you what a wonderful time
I am having on this delightful cruise. Next time
I will stay home with the twins, and you can cut
livers out of dead guinea pigs with a formalin-
injected corpse sitting on your shoulders.

During the last week of the voyage, the storm
began to slack off. The sun was finally spotted
pushing its way through the curtain of thunder-
heads, and the Campania's passengers began to
feel that perhaps they might not die after all.
The colonel revived sufficiently to take up cigars
again. And, unfortunately, the family of the
body in the morgue went to pay their respects
and discovered that he was traveling with guinea
pigs.

"It's no good, doctor. They're adamant." The

captain of the Campania crossed his arms on his chest to indicate that he was adamant, too. "They don't feel he is being given proper honor."

"His widow and his mother and father," the purser said. "And his eldest son. Traveling first class. Awkward. You understand."

Charley understood. If the Chinese family had been in steerage, the Campania's officers would have had very little interest in humoring them. Like some Americans, more than a few British considered the Chinese to be an inferior race; and steerage passengers were treated as barely human by the line anyway. A wealthy merchant family, however, traveling first class, was another matter. First-class passengers of any nationality, dead or alive, did not travel with guinea pigs—not on the Cunard Line.

"They have to go," the captain said. He brushed the gold braid on his sleeve as if brushing off the entire matter.

"Go where?" Charley demanded. "They've already been thrown out of my cabin."

"Overside, I'm afraid," the captain said.

"Oh, no, you don't!" Charley's temper boiled over. "I've nursed those blasted beasts for two weeks. They're half-dead from breathing formalin as it is. I've had to treat them and perform surgery on them in the most awkward possible circumstances, with a corpse for company, and now you tell me they're disturbing the corpse's family and you want to put them overboard? You'll have to put me overboard first!"

He looked ready to take a swing at the captain,

111

and the purser intervened. "Now, Dr. Lawrence, try to understand our position."

"Try to understand mine," Charley snarled. "I'm not traveling with the blasted animals because they're cuddly. These guinea pigs are important to research that may one day wipe out yellow fever. Now which is more important, that or someone's ideas of what's 'proper honor'?"

"The family's ideas," the captain said dryly. "On my ship. In a first-class cabin."

The ship's doctor, who had so far said nothing, looked uncomfortable at that. "The, er, animals, are important," he said now. "Perhaps they could be kept in the cargo hold."

"Passengers aren't allowed in the cargo hold," the captain said. "I can't permit Dr. Lawrence access to the area." He appeared to cling strongly to the idea of putting the guinea pigs overboard, the closer they got to Southampton and the possibility that word would get around that the Cunard Line transported diseased rodents.

"Passengers aren't allowed in the morgue either, strictly speaking," the doctor pointed out. "Not live ones, anyway. We've bent the rules this far. What about outside on the steerage deck?"

"They'll freeze to death," Charley protested.

"We'll wrap the cages up well at night," the doctor offered. "A little fresh air might do them good, after all that formalin."

"This is ridiculous! What if we have another storm?"

"Take it or leave it," the captain said. "On the steerage deck. That's my final offer."

"I thought you didn't want them around the passengers," Charley couldn't resist saying.

The doctor grabbed him by the arm. "Come on, old man, let's go get them." He lowered his voice. "We're not talking about disease; we're talking about people's refined sensibilities. On the steerage deck you'd better be more worried they don't cook them and eat them."

He dragged Charley away from the captain and down to the morgue, where they packed up the guinea pigs, leaving the corpse to lie in undisturbed honor. There were only four pigs left. On the steerage deck, Charley and the doctor lashed the hamper down under the curious eyes of a family of Italians and insulated the wicker with the Cunard Line's crested woolen blankets, which the ship's doctor helped Charley steal from the linen-storage room. The doctor seemed to be enjoying himself.

"Quite a show we've had getting these fellows across the Atlantic," he remarked jovially.

"Quite," Charley said. We, hell. He restrained himself. "I appreciate your help."

The weather held fair for five more days, during which time the steerage passengers—far fewer in their numbers on a ship bound away from American than to it—grew used to the eccentric doctor who came down three times a day to feed his odd animals. On the last day out from Southampton, a cold front moved in, and when the Campania steamed into port, the temperature was very nearly freezing. The guinea pigs were shivering and looked not overly long for this world.

They survived to disembark. Charley got his luggage, went through customs, and managed to get the hamper onto a coach on the London train. His fellow passengers were not pleased.

"What's that smell? Conductor, there's a mouse in here!"

"Certainly not, madam."

"There is. I can hear it."

"It's this gentleman here."

All eyes turned to Charley. He felt as if a large sign had been painted on his overcoat, labeling him a smuggler of diseased vermin.

"They have to go in the baggage car," the conductor said firmly when Charley finally acceded to the conductor's demand to produce whatever he was hiding.

"It's too cold," Charley protested. "They'll die. These are tropical animals."

The conductor produced a book of regulations and thumbed through it. The railway proved to be prepared for any eventuality, including guinea pigs. Reluctantly Charley carried the guinea pigs to the unheated baggage car and wrapped his coat around their cage, although with no real hope of preserving them for the last eighty-odd miles of their journey. Night was falling, and the temperature was dropping fast. Glumly he handed the conductor a message to send by wire to Richardson in London.

Charley drowsed as the train rattled north. He fell into a dream in which he was inexplicably forced to carry a farmyard pig in his pocket and to feed it pumpkins. He roused himself from this wearying task as the train slid into Paddington Station, and he hurried through the coaches to the baggage car before it had even come to a stop.

The car was icy, and the guinea pigs, when he pulled the overcoat away from their carrying case, appeared to be nearly frozen. Desperate, he put one guinea pig in each of his overcoat's pockets and moodily envisioned himself turning up in Harley Street thus attired.

But Charley had underestimated a man with whom he was only acquainted by correspondence. Israel Richardson was not a man for half measures. In a booming voice that could be heard the length of the station, he was hailing Charley as he stepped down from the baggage car. "I'm looking for Dr. Lawrence! This way, please! Dr. Lawrence!"

Charley discovered his host, a silver-haired man with a Vandyke and a vague resemblance to Robert E. Lee, had a London Medical Society ambulance waiting at the curb. A uniformed attendant stood by the open door.

"This way! This way!" Richardson helped him into the ambulance, and the attendant jumped onto the box where he shook out the reins and squeezed the horn. They sped away, to the excitement and interested speculation of the crowd on the platform.

In the ambulance Charley pulled the guinea pigs from his pocket, and Richardson popped them into a warming box.

"I don't know whether it's any use at all," Charley said. "I've had the devil of a time, I can tell you." He kicked the door frame of the swaying ambulance angrily. "And all for nothing, very likely."

"Not at all." Israel Richardson was bent over the warming box. "There's life in this fellow. Is he one of your sickies?"

"Yes," Charley said with relief.

"We're not quite out of the woods yet," Richardson said, rubbing the guinea pig's coat with a warm towel. "The other three are deader than doorknobs. We'll have to find a fresh pig pretty smartly to take sick from this fellow before he pops off. But I've got one of my assistants out after one now. I'm glad you wired me from the train."

Charley let out a sigh of mingled relief and lingering worry. "I apologize for my behavior. I've had these pigs nearly thrown overboard, poisoned with formalin, and frozen to death. I've worked on yellow fever for four years, damn well near died of it myself, and this strain from Baltimore is the first promising result of any research I've seen in the job."

Richardson chuckled. "Gets to be an obsession, doesn't it? Shall I tell you how long I've worked on it? No, perhaps I'd better not. I shouldn't like to depress you more than you are already. What do you think of Finlay's mosquito theory?"

"I suppose it's possible," Charley allowed. "But

no one's been able to demonstrate it. I've acted on it as a precaution when dealing with an outbreak, but I can't say I've seen any difference in the death rate."

"Difficult little buggers to get rid of, mosquitoes," Richardson murmured.

"Yes. And then there are these pigs. They aren't supposed to get it at all."

"Yes," Richardson said. He left the one remaining live guinea pig under the warming lamp and put the three dead ones in a bucket of ice. "Maybe they don't have it."

Charley groaned.

"Now don't be downhearted," Richardson said cheerfully. "They have something. Epidemiology's always a step backward and a step sideways for every two in the right direction."

VI

New York, May 1897

Janessa, chin on hand, sat at the kitchen table and watched the twins eat oatmeal. It was Kathleen's half day off. Brandon was a quarter of the way through his bowl, but most of the cereal was in his brown ringlets. Lally, who didn't like oatmeal, was patting hers with her fingers.

"Come on, darlings," Janessa said. "Eat some for Mama."

"No," Lally said distinctly. It was her best word.

The twins wore identical white dresses, according to fashion (Brandon wouldn't wear short pants until he was four or five), ribbed stockings, and high-buttoned shoes. Brandon's hair curled naturally, and Kathleen lovingly brushed it into ringlets each morning. Lally had finally achieved enough pale hair to see and then to tie into a ribbon on the top of her head, where it stuck straight up above the bow, an effect that Charley referred to as "Lally's palm tree."

Kathleen, who was inordinately proud of them both, had taken them in their pram to a phrenologist who had run his fingers over the bumps on their skulls and pronounced that Lally would become a scientist and Brandon the head of a divinity school. Janessa, who had very little patience with that sort of thing, had retorted that so far they seemed more likely to become demolition experts.

"Look. Mama's eating it." Janessa took a bite of oatmeal, which she loathed. "Yummy."

"No," said Lally. She dropped a handful of cereal over the side of the high chair.

"I can't say I blame you," Janessa said. She got up and took a skillet off the rack. "How about a nice eggie?"

"Eggie!" Lally banged her fist on the tray, and the oatmeal bowl flipped over onto the floor. "Mess," she said sweetly, looking down at it.

Janessa cleaned it up, then fixed scrambled eggs and toast, which was what she had been planning for herself anyway. Cooking wasn't very interesting while Charley was away. She gave Brandon some, too—he was always ready to eat twice—and then bathed the leftovers off them in the tin wash-tub, which served as the twins' bath.

Janessa sat and watched them playing in the water and wondered what was becoming of her life. It wasn't a matter of not loving the twins; she adored them. But her life was bounded by their needs and the endless parade of terrified, bewildered immigrants over whom she held so much influence. She agonized over what happened to the ones she sent back to their homeland. For that matter, what happened to the ones she passed? In six seconds she exercised awesome power over them and then never saw them again. It was difficult to feel that she was in any way benefiting humanity or even a few individuals out of that endless stream.

Brandon threw Lally's rubber duckie across the room, and Lally let out a piercing shriek of indignation. Janessa retrieved the toy. Why had she wanted to be a doctor? Her motivation had not been scientific curiosity; it was because her Indian mother had been a medicine woman, and Janessa had seen her touch lives in a positive way . . . when she had been allowed to practice. Living in self-imposed exile in Memphis with her half-white baby, among the white community, that opportunity hadn't come very often. Janessa had wanted to be what no one had ever let her mother be and to do what her mother had been stopped from doing.

Lally whacked Brandon over the head with the rubber duck, and Brandon howled. Janessa looked at them, and they smiled angelically and played pat-a-cake with the soapsuds. Janessa stood, lifted them from the water, and dried them off. She tucked them into dry diapers and flannel nightgowns that had been warming beside the kitchen stove, then carried them off to their room.

She sang to them and wondered, dreaming by the nursery window, what she was going to do about it all. " 'Baby's boat's the silver moon. . . .' " It was obvious that she was going to have to do something soon. She could pack Charley off to London to cure his doldrums, but that wouldn't work to cure hers. " 'Baby's fishing for a dream. . . .' " What was she fishing for? Motherhood was supposed to be the highest expression of female creativity. She had never doubted that. Even Elizabeth Emory's suffragist movement believed it.

" 'His line a silver moonbeam is, his bait a silver star. . . .' " The twins were asleep. Janessa got up, pulling her apron over her head, and found that Kathleen was watching her from the doorway.

"Ah, the lambs," Kathleen said. Her voice sounded on the verge of tears.

Janessa slipped into the hallway and saw that Kathleen's eyes were red with crying. "You're back early," she whispered. "Is something the matter?"

Kathleen sniffed and unpinned her afternoon-off hat, the one with the pink rose. "Ah, then, I didn't have the heart for it. I had a friend die. Me mum just told me the news. I've known Peggy ten years—we came over on the boat together, and she wasn't but twenty. It doesn't seem right, and the baby dying with her."

"Oh, dear." Janessa put an arm around Kathleen and led her down the hall. "Here, let's hang up your coat and sit in the kitchen."

Kathleen unbuttoned her blue wool coat and hung it on a peg by her bedroom door. She put her hat on the white wooden dressing table and looked sadly at Janessa. "Sure and it's not right, Dr. Lawrence."

Janessa towed Kathleen down the hall toward the kitchen and sat her at the table. "Tell me what happened." She put the kettle on the stove and poked up the fire.

Kathleen scrubbed her eyes with the heel of her hands. "It was that man's doing, that devil she married. He laid her in the grave. Always at her, he was, and then when the baby came, he drank away all their money and left none for the doctor. And then she took ill, and the baby was sickly, too. And now they're both gone. Aunt Eileen said it was the childbed fever."

Janessa closed her eyes. Puerperal fever was very likely, brought on by someone's dirty hands delivering the baby in a tenement where it was impossible to stay clean. "I'm sorry, Kathleen."

"Aunt Eileen did what she could," Kathleen said sadly. Kathleen's aunt was a nurse with the Hospital Service. "But she couldn't save her. That devil wouldn't let me aunt in when the baby was borning. He was drunk and roaring like always and didn't send for her till after Peggy took sick. Faith, and I'd go out now and shoot him dead if I didn't think he'd go to hell soon enough anyway, what with the drink."

The kettle, which had been nearly hot from Janessa's dinner, boiled now. Janessa threw a double handful of tea into the pot to steep faster. Then she poured a cup and put it in front of Kathleen. "Here, dear, drink this."

Kathleen sipped, and tears as hot as the tea slid down her cheeks. "It's bad enough being poor, but when it comes to dying of it, and nowhere that's clean and safe to be having your baby—I'd sooner not marry than give meself up to that."

Janessa looked at her sadly. She had no answers. Private hospitals didn't take charity cases, and public hospitals were pesthouses, which no one in their right mind would enter if they weren't dying. For well-to-do women like Janessa, babies were delivered at home, among a pile of clean sheets with a doctor in attendance; poor women had newborns on a bed that the rest of the family slept in, too. If they were lucky, a midwife was on hand to try to keep things clean long enough to get the baby into the world with its mother uninfected. Because of childbirth, the mortality rate for women was always higher than that for men. Among the poor women, it was astronomical, and their children were lucky if they lived through their first year.

Janessa gave Kathleen a second cup of tea with all the sympathy that she could offer, then sent her to bed.

Janessa retired also. She pulled on a nightgown and crawled into her bed—too big and empty without Charley. She folded her hands behind her head and, gazing at the thin bar of moonlight coming in the window, thought about poor young Peggy. All the women she examined so briefly on Ellis Island were at similar risk, moving into the tenements to die for lack of medical care.

She could save Kathleen from that if the poor girl weren't too frightened to marry—and Janessa wouldn't blame her if she was. But Kathleen was one among the millions, and any assistance there wouldn't solve the problem; it would merely remove it from in front of Janessa's agonized eyes.

Then it hit her. Feeling a new sense of purpose, she sat up, lit her lamp again, put on her slippers, and padded across the room to Charley's desk. It looked bare without his clutter of notebooks and papers. Janessa opened her address book and pulled out the box of good stationery she kept in the bottom drawer. After she had finished dashing off half a dozen notes, she wrote a long letter to Charley.

London

"I knew I shouldn't have left her," Charley told Israel Richardson. "She's going to start a hospital for slum women."

"She has notions like this often?" Richardson asked from his chair in the laboratory of his Harley Street offices.

"It's motherhood," Charley replied. "It hasn't exactly suited her."

"Dear me." Richardson cocked his head at Charley. "Well, she does have a medical degree. Stands to reason she might want to use it."

"Of course she wants to use it," Charley said. "I thought she would eventually open a private practice." He glared at the letter.

"Admirable cause, a hospital," Richardson said cautiously.

"For a millionaire philanthropist," Charley muttered. "But a very expensive cause for anyone else. We'll lose our shirts. How does she plan to meet the expenses of a hospital for people who can't pay?"

"Maybe you should read the whole letter. You haven't gotten past the first page."

Charley flipped it over. "She says she's going to solicit funds for an endowment. Good God, she doesn't know anything about that sort of thing. She didn't even consult me!" Charley looked up from the letter indignantly.

"You did say she was, er, independent," Richardson pointed out. He looked mildly shocked himself. Charley knew that the Englishman's wife had been dead for ten years. She had never, the man said, made any decision outside the kitchen or the nursery without first consulting him. "Perhaps you've allowed her too much latitude."

124

Charley got a grip on himself. "No such thing!" he responded, indignant now for Janessa's sake. "We don't run our marriage that way. We—we—that is, Janessa's capable of—"

Richardson burst out laughing. "Nearly anything, it appears to me, but that's your cross to bear, old man. You're outraged that she didn't consult you, and furious with me for suggesting she ought to have. Americans!" He threw up his hands.

"I've had a trying morning," Charley said with dignity. "Take a look at these results."

Richardson sighed as he glanced over at Charley's microscope. "I already have. Fascinating, but I'll be a monkey's uncle if I think it's yellow fever."

"Well, it's something."

"I think it's a ringer. Where's the incubation period?"

"Blasted if I know," Charley said morosely. "It occurred to me on the boat that the disease transferred mighty easily. But maybe we're wrong about the incubation period, too."

Yellow fever researchers seemed to have been wrong about everything else, so far. Scientists had noted that when yellow fever cases first appeared, there was a delay of between eight and fourteen days between the first cases and any further ones, even in the same neighborhood. In fact, as a rule there was the same gap between the first yellow fever case in a household and any other household members taking sick. That gap had been noticed as long ago as 1814, and researchers had come to the conclusion that the disease was incubating somehow, and somewhere.

"We're not wrong about the incubation period," Richardson said firmly.

"Well, we're wrong about something."

"Inevitably. Come and have some sherry, and we'll think about it. It's nearly teatime."

Charley stuffed Janessa's letter into his pocket and followed his colleague out of the laboratory, then up the stairs to a palatial suite Richardson kept over his offices.

"If we're lucky, I shan't have to go out," Richardson said, pouring golden sherry from a cut-glass decanter. "Lady Merton is getting near her time, but I think it will be another few days before her child makes its appearance."

The decanter spangled the Persian carpet with diamonds of light. Richardson handed Charley a glass and settled into a black leather wing chair in front of the bow window. Delivering Lady Merton's babies and attending her royal acquaintances' other ills and complaints paid Richardson very well. He had delivered a prospective duke only this morning.

Charley thought about his own house near the Hospital Service on Staten Island. Janessa and he had discussed the kind of clientele that Richardson enjoyed. They themselves could easily have had a similar practice, between Toby's Washington connections and Charley's Richmond family. The Lawrences occupied that most revered of postwar Southern niches, formerly wealthy old blood. They wielded social influence beyond their income on the newly rich. But Charley and Janessa hadn't liked the idea of treating old men's gout and bored debutantes' hysteria. So they had traded influence and money for professional satisfaction; now, stuck on Ellis Island, they didn't even have the satisfaction. No wonder Janessa wanted to start her hospital, Charley thought. But how was she going to get it off the ground without the influence and money?

"What?" Charley realized that Richardson had been talking to him for almost a minute.

"I asked you," Richardson said mildly, "where Hotchkiss in Baltimore got this yellow-fever strain."

"Sorry, I was daydreaming. From a family of Ecuadoran immigrants. It's almost endemic down there. Hotchkiss isolated them, treated them, and managed to keep the disease from spreading in Baltimore, thank God. The captain of the ship they sailed on called him in as soon as the first of them took sick."

"Do you find it sinister," Richardson inquired, "that Hotchkiss never managed to give yellow fever to his guinea pigs from any of the epidemics suffered in Baltimore?"

"Yes, blast it," Charley said. "I saw the victims, though. I went down to Baltimore when they first took sick. If they didn't have yellow jack, they had something awfully bloody like it." He grimaced.

Richardson nodded. Yellow fever had unmistakable symptoms: fever, jaundice, and black vomit. "Still, I've heard there are mimicking diseases in the tropics—all the symptoms of yellow fever, even in severe cases, yet not the same disease."

"If it looks like yellow fever and acts like yellow fever, then why shouldn't it be yellow fever?" Charley demanded.

Richardson chuckled. "For the same reason you were so almighty careful taking out that guinea pig's liver on board ship—because it might have been something else to which you had no immunity. And I must say I would have given a pretty penny to see you, with that Chinaman trying to dance the two-step around your neck! Oh, dear! Well!" Richardson shook his head in ill-concealed amusement.

"Believe me, it's funnier at a distance," Charley assured him. "Yellow jack is no laughing matter. You ought to try it yourself."

"I have," Richardson said. "Yellow fever researchers tend to die of it or survive and be immune. Nevertheless, I don't intend to take any chances, either, with what those guinea pigs are carrying. Fellows who have had yellow fever and ought to be immune have occasionally caught it again. To my mind that proves that one or the other wasn't yellow fever. We've established immunity pretty clearly."

"I know." Charley sighed. "So we've got some blasted tropical imposter. What are we going to do with it?"

"Oh, study it," Richardson said. "It's something, you know. And it appears to be particularly nasty. My dear Lawrence, don't be downhearted. We'll get old yellow jack eventually. And the Medical Society is extremely grateful to you for bringing this strain here. I trust you'll stay over here awhile longer and work on it with me."

"Of course, if you can use me," Charley said, wondering how much of his eagerness was attributable to scientific curiosity and how much was due to Richardson's palatial accommodations and his excellent cook. Despite Charley's decision to serve mankind, it was gratifying to perform the service over an old sherry and trout almondine.

"My dear fellow!" Richardson said, clapping him on the back. "You're a respected expert on the disease. I'm grateful to have you! I tell you what: Let's get hold of some mosquitoes and see if this can be transmitted by them. Maybe there's only a lag time in the incubation period when there's a mosquito in the middle. Who knows? Let me get Perkins."

Richardson, looking quite cheerful, rang the bell, and a solemn-faced, almost sepulchral butler appeared. "Tell Dawkins I want some mosquitoes," Richardson said. "Will you, Perkins? There's a good chap."

"Certainly, sir." The butler lumbered away.

Charley had learned that Perkins was not nearly as lugubrious as he looked. The butler had, Charley suspected, trained himself rigorously to maintain an expressionless visage while receiving orders for mosquitoes or vials of blood or a liver in formalin.

"I rather like the idea of mosquitoes," Richardson mused. "An enemy we can see, for a change."

"It would account for yellow jack being a tropical disease," Charley said. "Something about it is susceptible to cold. We did try keeping them out when I worked on it in North Carolina. Lord knows whether or not that helped, but it did disappear after the first frost, as always. It wouldn't take much to freeze a mosquito," he added thoughtfully.

"A great many diseases are endemic to the tropics simply because the people who live in the tropics aren't entirely tidy," Richardson pointed out.

"I'm not willing to buy the filth theory," Charley said stubbornly. "People who aren't entirely tidy also leave standing water lying around in old boots, too. And every village church in South America has its holy-water font."

"Personally, I subscribe to mosquitoes," Richardson said. "Patrick Manson has found filariasis in them, so why not yellow fever or malaria? Insect hosts are a credible theory these days. Ticks and tsetse flies. Quite a host of suspects."

"Most people think Manson's loony," Charley said.

"Pah! Most of the London Medical Society has been dragged kicking and screaming into the modern age of medicine. They all thought Lister was a crackpot. If they can't see it in front of their faces, they'll pretend it doesn't exist—until it's demonstrated so conclusively that even their ossified brains have to accept it. If I had a dollar for every doctor fifty years ago who didn't believe in microbes . . . I strongly believe that our man Ross in India is going to prove the malaria theory. I had the privilege of working with him and Manson both before Ross left for India. A most determined man, with the soul of a poet. Of course, all my dignified colleagues find him quite as laughable as 'Mosquito' Manson."

"I read an old report from 1848 by a fellow named Josiah Nott," Charley said. "He's been dead now for more than twenty-five years, but he practiced down in Mobile, Alabama, where they have a lot of yellow fever and malaria both. At that time no one had distinguished between the two. He said they were conveyed by the bite of an insect, and most likely mosquitoes. Everyone ridiculed him, in print as well as by word of mouth. Very much what they did to Manson: learned articles full of ridicule and condescending sarcasm. I'd be tickled if Nott turns out to have been right about both diseases."

"Well, Perkins will have the mosquitoes for us to play with tomorrow," Richardson said. "We'll see what the little devils can do. I have two suits of netting I've been quite eager to try out. Ah, here he is now."

"Dawkins informs me you will have mosquitoes tomorrow, sir," the butler reported. "And dinner is served."

An enticing smell lingered about Perkins, who had apparently come through the kitchen. Charley stood up with alacrity. Certainly it would be better to stay in England and work awhile longer while enjoying the labors of Richardson's cook. Particularly since Janessa appeared to have a very large bee in her bonnet. . . .

New York

"Mrs. Lawrence. How nice to see you. And how is your father the senator?"

"Quite well, thank you." Janessa didn't bother to point out that Toby hadn't been in the Senate since 1894. And she knew it was no use attempting to get Mrs. McLeod to call her Doctor instead of Mrs. Mrs. McLeod didn't approve of women being doctors. Janessa loathed Mrs. McLeod, but she sat on the woman's uncomfortable ivory brocade settee and balanced an excessively ornamented Bavarian china teacup because she wanted Mrs. McLeod's money.

"You're very kind to receive me." Janessa set the loathsome teacup down among the cucumber sandwiches. "It's so important to this worthy project to have the names of our leading citizens associated with it."

Mrs. McLeod appeared to be mulling that over. To be known as a philanthropist was useful, but it looked as if she was weighing whether she really wanted to waste her money on slum women. "And where is your husband, Mrs. Lawrence?"

132

she inquired, as if perhaps Janessa was involved in unauthorized activity in his absence.

"He's in London at the moment," Janessa replied. "Working on yellow fever research with Israel Richardson. Charley speaks very highly of him." She smiled ingratiatingly. "I understand you have a most charming new grandson."

Mrs. McLeod nodded regally. She was considered in New York society circles to have scored a coup by marrying her daughter, Cornelia, to the impoverished but blue-blooded duke of Manes, and the renowned Dr. Richardson had recently delivered an heir. "I should have liked to have been with my dear daughter for her confinement, of course, but my health has not been up to the voyage." Mrs. McLeod smiled regretfully.

"Of course," Janessa murmured. She had heard from Charley that Cornelia had utterly refused to receive her mother.

"Of course dear Cornelia writes to me every week."

Six years earlier, Cornelia, not yet out of her teens, had been forced, by her mother's social ambitions, into a marriage with a man fifteen years her senior. Janessa doubted that the young woman, having finally acquired some gumption, had anything further to say to her mother. She wondered if Mrs. McLeod still thought the marriage had been worth it. "You must be quite proud of him," she said as Mrs. McLeod produced a photograph of the baby, bundled in a white shawl. What appeared to be a disembodied pair of hands puzzled her. But then Janessa realized that they belonged to a nursemaid who sat, with a second shawl over her face, holding the child in her lap.

"Such a pretty baby, and born into such a fortunate family," Janessa said. *If you discount the fact that his parents don't love each other.* "There is such a desperate need to see that the children of the poor have a chance to begin life healthy and that their mothers don't die needlessly of causes that we more fortunate women never have to face."

"I have always held," said Mrs. McLeod, "that the poor have only to help themselves out of poverty by hard work and determination. No one who is not indolent need remain poor."

"In many cases you are quite right," Janessa agreed, resisting the urge to take Mrs. McLeod by the throat and shake her until she took notice of the real world. "But when a child begins life sickly, he or she never has a chance to work. When the mother is sickly, she produces only sickly children. We can do much with better health care and hygiene to stop the cycle of poverty."

"The poor have no notion of hygiene," said Mrs. McLeod. "You should see the utter squal-or of the homes in which my servants live."

"One of the purposes of our hospital will be to educate them," Janessa said. "Many of them, however, are fighting an uphill battle just to stay clean in a tenement filled with rats, where the water taps don't work half the time."

Mrs. McLeod shuddered delicately. "I feel sure

that with greater attention to morality, much might be accomplished. I do trust that your hospital will accept only deserving patients, of moral rectitude?"

"Mrs. Meigs asked me much the same question," Janessa said, after a calculated pause, "when she was agreeing to lend us her support." Mrs. Meigs was a friend of Mrs. McLeod's, and also of Eden's late grandmother Claudia Brentwood's. It was mainly Claudia's friends that Janessa was canvassing for her hospital. They all had money.

"Mrs. Meigs is joining you?" Mrs. McLeod inquired. She looked thoughtful.

"Oh, yes," Janessa said airily. "And we discussed the very point that you brought up. Mrs. Meigs felt much as dear Aunt Claudia used to: that one cannot turn away any desperate soul in an emergency, but that great improvement in moral conduct may be achieved with education and proper examples." She was immensely grateful that Charley wasn't there to hear her spouting platitudes. Or implying that a good-conduct investigation would be required of prospective patients. The poor were no fonder than anyone else of having their private affairs inspected by busybodies.

"I shall consider your proposal," Mrs. McLeod said. "One must be very careful, of course, where one bestows one's charity. But if Mrs. Meigs thinks highly of the project . . . You did say she was subscribing to the fund?"

135

"Oh, she's quite enthusiastic," Janessa said hastily. She rose to leave; the allotted fifteen minutes for a formal call had expired. "We are planning to name the establishment in memory of Aunt Claudia. Her son, my courtesy cousin Samuel, has made a very generous gift." He just doesn't know it yet.

"Indeed?" Mrs. McLeod, distracted from Mrs. Meigs for the moment, held out two fingers for Janessa to shake. An institution named for Claudia Brentwood was, of course, an endeavor with which one would wish to be associated. The newspapers would list all contributors. Mrs. McLeod was well aware that Claudia Brentwood had not liked her at all, but that was not the point. Claudia Brentwood had been rich, respected, and a power among the socially exclusive Four Hundred—all qualities that recommended a subscription in her memory.

Janessa went to call on Mrs. Meigs.

"How are you, dear?" Mrs. Meigs let Janessa kiss her cheek. "Are you still pursuing this notion of a slum women's hospital?"

"Of course," Janessa said. "In fact, I was just talking to Mrs. McLeod about it. She's very enthusiastic."

"Oh? Mrs. McLeod?" Mrs. Meigs's soft, wrinkled cheeks fluttered as she pursed her lips.

"And I've had the most wonderful idea. We're going to name the place for Aunt Claudia: the Claudia Brentwood Memorial Hospital for

Women and Children. I'm sure you'd like that. And my cousin Samuel has gotten the project off the ground already."

"Sam has contributed? I wouldn't have thought it."

Janessa chuckled. "Sam's not nearly the reprobate he used to be, I assure you. He's become a solid citizen, a gentleman planter."

"He could hardly have gone much farther in the other direction," Mrs. Meigs said dryly. Then a smile twitched at the corner of her mouth. "He was very handsome, of course. It's no wonder he was spoiled." She sighed, possibly for the days when she, too, might have been attracted to a dashing bad boy. "And you say Mrs. McLeod has subscribed?"

"She's been very generous."

"How generous?" Mrs. Meigs inquired.

Janessa took a deep breath. One might as well be hung for a sheep as a lamb. "Fifty thousand dollars."

"Fifty!" Mrs. Meigs blinked rapidly, then she, too, took a deep breath. "Well! I certainly wouldn't want her to put me to shame over dear Claudia's memorial. Fetch me my checkbook, Janessa, there's a good child. It's in my little secretary over there."

While Janessa was agonizing over how soon it would be permissible to call on Mrs. McLeod again—before Mrs. Meigs could contact her friend—a check for the exact amount arrived in the mail from that lady, who was not to be out-done. The New York grapevine moved in mysterious ways. Janessa took both checks and set out to display them to the other ornaments of New York society who decorated her list and who wouldn't want to be outdone, either.

VII

When Janessa had, as Charley put it, a bee in her bonnet, she was a force that very few people could reckon with. By mail she ruthlessly shook down her courtesy cousin Sam, then paid personal visits to his grandmother's cronies and her father's political acquaintances. The politicians included Theodore Roosevelt, whom she cornered one afternoon at his house in Oyster Bay.

The assistant secretary of the navy had been joined by his wife Edith. "You do realize, my dear"—he bent a bemused gaze on Janessa's prospectus—"that I have a large family to support."

"Then of course you will be sympathetic to the plight of these unfortunate women who lack such a conscientious provider," Janessa said, brooking no argument. She thought she saw a flicker of amusement replace Edith Roosevelt's normally self-restrained expression. Edith seemed always to have a baby on her hip, or one on the way, or both.

After Janessa had wrung sufficient funds from her victims to make the hospital a real possibility, she handed in her resignation from the Hospital

Service to Dr. McCallum, her commanding officer. He was not surprised; Janessa did not keep secrets well. Then she set about raiding his staff for doctors.

"McCallum warned me about you," Steve Jurgen said. "He's promised me first choice of all future assignments if I refrain from jumping ship with you for this harebrained scheme."

"It's nothing of the sort," Janessa said indignantly. "You would be doing some very real good, desperately needed."

"I'm doing some very real good in the Hospital Service," Steve pointed out. "I didn't go and have twins." He adjusted his gold-braided uniform cap and shook his head sadly. "Fancy you in civvies."

The next day Janessa thought about his remark and looked at herself in the mirror. She wasn't sure she fancied herself in civvies, either. Hospital Service doctors were commissioned officers in fancy uniforms. Now, in her plain white shirtwaist and blue serge skirt, she looked like someone's middle-aged mother. How much would the lack of the uniform cost her in terms of perceived authority? She felt a little naked without that outward and visible sign that she stood on an equal footing with the male doctors. Now people would take her at first glance for a nursing sister, and she would have to explain over and over that she wasn't.

Calm down, Janessa. She felt as if she were standing on a swinging bridge; it was a very heady sensation but one that she did not entirely trust.

The combination of fear and exhilaration was too unsettling. She shored up her determination with the paperwork involved in creating the Brentwood Foundation, with hiring an administrator and a head nurse, with interviewing doctors.

Most of her candidates were either just out of medical school or Hospital Service doctors tired of being sent on a moment's notice to Timbuktu. Janessa had found a building, a creaking tenement on Cherry Street. The structure might be rehabilitated, given a contractor whose crew wasn't afraid of rats. She hired a night watchman next, to keep everything that had been installed during the day by the builder from being stolen at night.

Janessa's list of applicant doctors decreased by two-thirds when they saw the building. Patiently she explained that poor women had no use for a hospital they couldn't get to. With equal patience she explained that expecting the denizens of Cherry Street to be immediately grateful and therefore to refrain from robbing their intended benefactors blind was unrealistic. She hired a preacher's young son just out of medical school; he had his pocket picked on the way home from his interview. She also hired a middle-aged socialist whose street-corner clinic had not been able to survive financially; and a former Hospital Service doctor who had recently married and who spoke Yiddish, German, and Italian. The New York newspapers picked up the story, labeled her a crusading lady physician, and printed a long biography of Claudia Brentwood and a list of the hospital's patrons.

The ribbon was cut on a brilliantly sunny day in July. Charley was still in London with Israel Richardson, dissecting mosquitoes, but he sent a telegram of cautious congratulations.

"He's afraid to come home," Janessa's brother Michael suggested. He and Eden had turned out for the well-attended ceremony.

"Nonsense," said Janessa. "And don't think you're going to come lurking around, either, trying to make moving pictures of people's gall bladders. I won't stand for it."

Mike had recently begun a new moving picture, which, he said, mirrored real life. Because the public rarely appreciated real life, he had also begun another, which featured vaudeville pratfalls and pies in the face.

"I'm impressed with you, Janessa." Michael looked up into the bright sunlight, toward the top of the brownstone building. All its windows were newly glazed. A stiff breeze whistled down the canyon of the street and tried to take his hat off. "You need a flag, though. A pennant, with the symbol of a mule rampant. The motto could be 'I will.' "

The breeze also lifted the strewn trash of Cherry Street. The ambulance horses, drawn up proudly in front of their newly painted, secondhand ambulance, shook their heads in clouds of flies.

Slowly Janessa walked to the ribbon-decked podium and accepted the gathering's applause. A

New York Times reporter duly wrote down the names of the social luminaries who had graced Cherry Street with their presence. The article would appear in the next day's edition.

"Ladies and gentlemen," Janessa began, "thank you for coming here today and for the funds you have so generously given to make the Claudia Brentwood Memorial Hospital for Women and Children a reality—"

What is Kathleen thinking? she wondered after she finished her less-than-brilliant speech and was cutting the ribbon to the applause of the donors. Did the girl understand the role she had played in it all? Kathleen had not wanted to bring the twins in their pram to the ribbon cutting. "I'll not be taking me darlings down there in that nasty neighborhood," she had said.

Many of the donors appeared to feel the same way, but they stayed for a tour and a reception. Then the hospital was officially opened for business.

"Lord God," Anna Williams, the head nurse, said. "I feel like Cinderella come home from the ball. The party's over. Let's get down to work."

But the first day there were only two patients. The hospital had appeared overnight like a mushroom on Cherry Street, and the people it was designed to serve eyed it warily and were afraid to go in. A few days later word had gotten around that the hospital truly didn't charge its patients money and didn't preach sermons like the Rescue League did. Suddenly the place was inundated.

Janessa went home exhausted and blood smeared, but whistling. At last she had the satisfaction—work with results, work with a purpose. She had delivered two babies in antiseptic surroundings (one over the furious protests of its father), cleaned and stitched a cut thumb that would almost surely have festered, and admitted and prescribed morphine for a woman with an advanced and inoperable tumor. She came home, wolfed down the dinner Kathleen had fixed her, and played bears under the table with Lally and Brandon.

"You're a sight, Dr. Lawrence." Kathleen giggled. "Sure and you ought to see yourself."

Janessa stuck her head out from under the tablecloth. Her eyes shone. "Oh, Kathleen, it feels so good to be doing something useful!"

This state of bliss continued for nearly a month until a thin and shadow-eyed patient named Araminta Haggerty crept into Janessa's office.

She said she was thirty but appeared closer to fifty, with the muddy skin and missing teeth of bad nutrition. She looked as if she had had too many babies too close together. Araminta glanced nervously over her shoulder, twisting her neck as she sat down. "My husband don't like that I'm here," she said. "He said he'd flat kill me if I told some doctor all our private business. But I'm that desperate I come anyway."

"What are your symptoms?" Janessa asked gently.

"I don't have no symptoms," Mrs. Haggerty said. "Exceptin' that I'm so tired all the time I just want to die."

"That could be a symptom of anemia," Janessa suggested, although she suspected it was more likely a symptom of overwork. "Is that why you have come to us?"

"No. I want you to take my womb out."

"I beg your pardon?"

"I want it out. I know there's an operation for that, because my cousin's sister-in-law had to have it. I want mine out, too."

"Mrs. Haggerty, we can't do that."

"Why not?"

"We don't remove healthy organs. That other woman's womb must have been diseased."

"But I got to have it out. I got seven kids. And I birthed three more that died. The last one went two days ago. I can't take no more. I get in the family way the minute he looks at me, seems like."

Janessa regarded Araminta Haggerty's worn face. What kind of worm was her husband? she wondered, indignant. "Mrs. Haggerty, I can't remove your womb. What I can and will do is write a letter for you to take to your husband informing him that it is essential to your health that you do not become pregnant again. Ten babies in what—ten years?—are far too many."

"He knows that." Mrs. Haggerty looked embarrassed.

"Then he will simply have to leave you in peace," Janessa said.

"That's all you're gonna do for me?" Mrs. Haggerty demanded angrily. "Tell me I ain't supposed to let my husband in my bed? He told me that was all you'd say, but I didn't believe him."

Janessa thought about that. Maybe she had been making the wrong assumption. "Mrs. Haggerty, you are going to have to be very frank with me. Do you want to continue to have sexual congress with your husband? I don't mean does he; I mean do you?"

Mrs. Haggerty's cheeks flamed red, and she looked at her hands, which she was twisting in her lap. "Well, it seems like we don't have no other pleasures. And it is nice to lie down next to him, at night, after work's done. But I'm so afraid of getting in the family way again, that I can't bear to let him touch me."

"I see." It wasn't the story she heard from most of her patients, who would have been grateful if their husbands lost their sex drive entirely. But for every three wives who submitted only because it was their duty, there was an Araminta Haggerty. And it seemed that her husband wasn't such a brute, after all.

"Doctor, are you married?" Mrs. Haggerty asked.

"Well, yes." Janessa displayed her ringed left hand.

Mrs. Haggerty looked embarrassed, but she persisted. "Do you like it? With your husband? What you call sexual congress." She blushed. "I never gave it no name before."

"It is necessary to speak openly if we are to help you," Janessa said.

"Well, then," Mrs. Haggerty said, "do you like it?"

This time Janessa blushed and was furious with herself for being embarrassed. "Yes, I do."

"Then you ain't gonna tell me I'm depraved and unnatural 'cause I want to keep doing it with my husband but don't want no more babies," Mrs. Haggerty said flatly.

That was exactly what many social reformers preached. The doctrine of "voluntary motherhood," a phrase coined in the seventies, had been around for years in feminist and other reform circles; but they preached self-restraint as the way to achieve it. The Comstock Law of 1873 had defined contraceptive devices, or even information, as obscene and prohibited their public distribution. That didn't mean they weren't available, of course; just that women had no idea what they were or what to do with them.

"No, I'm not going to tell you that you're depraved," Janessa said. "I'm going to tell you what I use. But you have to be very sure to use it every time."

Mrs. Haggerty nodded. She seemed both eager and apprehensive, rather like someone contracting with a wizard for a spell.

As Janessa wrote on a prescription pad, she said, "There are several possibilities. You and your husband will have to be prepared to talk openly with each other, too, and discuss which you like the best." Janessa instinctively lowered her voice. Dispensing contraceptive information was not part of the hospital's mission. If Horace White or Adam Sells, two of her fellow physicians, overheard her, they would probably be horrified. But this kind of information was always given woman-to-woman, in a kind of wives' network. Janessa was just playing her part in that. She had given the same information to Eden when Eden had married Mike.

"First of all, there are condoms—rubber sheaths that the man wears. They are the 'obscene rubber goods' that are written about in the newspaper when Mr. Comstock's agents have staged another raid on some hapless druggist. They are perfectly legal to buy for the prevention of infection. They also do nicely to prevent pregnancy, which is no one's business but your own."

"I'd be ashamed to ask for them," Mrs. Haggerty whispered.

"Then have your husband do it," Janessa suggested.

"I doubt he would, either. Askin' for something like that in front of all those people."

"I am sure a great many women have found that preventing pregnancy is a matter best not left to their husbands," Janessa said with some asperity. "Very well, there are several methods for you to use yourself. Using a syringe to wash yourself with vinegar immediately afterward is effective. Or you can make up a soluble pessary—that's a suppository—in these proportions. . . ." Janessa began to write out the formula. "Six grains of citric acid and one dram of boric acid in ninety grains of cocoa butter. Or insert a sponge dipped in vinegar beforehand. You'll find them in drugstores, in little silk net bags, with a string attached for removal. Or you can wipe the sponge with eighty grams of quinine mutate to an ounce of petrolatum." Janessa wrote down "quinine mutate."

Mrs. Haggerty was beginning to look bewildered and disappointed. "I don't know what all them words are."

"The druggist will know," Janessa said, writing. Then she looked up and caught sight of Mrs. Haggerty's face.

"I thought you meant you'd give me somethin' to take away with me." Her mouth trembled with disappointment. "I don't have no money, either."

"Oh, dear." It was obvious that even if Mrs. Haggerty had had the money, she wasn't capable of going into a drugstore and ordering a pessary made up, or even quinine-laced petrolatum. "I suppose we could provide you with some method," Janessa said dubiously. "As being necessary to your health. There is another way, the method that I myself use most often; but it has to be fitted by a doctor. It's called a womb veil, and it's a kind of rubber cap on a spring-steel circle. It fits over the mouth of the womb and prevents the seminal fluid from passing through. You rub it first with the same mixture of petrolatum and quinine mutate." She found Mrs. Haggerty looking blanker

148

than ever. "Here," Janessa said. She took down an anatomy text from the shelf behind her desk and opened it to the relevant illustrations.

"Lordy," breathed Mrs. Haggerty.

"Now. This is the vaginal passage, and this is the cervix and the womb. The womb veil fits here, do you see? And every woman is a different size, so it has to be fitted specially."

Mrs. Haggerty bit her lip. "And I put this contraption up into myself and take it out again?"

"You wait several hours before removing it." Janessa saw that Mrs. Haggerty's face was flaming. "I assure you it is a much less drastic and embarrassing process than removing your womb. Maybe you should start with the sponge, though, and see how you and your husband react to it. If you'll come back tomorrow, I will have one for you, and you can dip it in plain vinegar. But take a good look at this illustration. This is where you want it, do you see? Don't push it too far up, or it won't work."

Mrs. Haggerty nodded mutely, then fled, mortification finally winning out over determination. Janessa thought the woman would be back the next day, though. She had been desperate enough to overcome embarrassment in visiting the hospital in the first place. If she hadn't had a woman to talk to, she wouldn't have come at all, Janessa thought. Ever since Janessa became a doctor, she had treated epidemic diseases, microbes that made no distinction between the sexes. She had never had private patients. Epidemiology allowed no space for obstetrics or gynecology. Those were specialties for the everyday world, when the plague had passed by.

It was nearly the end of the day, and Janessa let herself out of her office and, prowling the halls, moved through the bloodstream of her own creation. The night-shift nurses were coming on, turning up the gas lamps in the corridors. Janessa was the last of the day staff to leave.

Brentwood Hospital had been created in the skeleton of what had once been a rich man's house, and its wings were well spaced and open to the light, unlike the airless tenements that had grown up around it as the neighborhood decayed. Renovated, with its wings turned into wards and its gardens replanted with trees and flowers, the hospital was a self-enclosed world, a haven of cleanliness. An orderly was pushing a mop down the hall, and Janessa pulled her skirts away from his soapy bucket.

Cleanliness was the watchword by which Nurse Anna Williams lived—cleanliness and fresh air and no nonsense. She was a big, starched woman who rustled when she walked. She would have rustled with efficiency even if her skirts had not.

"Good night, Dr. Lawrence," she said as Janessa passed. "Kiss the babies for me."

"I will," Janessa said, thinking of Araminta Haggerty. It must have taken a lot for the woman to come to the hospital two days after her child's funeral. But then, she was desperate for the

150

strength to care for the babies she already had, while not letting any more slip away from her.

London

Dear Charley,
   I provided instructions on contraception today to a woman who came to the hospital. We had the most amazing conversation.

Charley groaned and slumped in his chair.

"What's the matter, old man? Not bad news from home?" Israel Richardson bunched gray brows in avuncular concern.

Wordlessly, Charley handed him the letter.

"You don't want me to read—well, if you're sure. . . . Hmm, oh, dear, yes, I see." He took off his spectacles and handed the letter back. "A trifle rash, perhaps, but not illegal, you know."

"It's illegal in America," Charley said grimly.

"Oh, yes—Mr. Comstock," Richardson muttered. "Americans are a mystery to me. Still, do you feel you ought to go home?"

"If I go home," Charley said, "everyone will think I've come to keep Janessa in line, which is insulting to us both. Worse yet, they'll expect me to. Janessa's very naïve in some ways. Like me, she's had her head in a cloud of microbes. She may not realize the criticism she's let herself in for."

"I expect she has by now," Richardson commented, looking at the postmark on the envelope.

Araminta Haggerty came back the next day, and to Janessa's surprise the woman painstakingly copied the illustration from Janessa's anatomy text, so she would be sure to know exactly where to position the sponge.

"That ought to shock my mister something fierce, that drawing," she said with a shaky laugh. "Maybe I better not show it to him."

"Now remember to soak it in vinegar first," Janessa said. "You can wash the sponge and reuse it, but disinfect it with carbolic soap every time. And be very certain your hands are clean. That's extremely important to avoid an infection."

"I'll remember it all," Araminta promised.

Janessa didn't think about her again until the end of the week, when two more women appeared asking for what the doctor had given Araminta Haggerty. And the next day, four more walked in.

"I try, but I can't keep him off me. He's too strong," whispered a thin woman with bruises on her wrists.

"The doctor said I wasn't to have no more. But when I asked him how to stop it, he said I was debased," a stocky woman with red, chapped hands and indignation in her eyes confided.

"I've got rid of two already, but it breaks my heart to do it. The last time I almost died into the bargain. These are all I can tend to." The woman nodded at the four shoeless girls hanging on her skirts.

A pale sixteen-year-old with straw-colored hair and a fragile beauty was the next to arrive. Janessa thought her loveliness might bloom for two or three years before it faded and she looked like Araminta Haggerty.

After her last patient had left, Janessa was sitting at her desk when Horace White appeared in her office doorway. Adam Sells was behind him.

"Dr. Lawrence, we must speak with you. Immediately."

"Certainly," Janessa said. An inkling of what was to come crossed her mind. "You look like your boots are on fire, Dr. White. What can I do for you?"

"It has come to my attention," Horace White said with as much dignified outrage as he could muster, "to our attention, that you have been disseminating information on—" He choked on the word in front of a female. He was, after all, a preacher's son. "Information that will allow wives to shirk their duty."

"Shirk their—" Janessa glared at him. "Dr. White, when you have attained the age I am now and you have been married as many years as I have, and when you have been a female, I will allow you to discuss the 'duty' of wives with me."

"Dr. Lawrence." Adam Sells folded his arms across his chest. "I agreed to take a position with this hospital because I felt that you had a clear vision and a genuine wish to help the poor. I have no intention of countenancing illegal and immoral activities."

"Would you rather countenance unwanted children raised in deplorable conditions, so, if they are 'lucky' enough to grow up, they can have more unwanted children? Have you seen the women whose health is being ruined by too many babies? Would you rather countenance abortion?"

"Certainly not!" Dr. Sells was horrified. "That is disgusting!"

"Well, it happens all the time," Janessa snapped. "Rich women can find an accommodating doctor to help them. The poor ones do it themselves, with a knitting needle."

"Are you claiming to approve of that practice?"

"Of course not, you idiot!" Janessa found herself getting louder and lowered her voice. "I'm trying to stop it, by preventing the necessity for it."

"There are other options open to couples who wish to space their children," Horace White said icily. "Options approved by the best moral thinkers and reformers. These women may easily practice those by employing the proper restraint."

"Tell that to their husbands," Janessa suggested.

"These people are in need of moral education," Dr. White said with perfect sincerity. His youthful face was shining and earnest.

"Good," Janessa said. "You go out and educate them. You might want to carry a good stout stick."

"It's not necessary to refrain permanently," Dr.

Sells said irritably. "Only during the fertile time of the female's cycle."

"Excellent," Janessa said sweetly. "Do let me know as soon as you have accurately figured out when that is."

"Certainly there is some debate," Sells acknowledged. "I hold with Hollick's theory that the safe days are from the sixteenth to the twenty-fifth day after the monthly flow has stopped."

"Pouchet holds that the fertile period is just prior to and during the flow," Horace White supplied, his interest in alternate theories momentarily overriding his outrage. "Perhaps it would be safer to avoid both periods."

"Leaving the happy couple approximately two days per month in which they may consider themselves safe," Janessa said. She looked with interested skepticism at Adam Sells. "Is that how you manage it, Adam?"

"Dr. Lawrence, I assure you my wife would have it no other way." Dr. Sells straightened his tie and looked straight ahead. He coughed. "Simple withdrawal by the male also offers an option that does not require obscene devices or provide women with the opportunity for sustained debauchery."

"It also puts the responsibility in the hands of the man," Janessa pointed out, "which I am beginning to feel is not such an excellent idea, given the tenor of our conversation just now."

"I disagree, Doctor Sells." Horace White looked earnestly at his male colleague. "Withdrawal causes nervousness and ultimately impotence in the male. Worse, it produces diseased thoughts, which will eventually result in mental degeneration."

"It does nothing of the sort," Dr. Sells said irritably.

"None of which allows the woman any rights at all over her own body," Janessa remarked.

The men quit arguing with each other and swung around to stare reprovingly at Janessa.

"Motherhood is woman's highest and best function," Dr. Sells announced. "In cases where the mother is delicate, it is permissible to space children by the use of moral restraint. Or withdrawal." He glared at Horace White. "I cannot argue with that. I am not a brute." He looked at Janessa, reading the stubbornness in the set of her jaw. "But artificial means of preventing conception are against the laws of man and nature. I am firmly convinced they will result in the degeneration of the woman's intellectual and moral capabilities and render her unfit for her calling."

"Oh, stuff!" Janessa stood up and slapped the well-used anatomy text down on her desk. The ink bottle rattled. "That's what men said about women's education. If it is necessary to drag the male gender kicking and screaming into the next century, then I suppose women must be prepared to do so. But I thought you two would have had more sense."

Dr. Sells folded his arms again. It seemed to be his position of advantage. "I conversely, assumed when I accepted this position that you had a modicum of sense. I am not prepared to be associated with a colleague who is engaging in activity that is immoral and illegal. Think of the reputation of the Brentwood Foundation, if nothing else."

"I built the Brentwood Foundation," Janessa informed him.

"You don't run it," Sells shot back. "The foundation board does."

Janessa took her cloak from the hook behind her door. "This is a private matter between my patients and me, and no more the board's business than it is yours. The hour is late, gentlemen, and I want to go home. If you have any further moral or religious questions, I suggest you take them up with your respective clergymen. That's their bailiwick. Mine is medicine. Good night." She swirled her cloak around her in an irritable flurry and stalked out.

Outside the hospital front door, a woman was waiting for her on the steps. She wore a shabby blue serge suit and shoes nearly worn through at the toes. Her hair was piled under a brown felt hat with a spotted band. She clutched at Janessa's elbow.

"I'm just leaving," Janessa said, taking her to be another in the seemingly endless parade of exasperated wives that had begun with Araminta Haggerty. "I'll be glad to give you an appointment tomorrow."

"I don't want an appointment," the woman

seethed. "I'm here to tell you you're a disgrace to womankind. And if you tell my daughter any more of your dirty, unnatural notions, I'll have the police on you!"

Janessa yanked her arm away. "If your daughter is a married woman, ma'am, she's entitled to make her own decisions—" was all she could find to say.

"She won't be consorting anymore with the likes of you! And you a doctor! You ought to be ashamed!" The woman stalked away, her footsteps sharp as hammer strokes up the brick walk.

Janessa, bewildered and furious, fled in the other direction. She took the ferry home. As she wearily hung up her cloak and hat by the front door, the twins rocketed down the hall and flung themselves at her.

"Mama! Up!"

Janessa picked up Lally and gave Brandon her other hand.

"Up!" Brandon said indignantly.

"I can't pick you both up at the same time," Janessa said reasonably. "I'll carry you next."

"Up!" said Brandon, reminding her of Adam Sells. Really, Adam had been acting like a two-year-old.

"You look done in," Kathleen said, fussing over her. "Sure, and that place is wearing you to the bone."

"It was just a particularly aggravating day," Janessa said, unwilling to explain further to Kathleen. What would Kathleen think of it all? Janessa wondered.

158

"Maybe you ought to be staying home with the babies instead of working in that place," said Kathleen. She had not been with Janessa for very long before she felt it her privilege to offer advice.

"If I did, I couldn't afford you," Janessa pointed out. "I wouldn't need you, either." It baffled her how Kathleen could be so distraught over her lost friend Peggy and so unfeeling about other women suffering or dying from the same plight. Kathleen's world was very tightly bounded. Maybe that was the trouble with Adam Sells, too, Janessa thought. She felt rocked by the depth of Adam's hostility, by the vitriolic anger she had stirred up. She wouldn't have guessed the subject would be so threatening. And why would women argue so vehemently against freedom for other women? How could that woman on the hospital steps have wanted any less than sexual self-determination for her daughter?

Maybe I haven't been paying attention, she thought. Some chance remark of Elizabeth Emory's crossed her mind, a snatch of conversation overheard at the rehearsal dinner: "Plenty of women are terrified at the idea of voting, even in this day and age—it argues too much responsibility, too much aloneness. If a man doesn't make the decisions for us, then we haven't got a man to lean on. Ultimately that means women can't demand keep and protection from him. That frightens many women. They fear that they'll be swept into the void."

Rafe Murray had laughed and said, "That

159

frightens men, too. If we don't have women to protect, how can we men justify all our pomposities?"

Everyone had laughed then, some uneasily. The conversation had naturally flowed to other things.

But now Janessa wondered what even Elizabeth and Rafe would think of her and what she had done. Did contraception offer too much freedom and aloneness, even for feminists? The women's movement supported—indeed was adamant about—voluntary motherhood. But most reformers' solution to the problem was that the husband behave himself. Janessa had never really taken the notion seriously because contraception was so simple and so easily available to anyone with the proper information.

Janessa, still pondering what Elizabeth had said, put Lally down and bounced Brandon in his turn on her knee. "'How many miles to Babylon?'" she chanted. " 'Threescore miles and ten. . . .' " She kissed the top of his head. And yet . . . maybe cutting loose from this deepest dependence on men, making motherhood a woman's choice while leaving her free to indulge in the sexual act— was that making women too alone in the world, taking away their oldest, surest coercion to marriage: "There's a baby on the way"?

Janessa discovered the force of that viewpoint the next morning when she found the head nurse in her office. Anna Williams's face was grim, and her jaw was set. She marched to the visitor's chair

160

when Janessa gestured to it. She sat down, feet together, hands clenched in her lap, argument in every bone in her body.

"You're wrong, Dr. Lawrence. You're doing a wicked, immoral thing." She let out her breath. "There. I've said it."

"Anna." Janessa spread her hands out. "Nurse Williams. Perhaps you could explain to me why you think so."

"I wanted to tell you what I thought first," Anna said. "To make sure I said it plain. I've tremendous admiration for you, Doctor, and I wanted to be sure I didn't weaken at the last minute."

"Did Dr. Sells and Dr. White send you in here?" Janessa asked suspiciously.

"They did not. I came myself to make you listen to reason before you throw away everything we've built in this place."

"If you're concerned with the legal issue—"

"I'm not concerned with the legal issue!" Anna was indignant. "I'll have you know I've campaigned for women to vote, to control their own property, and to have some protection against husbands who abuse them—and a great many other things that the law said we mustn't have! I've worked for social purity since I was a nursing student! And you're prepared to put wives into the same category as those pathetic, degraded creatures!"

Anna's argument was laced with euphemism, but Janessa had no trouble in deciphering it. Social purity was the polite term for the campaign against prostitution. Male reformers had suggested that prostitution be regulated and controlled through legalization, but feminists had risen up in fury. They objected both to the idea of any woman's being seduced into that pitiful life and to the danger presented respectable wives when philandering husbands brought home venereal infections. Contraception, particularly in the form of condoms, was inextricably associated with prostitution. The social purity movement intended to abolish all forms of sexual philandering as well as to promote sexual moderation in marriage. The movement wanted no part of contraception.

"Anna," Janessa said gently, "it isn't wrong or degrading for women to wish to space their children. You know what happens to a woman's health when the babies come too fast. And the women we're seeing here can't even afford to feed their babies!"

"It's them I'm concerned about. Can't you understand?" Anna wrung her hands. "If men and women behave like the animals—with no restraint or decency—then they undermine the strength of the family and woman's safety and security. If men can take their pleasures anywhere they feel like it, with no responsibility, then why should they marry? You're proposing to take away the very foundation of marriage. You'll leave women entirely without protection."

"I am doing nothing of the sort," Janessa said crossly. "I'm proposing to put the means of controlling their own destiny in the hands of the women, not the men."

"By removing their moral compass," Anna said sharply. "That's as useful as freeing a slave by throwing him naked out in the snow. Where is women's protection? Where is the decency? A woman who has relations with a man for nothing but selfish physical sensation has lost all claim to being better than an animal."

"We are animals in that sense," Janessa said. "We have the same physical urges they do."

Anna's hands tightened in her lap, and she looked at Janessa with bewildered outrage. "Men and women have souls and higher purpose. We have been given understanding, the capacity for love, and the ability to practice restraint and sacrifice. If we throw those over, we surrender our very humanity. When it is not advisable for a man and a woman to have a child, then they have the capacity to prevent it by those very qualities of restraint and moderation—"

"Before you get too far along this path," Janessa said dryly, "let me point out that you are on the verge of insulting me and most of the other married women of your acquaintance."

"I don't mean to," Anna said stiffly. "But what is a matter for a couple's individual conscience has no business being distributed wholesale."

"I see," Janessa said. "Those of us who are educated enough or well off enough to solve our own problems may; but heaven forbid we should help the poor, who need it most."

"You are not helping them!" Anna's voice rose. "You are offering them degradation and taking away their safety. You are undermining the very institution of marriage and the sanctity of the family. If you pervert motherhood—woman's highest purpose in life—with artificial means, you pervert her very being!"

Janessa sighed. "Thank you for your opinions," she said. "I do appreciate your coming in, Nurse Williams. But I am afraid I cannot share them."

Anna stood up. "You'll find yourself alone on that. I admire what you've done here. But if you don't come to your senses, you are riding for a fall, Dr. Lawrence. A hard one."

After Anna had gone, Janessa closed the office door, went back to her desk, and thought. She leaned back in her chair, folded her arms across her chest, and glared at the closed door. Everything Anna said made some sense, but when you analyzed it, Janessa thought, you had something that sounded suspiciously like a man's argument—similar to men's arguments against everything else women might want to do. They shouldn't vote because they were too fine and delicate to expose to the brutality of politics . . . they must not practice contraception because they were too refined and noble to be interested in sex for its own sake—unlike men, who, as everyone knew, were beasts anyway and got to have all the fun.

"I don't buy it," Janessa muttered. "The notion of people enjoying themselves immediately convinces everyone else that they must be immoral. What on earth is the matter with us?"

Irritable, she turned her attention to her morning stack of mail. It contained the usual advertisements for patent medicines, which their suppliers hoped she would recommend, and requests for contributions or the lending of the Brentwood Hospital's name to every imaginable cause from fresh-air country vacations for slum children to spiritual revival through meditation and herbal enemas. Janessa passed the requests for sponsorship or donations on to the hospital's administrator, Reuben French, then slit open the last envelope. The Thursday Morning Women's Club wanted the hospital to send them a speaker to discuss the subject of "social reform."

Janessa uncapped her fountain pen. Since she had been accused of being a troublemaker, she might as well make some trouble.

Dear Mrs. Bent, I should be delighted. . . .

VIII

Seattle, Washington, July 17, 1897

Frank Blake stood staring in the middle of the street. His bedroll dangled from one hand. No circus could compete with this, he thought. The street near the docks was jammed so closely that horse-drawn traffic couldn't get through. Some drivers had simply dropped their reins and left drays, wagons, and hackney coaches standing in the road. The drivers were presumably inside the Northern Pacific ticket office or in the swarm of humanity that surged outside it, trying to get in.

Frank already knew why. He had heard the newsboys shouting the headlines: " 'Klondike Strike! Gold Ship Docks Today!' "

The rumors in the wind had proved correct. Five thousand people had already been waiting on Schwabacher's Dock at six in the morning when the Portland steamed in with sixty-eight triumphant miners and two tons of gold. The Portland had been booked for her return voyage before she had even docked. Now the whole wharf was a solid mass of would-be prospectors, trying to buy passage on anything that would float.

Frank had $254 in his pocket, so he bypassed the Northern Pacific office—the fare posted in the window was being changed from $200 to $250. As he watched, a hand reached out again and made it $300. Next door the sidewalks outside Cooper & Levy Pioneer Outfitters were lined with stacked bales and boxes and hopeful miners awaiting transportation to the docks. Some looked as if they might have prospected for gold before, but most looked like bank clerks. Frank noted a few of the most enterprising box-house girls from the skid row, perched on packing crates, pocketbooks firmly clutched on their laps.

"Where can a fellow still find fare?" he asked one at random.

The girl smiled at him. She was a gaminlike waif with blue eyes and the cheery hopefulness of a dreamer. She seemed to like his looks. "Down at the docks maybe. Try the Barbry Allen. She's an awful old scow, but she floats. You could tell Luther that Lulie sent you."

"Lulie!" The young woman with her straightened up from tightening her trunk strap. "There's plenty of men going north. You don't have to recruit no more, and God knows who into the bargain—"

The touch of Irish in her voice caught Frank's attention, and he burst out laughing. "I'm the bad penny, Peg," he said helplessly. "You should have known."

She snapped her head around and stared at him. "And what in the blue blazes are you doing here?" Peggy Delaney asked, delighted. She flew into his arms, and still laughing, he swept her up and swung her around. "And you were supposed to be going north last year. I thought sure you'd be one of these fellows come in on the Portland."

"Not I," Frank said sorrowfully. "Late as usual."

"Well, I mean to get rich," Peggy told him. "You're the one who told me about it in the first place. But I come to find out that there wasn't any rush to head up there. A laundry's no good without dirty men to wash for."

"So what have you been doing?" Frank asked. "I've thought about you often."

"I set up here in Seattle for a while to see which way the wind was going to blow."

"Now we're going north," Lulie said happily.

"To do laundry?" Frank raised his eyebrows. Lulie did not look like a laundress. Her blond hair was pinned under a fancy black velvet hat. She wore a black wool skirt and a cerise taffeta basque with puffed sleeves. A soiled purple velvet shoulder cape completed the outfit.

Peggy looked more the role. She wore a sensible, serviceable suit and a black felt hat over her flaming hair. "Lulie's going to help me out in the laundry," she informed him stiffly, although it seemed more for Lulie's benefit than for Frank's. "I got my own business here, or I did have. I just sold out. Did all right, too, without Pa drinking up every blessed nickel."

"Where is your pa?" Frank asked.

"I don't know," Peggy said. "He never came back to Sierra?"

Frank shook his head. "Not as far as I know, but I left, too, after. . . ."

Peg nodded, understanding. Her pa was probably dead or would never be seen again.

"I haven't quite decided what business to go into," Lulie confided, casting a quick glance at Peggy. "I'll see how things look when we get to Dawson. That's where everybody's going," she added.

Without actually moving, Peggy gave the impression of throwing her hands in the air. "Just use your head." She looked as if she didn't have much hope of Lulie's being able to do that. Instead, Peggy turned her attention to Frank. "If you want passage, Luther might squeeze you in. But you'll have to buy supplies and be quick. Luther's planning to beat it out of here on tonight's tide. He's as hot to go dig gold as the rest of the people in this city. I swear, Frank, you've never seen anything like it. Old nags that aren't worth more'n five dollars are going for thirty. Nobody's dog is safe if it's bigger'n a beagle. I saw one fellow trying to sell a sheep to carry packs. I'm thinking some fool probably bought it, too."

"Should I try to buy dogs or a horse?" Frank asked.

Peggy shook her head. "Save your money to pay the Indians to pack your goods over the pass. That's what a fellow off the Portland told me, and I figure he knows more than these yahoos." She shook her head pityingly at the bank clerks and farmers still milling outside the steamship office. "He says you can't get a pack animal over the pass, and stateside dogs are useless."

A few Seattle residents had consulted returning prospectors before laying their plans, but uncounted hundreds hadn't. Prospectors off the Portland were reporting that the worst part of working a claim once you got to it was digging through the frozen ground. As Frank was about to pay for some supplies, one enterprising speculator handed him a flyer inviting investment in the Trans-Alaska Gopher Company, shares one dollar each. The company proposed to breed these rodents and train them to tunnel through permafrost.

Another fellow, in a hunting cap with earflaps, was demonstrating an "ice bicycle" with stubby skis in place of the front wheel. He rode round and round on the dock. Yet another man claimed to have an X-ray machine that could locate gold, and the Jules Verne-like quality of his product brought him a brisk business.

The whole adventure had a lunatic cast to it. Later, squeezed on board the Barbry Allen, a leaking oyster boat that might possibly make it from Puget Sound to Skagway in the protection of the Inside Passage, Frank watched the hysteria on the docks and the bay full of boats. Rampant lunacy seemed to have touched everyone. Ten feet across the water, a man was trying to coax a billy goat up the gangway. Entrepreneurs had sprung up like mushrooms on shore, their numbers keeping pace with the would-be miners. Their schemes grew more bizarre by the moment, or so it seemed to Frank. Hardened from his year on the road, he looked apprehensively at the boats full of preachers, clerks, accountants, cooks, even, someone said, the mayor of Seattle. How were they going to fare? he wondered. They were ready for adventure, cheering as each boat, loaded with picks and shovels, hammer and nails, saws, pitch, rope and drills, and food, pulled out from the dock.

The merchants of Seattle were stripped clean but made wealthy by the end of the first day. The gold seekers, eyes shining, steamed out into Puget Sound.

There were two routes north to the ultimate goal of the Klondike, the Yukon Territory of Canada. The more expensive was the all-water route to St. Michael on the Bering Sea and up the Yukon River to its confluence with the Klondike, a way only open from June to September. The other was the poor man's route, the direct or impatient man's route: north along the Inside Passage, between the continent's edge and the offshore islands, to Skagway or Dyea and then overland through White Pass or Chilkoot to the Klondike. The route appeared deceptively short on a map, on which it was difficult to discern that much of the way was vertical. But it was open all year, and for scows like the Barbry Allen, the Inside Passage was the only possible route. The well-used vessel would have disintegrated on open water. Actually, the Barbry Allen wasn't a sure bet even in the Inside Passage, but Luther said he thought he could get her to Dyea. He wasn't planning on going back anyway.

Luther was a big barrel of a man, with a scarred cheek and a missing tooth. He gave the impression that these had been sustained in the same knife fight. For a hundred dollars he cheerfully sold Frank a ticket for enough space in which to set down his supplies and sleep on top of them.

By the time they made Wrangell on the south-

171

ern Alaskan coast, Frank had won forty of it back, and Luther had quit playing poker with him. Despite an almost complete lack of privacy, Lulie had managed to make some money, too, wandering off behind jury-rigged screens that blocked her and her partner from curious eyes.

"You got no sense!" Peggy told her later. "You're going to get hurt! That's no way to live."

"I don't go with but nice fellows," Lulie protested.

Frank knew better than to get in the middle of an argument that Peggy was already managing very well by herself, but he listened with fascination to Lulie's saga. She had been working in a Seattle laundry when Peggy had set up her own business. Lulie hadn't liked the work, so she had tried prostitution at night and liked that much better. The money was easier, she said, and some nice fellow was always bringing her a present.

Peggy snorted. "And how long do you think you could have worked on your own before the madams and the pimps ran you out or had you beat up? Or before some man wanted some favor you didn't like and killed you for it?"

"Nothing like that's ever happened," Lulie said.

"It would have if you hadn't left," Peggy said, exasperated. "You aren't fit to be out on your own! You don't know anything!"

"I'm going to get rich in the Klondike," Lulie replied calmly. "Then I won't have to worry."

"You're dumb as a box of rocks, that's what you

are," Peggy said, but she was talking to Lulie's back. The girl had already drifted off.

"If you're going to try to reform her," Frank said, "you've got your work cut out for you."

"She's like some half-fledged chicken standing in the middle of the road, waiting to get run down," Peggy fumed. "I should never have let her come with me." She stared irritably at the passing scenery, which was not of the soothing kind. The ship's passage was exotically bewitching—a place of unbroken dark forests and deep, green water through which porpoises occasionally flung their silver shapes. Once in a while they would glimpse an Indian village on the shore, with its totem pole staring, fiercely beautiful, toward the sea. Or Frank would see a canoe shoot suddenly from the shadows of the trees that overhung the water, its hull blackened with soot and seal oil, a dark-eyed painted face above it. As a vista, it was enthralling but not reassuring.

"And how would you have stopped her from joining you?" Frank inquired practically.

"Well, at least I didn't have to let her come with me. Now I'll be looking after her forever, as if I needed that."

"You've gotten tough in the last year." Frank slipped an arm around Peggy's waist and, ignoring the forty other voyagers on the Barbry Allen, nuzzled her ear.

"I haven't gotten tough," Peggy protested. "But I wish I had. I paid my dues with Sid and Payou know that. I'm entitled to have just my own self to look after." She gave him a sideways glance. "No one else is going to."

"That's right," Frank agreed good-naturedly. He kissed her earlobe.

Peggy grinned. "Not that I asked you to. I know a man with a wandering foot when I see one. And you quit that! Leave my ear alone."

Frank stopped, but he didn't take his arm from around her waist. "You feel awfully good, Peg," he whispered. "And who else here is going gold hunting, on her own two wandering feet?"

"I didn't wander out of Sierra," Peggy said flatly. "I was run out, same as you. And I been making an honest living in Seattle ever since, not trooping around with snakes and tattooed ladies."

"We'll see stranger things than that on this road, I imagine." Frank held out one last inducement. "I brought some books, Peg. I'll read to you like I used to. Remember Omar Khayyam? I brought him."

"That might be nice," Peggy mused. "If life gets dull."

It was the closest she was going to get to telling him she would let him in her bed again. Peggy wasn't Lulie. Actually, Frank was relieved. Hot-footing it out of Sierra the way he had, he felt that he had run out on Peggy, and just when her brother had been found dead. Of course, she hadn't asked him to stay. And Frank would have been murdered, too, if he had lingered. Still, it was a great relief to see she was all right and as self-willed as ever.

The voyage to Dyea—Luther wanted to go to Dyea; therefore that was where his passengers were going—took two weeks, punctuated by ports of call that began with Wrangell on the Alaskan coast, a ramshackle collection of cabins that appeared on the verge of falling down at any moment. The inhabitants, accustomed to subsistence, were newly prosperous, however, from the sale of Indian trinkets, prospectors' supplies, and medicinal whiskey. In theory, Alaska was dry. In fact, it was possible to buy all the whiskey you wanted as long as you claimed it was for your health. As a result, every man was his own physician. Northwest of Wrangell was Sitka, the former Russian capital; Juneau came next. More supplies could be purchased there, but the prices took into account—several times—the commodities' distance from the States.

Dyea had no natural harbor. Boats were anchored offshore, then all passengers climbed over the railings and into the mud flats, to drag their possessions to shore. The cargo was simply dropped overboard. Frank learned within seconds that if Alaska was an icebox in the winter, it was a swamp in the summer. Mosquitoes—big, voracious ones—were everywhere. As Frank towed one of Peggy's tin washtubs loaded with flour sacks, he stopped to wonder what on earth he was doing there. The women were in the water, too, trying to drag their trunks ashore and cursing at Luther. They eventually got everything hauled to dry land, where they stood dripping icy water and staring despondently at the pile. All around them, soaking Klondikers were doing the same, while the local Indians watched with interest.

The Chilkats were a Tlingit tribe, short and broad shouldered and smelling strongly of fish. Until recently Dyea had been their town, with a population of no more than two hundred and fifty. Now it was overrun by white men putting up tents along the edge of the sea wrack and building wooden cabins along the muddy main street that had become the road into the mountains.

As the Klondikers stared dismally at their impedimenta and the vertical walls of the mountains rising in the distance, the Indians announced their availability as porters: twelve cents a pound to carry goods the twenty-seven miles through the pass to navigable water at Lake Lindeman.

Frank's guess was that their offer would be viewed as a bargain by later arrivals, who would surely be charged a dollar a pound as the demand and the Indians' boldness grew.

The only alternative was to carry one's own goods without help, making ten to twenty trips. Many did just that. Peggy and Lulie hired Indians, and Frank, because he had won back his forty dollars from Luther, went along with that scheme. Without ever having made any verbal agreement, he and the women seemed to be three-way partners for the trek. Frank wasn't willing to lose track of Peggy again, and he knew that Lulie was part of the deal.

"Why do you want to baby-sit for that flighty

tart?" he demanded, swatting mosquitoes away with his hat and talking over his shoulder to Peggy, who was trudging behind him. Lulie was three or four paces back, with the Chilkat porters between them . . . when she wasn't off in the bushes with one. Peggy didn't answer, and he couldn't see her expression through the mosquito veiling she wore. Her silence didn't really matter; his had been a rhetorical question, posed out of boredom.

For the first few miles, the trail out of Dyea was an easy one, and they had walked three abreast singing "Froggy Went A-Courting" and commenting on the midsummer warmth. Five miles from the tidewater, however, the town of Finnegan's Saloon marked the edge of hell. Beyond Finnegan's, the trail narrowed to a quagmire at the bottom of Dyea Canyon—a chaos of mud, boulders, and the Dyea River, entangled in a thicket of spruce and hemlock. Those who had managed to drag wagons this far were forced to abandon them now. They whipped their unfortunate teams, used as pack animals, up the trail. Thirteen miles from Dyea, at Sheep Camp, not even horses could conquer the terrain, and the beasts, too, were abandoned there, usually to be rounded up by enterprising Tlingits, taken back to Dyea, and resold. At that, the horses fared better than those abandoned at White Pass, where their bones clogged Dead Horse Trail.

In Sheep Camp was a so-called hotel, but aside from desperate men who had walked from Dyea, no one would pay to spend the night. Frank, Peggy, and Lulie spent seventy-five cents apiece for a meal of beans, bacon, and tea, and a place on the floor to sleep when the tables had been cleared away.

Frank, whistling, unrolled his blanket, and after a moment the other diners picked up the tune, that year's popular nonsense song:

"The chambermaid came to my door,
'Get up, you lazy sinner.
We need those sheets for tablecloths,
And it's almost time for dinner.' "

Frank put an arm around Peggy and Lulie each. The room was warm and smoky.

"She's the only girl I love,
With a face like a horse and buggy,
Leaning up against the lake,
Oh, fireman, save my child!"

They lay down, crowded nearly wall to wall, in the glow of the banked stove. Shoes, hung from the rafters to dry, made ungainly shadows like the wandering trunks of elephants on the walls.

Am I going to get rich? Frank wondered sleepily. Oddly enough, at the moment it didn't seem to matter. As the temperature began to drop, he cuddled Peggy and Lulie, one into the crook of each arm, then slept, lulled by the gentle rise and fall of their breath. . . .

No animal but man could scramble from Sheep Camp to the summit. For the first three miles, the grade was between twelve and eighteen degrees; then it steepened to twenty-five until the flat ledge known as the Scales. There the Indian porters rearranged their packs, reweighed them, and held out for double or nothing.

"We had a deal!" Frank protested. "I'll carry it up myself for that."

"Good," said the Chilkat, taking a step back. "You carry."

"I will!" Frank bent to pick up the first pack.

"And what are we supposed to be doing at the top, Frank?" Peggy demanded. "Wait three weeks for you to carry up all this that's taken ten Indians to get here?"

"You mean you're going to pay it?" Frank exploded.

Peggy gave him a look of elaborate patience. "Are you looking at that closely?" She pointed over his shoulder. Above them rose the final ascent of Chilkoot Passa slope of mud and slippery shale set at an angle of thirty-five degrees, a trail out of a nightmare, along which antlike figures zigzagged in lockstep, one behind the other, the pace set by the slowest in the line.

A man stomped past Frank. The traveler had a heavy grindstone on his back. Another trekker passed with a cageful of cats. It looked to Frank as if the road produced its own mental aberrations before one had even set foot on it.

"I'll climb that path once," Peggy said, "to be saying I've done it and because I've come this far already. But to go down it and back up again, that I will not."

"Well . . ." Frank couldn't say he wanted to, either. He wanted to push on for Dawson before all the good claims were staked. Less fortunate Klondikers were climbing and reclimbing the trail, and they would be there long enough to get caught by winter. While Frank was thinking, the Chilkats picked up his packs and started up with them. "Well, all right." He surrendered and went after them.

After reaching the top, he knew that desperate men were coming to dig gold in Dawson, and he was not one of them. He was not desperate enough to climb Chilkoot Pass again.

At the top was a station of the Canadian Mounted Police. The Mountie on duty looked gloomily at the staggering Klondikers. Not one in five had brought enough provisions to last through the winter. "I hope these greenhorns can hunt," he muttered.

"I hope they can, too," Frank said to the lawman.

Food had been among the goods abandoned on the slopes of Chilkoot Pass on the blithe assumption that one could always buy more. And, the reasoning continued, provisions would cost less than the Indians would have charged to pack and carry it to Dawson City—assuming they got to Dawson. Frank didn't like to think about these cheerful, determined city slickers starving to death in the Yukon wilderness.

"There's talk of making everyone bring provisions for a year with them," the Mountie added, "or turning them back at the border."

Peggy looked at the river of men flowing past them. "That would take a lot of Mounties, I'm thinking."

The tall policeman snorted. "I know. And we haven't got but nineteen constables in the whole Northwest. They'll hire more if this keeps up, though. There'll be chaos if they don't."

"That constable was awfully nice to me," Lulie said later. "He says it's downhill most of the way to Dawson from here." She looked cheerful and excited, as if the downhill slope was not five hundred miles long.

"I know," Frank told her gently. "It would have to be. Otherwise, we wouldn't be going downriver."

"Oh," Lulie said.

Most of the rest of the journey would be by boat—which first had to be built. The trail to Lake Lindeman ended at another saloon on the shore, where the weary could fortify themselves before tackling that task. Frank, gazing at the dwindling supply of trees around the lake, shook his head at the thought of further depletion. But he went ahead and cut wood, using the tools he had paid the Chilkat to haul over the pass.

Peggy came and, arms folded, stood over him.

"I don't know how to build a boat; but if you'll show me, I'll work till I drop. It's not right for you to do it for all of us."

"Who said I was?" Frank asked. "Did I invite you to share my boat?"

"There's Lulie, too," Peggy said, ignoring that.

Frank grinned. "She can pay me in kind."

Peggy gave him such an outraged look that he threw his hands up, laughing. "Cook! She can cook!"

"Show me what to do," Peggy urged. Her expression gave him to understand that he was too juvenile to argue with further.

Frank had never worked side by side with a woman before, not at the kind of backbreaking labor that Peggy insisted on sharing. She claimed that the tree he set her to felling was less work than bending over a washtub to scrub clothes. Through Peggy he began to gain yet another perspective on the world and its inhabitants, and out of that there grew between them the kind of companionship that formed between men on the trail. His skill at carpentry canceled out the fact that he was the younger, and the muscles in her forearms as she swung the ax negated the fact that she was female. It created a camaraderie between them that made them glance interestedly, in appreciation, at each other now and again.

As the work progressed, the weather remained hot. The mosquitoes that bred in the muskeg swarmed all over, as vicious as flying needles. Old hands told them that winter, when it came, would come quickly. Peggy, Lulie, and Frank equipped their boat with a blanket sail and christened her the Lucy Annie Pearl with a shot of saloon whiskey. She was a catboat of the sort that Frank had learned to pilot in his wanderings along the California coast. She had barely enough room for the threesome and their cargo. Worse, she leaked, requiring periodic determined bailing. But in four days she took them damp, bitten, but undrowned, downriver. They passed from Lindeman through a string of mountain lakes—Bennett and Tagish and Marsh—to the beginnings of the rapids.

Now, at dusk, Frank stood gnawing his thumbnail and looking down at the white foam boiling between the walls of Miles Canyon. Lulie, chirping happily to herself, was baking biscuits in a Dutch oven over the fire. Her capacity for wide-eyed cheerfulness never ceased to amaze Frank; but lately it had begun to get on his nerves.

Peggy appeared at his elbow. "I heard a man got smashed on the rocks yesterday. I reckon we haven't got any choice but to go on, though."

"It's going to be a hell of a ride," Frank confirmed.

They stood in respectful silence and looked at the roiling river. "I reckon we better lash everything down good. . . ."

He nodded. "All we can do is shoot the rapids and pray the current takes us down safely. If we fight it, we'll end up on the rocks like that poor

183

fellow yesterday. I heard about him, too, and I've been thinking ever since how to do it alive."

Lulie called out. "Supper's ready. Beans again. Isn't it a good thing we all like beans?"

"Oh, yes," Frank grumbled.

"Look how fast the river's flowing," Lulie enthused. "I saw you watching it. It's moving so fast we ought to get to Dawson in no time, shouldn't we?"

"If we don't die first." Frank bent and whispered in Peggy's ear, "Why do I keep feeling as if you and I got married and had a kid?"

Peggy sighed. "I been wondering since I met her how she lived to grow up, but she's so good-hearted it's hard to fault her."

"There's such a thing as being too good-hearted," Frank said. "She hasn't got any sense."

In spite of his reservations about her, when it came time to venture onto the river the next day, Lulie sat herself firmly in the bottom of the boat where Frank told her to and without complaint braced herself for the wild ride. His first impression was that she wasn't smart enough to be scared; then he saw the white line around her clenched lips and the tic in her jaw. He relented and brushed her shoulder with his fingers. "We'll be fine."

Fine was a relative term. Crouching in the boat while Frank guided it down the roaring channel left all three of them white-faced and panting with sheer terror by the end of the canyon. Then the horrific experience was promptly repeated in the boiling waters of Squaw Rapids. But looking at the vicious torrent that lunged and howled its way down White Horse Rapids, they felt that their previous voyage had been a picnic. Frank eyed the black rocks that jutted like rotted teeth from the milky water. Between them the channel was studded with whirlpools. He watched one suck in a log, then spin it like a top. Eventually the water spat it out again, spewing the log high in the air, tumbling it under the flow, and breaking it into splinters on the next set of fangs. Frank felt his stomach tumble and surge like the water.

"I ain't going over that," a man beside them quavered. He sat on his beached boat and cradled his head in his hands.

"Of course you are, you danged fool," Peggy said. "You can't go back before winter sets in."

"Then I expect I'll just set here till I freeze solid," the man said glumly. "They'll find me here with my arm stretched out, pointing the way."

"Oh, for—" Peggy gave up on him. They never did find out whether he continued on or went back.

The man with the cats passed them on the river. His soaking, furious cargo was lashed to the deck, and his gaze concentrated on the rushing torrent.

"Those are going to be about the maddest cats that ever went traveling," Peggy said. "Come on, me dashing pilot. If that loony can do it, so can we."

They crouched in the boat again, and Frank pushed off. The Lucy Annie Pearl shot into the water, and Frank aimed her nose at the fastest running channel. The women agreed with Frank's prognosis that the best way through was just to let the current take them. If they tried to fight it or if they slowed, it would grind them up like powder. The icy water boiled up around them in spray so thick they could barely see past the boat's prow. Frank's eyes were squinted half-shut against it, and his hand, on the tiller, was white knuckled. The boat shot past the first whirlpool, skimmed over the howling water, and dodged the rocks that loomed open-jawed on either side. The riverbank was fanged with rocks, and at intervals the mountain's bony spine pressed into the center of the channel, threatening to smash boats, compressing the water, flinging it on ever faster.

Three men in a canoe were shooting the rapids ahead of them. For a moment Frank thought they had swamped, but then the canoe leaped like a salmon out of a cloud of spray and sailed down the next drop. The man at the tiller had a wide-brimmed hat jammed over his ears, and Frank couldn't help but wonder how he kept it on. He had stuffed his own into one of Peggy's washtubs. Peggy and Lulie had tied their bonnets under their chins, and the sodden brims drooped. They looked like the human counterparts of the wet cats in their crate.

The Lucy Annie Pearl slewed sideways and began to founder. With all his strength, Frank dragged on the tiller and prayed. The boat shifted again, and the current caught her and hurled her on, out of the whirlpool that had been fishing for her. She twisted like a fish in the current, and Lulie lost her grip. She fell, splayed sideways, and became wedged between a lashed trunk and Peggy's washtubs. Her fingers scrabbled for a grip, but the wood was wet. The boat rolled the other way, slamming into a wall of spray. When it righted, Lulie was half over the edge, a mass of dripping petticoats pulling her down into the water.

Frank, clenching the tiller in both hands, was unable to let go, or they would all be dead. Peggy, beaten to her knees by the water, pulled and tugged on Lulie and wrestled her back in. For a moment he thought both women were going over the side. He got ready to go after them and sacrifice the boat to the rocks. Then Peggy toppled backward with Lulie in her arms, and they were rolling in the bottom of the boat, drenched and safe.

Frank directed his eyes forward again, just in time to see a tower of rock looming up. He yanked the tiller over, and the boat shot by it in a roar of spray, then out into the steady flow of the river at the cataract's foot. The water shimmered, crystalline, and light reflected into his eyes from its rippled facets. They had made it! He felt giddy, all his nerves humming, and then quite suddenly faint. The sparkles grew on the water. Frank beached the Lucy Annie Pearl on the first mud flat he came to and staggered out of her. He looked at the women in the bottom of the boat.

"I'm going to . . . build a fire. Get dry. Stay there. Don't . . . go anywhere."

He pitched forward, to his knees, then onto his face. The women shook their heads solemnly and didn't move.

IX

Dawson City, Yukon Territory, September 1897

The rest of the run to Dawson took a week and a half, and they made it with snow biting at their ankles. The late starters were left behind to winter at Lake Bennett. Peggy, Lulie, and Frank had come three hundred and sixty miles to end up staring at the muddy main street of Dawson as if it were El Dorado. Front Street was a jumble of canvas tents, cabins, half-and-half structures, and buildings put together of whatever had come to hand. It was a vernacular architecture of oil barrels, torn-up boats, and tin pie plates. There were four saloons, a tent church with a banner promising "Revival Tonight," a store for dry goods and miners' supplies, the land recorder's office, and a half-framed building that was going to be the Odd Fellows Hall. The wonder wasn't that Dawson City was so raw but that it was there at all, and growing with each new boatload of miners in this almost inaccessible place.

Everything was at a premium there, even companionship. The man with the cats suddenly turned from a loony to a perspicacious soul with a head for business—he was getting an ounce of gold apiece for those cats. Peggy found a side street on which to set up her laundry and was almost immediately swamped with business. Lulie helped her reluctantly. Frank could see her heart wasn't in it.

Scuttlebutt at the recorder's office said a man could still find a claim on the network of creeks that fed the Klondike River, but they were getting fewer and farther from Dawson. Hopeful miners asked the men in the Monte Carlo Saloon how long it should take them to dig, say, twenty thousand dollars. A rude awakening met Dawson's greenhorns. Frank staked a claim on five hundred feet of Caribou Creek and broke up the Lucy Annie Pearl to make himself a sled, with extra wood for a shelter.

"I've got to build a cabin before the weather gets too cold," he said, warming his hands over Peggy's hot wash water.

She was making good money already. The traffic of Dawson went by outside the tent. Soon she would pay to have her own cabin built. It had occurred to Frank, although he was not about to admit it, that shop owners were the ones who got rich in a gold rush. But there was no adventure to running a shop—or at least not enough.

"You'll freeze yourself to death out there," Peggy warned, "and then come into town like all the rest, smelling like a moose and with clothes that haven't seen soap in three months."

189

"That's right," Frank agreed. There was no one around, and he licked her ear. "But I'm clean now."

"Cold, too!" Peggy yelped when he had stripped off his shirt and inveigled her under the pile of blankets that served for a bed. "You got hands like ice."

"Warm me up, then." Burrowed in her arms in the thick wool blankets, Frank knew yet again that life was magical, an adventure not to be missed.

In the morning, dragging the sled with all his worldly goods piled on top, Frank set off for his claim. Winter was dropping on them quickly—a cosmic hand turning down the gas lamp and the heat. White birch, cottonwood, and spruce covered the low hills, and the deciduous trees seemed to burst into flame and lose their leaves overnight. As the winter twilight came and stayed, the small game, moose, and caribou grew harder to find, and the trout and salmon streams froze over. Frank used wood from the Lucy Annie Pearl to build a twelve-by-twelve-foot cabin, then finished it off with green tree trunks chinked with moss. For windows he used empty glass bottles gathered outside a saloon and held together now with mud. A fireplace of stone and mud also provided his oven.

He was proud of that house, proud that he had built it. In its green wood and the whack of the ax blade, he found a strong sense of connectedness with the ghosts of his pioneer grandfathers. Everyone in the family knew about Whip Holt, his maternal grandfather; but Frank had never given much thought to his paternal grandfather. Henry had been adopted as a teenager by Lee and Eulalia Blake. Now that Frank thought about it, nobody much talked about Pete Purcell, Henry's real father, although Peter was named for him. Frank sat down on his bed by the newly made fire and thought about Pete Purcell.

Two dogs, his newest acquisition, flopped down, steaming warmly. By the first snowfall, he had not worked his claim, but he had bought the dogs, no more than eight months old, from a passing stranger. They were probably not full-bred malamutes, and their ribs stuck out under their heavy silver coats; but they had been half-trained, and the price was low—possibly because they had been stolen. Frank counted out the money while the dogs watched him, their tongues lolling happily and their breath making clouds in the air. After the stranger had gone, they followed Frank into the cabin and sniffed the bacon hopefully.

I'll have to hang it from the rafters, he thought, then gave them a meal of beans and cold biscuits, his dinner leftovers. "Didn't feed you any more than he had to, did he, fellas?"

They wolfed it down and settled with little canine sighs of contentment by the fire. There they stayed, unless Frank pushed them out or brought out the sled harness. For some reason they loved to pull the sled and would race happily for hours over the snow.

Frank shot a caribou and dressed it. He made snowshoes and skis and began to understand the ways that men moved across the countryside in winter. The cold was shattering, and there was no thermometer capable of measuring it—mercury turned solid at -38 degrees. The miners had, however, learned to gauge the cold by other means: When whiskey froze, it was -55 degrees; when kerosene hardened, it was -65 degrees; the most popular medication at the Dawson City drug store was a vicious concoction known as Perry Davis's Pain-Killer. It was nearly all alcohol and wouldn't freeze until -75 degrees. In the meantime, it killed pain and nearly anything else. The days never got all the way light until about noon, which made them depressing. In summer it had been light nearly all night. Frank felt as if his internal clock and emotions were out of synchronization with the world.

Now, having food and transportation, he began to work the creek bank. The muskeg moss, which bred mosquitoes in summer, froze in winter, over a foot deep. Below it was permafrost, the rock-hard subsoil that never thawed, even at midsummer. Beneath the permafrost, ten to fifty feet down, lay the gold—if there was any—atop bedrock. The old hands told Frank that fire setting was the only way to tunnel through the permafrost. A fire laid at nightfall at the bottom of the shaft would burn to ash by morning and thaw as many as six inches of soil. After a month or so, a man might reach bedrock, and tests could be conducted indoors, in buckets of melted snow; but the experiments were generally inconclusive.

In winter the soil immediately refroze after it was brought to the surface, and miners' cabins sat amid frozen dumps of dirt waiting to be sluiced in spring. Outside his cabin door, Frank built a strange, miniature city of frozen lumps of dirt like sand castles made on a warm beach.

When he tired of the hard, cold work, he ventured into Dawson with the dogs to soak at Peggy's, in the luxury of hot water. Peggy had a cabin now, and recognizing opportunity when it presented itself, she had opened a bathhouse attached to the cabin, where she charged an exorbitant rate for the privilege of bathing in the warm, once-used laundry water.

"And it's cleaner than you are," she informed a customer, new to Dawson, who had the nerve to complain.

"Cleaner than I am, too," Frank said, coming up behind her. "Where's the soap?"

Peggy's face lit up. "Where did you blow in from?" She sniffed suspiciously. "Lord God, but you aren't joking. You smell like a vulture."

"The pups found a dead caribou to roll in," Frank said apologetically. Any man who had dogs slept with them for warmth and was grateful—up to a point.

"Get in the water, then," Peggy said. "And hand me out those clothes."

Frank slipped into the tub while the other customer watched dubiously.

"Ah . . ." Frank looked up, his nose just above the soapsuds. "When you've been here as long as I have," he told the newcomer, "you won't care what she's washed in it."

He emerged after a long soak, to find his clothes boiled and hung by the laundry fire. The spares he kept at Peggy's were laid out for him.

"Are you rich yet?" Peggy laid a plate of stew on the table as he sat down. She didn't feed her other customers; Frank had special privileges.

"I have a pile of frozen dirt outside my door the like of which the world has never seen," Frank said. "I feel certain it's full of gold. I'll hold my breath until springtime."

"You could hold your breath just because of the dogs." Peggy gave a disapproving look at Frank's malamutes, who were flopped at his feet and still redolent of the caribou.

"It'll wear off," Frank said. "I hardly notice it myself now, except at night."

Peggy put her hands on her hips. "If those dogs are going to sleep with you, Frank Blake, you'll be sleeping right here on the floor."

Frank shook his head regretfully at the dogs. "Sorry, boys. You'll have to go find your own girls." He shut them in the bathhouse.

They snuffled outside the door and poked their paws under the bottom. The door was a rough fit, like those in every other cabin in Dawson, built of green wood one step ahead of the cold. The wood changed its shape all winter.

From her bed Peggy watched the gray paws slide in and out over the sill. Her red hair hung loose like a cascade of fire over her shoulders. "It gets lonesome out there, doesn't it?" she asked him.

"Lonesome as hell," Frank confessed. "It's so quiet sometimes, you start to hear things that aren't there, and the moon on the snow looks like ghosts. Pretty soon you think they're in the cabin with you. And you wonder why I sleep with dogs."

"I'm cold." She burrowed down under the blankets, then pulled a fur rug up over them both. "I've never been so cold. I didn't know it got this cold."

"It doesn't, in California."

"It doesn't get this cold any place you've ever been, either," Peggy said. "Quit acting like you know everything."

Frank looked at her thoughtfully. "What gives you this urge to talk to me as if I were twelve?" he inquired. "Particularly in bed?"

"It's a precaution," Peggy answered immediately. "To make sure I don't fall in love with you." She burrowed farther down in the fur until only the top of her hair showed.

Frank pinched the candlewick out, and the room turned black and silver. He lay awake for a while and wondered how serious she had been about that. He drifted off with his questions unanswered.

Sometime in the night, he woke to find both dogs snoring warmly, in bed. The beasts had jiggled open the door latch.

"Get off!" he hissed, prodding them with his toes. "Get out of here!" Peggy was asleep spoon fashion in front of him, pinning down one of his arms.

The dogs didn't budge. Frank struggled up on one elbow and woke Peggy. She glared at the dogs over the top of her fur rug, through the winter dark.

"Get those dogs off my bed," Peggy said. "I got limits. I told you I wasn't sleeping with dogs."

"Calm down," Frank said. "They're going. Get off, damn you." He jabbed his foot into furry ribs, considerably better padded now, and one dog hopped down. It sat on the braided rug by the bed and yawned, a giant, cavernous yawn. Frank shoved the other off. Then he rolled over and wrapped his arms around Peggy, trying to find his way through the two layers of long underwear they both slept in.

"Oh no, you don't," she said. "Not with those dogs watching."

"For Pete's sake, Peg, they're dogs," Frank protested.

"It gives me the creeps," Peggy said. "It ain't decent." She sat up and pulled her shift over her head and a quilted wrapper over that. "I got work to do, anyway. I can't spend all morning lolling around in bed with you." She pulled on fur-lined slippers and padded over to the chest of drawers

196

Frank had made from a packing crate for her. The water in the pitcher on top had a layer of ice on the surface. Peggy pierced it with a buttonhook, poured some into the basin, and gingerly splashed her face with it.

"Oooh! Eee!" The stove in the corner had nearly gone out. She poked the embers up and put some more wood in it. She looked over her shoulder at Frank. "Get up. Soon there'll be customers here with their wash, and I'm not going to have them find you in that bed."

"All right, all right." He swung his legs over the side of the bed and pulled his pants on. They felt as if they had frozen solid overnight. "You're awfully fine haired," he grumbled.

Peggy was pulling on black stockings over her long underwear. "I got to live in this town," she informed him. "And make a living here. What I do is nobody's business but mine as long as I don't stick it in people's faces. I like to live private. I guess being a man you don't understand that. But if I act like a tart, I'll get treated like one. I won't put up with that."

"I'm sorry, Peg." Contrite, Frank came over to her. "I don't want to embarrass you in front of people."

"I don't guess you do, really." Peggy took off her shift and wrapper, then stepped into a flannel petticoat, fastened over a red flannel undershirt. Over that she pulled on a black wool shirtwaist. She bit her lip. "I'm just so outdone with that Lulie, I reckon I'm going overboard in the other direction. Next thing you know, I'll get saved."

"You'd have to give up too many things you like," Frank teased. "What's Lulie done? Where is she, anyway?" The night before, he had thought about her just long enough to feel grateful for her absence.

"She's been working nights at the Daybreak," Peggy said. "Pouring drinks and dancing with the men. She moved in there because it was more convenient."

"Uh-huh," Frank said.

"She says it's easier work."

"Uh-huh."

"Oh, hell, I suppose it is." Peggy handed Frank a washtub. "Go dig me some more snow. But I just know she's going to get in trouble. Winter's setting in good, so there won't be so much business for a while. She won't be able to pick and choose her partners."

Frank went out the back door and shoveled snow into the washtub. Peggy was already heating a big brass can of it on the stove when he came back. The fire was going in the fireplace, too, under a caldron. With Peggy's wash water starting to boil, the cabin became as steamy as a Turkish bath. Then the water condensed again on the cold walls and froze into icicles. Peggy chipped them off and melted them for drinking water.

"You can't spend your life trying to be her mama," Frank said.

"I'm not!" Peggy said indignantly. "I wish I'd

never seen her. But since I have, I can't help but to take an interest."

"You're the one who couldn't wait to have just yourself to look out for," Frank pointed out. "Are you trying to chain Lulie around your neck to make up for losing Sid? That's a hell of a price to pay."

"Look at you and those mutts." Peggy pointed an accusing finger at the dogs, who were sleeping in a pile of dirty clothes. "You told me all about how you lit out from home and didn't need your kin. And now you've got a pair of dogs sleeping in bed with you."

"The dogs pull a sled, which is more than Lulie does," Frank said.

"Oh, leave me alone about it," Peggy said. "It's lonesome up here, and that's a fact. If you don't make friends, you could die of loneliness."

"Yeah, I know." Frank, behind her, put his arms around her waist. "I'm sorry I deviled you. You go right on and keep the little birdy brain for a pet if you want to." He kissed her cheek, then whistled up the dogs. He knew that he had better get out of there before he started to dwell upon just how empty his cabin was. The weather was making travel harder and harder, too, so his trips to Dawson would be fewer.

He passed Lulie in the doorway and shook his head. Peggy wasn't ever going to make a wash-woman out of that one. Lulie was wearing a new fox-fur cape over the cerise shirtwaist. He heard Peggy's little murmur of envy and admiration.

Frank grinned. Peggy could have a fox-fur cape, too, if she was willing to put up with what Lulie did; but she wasn't. Frank didn't blame her. Peggy was nearly as pretty as Lulie, and prettier by far than most of the saloon girls who bore such uncompromisingly descriptive nicknames as Dog-faced Kitty and the Oregon Mare. But Peggy had a temper, and her attitude toward sexual relations didn't extend to letting some man pay to paw her. Frank knew that the privileges she accorded him in her bed had nothing to do with the wood that he chopped for her as a favor. It was based instead on the poetry he read her, the jokes that he told, and his willingness just to hold her those nights when she was tired or not in the mood.

On the other hand, Lulie liked presents.

"I know just what to do about this winter!" Lulie informed Peggy after the door had closed behind Frank. "I heard of the cleverest thing this girl did down at the Monte Carlo."

"She packed up and went home while she still had some sense?" Peggy guessed.

"Oh, don't be such a stick-in-the-mud." She giggled. "Though anybody would stick in this mud, wouldn't they? And if we get any more snow, it's just going to be worse. None of the men will be able to get into town most days, will they?"

"No, they won't," Peggy said cheerfully, "and maybe then you'll finally understand that this laundry is a solid business. Men who get into town just once a month still bring all their dirty clothes with them. I can wash a month's laundry in a day. But they can't make up a month's lost time with the girls on skid row."

"I know," Lulie said mournfully. "All the girls say that business is awful in the winter."

Peggy shook a soapy finger under Lulie's nose. "Then you'll have to find another line of work, something self-respecting!"

"I have respect for myself," Lulie protested. "I don't see anything wrong with nice men giving me presents. Besides, I got a way to get through the winter. This girl named Mabel LaRose down at the Monte Carlo thought it up first, and she made five thousand dollars!"

"How?" Peggy asked suspiciously.

"By getting herself married for the winter, that's how!"

"What?"

"And I'm gonna do it, too. If the men can't get to Dawson, then I'll just pick a nice one and go where he is. I'll live out at his cabin and keep it clean and cook for him and sew his clothes, just like a wife." Lulie's eyes were bright. "It'll be fun. Like playing house when I was a girl."

"Mother Mary." Peggy rolled her eyes heavenward. "Cooking and cleaning isn't all he'll want, you puttyhead."

"Well, I know that," Lulie said. "But I don't mind that."

"I know," Peggy muttered. She poured soapflakes in the boiling wash water, but her mind wasn't on her work. "Getting married isn't some game," Peggy said. "You get married in the sight of God and everybody."

"I don't mean really married, silly. Just pretend married, for the winter. Though I heard of another girl once—she ended up married for real. He was rich as anything." Lulie stroked her fur cape. "They lived happily ever after."

"Ha!" Peggy said. "My ma was married to my pa for real."

X

Dawson City, October 1897

Throughout Peggy's relentless efforts in favor of common sense, Lulie remained unconvinced. But she didn't strike a bargain with anyone, either, so Peggy became hopeful that maybe the girl had reconsidered. Lord knew the pickings were slim— most of the Klondikers stank like skunks and spent their gold in the Dawson City saloons and brothels as quickly as they could dig it up. If they happened to have any left over, Peggy told Frank during a visit to his cabin, the miners lost that at poker. And many of them were already legally married into the bargain, to women back home in the States.

"I told her if she took up with one of them, I'd put her over my knee," Peggy reported to him. "Here, come on up out of that hole. I've made you some tea."

Frank crawled up the toeholds hacked in the sides of his twenty-foot shaft and stuck his nose over the edge. The tip of his nose was blue.

"Get inside," Peggy said. She poured him a cup of scalding tea from the pot she had heated over his fire. If it occurred to either of them that they had a kind of Klondike marriage of their own, neither one wanted to disturb the arrangement by mentioning it.

"I came out here on business, not just to see if you're froze yet," Peggy had said, pulling a sheaf of flyers from her saddlebag. The borrowed donkey that she had ridden was tied outside under a spruce tree. Now Peggy spread her flyers on the table.

"Warm Up Old Man Winter," the headline invited in curlicued Old English type.

"I designed these myself," Peggy said proudly. "Fellow came into town with a portable press and all kinds of fancy lettering."

Frank read the newsprint sheet with interest. " 'Old Man Winter Wingding & Dance. One last soiree at the Daybreak Saloon. Indian wrestling contest and hoedown. Games of chance. Gypsy fortune-telling. The most beautiful girls in Dawson.' "

"I'm going to tell fortunes," Peggy explained. "I thought up the idea myself when Heartache said he was going to throw a party." Heartache Johnson ran the Daybreak Saloon as a distraction from his alarming string of busted love affairs. Every saloon girl in town had been Heartache's mistress until he drove her crazy.

Frank wrapped his mittened fingers around the hot mug. "You don't know the first thing about fortune-telling," he said.

Peggy snorted. "I know just as much as anybody. You just tell them what they want to hear, and that's easy enough to figure out. I need a top-notch name, though. Something kind of mysterious."

"Madame Blavatsky," Frank suggested.

"Oh, that's just right!"

Frank wondered if he had gone too far. Madame Blavatsky was the founder of the Theosophical Society and an occultist of some note. But she was also dead, so he supposed it wouldn't do any harm—unless Peggy found out he had been pulling her leg.

"Just another way to get the poor miner's gold," Frank said. "I know who's getting rich in Dawson, and it's not me."

"I work for my money," Peggy told him. "I got to last out the winter, too. If Heartache gets all these dirty old sourdoughs into town for a party, they'll want to get cleaned up for it, and they'll use my laundry and my bathhouse."

"You better have some spare wash water," Frank said. "Those soapsuds aren't good for more than five customers. I don't want to end up dirtier than when I started."

"I'll save you the first crack at it," Peggy offered. "You'll come, won't you? It's going to be the biggest, loudest party Dawson's seen."

Frank put the teacup down and, grinning at her,

folded his arms across his chest. "And how am I going to dance the hoedown with the most beautiful girls in Dawson with you keeping your eye on me?"

"I don't own you," Peggy said airily. "Dance with who you like. Dance with Lulie, for goodness sake. Maybe she'll make enough money on dancing that she won't be stuck on her dern-fool idea."

"Don't hold your breath," Frank warned. "But I'll come in for the doings. I wouldn't miss them. You can tell my fortune."

"I'll tell your fortune if you get drunk and dance with those Daybreak girls. You won't have a nickel left, that's what. They've got rolling drunks down to a fine art."

"You pick nice pals," Frank commented.

"Aw, they got to make a living same as anybody," Peggy said. "It doesn't sit right with me, but if I got snooty in this godforsaken place, I'd have no friends. I can't be setting rules for anybody but my own self."

Frank, deciding not to pick a fight, refrained from mentioning her attempts to set Lulie's rules for her.

Frank didn't see either Peggy or Lulie again before the night of the soirée at the Daybreak Saloon, but Peggy's flyers appeared to have done their job. And where she and her donkey hadn't gone, word of mouth did. Three days before the party, bored, lonesome Klondikers began to trudge past Frank's claim on their way into Dawson. By that same evening, there was a steady stream of men, from newcomers unstrung by the loneliness of the north to old, backcountry sourdoughs whom no one had seen in years. A miner in his seventies trudged by on snowshoes. He wore a top hat, a worn, outdated black coat, and a pearl stickpin in his cravat.

"Evening." He tipped the top hat.

"Evening." Frank was just climbing out of his shaft to get more kindling. The hole was deep enough now that packing it with a charge of wood that would last through the night was a wearisome project. Frank had rigged a pulley by which he could raise and lower himself in the shaft, but starting the fire still had to be accomplished while hanging nearly upside down in the sling. It was like trying to make a fire in a fireplace while hanging upside down in the chimney.

"Hit any pay dirt?" the old miner inquired.

"Not so far," Frank answered. "I've washed out some dust in a bucket that's halfway promising. I'm not down to bedrock yet."

"Runs mighty deep along this creek," the prospector said. "Knew a fellow who went stark starin' mad trying to get to it. He got convinced there wasn't any bedrock, just permafrost clear down to hell. He up and went back to the States, and the next fellow to work the claim found bedrock in eight inches."

"Any gold?" Frank asked hopefully.

"Naw. Just bedrock. You going to Dawson?"

"The party's not for three days."

"I know. Just thought I'd get an early start on it." The old man tipped his hat in farewell and trudged on. The angle of his top hat was jaunty.

Frank stuffed more kindling into the bottom of the shaft and laid logs on top of it. As soon as the wood was arranged to his satisfaction, he pulled sulfur matches from his coat and struck one, teased flame from the kindling, and retreated up the shaft as it caught. He squatted by the lip of the shaft and watched. Little flames licked at the logs. Frank set a piece of tin roofing with curved edges in the sling, then with gloved hands he dumped a can of coals from the cabin fire into it. He lowered it into the shaft and spilled hot coals onto the intensifying fire. The fire, growing steadily, licked them up. Frank lowered a pair of heavy logs now, tipping them carefully from the sling. He watched awhile longer, decided it was going to take, and backed away from the smoke that rose up the shaft. The malamutes got up off the cabin doorsill and drooled hopefully. It was always dinnertime after the fire had been set.

The dogs padded inside with him and sat by the cabin fireplace while Frank took down a haunch of caribou from the rafters. He hacked frozen chunks from it and put them in a skillet on the fire. A can of peas and a can of tomatoes went into the mixture, and while it stewed, Frank made biscuits. He had become a reasonably proficient cook, he thought. Of course, the dogs weren't connoisseurs.

They shared the stew, then Frank hacked

steam-formed ice off the cabin walls and melted it for dishwater. The dogs' water bowl had iced over again, and he stuck a hot poker through the crust. After the dishes were done, he dragged a chair he had made from green wood and leather thongs onto the cabin porch. Bundled to the eyebrows, Frank sat and watched the night sky.

To the north, drowning out the stars, sheets of flaming, translucent red and green wavered across the sky—the aurora borealis signaling some mysterious message that could only be read with the heart. Frank never tired of watching it. If he could only decipher its dance, he sometimes thought, he might have the key to the universe. It might be as simple as that—God's message written in the night sky, for anyone hardy enough to go north and see it. Or it might be that he was going crazy with the cold, he thought.

Winter was, he was learning, the single most significant factor of life in the north. If man or woman survived it, they could surmount almost any other challenge. Just the absence of light was enough to leave a soul shivering in the outer darkness, cowering on the brink of sanity before the fiery curtains of the aurora borealis. On the far North Slope the sun set in mid-November and did not rise again until late January. Here, near Dawson, midwinter would offer only two hours of light a day. But life, even civilization of a sort, went on without it. If it was dark all "day," then business was conducted in the dark, much the same way it had been carried out in the nearly endless days of summer. During the summer one slept by daylight; throughout winter one dug by lantern light.

The dogs crept up and stuck their noses in his mittened hand. He scratched their ears. What was he doing, digging up in the Yukon in the snow? It was hard to say, but he had a feeling he was accomplishing something. He sat watching the northern lights until they faded. Inside, he sipped from a hoarded bottle of whiskey, then whistled the dogs into bed. They curled up one on each side of him and went to sleep, twitching and pawing their way through dreams of sled runs. Frank finally slept, too, and dreamed he was one of them, flying on the open snow.

Three days later Frank doubted that anyone was working a claim within a fifty-mile radius of Dawson. By the time he hitched the dogs to the sled, nearly a hundred men on skis, donkeys, snowshoes, and dogsleds had gone by his cabin. One pair of Klondikers were taking turns pulling each other on a sled. Fortified by a whiskey bottle they were passing back and forth, they didn't seem to mind not having dogs. Snow had fallen again in the night, and the low hills were sculpted with it, then laced with the monstrous stone rings called nets: Frost heaves pushed stones to the surface, then rolled them down to encircle the hills. On mild slopes they made looping garlands among the delicate branches of labrador tea and blueberry.

As the dogs lumbered down a well-packed path toward Dawson, Frank watched the snowscape fly by. He knew that his mother would love it here. Cindy was an artist, and the wildness of this country would have caught at her heart. She would appreciate it in a way his father could not. Henry would define only the practical aspects: the climate and the presence of useful metals. His mother, though, would know the magic in the aurora borealis and the stone nets. She would peer into the fissures made by freezing and thawing ice and listen to the voices of the wolves. If he went home again, he would tell her all about it.

Was he going home again? He wondered. Lately he had realized that while his anger at his father remained unthawed, he felt a longing for his mother. He knew she would not be happy until he came home again. Frank shelved the idea. In a couple of years, maybe, he'd go back—when he was twenty-one, when his father would have had to give up the idea that he could compress his children and pour them like molten metal into the molds of his own choosing. Would Henry give that up? Frank wasn't sure his father was capable of doing so.

A snow-laden branch of spruce smacked him in the face and ended that reverie. Ahead, Frank could see a four-dog sled overtaking a man on skis. Behind him sounded the happy caroling of another sourdough who'd brought his whiskey bottle along for the ride. Frank hoped the reveler made it into Dawson before he fell off his donkey.

The path into the city was churned to mud by heavy traffic. Dirty snow was banked on either side of Dawson's streets, and Heartache Johnson had thoughtfully shoveled a route to his saloon. The Old Man Winter party wasn't supposed to start for another four hours, but from the noise blaring from the Daybreak, it sounded as if the customers had been getting a head start on the celebration. The staff of the Monte Carlo Saloon, which had a theater and an organ and considered itself higher class, were disgruntled that they hadn't thought of the idea first; but there appeared to be enough party goers to make both establishments happy. From end to end, Dawson was full of merrymakers howling in the two o'clock twilight.

Frank stuck his nose in Peggy's bathhouse, recoiled at the state of the water—even now he was cleaner than it was—and went next door to the laundry to cajole a fresh tub out of her. She let him in, guiding him past mounds of laundry tied like hoboes' bindles, which half filled the room.

Frank stared at the accumulation. "Lord, Peg, why don't you close up? You'll never wash all this in a month."

"I'm not going to turn down any work," she told him. "I got the winter to get through."

"You won't even get through this," Frank said. "You'll miss the party."

"I aim to finish tomorrow," Peggy explained. "These boys will be sleeping it off tomorrow. They

211

won't be in a hurry to leave. Are you wanting a bath?"

"Not in that sludge next door."

"I said I would save you a tub." She led him behind a screen of slats stretched with calico and to an empty tub beside her bed and dresser. "I just made this screen," she told him proudly. "Got tired of having the wash in my bedroom like, and every Tom, Dick, and Harry looking at my things."

"Very posh." Frank peeled off his clothes. She came back around the screen with a can of hot, soapy water. She filled the tub with four more cans, and he sank blissfully into it. On the other side of the screen, he could hear miners coming to pick up their wash or bring her more bundles. He didn't bother to scrub. He just lay floating like an alligator in the warm water and let the soapsuds dissolve his outer shell of grime and sweat.

Finally the tub got cold. "I need more hot water, Peg!"

"Hush!" She came flying around the screen. "Someone'll be hearing you!"

"I waited till I didn't hear anybody," Frank said penitently.

"You've been in there an hour." She gave him a disapproving look.

"It's the only time I've been warm in weeks. Aw, come on, Peg. Just one more can." He smiled hopefully, coaxingly.

Peggy inspected him. "You look like a prune."

"If you don't give me some hot water, I'll jump out and go 'boo!' at your next customer."

Peggy removed a can of cooling water from the tub and pitched it out the cabin door and into the street. She smiled thoughtfully and hung the Closed sign on the door. She dipped another canful of water from a tub that had barely begun to heat; it was snow just a degree warmer than freezing.

Frank saw her coming. He smiled gratefully. "Thank you, darling."

She poured it on his head.

Frank, spluttering and howling, leaped out of the tub, then shot around the screen in pursuit of Peggy, who had retreated toward the door. He caught her before she could open it.

"Get away from me!" She tried to dodge him. "You're all wet!"

"Not as wet as you're going to be."

"Let me go!"

"If I let you go, you'll run away. And you probably hid my clothes."

"Did not!" She wriggled, laughing, in his grasp. Frank began to drag her toward the tub. "Oh, no, don't! Nooo! The water's all dirty."

After all those years of scrubbing clothes, Peggy was nearly as strong as he was. If Frank hadn't been taller than she and well muscled himself, she could have pinned him. She pulled one arm out of his grip and stuck her foot between his bare, wet legs. He slipped on the soapy floor, and they fell in a tangle into a pile of dirty shirts.

213

"You're a devious wench, and I'm going to stick you in that tub," Frank threatened.

"Try it! And it was time you were getting out, anyway. I've got me own bath to take."

They wrestled in the shirts, first one on top and then the other. Not surprisingly, in a minute or two Peggy wasn't trying to get away, nor was Frank trying to heave her into the tub fully clothed. He was unbuttoning the front of her shirtwaist, then the red flannel camisole under it. "I'll help you draw a new tub," he suggested, "if you'll let me back in with you."

Her eyes glinted up at him. "All right."

He let her up, and she unbuttoned her skirt and with some dignity peeled off her long underwear and stockings. The washhouse was warm and steamy with the hot water. A tub of soapy water stood by the stove, ready for the next load.

"Here, come get in this," Frank cajoled. "I can't very well empty the other outside."

"Not in that state," Peggy said, eyeing him.

He climbed in, and she settled down in front of him, her back against his chest. They barely fit.

He began to nibble the back of her neck and let his hands slide over her soapy body. She felt for him in the suds. The water began to slosh dangerously. A washtub was not the easiest thing to make love in. They foundered, lifting themselves half out of the water, and slid, slippery, from each other's grasp. He leaned toward her, overbalanced, and tipped, washtub and all, in a spray of suds.

A planer from the sawmill, his Sunday shirt in hand, opened the door as the naked couple fell from the tub.

"Get out of here!" Peggy shrieked. "It's closed! Can't you see the sign?"

"Door warn't locked." He stood clutching his shirt as if unsure of what etiquette demanded and wondering whether she might be willing to wash his shirt after all.

"Get out!"

The intruder retreated. Frank lay on the floor with his feet still in the tub. Water was pooling under him, and soapsuds ran from his hair.

Peggy sat with her legs splayed, but, covered with soapsuds, she maintained modesty. Her red hair dripped in her eyes. She put one hand on her brow. "I'll never be able to hold my head up in this place again," she said despondently.

Frank extracted himself the rest of the way from the tub. He went over to the door and dropped the bar. At its thud Peggy looked up. "You're a mite late with that," she said irritably.

Frank's mouth twitched. He did not remind her that she had been the one to leave the latch off.

She looked at him, crossing her arms in Irish wrath across soapy breasts, lips compressed.

Frank cocked his head at her. "Come on, Peg. . . ."

She gasped and burst out laughing. "You—you

have soap on the tops of your ears," she spluttered. "You look like a bobcat!"

Frank wiped the fog off the tiny square of mirror on the wall, then peered at his reflection. He rather liked the effect, but he grabbed a towel and dried himself anyway, brushing away the suds. He wrapped the towel around Peggy and pulled her to her feet, patting her gently, stroking her shoulders and her thighs with it, murmuring distractions. There wasn't much point in getting dressed now and looking pious. They were already a scandal.

The rest of Dawson was well on its way to its own scandals by the time Frank and Peggy made their appearance at the Daybreak, but word had apparently gotten around. The couple was greeted with appreciative hoots of laughter and offers of advice.

"You get him clean, Peggy?"

Peggy ignored the jokers and swept across the crowded dance floor to the bar. She was wearing her best dress, which she had bought in Seattle, an emerald silk that set off her fiery hair and rustled luxuriously when she walked. She let Frank buy her a whiskey—she usually didn't drink—and sipped it regally. Her eyes dared anyone else to comment.

They gave up, since she wasn't going to be baited. It was no fun if you couldn't get a fight going. Frank just looked pleased with himself.

The Daybreak was packed to the walls with

miners and merchants, dance-hall girls and the girls from upstairs, who sold more than dances. Even the respectable women of Dawson were there. They were few and far between and were cooks and laundresses and boardinghouse keepers. Dawson didn't have an upper crust yet, unless the newly rich wives of the miners who had struck it big were so perceived; they had mainly started as saloon girls, though, and still felt at home. Dawson was a high-living town. As Peggy had said, if she tried to keep her nose in the air, she would never have company. There was only one preacher's wife in town, and she barely ventured out the front door. Poor thing, said Peggy.

Musicians with a fiddle, a string bass, and a banjo were playing in the corner, and every woman was scooped up into some man's arms as soon as she came in. Frank grabbed Peggy and danced her into the thick of the crowd to howls of protest from the other males and renewed ribaldry.

"Give someone else a turn!"

"I'm cleaner'n he is!"

"If I come over, will you wash me, too?"

Most of the partnerless men were dancing with one another, galumphing from one end of the room to the other. Some of them had decided to remember who was supposed to be the girl by tying bandanas around their wrists. Most of them had their hats on, and they danced with enthusiasm if not lightness of foot. The plank floor shook as they thundered across it, raising clouds of sawdust, to the rollicking tune of the fiddle.

"Me and my wife and my wife's pap,
We all live down in Cumberland Gap."

Lulie danced by, as ethereal as a butterfly—a slightly drunken butterfly—in a dress of pale lavender silk and a froth of white lace floating at her breast. Her pale face was flushed, and her eyes shone as she spun among the dancers in the arms of a brawny Klondiker with a beard. He held her close to his chest, nearly lifting her off the floor.

Frank let go of Peggy, and she was pulled into the whirl again and again by other partners before he could reclaim her.

Most of the miners paid for their drinks with gold dust, and rumor had it that Heartache Johnson made a hundred dollars a week just panning his floor. Heartache was a burly man with the mournful countenance of someone who expects life to poke him in the eye. His brown hair rose off his forehead like a cockatoo's crest, and he wore long muttonchop whiskers. Frank wondered what it was about Heartache that drove women away. Maybe it was those whiskers that gave women the willies.

Heartache was wearing his best clothes, a natty Prince Albert coat over a pearl-gray waistcoat. Gray spats peeped from under his dark gray trousers. He sighed wistfully at the fleeting form of Gussie Lamore, a nineteen-year-old temptress who had recently abandoned him for Swiftwater Bill Gate—slured away, so Heartache said, with eggs. Gussie had an insatiable appetite for that almost unavailable item, and Gates had cornered the market in Dawson.

"Cheer up, Heartache," Frank called over Peggy's shoulder. "There are more fish in the sea."

Lulie whirled by again with another miner, this one incongruously dressed in a naval lieutenant's dress uniform that must have been twenty years old.

"Maybe we ought to fix Lulie up with Heartache," Peggy said.

Frank dismissed that. "Nah, Heartache's got some secret weirdness. He must bite his toenails or something. I never saw a man get reshuffled so fast." He noted Lulie disappearing up the stairs, her arm linked with the erstwhile naval lieutenant's. "Besides, Lulie hasn't got time."

Neither did the other girls. There was a constant stream up and down the staircase. The respectable women chose to ignore the traffic; they couldn't very well stop it, and any other form of acknowledgment would be undignified. There was only a fine line between the upstairs girls and some of the dancers anyway. The dance-hall girls got paid to dance with the customers and to flirt with them, to cajole them into buying drinks and keep them spending money. It wasn't an arrangement entirely on the up-and-up. When a customer bought a dance-hall girl a whiskey, she got cold tea in a shot glass and thus could drink all evening for the profit of the saloon. But she wasn't exactly a prostitute. If she chose to go upstairs with a customer, the bar charged her rent for the room. And most of the dance-hall girls took their pay in the form of "presents"—it was considered nicer that way.

Lulie hovered somewhere between the status of the dance-hall girls and the out-and-out prostitutes. With a vague confidence that everything would turn out fine, she slept with any man who asked her. Her ingenuous pleasure both in their company and their "presents" flattered them into kindness. She received a dance-hall girl's pay, and any other operations were on the side. Heartache was aware that her wistful beauty drew men into the Daybreak.

A dancing male couple caromed now into the string bass, and the music ceased abruptly while the bass player swore at them. Another couple, oblivious to the collision, went on with their polka, while a third, attempting to correct course and avoid the pileup, overshot and crashed into the poker game in the corner. By the time the musicians had themselves straightened out, fortified with a little Perry Davis's Pain-Killer, and were playing "The River in the Pines," someone had cut in on Frank. He suddenly found himself holding the reins of a donkey handed to him by the usurper.

"Get that animal out of here!" Heartache shouted.

"Hell, she's better looking than some of your customers," Frank said. He shook the reins and did an experimental dance step in a circle. The donkey obligingly turned with him. "See? She dances better, too."

The donkey snuffled the sawdust on the floor and then, clearly about to make a mess, hiked her tail.

"No! Get her out!"

Frank tugged on the reins and persuaded her out the door before the dance floor was befouled. He tied her outside, then went back in, stumbling a little against the door frame. He wasn't entirely sober himself, but it didn't seem to matter. The evening had a last-fling excitement that promised that all sins would be forgiven on the morrow.

He looked around for Peggy, prepared to do battle with the interloper and take her back, but he didn't see her. The room was full of howling drunks and cavorting dancers, and someone was pouring whiskey from a shot glass down the fiddler's throat while he continued to play, head tipped back and eyes closed. One of the dance-hall girls, her skirts held up to show shapely ankles, was doing a ragtime dance on the bar.

"Gentlemen! Ladies of the fair sex!" Heartache Johnson clambered up beside her onto the bar. "Excuse me, dear. Gentlemen, the Daybreak Saloon presents the mystical seeress of the Klondike, the oracle of the frozen North!"

Frank followed Heartache's pointing finger and saw Peggy now, sitting demurely at a table at the

221

end of the bar. Her red hair was hidden under a paisley shawl, and another shawl was twisted around her shoulders, over a deep green blouse and a skirt of red and black flounces. She wore gigantic gold hoops in her ears, and her cheeks were reddened with rouge. A dark pencil had transformed her pale brows into winging black ones. She moved her hands, winking with glass jewels, over a crystal ball, which looked suspiciously like the ground-down globe of a lamp shade.

"For only a dollar Madame Blavatsky answers all your questions! Are you crossed in love? Is your test hole a skunk? Madame Blavatsky knows."

"How come you don't ask her where your lady friends keep a-goin'?" someone chortled.

The other revelers guffawed.

"I have already consulted with Madame Blavatsky," Heartache said with dignity, "about my financial affairs and my personal life. I would not recommend to you a service I could not personally endorse."

"Well, what did she say? You ever gonna git a lady to stay put in your bed?"

"She says you're going to get skunked and die of the d.t.'s, that's what she says," Heartache snapped. He jumped down to glare eyeball to eyeball at his tormentor.

"You leave Heartache alone," Frank said. He climbed up on the bar and tipped his felt hat to the rakish angle of a sideshow pitchman's. He spread his arms. "Ask not for other men's fate!

Inquire into your own! Madame Blavatsky knows the secrets of the universe, and for a dollar she will tell them to you! Are you going to be a rich man? Or does a pitiful fate await you somewhere on the frozen tundra? Find out before it's too late!"

Heartache tugged at Frank's trousers as miners, clutching their pokes, began to converge on Peggy's table.

Frank leaned down, listened to instructions from Heartache, then stood up. "Indian wrestling will continue in the far corner, for a purse of fifty dollars and fame throughout the territory."

Frank watched as a young blond miner with a scrubbed face held his palm out to Peggy. "Kin I win that Indian wrestling?"

Peggy took his dollar and consulted her crystal ballor lamp globe. Then she felt his forearm thoughtfully. "Madame Blavatsky sees victory ahead. But it is hard to tell if it will come this night or some other. Persevere."

Frank chuckled appreciatively at Peg's advice. She bent over her crystal ball, apparently deep in trance. She was pretty good at that, Frank reflected. She had the touch and could have done fine with the sideshow. She seemed to have acquired a mysterious accent. She sounded like the Russians from Sitka.

Frank climbed down from the bar and, finding himself behind it, helped himself to a shot of whiskey as pay for giving his spiel. He accidentally knocked over a row of shot glasses but carefully set them back up again. The Daybreak was noisier than ever, with dancers still thundering across the cleared floor and shouts of encouragement erupting from the Indian wrestling across the room. He leaned against the counter because he seemed to sway a little.

A shout from the far corner announced the winner of the Indian wrestling match. The musicians stopped to have another drink. Into the comparative silence that prevailed, a woman's voice cried, "Hey, boys! Listen to me!"

Frank scanned the room, squinting through the smoke and kerosene fumes and saw Lulie atop a table. Her cheeks were redder than before, and her eyes glittered.

"Listen up, boys, because I got an offer to make you!"

"Oh, no," Frank heard Peggy say behind him.

"That's right," Lulie called. "Now I know it ain't ladylike to toot my own horn. But up here if a girl doesn't do that, who'll do it for her?"

"Hell, I would!" someone shouted. "You're about the purtiest thing I seen!"

"Thank you," Lulie said, smiling demurely. "You're gonna get a chance to prove that, sugar, cause here's what I aim to do: I aim to get married for the winter! Unless I don't like his looks, I aim to marry up until spring thaw with the highest bidder."

"There hasn't been anybody yet, she didn't like his looks," Peggy groaned, accent forgotten. She had come to stand by Frank. "I got to stop her."

"And I'll cook for him," Lulie went on, "and keep his cabin clean, and everything a real wife does, till spring."

"Everything?" another man shouted.

Lulie lowered her lashes as if she were blushing. "That's right," she murmured. "Everything."

"Eeeeyow!"

"I'll bid! I'll bid!"

"A hundred dollars!"

"Five hundred!"

"Now you boys just wait a minute. We're going to do this orderly." Lulie scanned the room, and her eyes lit on Frank.

Peggy stalked over to her friend, reached up, and grabbed Lulie's pale silk skirts. "You aren't going to do it at all!" she scolded. "You lost your mind? Get down from there!"

"I ain't," Lulie said, yanking her skirt aside. "I told you I was gonna do it."

"Not like this!"

"Leave her alone!" Men were pushing around the table, pulling Peggy away. "Stay out of this! It ain't your business!"

Peggy pushed back. "You can't do this, you ninny! There's no telling who you'll get."

"I'll get more money this way," Lulie hissed. "You leave me alone. Frank, you make her leave me alone."

"Me?" Frank blinked at both women. "She's a grown woman, Peg. You can't stop her."

"That's right," Lulie said. "Now then, boys—"

There was an immediate and attentive silence. The musicians crowded closer to hear, and even the poker game in the corner had broken up, its players stuffing their pokes in their pockets and picking up chips.

"We're going to have an auction," Lulie continued. "A proper one, with an auctioneer. Frank Blake, you come on up here and be my auctioneer."

"Me?" Frank looked taken aback.

Peggy stabbed a finger at him. "Don't you dare!"

"Lulie, I've never been an auctioneer." Frank tried to wriggle out of it.

Heartache Johnson bowed to Lulie. "I count that among my attainments," he said portentously. "I would be glad to do the honors. For a commission, of course."

"I want Frank," Lulie said. "And I know what your commissions are like."

That drew laughter from the other girls, except Peggy, who put one foot on a chair and tried to get up on the table with Lulie. "You've run plain crazy. You get down from there."

"I ain't!" Lulie said.

Peggy whirled around at Frank. "And if you take any part in this harebrained scheme, I'll tear your head off."

"Get back, Peg!" someone yelled. "Lessen you want to play the same game. You got an Irish temper, but I'd bid on you."

"Hell, that ain't Peggy, that's Madame Bla-

226

vatsky," someone else said, then guffawed. "She can see in her crystal ball you ain't got no money."

"Come on, Peg, you can't stop her." Frank managed to lure Peggy off the chair and away from the table.

"You aren't going to help her?"

"He is too!" Lulie said.

Frank looked at the ceiling. Clouds of cigar and lamp smoke floated there, as amorphous as his brain. Someone opened a champagne bottle, and the cork arced across the clouds. Frank was too drunk to know clearly what he ought to be doing. It was easier just to let events flow.

"At least I won't charge her any commission," he pointed out to Peggy. "Somebody else is going to do it if I don't."

Peggy let out a long breath. They both knew she could never win an argument against a roomful of drunken miners and a girl who was determined to be foolhardy. "I don't see anything good coming of it," she said at last, then shrugged her shoulders. "Go ahead."

"Yow!" The miners started to stamp their feet and cheer. One of them handed Lulie a glass of champagne.

"Now you all just shut up!" Frank shouted. He leaped onto the table, beside Lulie, then tipped his hat to one side again. "Now this here lady is a lady, and there's not going to be any dirty talk, you understand? All right, who's going to give me five hundred dollars? I heard five hundred already.

Who was that from? Okay, we've got five hundred from Jake."

The old miner with the top hat and the pearl stickpin smiled. He had a bottle of champagne in one hand, and his nose was as red as Lulie's cheeks.

"I got five hundred. Now that isn't near enough. This here's an angel in human form, come to the Klondike just to make some miner die of happiness. And she can cook. Seven, I got seven. Who'll give me a thousand?"

It was easy to fall into the rhythm of the patter, just like ballyhooing the reptile show: "Step right up and see the beauteous wonder of the Klondike—all natural, all real, nothing hidden, nothing enhanced! I've got a thousand; I've got fifteen hundred! Somebody give me two!"

Lulie turned this way and that on the table, simpering. Her eyes glowed over the rim of her glass as she sipped champagne, little finger stuck out.

"Two thousand! Twenty-five!"

Everyone cheered every time Frank accepted a bid. He danced on the table, showing off Lulie, drawing them in. Eight or ten men had gravitated to the front of the crowd. Old Jake in his battered top hat was still among them. At three thousand, four of them dropped out, but the rest stayed in, eyes fixed avidly on Lulie's lavender silk. Everyone else offered advice and comment.

"You won't live through the winter, Jake, if you hook up with that young thing!"

"Hell, he'll die happy!"

"Stone cold in the sheets with a smile on his face—that ain't no sight for a purty young thing to wake up to. Jake, you better back out now!"

Jake raised his bottle of champagne. "I'll have you know I can whup any one of you with one hand." He hiccuped, then tipped the bottle and took another swallow.

"Thirty-five! Who'll give me four?"

"Four!" The bidder was a tall man, as solidly built as a tree. He had a straight cap of hair the unusual bronze color of autumn leaves, parted in the middle and hanging over his collar.

"Four from this gentlemen. I don't know you, sir." Frank bent down toward him.

"The name's Dahl."

"Four thousand from Mr. Dahl."

"Forty-two!" That came from a young man with dark, curly hair. He wore a flannel shirt and overalls, from which he pulled a poke to prove he had it.

"Forty-five," Jake called out.

"Five thousand," Dahl said.

"Five thousand! I have five thousand. Now that's not enough for so much beauty at your beck and call all winter—the best deal this side of heaven!"

"Fifty-two!" said the young man in the flannel shirt.

"Fifty-three!" Jake yelled. He took another swig of champagne.

"Fifty-three! Who'll make it fifty-five?"

Except for the curly-headed boy and Dahl, the

others shook their heads. "Fifty-four!" the younger man shouted.

Dahl came closer and studied Lulie, looking her up and down.

"I don't like him," Peggy said to Heartache. "He hasn't even cracked a smile. Can't you stop this?"

Heartache shrugged. "She can turn him down if she wants to."

Dahl was still looking at Lulie. "Six thousand!" he said abruptly.

"Sixty-two!" Jake poured the rest of the champagne down his throat. Then he sank slowly to the floor. A snore like a warthog's escaped him.

"Seven thousand," Dahl said contemptuously.

Frank looked at the curly-haired boy.

The boy shook his head. He held up his poke balanced on one palm. "I won it in a poker game. I ain't got no more."

Frank scanned the crowd. "I have seven thousand! Seven thousand! Who'll make it seventy-five? Take a look at this beautiful lady, ready to be your heart's companion. Guaranteed to be just as you see her—no deceptions!" Lulie spun gracefully on the table, all swaying hips, blond hair, and lavender silk. "Hair and teeth and all other attractions guaranteed to be her own. She'll rise in the morning just as you see her now. Who wouldn't pay seventy-five for such pulchritude?"

"Jake would if he was awake!" someone shouted.

"Well, he's not," Dahl said. He folded his arms

and with a proprietary air stood next to Lulie. "Seven thousand. Is anyone going to top it?"

Peggy knelt beside Jake and shook his arm. "Wake up, you old buzzard." Jake let out a long snore of contentment and then rolled over, his face in the sawdust. Peggy shook him again. "Jake! Wake up and bid!"

"He's out," someone said. "He ain't going to wake up till Sunday."

Peggy looked at Frank, panic evident in her face.

"Seven thousand," Frank said. Something about Dahl made him uncomfortable, but maybe it was just Peggy's reaction rubbing off. "Seven thousand," he said again, slowly, "going once."

There was silence in the room. Lulie stood still, posing, smiling, oblivious.

"Going twice."

Dahl didn't pay any more attention to Lulie. He just stood waiting.

"Seven thousand dollars, going three times. Gone! Gone to this gentleman here, to Mr. Dahl."

Dahl turned around and motioned for Lulie to get down off the table.

"Just a minute!" Peggy said. "You just wait! She's got the right to reject the high bidder if she doesn't like him!"

Lulie looked at Dahl with curiosity and then at Jake, passed out on the floor. "Well, I don't reckon I could take a whole winter of that," she said.

231

"Jake's out of the running," Frank judged. "He defaulted on account of champagne."

"This fellow was the next bidder," Peggy said desperately. She dragged the curly-headed boy forward.

He smiled sheepishly at Lulie. "I'd of gone higher if I'd had it, ma'am," he said. "You sure are a wonder."

Lulie looked at him, vaguely interested. "How much did you bid, sugar?"

"Fifty-four. But I got fifty-five."

"I bid seven," Dahl said. "You come with me."

Lulie's face took on a concentrated expression for a moment. Then she smiled at Dahl. "Okay," she said. "You look nice."

"Where's your diggings?" Peggy demanded of Dahl.

Dahl looked at her as if trying to decide whether to bother answering. "Out the far end of Eldorado Creek," he said. "It ain't your business."

Lulie was humming to herself, patting the purse he had handed her.

"Get your coat on," he told her. "Let's go."

"I'll drive her out in the morning," Frank offered. "You don't want to go all that way tonight."

"Bring her things in the morning," Dahl said. "I paid for tonight—not for tomorrow or next week."

One of the other girls brought Lulie's coat down to her, and Dahl put it around her as if he were wrapping a package. Then they went out into the street, and their departure left a still hole at the center of the nightsome dark arrangement with which no one was comfortable, but no one could say why.

"He looks all right. . . ." Heartache Johnson said dubiously.

The curly-haired boy went up to the bar and laid his poke on it. "Give me a whiskey."

Two miners picked Jake up and dragged him off to a corner, out of the way. The fiddle and the string bass struck up again.

"He looks all right. . . ." Heartache said again, staring uneasily at the door.

XI

Sierra, California, October 1897

Henry Blake strode along the wooden sidewalk built to protect ladies' skirts from the dust of Sierra's shopping district. Actually, stomped along was a better description. It was October, but what kind of fall was this? he wondered. Where were the red and orange trees? The live oaks didn't even bother to shed their leaves. The trees that did, their leaves simply turned a sickly yellow, then dropped off. The citrus didn't shed leaves, either. There they sat, bright green, hung with fat fruit. They looked as if they'd been painted by those fellows whose work Cindy hung in her gallery—nothing they painted ever looked real. Cindy was still in Portland, at the Madrona with Eulalia. Henry had tried to get her to come home. She had refused.

Henry glowered into the window of a milliner's shop and then turned the corner. The streetlights were being lit, and the temperature was finally beginning to drop. What did Cindy think she was doing at the Madrona? She'd had two postcards from Frank, one mailed to Washington, D.C., from somewhere up near Point Sur; the other mailed in Seattle, sent to Washington, then forwarded to Portland. Frank had been traveling with a circus, of all the disgusting things. And Cindy had become hysterical when she realized that it had played Portland but Midge and she hadn't gone because the child had a sore throat.

Had she wanted to find Frank like that? Henry wondered, shooting a fiery look up and down the street. Would she have enjoyed some sick satisfaction from seeing her son eking out a hand-to-mouth living in some squalid carnival? Probably, he decided angrily, so she could hit him over the head with it.

No telling where the boy was now, but Cindy ought to know he wasn't going to come for dinner in Portland just because he had been sending her postcards. Henry felt aggrieved. What in blazes did she expect him to do that he hadn't been doing? There was only so much one man could do; he had just begun to root around into the problem of Sierra Oil when he had received orders from Washington to go to Cuba.

"Go down there and find out what the devil is

really going on" was the way his assignment had been explained to him.

He had gone, of course, but first told Peter to lie low until he got back: Say "Yes, sir" to Sanford Rutledge, pay his share of the negligence settlement, and not sell his stock. Peter had grudgingly agreed to comply, but while Henry was in Cuba, he had felt the hair prickle on the back of his neck every time he thought about Peter.

He had skulked around Cuba for an entire mosquito-infested summer, looking for the Spanish atrocities that were being trumpeted daily in William Randolph Hearst's New York Morning Journal and Joseph Pulitzer's New York World. When the country had worked itself up in 1895 to fight Britain over a boundary dispute in South America, Pulitzer had used common sense to deflate the war hysteria. The tactic must not have sold papers. Now Pulitzer was doing his best to outdo the rival Journal with bloodcurdling descriptions of Spanish brutality:

The skulls of all were split to pieces down to the eyes. Some of these were gouged out. . . . The arms and legs of one had been dismembered and laced into a crude attempt at a Cuban five-pointed star . . . The tongue of one had been cut out and placed on the mangled forehead. . . . The Spanish soldiers habitually cut off the ears of the Cuban dead and retain them as trophies.

Henry had found no severed ears. Spain was

fighting to maintain its colonial rule, while the Cuban insurrectos were fighting to throw it off. Henry found the state of bloodshed and chaos that might be expected under the circumstances, but no atrocities of the sort with which Hearst and Pulitzer were making American civilians shiver at their breakfast tables every morning. The Spanish general Weyler was loathed, and Henry had a low opinion of him; but he had an even lower one of Hearst. During the summer he had met an artist, Frederic Remington, sent to provide illustrations for Hearst's paper. Remington complained that he had cabled Hearst that he could find no material. Hearst had cabled back, "You furnish the pictures, I'll furnish the war."

In the early fall, Henry had returned to Washington and reported to President McKinley. Henry believed that a settlement could be worked out because Spain had inaugurated Sagasta, a political moderate. Of course, Henry went on to say, if President McKinley wanted a war with Spain, then American sentiment would certainly support it. Henry did not consider it his job to tell President McKinley which course to take.

Henry had deliberately bypassed visiting the Holts. He was well aware of Toby's strong opinions that a war with Spain was inadvisable. Toby was telling his opinions to anybody who would listen. Henry secretly wanted a war; he wanted to fight somebody. In any case, Toby and he had parted on bad terms after Tim's wedding. Lastly, he needed to be in Sierra; he had no time for Washington socializing.

As soon as he was able, he had taken the first train west. He couldn't imagine what else Cindy thought he had time for, between Sierra Oil and Cuba.

Of course, she had been unreasonably furious that he hadn't told her in advance that he was going to Cuba. Cindy was always informed of these quiet government missions, even though no one else in the family was. This time, however, Henry had taken perverse pleasure in getting on a ship without notifying his wife. He hadn't been able to explain his secrecy, other than simply wanting to strike out in some way at her.

Now Henry stalked past another Sierra saloon. He was heading into the roughest part of town. Saloons such as the Miners' Rest on the corner of Main Street and Avenal actually served dinner, and a miner might bring his family. Saloons like the Wellhead at the far end of Avenal served trouble. That made them magnets for Henry; trouble was what he looked for. Trouble gave him a stick to beat any dog who might have the information he needed but was afraid to have his name mentioned to the police.

Henry stopped about a hundred feet away from the door of the Wellhead and inspected the entrance. He had learned never to keep an appointment requested by another man unless he went armed with a surprise up his sleeve, just in case. Henry knew he had attracted attention just by nosing around Sierra and the burned-out refinery. As he had hoped, his acting the bird dog had come to the notice of people with an interest in Sierra Oil. The man he was meeting tonight—he was the third such contact—had offered to sell information. The first two hadn't had anything except a desire to make some money. This one, Henry believed, might actually know something, particularly since he appeared to be waiting in the shadows in the alley that ran beside the Wellhead.

Henry's eyes narrowed, but he didn't let them linger on the man he had glimpsed. The watcher in the alleyway was no more than just a darker shade of gray—night had come down around them, and the streetlights made bright pools that cast everything outside their boundaries in shadow. Henry drew a cigar from his coat pocket, and as he lit it, he held the match so that the man in the alley could be sure of his face. It would be a pity to have him jump some other poor bastard out of sheer nerves.

Then Henry tucked the box of matches back in his pocket and ambled toward the Wellhead. His hand grasped the blackjack tucked in his pocket with the matches.

The man in the shadows lunged at him. The knife in his hand flashed briefly in the light from the streetlamp. Seeing it, Henry smacked his blackjack down efficiently on the shadow's knife hand, then flung the blade into the alley while the man howled in pain. Henry got his assailant by the coat collar and shoved him down the alley, where a thick stew of spilled beer and horse manure from the brewery wagons clung to the cobbles. The man writhed in his grasp, and Henry, to subdue him, punched the man in the jaw.

"Shut up and listen." Henry kept his voice low. He didn't want to be interrupted by the police until he had got his message across—assuming the police took any interest in the doings of lower Avenal Avenue, which was doubtful. The other patrons of the Wellhead might, though. "Go tell whoever sent you that if I see your face again, I'll split it in two with a hatchet. And if you're considering laying a finger on my son, I'll find you and split your skull four ways."

The man wriggled in his grasp. "I wasn't trying to do no harm! I was s'posed to meet you here. I was just comin' up to—"

"Stow it," Henry snarled. "When you come to, do what I said. Now hold still so this won't hurt as much."

The blackjack came down so quickly that the man didn't have time to move. He went limp, then Henry hauled him far down the alley and tucked him out of the way of carriage wheels. After brushing himself off and inspecting his trousers for traces of horse manure, Henry sauntered, satisfied, into the Wellhead for a drink.

"Hey, Nate! What happened to you? You look like you got chewed by a bear."

Nate glowered and bared his teeth at the roughnecks in a corner table of the Wellhead. "Don't mess with me."

It was twenty-four hours since his encounter with the blackjack, and Nate was nursing a split lip as well as a painful knot at the back of his head. His hat was angled; pulling it all the way down hurt too much.

The roughnecks went back to their drinks. They were oil-field workers, grimy and well muscled, with hamlike hands and black-rimmed nails. But Nate had a reputation. There wasn't any point in taking him on for no reason.

Another man wandered in, and the roughnecks watched with interest. He had chewed-looking sandy hair and a broken nose. He glared upon the world with the same malevolent glitter as Nate, daring it to try something. "Heard you got horsewhipped," he said, smirking. He studied Nate. "You look like it, too."

Nate made a noise in his throat like a dog that had been tied up too long. "Son of a bitch was ready for me," he muttered.

"Heard that, too," his crony said. "Heard he came in here and asked for a drink afterward, smooth as silk. Heard he was dressed like a dude and nobody messed with him."

"You heard a lot," Nate growled. He flicked a glance at the roughnecks, who were listening interestedly while pretending not to.

"And all while you was out in the alley, probably puking your guts out. Thought I'd do you a favor."

"Yeah?" Nate eyed him suspiciously. "What for?"

"Keep the boys in the corner from laughing themselves silly over you." The roughnecks turned away in a hurry. "I might want something myself someday. You'll stir up big trouble if you keep on the way you're going, and I don't want to get sucked up in it."

"All right, all right. How come you know so much?"

"Like how come he was waiting for you? Cause he's a professional. You got to watch yourself."

Nate shrugged. "Ain't nobody ever surprised me like that before."

The man snorted. "You probably never got hired to put the finish on a government man before."

"Government man?" Nate looked puzzled. "Like a marshal?"

"Naw, he's higher up than that. He's a goddamned colonel in the army, and he didn't get there pushing papers across no desk."

"That ain't what R—what the old man told me." Nate looked indignant.

"Well, of course not. He ain't going to tell you to go after somebody that's already killed more poor fellows than you can count on both hands. God deliver me, but you're dumb. You listen to what I say. Stay away from Blake. You get him riled, he'll dig deeper than what I think he's after and land us all in the can for arson and murder." He lowered his voice. "If Blake don't murder you personally, I'll kill you. What you did to Sid Delaney, I can do to you." He moved off and got a drink of his own, then sat nursing it while Nate stared furiously into his.

Nate confronted Sanford Rutledge across a vast expanse of mahogany desk. Rutledge was engaged in sorting its contents into small piles—rubber bands with rubber bands, and red and blue thumbtacks by color.

Nate slapped a handful of cash down on the desk. "It's all there. You never told me about this Blake, and I'm not gonna get my head knocked off. I coulda got my head knocked off!" He scowled at Rutledge reproachfully.

Rutledge looked up, jutting out his chin and beard like an accusing flag. "I don't know what the world's coming to. You were highly recommended, but this is the second job you've bungled."

"I ain't bungled it. I quit!"

"You bungled young Mr. Blake," Rutledge pointed out. He arranged three red thumbtacks in a pattern, then flicked one of them furiously across the desk at Nate. "You bungled him! You admitted it."

"I chased him clear up to Canada," Nate protested. "I tried killin' him with tent poles, railroad cars, an' snakes. It ain't my fault if none of 'em took."

"You might have tried bullets."

Nate was furious. "You said to make it look like

242

an accident! And then you wired me to leave him alone and come on back, long as he got on a boat."

"Nonsense." Rutledge tented his fingers together in front of his beard. "Anyway, now I want you to deal with his father and his brother. I am aggravated with Mr. Peter Blake. He behaves as if this company were a charitable institution instead of a corporation." Rutledge pushed the bills back across the desk at Nate. "Don't argue with me."

Nate looked uneasily at the old man. Something about him was strange. Nate couldn't put his finger on it, and it didn't give him the creeps as bad as his crony's information concerning Henry Blake; but it bothered him enough to push the money back again.

"I ain't gonna do it. I ain't gonna try anything on the son, neither."

"You have already been paid."

"Well, I'm givin' it back, you crazy old coot! There, see?" He pushed the money more emphatically at Rutledge.

"You can't give it back," Rutledge said in reasonable tones. "I won't take it."

"Then you can just leave it lie there!" Nate snapped.

"You'll have to find me somebody else." Rutledge was back to sorting rubber bands, this time by size. "I might let you off the hook if you do that." He looked up briefly and then down again. "That will be all. Send your replacement to my office."

"He's crazy, that's what he is," Nate muttered into his whiskey in the corner of the Wellhead. "Where am I gonna find him somebody else?"

"Danged if I know," said his pal, running his hands through his dark hair. "But there's more fools out there than you'd think."

"Yeah, I know, but none of 'em's that big a fool. I tried 'em all. Seems like I was the only one who didn't know who this Blake fellow was. The old man keeps sendin' me threatening notes," he said nervously. "I don't like it."

"You're in a pickle, ain't you?" his buddy said sympathetically. "You're going to have to kill somebody now—either Blake or the old man."

Henry Blake contemplated the envelope delivered to him, in care of Peter. It was fortunate, Henry thought, smiling wolfishly, that Peter wasn't at home to see it. So Sanford Rutledge wanted him to stop for a chat the next morning, did he?

Henry put the envelope on Peter's parlor fire, then trotted up the stairs two at a time to the guest bedroom, which he was once again inhabiting. It was fortuitous that Peter was at a company banquet with a representative of Standard Oil; Rutledge would undoubtedly be there, too, if only to keep the devil at bay. Standard was still interested in acquiring Sierra Oil, preferably before Sierra got back on its feet financially and had the luxury of declining the offer. A Standard representative had been in town for a week, for courting purposes. Peter had told his father that Kemp was edging toward selling and that Rutledge was getting frantic over it.

On Henry's orders, Peter had refused to commit one way or the other, but he was going to have to soon. "I look like an incompetent," Peter had said grumpily earlier that evening as he fastened his shirt studs. "Let me off the leash, Dad, or I'll do it anyway."

"Soon," Henry had promised. Now he grinned again. Tonight maybe. . . . He slipped off his gentlemanly white shirt and tugged a dark knitted pullover over his head. He added a navy-blue fisherman's cap over his pale hair and looking purposeful, left his son's house by the back door.

Kemp, a country boy and a local son, had a ranch and an orange grove outside town. But according to Peter, Rutledge, with his passion for modernity and his treasured new refinery at Oleum, settled his family in San Francisco and periodically traveled north on the train to see them. Consequently, no wife and children would be at home in Sierra, waiting for their provider to return from the business dinner. The house could be counted on to be empty tonight, despite the electric lights left burning in the front parlor by the housekeeper. Henry slunk around to the back door, which was not so well illuminated. Using a set of tools that would have done a burglar proud, he picked the lock, blessing the fact that Mr. Rutledge did not keep a dog. Lock picking was a skill that Henry would have considered morally deplorable in anyone else, but for him it was a necessity.

Henry was operating on the assumption that Rutledge kept records and that he was too astute to keep them at the company offices. A man who was truly intelligent wouldn't keep records at all, but it had been Henry's experience that a man accustomed to running a business treated all his affairs similarly and kept books. Why was a mystery to Henry, but he was immensely grateful for the idiosyncracy in certain otherwise crafty criminals.

Henry prowled into a first-floor office and peered through the gloom. He didn't like the idea of switching on the lights, so he felt his way to the desk, then began sliding the drawers open. He lit a series of matches and held them cupped above each drawer while he flipped through the contents with his other hand. The unlocked drawers contained a rat's nest of oddments and correspondence with Mrs. Rutledge in San Francisco. Henry grinned. It appeared that Rutledge wanted to electrify the house completely, and she was having none of it . . . their daughter was going out with an unsuitable young man . . . there were rats in the attic, and poison would have to be put down. . . . Henry, having decided that Rutledge had not confided murderous intent to the missus, went on. The last drawer was locked—an excellent sign. Henry picked it, too.

Inside was a boxful of cash and a small notebook. Henry at first thought it contained notes for a church class, since the first page was filled with biblical-sounding exhortations to stand off evil, "the many-headed hydra and the devouring serpent." Apparently, however, the serpent that Rutledge had in mind was Standard Oil, and the next pages contained jottings of sums of money, opposite names, with the scrawled notation "to fight Rockefeller" beside most of them. The appearance of Sid Delaney's name on the list caught Henry's eye. He stuck the book in his pocket and investigated the rest of the room, seeking something more concrete.

The office walls supported elaborate shelving of the sort considered appropriate for a gentleman's library. Like many prosperous fellows who wished to be admired for maintaining a library, Rutledge appeared to have chosen his books according to how well they would look on his wall rather than with any real intention of reading them or concern for their content. Elegantly gilded spines marched in neat rows down the shelves. Most of them were subscription sets, matched in size and color. They included Shakespeare's plays in teal blue, the major British poets in scarlet, Dickens in green, and Plutarch's *The Parallel Lives* in brown. The volumes of the collected sermons of Henry Ward Beecher and other notable theologians were, of course, in sober black. Henry reached up for a volume and bet the pages hadn't even been cut. After proving himself right, he investigated further and found that the Reverend

247

Mr. Beecher and his colleagues hid what Henry was looking for: a wall safe.

Henry dragged the rest of the ministers' work off the shelf and pulled a chair near the wall. He stood on the seat and, sticking his ear against the safe, twiddled the dials experimentally. It wasn't a particularly complicated apparatus and had probably been ordered from Sears, Roebuck. Simple, he thought. Of course, on the off chance that Rutledge came home unexpectedly . . . Henry, having been to his share of banquets, knew that unless the old man got sick, he wouldn't be home for a while. Banquets went on and on as long as anyone present had enough breath left to make a speech. He was devoutly glad to be here burgling Rutledge's safe rather than at that dinner and going to sleep over the port.

Henry gave the dial a last twitch, and the door swung open with gratifying ease. He pulled out the contents and lit another match.

Henry found a pair of diamond cuff links vulgar enough for a silver nabob—he couldn't imagine Rutledge wearing them—and a stack of canceled Sierra Oil Corporation checks. They were made out to the names in the notebook, including Sid Delaney's, and were variously signed by Sanford Rutledge and the entire board of Sierra Oil directors—including Peter Blake.

Henry stood back, looking at the signatures and getting more and more enraged. The match burned down and singed his fingers. He swore and dropped it. Before he could light another match, he heard carriage wheels. Quickly he stuffed the cuff links back in the safe, clicked it shut, and spun the dial. The books of sermons were jammed onto the shelf, and Henry darted for the back door just as someone came in the front.

Henry slipped out the back gate and, strolling casually, doubled around the house, to see if the arrival—Rutledge, most likely—was going to raise an alarm. A hack was just pulling away from the door. Inside the house, a light went on upstairs, shortly after the downstairs one went off. Henry shot one glance over his shoulder and set out toward Peter's house.

Henry found his elder son smoking a cigar by the fire. His look of blissful ignorance served to madden Henry. "What in the hell do you think you've been doing, Peter?" he demanded.

Peter, eyes widening, peered at his father. "What do you think you've been doing? You look like a waterfront thug."

Henry pulled off his cap and tossed it onto the table. His hair stood up stiffly, as if in indignation. He extracted the sheaf of Sierra Oil Corporation checks from his pocket and shoved them at his son.

Peter's expression was of mild curiosity as he inspected the top check, signed by Rutledge. "Rutledge was very strange at dinner tonight. He was nearly raving at Standard's rep. Extremely embarrass—" When he looked at the signature on the second check, his brows went up. "But I didn't think—Hatch Hey!" Peter sat bolt upright, clutching a check that bore his own signature. "Why that slimy, conniving, murdering son of a bitch!"

"Did you write that check?" Henry demanded.

"What the hell do you take me for?" Peter shouted, jumping up from the chair. "No, I didn't write this check, and Kemp didn't write this one, I'll bet." He was nearly dancing with fury as he waved another check under Henry's nose. "Where the hell did you get these?"

Henry folded his arms. "From Rutledge's wall safe."

Peter looked him up and down. "Good God, Dad, what if you'd been caught?"

"You might be a little more grateful," Henry commented.

"Grateful! Coming in here accusing me of— of—" Peter was nearly choking with outrage.

"Simmer down," Henry said. "I didn't accuse you. I just wanted to see what you'd do. It looks like your signature to me, you know."

"It looks like my signature to me," Peter admitted, gaining control, "but it isn't."

"That's all I wanted to know."

"Don't you want some proof?"

"Certainly not," Henry said. "I raised you properly." He turned and went upstairs, leaving Peter looking puzzled.

Peter was still asleep when Henry left in the morning. Henry presented himself at Rutledge's Sierra

Oil headquarters at eight o'clock as requested, and a clerk showed him to the second-floor offices. The corporate headquarters building was made of gray fieldstone below and red brick above. Arched windows alternated with overhanging Italianate bays on the second floor. Above the bay window on the corner the Sierra Oil flag was waving. This corner room was Sanford Rutledge's office.

"Good morning, Colonel. Pleasant weather we've been having. Good of you to come." Rutledge stood and shook Henry's hand. Rutledge's fingers felt hard and knobby, as if the bones were just beneath the skin.

"Good of you to invite me." Henry contemplated asking Rutledge why he had, but decided to see how the man would broach the subject.

"Knew you'd come, of course. Can't imagine why the government should be interested in our operation, but I'm always glad to help."

"I wasn't aware that the government was interested," Henry replied genially.

"But it's what you're doing here, isn't it? Investigating the saboteurs who're trying to ruin me? I take it kindly."

"Not exactly," Henry said. Rutledge hadn't sat down again, so Henry didn't. He wondered if Rutledge could possibly be as naïve as he sounded. There was something very peculiar about the man. It gave Henry an itch between his shoulder blades. "I take it you are referring to the refinery fire?"

"Saboteurs everywhere," Rutledge said darkly. "Waiting to devour us. The fire was a blessing."

"That 'blessing' killed several people."

"Certainly. Difficult for them." Rutledge peered at Henry from under a hedge of eyebrows. "But the refinery had to go. Standard Oil blew it up. Saboteurs everywhere."

Henry tried to sort that out and failed to find the logic. He looked at the man with growing unease. There were differences between a man who was merely a little eccentric and one who might be literally insane. For example, unlike the eccentric, the insane cannot assess consequences and thus are capable of anything. Henry edged away, just a little at a time, until his back was against the wall.

"Saboteurs," Rutledge continued. "Mark my words, Colonel—saboteurs, the hand of Rockefeller. You know who I mean."

"I'm not sure I do," Henry said. "Do you honestly believe that John D. Rockefeller had your refinery burned down?"

Rutledge's eyes grew crafty. "Of course not. He used his agents. Kemp is one. No one's to be trusted." He sat down abruptly at his desk and began to play with the items on the blotter—thumbtacks, rubber bands, a ruler, pencils—moving them with his fingertips like a shell-game operator.

Henry eased himself into the visitor's chair and wondered what the hell to do next. Now Rutledge

252

was fidgeting with the brass letter opener shaped like a chicken foot. Was the man planning to stab him with a letter opener, or did he have a gun in his pocket? Was Rutledge crazy or murderous? Or worse, was he both?

"God's plan for mankind is oil, Colonel," Rutledge said. He stood up and began to pace, combing his beard with his letter opener. Henry got up, too. Having Rutledge wandering around behind his back made him uncomfortable, especially after the man tossed the letter knife back onto the desk top. That argued the possibility of a gun.

Henry took stock of his host as a possible combatant. Rutledge was as tall as Henry but bony and much older. But possibly mad. Henry would have preferred a heftier, younger opponent of undoubted sanity. Maybe he wasn't as crazy as he sounded? . . . Henry narrowed his eyes at Rutledge and decided that that was wishful thinking. Something had sent Rutledge over the edge into a madness that he was incapable of seeing himself and therefore incapable of hiding. He was a bomb waiting to explode.

If I don't see this through, Henry thought, the next fellow who gets in his way is a goner. And it might be Peter.

But without some evidence of either lunacy or homicidal intent, there was nothing he could do. Wait, he told himself. Just wait. The way Rutledge was behaving, something would erupt soon.

Rutledge sat down again at his desk. "I'll tell

you about the importance of oil to the nation's economy, Colonel," he said. "And you can pass it along to your governor's friends." He looked at Henry as if to be sure he was attentive. "I'll begin with the causes of the current recession. . . ."

"Dad?" Peter, in his nightshirt, wandered into the kitchen. "Dad, I've made up my mind. I'm going out. That old devil's gone too far. His behavior last night was inexcusable, but forging my name on those checks was. . . ." He noticed the empty plate on the table. "Dad?" He went back upstairs and peeked into his father's room.

Well, that simplified things. If his father chose not to tell him where he was going, then Peter was under no obligation to tell his father.

Peter got dressed, hurrying, only a little guiltily, to be gone before his father came home again. He had lain awake till nearly dawn thinking it over and wakened still determined: He wasn't going to hide behind his father or wait for him to make up his mind any longer. Rutledge had stepped over the line, and Peter was going to have it out with him.

Peter was well aware that the checks had been the old man's insurance policy—forgeries with which he would have tried to prove that all the Sierra Oil directors were in on the burning of the refinery. Well, now that the checks were in Henry's hands, Rutledge couldn't get away with it. Peter yanked his socks up, then stepped into clean trousers and tugged them up to his waist. The thought of his name on that check maddened him.

As he stormed from the house, he rehearsed what he was going to say to Rutledge. He was going to say it loudly and clearly, and Rutledge, by God, was going to listen to him! He didn't bother to wait for a hack. He walked, the morning's crisp fall air fueling his anger. He approached the company headquarters and was prepared to push his way past any guardian clerks or other visitors.

An oil-field worker was turning in the front door ahead of him. Peter stopped just short of elbowing past the man. There was something familiar about his face, something that penetrated Peter's cloud of anger. Then a name came back to him: Nate Sawyer. He had been a crony of Sid Delaney's; Peter had seen him at Sid's funeral. What was he doing here?' Peter wondered. Roustabouts didn't have business at company headquarters; they got their pay and their work orders in the field. Besides, Nate seemed to know where he was going. Peter looked down the hall. The clerk in the front office was just disappearing into the washroom, and Nate didn't bother to wait for the fellow's return. Instead, he headed purposefully up the stairs.

What the hell? Caution slowed Peter's self-righteous steps toward the second floor. He let Nate get ahead of him and watched the man's footfalls grow stealthy. As Nate turned the corner at the last landing, his hand came out of his jacket pocket and encircled the blunt shape of a pistol.

Peter caught his breath. Was he going to shoot old Rutledge? He must be. Peter's face grew furious. Not before Peter had his chance, he wasn't!

"And of course we will provide the fuel that is the future of transportation. . . ." Rutledge, still lucid, had risen again from behind his desk and was pacing, hands clasped behind his back.

Henry listened helplessly. Rutledge had been lucid for the last half hour, lecturing interminably about the history and future uses of petroleum. Henry was beginning to wonder if he had been mistaken about the man. And might Henry himself go mad before Rutledge shut up? What was he planning?

"Ships, Colonel! Ships with oil-fired burners—" Rutledge's fingers twirled in enthusiasm before him and then suddenly flashed across his desk. His sentence unfinished, he seized the heavy onyx ruler and hurled himself at Henry, who sat half-hypnotized by boredom in the pool of light that flooded through the bay window.

Damn it! was all Henry had time to think. He leaped up and dodged the flying ruler, then grappled with Rutledge for it. The men staggered against the window seat.

Suddenly the office door was flung open with a bang, and a man loomed in the doorway. A gun showed clearly in his hand, the black muzzle pointed at the struggling men. Henry realized im-

256

mediately that it was the thug he had knocked out in the alley.

Henry jerked on the ruler, but Rutledge held on and pulled back. Henry felt astonished only momentarily as Peter flew through the door behind the stranger and flung himself on the man's back. As Peter fought for possession of the gun, his eyes met Henry's in equal astonishment. Then Peter and the gunman fell wrestling on the floor.

Henry had a gun in his own pocket. Now he quit trying to decide whether or not to use it. He let go of the ruler and ducked to reach for his weapon before Peter's opponent could free his own.

Rutledge's grip on the onyx ruler was his undoing. As Henry released it, Rutledge flew backward, pulled by his own momentum, and plunged in a hideous shower of breaking glass through the second-story window.

There was a single frozen moment, and then the sound of someone screaming from the sidewalk below sounded clearly in Rutledge's office. The gunman recovered from the surprise and threw Peter from him. As Peter crashed hard against the wall, the thug stumbled toward the door. He swung around in the doorway and looked at Henry. "You didn't ought to have been here," he said, gasping, and leveled the muzzle in deadly aim.

Peter, bent double in pain against the far wall, was staring, horrified, at the broken window. Then he turned and saw the gun. He pulled himself up and ran at the thug. Peter hit him low, like a football player, and the gun discharged with a blast that reverberated in the room.

"Peter!" With a howl Henry launched himself at the gunman, and the weapon, knocked loose from the impact, skittered into the hallway.

Henry, in a rage, pounded Nate's head on the floor until Peter, chalk white, pulled at his sleeve.

"I'm all right, Dad." He pointed at a hole in the ceiling, whence a fine drift of plaster rained down.

"I wasn't after you! Wasn't after you," Nate gabbled through a split lip.

"You should have been," Henry said grimly.

"Dad—" Peter looked at the window.

Footsteps pounded up the stairs, and a policeman appeared in the doorway. The front-office clerk peeked into the room from behind him and gaped at the window.

"Mr. Rutledge had an accident," Henry explained. He poked a finger at the gunman. "This fellow tried to shoot him."

"The amazing thing is, I think—what's his name? Nate Sawyer?—did try to shoot Rutledge," Henry said in a low voice to Peter. "I don't think he was after me at all." They were looking out the broken window, down at the still body on the sidewalk. "I think Nate got in too deep and couldn't see any way out."

A crowd was milling on the sidewalk, and another policeman worked to keep them back from Rutledge's body.

"What in the name of God just happened in here?" Peter whispered. He was shaking.

"I'm not quite sure," Henry admitted. He looked at his son. "I think you saved my life." Henry's face was taut, and there was a twitch by his eye.

"Are you all right, Dad?"

"I don't like crazy people," Henry muttered. His stock-in-trade was knowing what his adversary was going to do before he did it. His experience with Rutledge had demonstrated a gaping hole in that ability. For the first time, he had found something he didn't know how to fight—something that drifted like smoke through his fingers.

"Dad? You don't look good. Here, sit down."

"I'm all right," Henry grumbled. He felt awful but wasn't going to admit it.

Behind them, two detectives were interrogating Nate Sawyer. Peter listened with horror as Nate confessed everything. When the machinations were detailed in the newspapers, the reputation of Sierra Oil Corporation would, he knew, be ruined beyond repair. It was some comfort to Peter that he was exonerated—he hoped.

"Dad, what did you do with those checks?"

"Burned them," Henry murmured.

"Oh." That probably wasn't legal, but neither was breaking in to Rutledge's house. Peter decided not to argue. He sneaked a tentative look out the window again. "He's dead, isn't he?"

Henry peered down at the body and the unnatural position of the neck and head.

"I hope to hell he is." He took a deep breath and schooled his face into its usual unruffled expression. "It'll save deciding what to do with him." He caught sight of his son's face and set a hand on Peter's shoulder. "He wanted you dead, you know. I wasn't going to stand for that." He steeled himself to mention his other son. "He tried to have Frank killed, too."

Blood was pooling now on the sidewalk under Rutledge's head. Peter's stomach lurched, and he forced it to behave. As he watched, a policeman draped a blanket over the still form. There was a certain poetic justice in Rutledge's death, he supposed. Frank would have appreciated it. Something in Frank's temperament was far closer to the nature of their father's than Peter's was. But I'm the one who was here, Peter thought. I'm the one who jumped the man with the gun. He would feel good about that, he thought, after he quit remembering what Rutledge looked like on the sidewalk.

Father and son considered each other. "What are you going to do now?" they asked simultaneously.

"You'd better sell out," Henry said.

"You'd better go to Portland," Peter said.

They looked at each other gloomily. "He was so obsessed with the idea of a takeover by Rockefeller that he made it inevitable," Peter said, and shaking his head, he turned away from the window.

"Why should I go to Portland?" Henry asked.

"Make your peace with Mother," Peter told him. He managed a shaky smile. "Take her Rutledge's head on a plate."

"She won't care," Henry said. "I didn't get her Frank back."

"Go anyway," Peter urged. "Try." For a fleeting moment he felt older than his father, and desperately sorry for him.

XII

Washington, D.C., October 1897

"Cindy says that Henry is coming to Portland." Alexandra looked up from the folded, butter-colored stationery and at Toby, across the breakfast table. It was one of those fall mornings when everything outside was gaudily dying, racing toward destruction in a flurry of red and topaz leaves. The light from the breakfast-room windows glowed on Toby's graying, sandy hair as he read the newspaper. Alexandra handed the letter across the table. "Do you think they'll patch it up?"

Toby appeared not to notice the envelope. He reached for his coffee cup, eyes on the newspaper. "Maybe."

Alexandra looked exasperated. "Don't you care?"

"Not a lot." Toby folded the newspaper, creased it carefully, and continued his reading.

"Cindy will do what she has to. Henry brought this on himself."

"I know, but—" Alexandra, troubled, pleated the tablecloth into thin folds between her fingers. "It just seems as if everything is falling apart. Your turning down that post in Theodore's department—"

"Theodore and I don't see eye to eye," Toby said brusquely.

"On what?"

"On practically anything. Particularly, at the moment, Cuba. He's frothing to fight Spaniards with his bare hands. Says it would be 'bully.' " Toby snorted. "I have no patience with him. We'd be at each other's throat in a fortnight. It was kind of him to offer the position for friendship's sake, but I knew better than to accept it."

"Oh." Alexandra looked out the window. Toby still spent his days at the Capitol or in the political clubs or the informal committees that met over steak and cocktails in Washington restaurants. He was still nearly as influential as he had been during his tenure in the State Department. But would that fade? she wondered. Would he be miserable when he had no more power to wield? He was gone from the house so much, she didn't feel she knew his thoughts well enough to predict. Nothing seemed the way it had been when they had first moved here.

"I've been offered another job," Toby said, cutting across her thoughts.

"What is it? Will you take it?" Alexandra wondered how long he had known about it. Probably long enough to make up his mind before he told her, she thought.

"It's with the Foundation for International Relations. They're a private foundation, philanthropically supported. The major goal is long-term understanding and mutual benefit among nations. Their immediate agenda is to prevent an idiotic war with Spain."

"That's a very unpopular opinion," Alexandra said.

"True. It also happens to be my opinion."

"Of course," Alexandra murmured. "I didn't say you shouldn't take it." It wouldn't have done any good anyway—nothing had ever deterred Toby from what he perceived to be his duty. She thought about how things had been with his other wives, before she had met him. Toby had ranged across the country, doing government work and leaving the wife at home. When Tim was a child, he rarely saw his father. That incessant traveling had nearly stopped after he married Alex. But now he seemed to be reverting to the old ways.

"I'm glad," Toby said. "Since I've accepted the job."

He flashed a smile as he laid the newspaper down. "I begin today. The foundation has a lot of organizing to do if it's to be effective." He glanced across the table at her. "What are your plans for the day, dear?"

"I don't really know." Alexandra looked down. She had always been so busy in Portland, with her horses and the ranch. Now . . . "Sally has dancing class after school, but Juanita will take her. I guess I'm just feeling a little low today. Did I tell you Mr. Nakamura has been recalled?"

"I'd heard that." He didn't sound particularly interested. Mr. Nakamura, the ambassador from Japan for a number of years, was more Alexandra's friend than Toby's. They had had an odd, unconventional acquaintance and took tea together once a week, to the amusement of Washington society. He taught her flower arranging. "I'm sure you'll find another interest. There's always been plenty for you to do here."

"Oh, yes." Alexandra lifted her face for his good-bye kiss, then stared listlessly out the window until after his carriage rolled down the drive. What on earth was the matter with her? she wondered. She couldn't quite put her finger on it, but everything seemed flat. She took a bite of her toast, found that it had turned cold, and stared again at the leaves settling into stillness beyond the window.

When the Holts had first come to Washington, the capital city had seemed to Alexandra to glow, to hum with energy. She had thrown herself into life there, planned parties, been a political hostess, and known with satisfaction that she was considered one of Senator Holt's greatest assets. But slowly it had all grown stale. There was nothing for women to do in Washington except plan parties and charity balls with other wives. Most of them were content to compare clothes and bask in their husbands' success. But to Alexandra, being an asset made her feel like a bank account or a favor owed someone, not like any sort of real person. In Portland she had been occupied with her horses, show animals that she raised and trained herself. There was no room for them in Washington, and no time left in her social schedule of events, which she didn't really enjoy. At these gatherings, her primary function was to be an asset.

Her mood had worsened since Tim's wedding, after which Cindy Holt had moved away. Cindy had been a real friend. Of course since Frank had gone, Cindy had lost interest in almost everything. She was in Portland, and her art gallery was run by a manager. Alexandra missed the afternoon visits with her sister-in-law. Their conversation was stimulating, never limited to gossip and clothes. And now Mr. Nakamura was leaving, so there would be no more tea ceremonies and lessons in Japanese, no more exploration of his hidden and mysterious world.

The telephone rang in the hall, and Alexandra let Juanita answer it. Juanita was her personal maid, who doubled as a duenna for Sally; but she really ran the household, coordinating and overseeing the efforts of the housekeeper, the upstairs and downstairs maids, the cook, the gardener, and the stable boy. Alexandra ran nothing, so far as she could tell. She gave the orders; but even when she issued none, everything still went on.

In fact, at this point Alexandra wasn't sure that

anything she did was essential. Sally had her own friends, parties, outings, and dancing lessons to occupy her. At first Alexandra had escorted her to these but had found herself the only mother there. The other girls were accompanied by their maids and governesses. Convention decreed that the employees did not engage in conversation with Alexandra, and so she had stopped going and sent Juanita instead.

Juanita came into the kitchen and waited for Alexandra to look up. "It is Mrs. Hoffman, Mrs. Holt." Even Juanita had become a Washington servant and called her Mrs. Holt instead of doña, as she had when she first started working for Alexandra.

"Thank you." Alexandra took her coffee to the telephone table and put the receiver to her ear.

"Well, thank goodness!" Lucinda Hoffman's voice chirruped at her through the receiver. "You wouldn't believe the trouble I've had just trying to make up two tables of bridge for this afternoon. Now, Alex, you mustn't let me down. . . ."

It was something to do, of course, and better than feeling sorry for herself.

Alex was pinning on her hat when Sally came home from classes—at an exclusive and expensive girls' school attended by politicians' daughters and a smattering of ambassadors' children.

Sally jettisoned her schoolbooks with a disdainful thump. "I don't see why I need to know what Charlemagne did," she complained. Her eyes lit on Alexandra's hat, a new one of velvet and taffeta with a stiff lace aigrette. "Oh, that's a smashing hat, Mama. Can I have one like it?"

"Certainly not," Alexandra said. She looked at Sally's school dress and felt uncomfortable. It was also too old for her, although not so outrageously as the hat would be. She found it impossible to persuade Sally to agree to any frock suggested by the dressmaker as suitable for a fourteen-year-old.

Sally pouted—the face of a Botticelli maiden, sulky and beautiful. Alexandra caught sight of her own face in the mirror above Sally's rose-gold curls and plaid tam. There were lines that hadn't been there before, and gray in the auburn tendrils beneath the new hat. Even in the dashing hat, which had looked so wonderful at the milliner's shop, Alexandra thought she looked dispirited. Not so much old, perhaps, as listless. Maybe she needed some kind of tonic.

"Where's Juanita?" Sally asked. "Isn't she ready? I have dancing class in half an hour."

"She'll be here in a minute, dear." Sally, Alexandra knew, considered the latest dance steps, unlike the deeds of Charlemagne, to be essential knowledge.

"Well, she ought to hurry," Sally said. "Where are you going, Mama?"

"To play bridge with Mrs. Hoffman," Alexandra answered. "I suppose." It didn't seem worth the trouble somehow.

"Milly Hoffman's teaching me to play bridge," Sally said. "At lunch every day."

"Miss Sally." Juanita sailed in from the breakfast room, her stout figure encased in a blue serge suit with a high starched collar—the attire of a proper Washington nursemaid. "Are you ready? It is time we go."

"I've been ready," Sally said. "Where are my dancing slippers?"

"You should have them," Juanita said.

"Well, I don't. Get them for me."

"You go," Juanita said firmly. "They are your shoes." She folded her arms and waited.

Alexandra picked up her pocketbook. Her carriage was waiting in the drive. Juanita would manage Sally; she always did. Alexandra didn't even seem to be able to do that anymore. Maybe she should see a doctor. It was awful to be so tired all the time. But how could anyone feel lively when there wasn't anything to do but play bridge?

"We're delighted to have you on board, Mr. Holt." Lynford Sorel shook Toby's hand, and the other members of the foundation nodded in agreement. "We're in a minority here, but we intend to be a very vocal minority."

Toby sighed. "In my younger days I can't say I would have given five minutes' thought to the notion of pacifism. I was hot to fight in the first war that came along."

"That was the War Between the States, was it not?" Sorel smiled sympathetically. "That experience would temper any man's opinion."

"It tempered mine," Toby said.

"It was an unavoidable conflict," Aaron Leverage said. "That one had to be fought." For a moment he bowed a dark, graying head to some recollection. "I fought in it myself."

"I was too young for it," Sorel murmured. "But it took my father and my two older brothers. One of them is still alive. But he has no legs."

"I'm still certain that it had to be fought," Toby said. "It was fight or die as a nation. I come from a family of fighters—warrior statesmen, if you will. I am not certain that even now my father isn't spinning in his grave about my being here."

"Consorting with pacifists?" Leverage chuckled. "We aren't that; you may assure him in your prayers. If Spain were to invade the United States, actually threaten us directly, you would blink to see how fast I'd have a rifle in my hand. What we question is sending our young men for cannon fodder over an issue that is not ours, one that may yet be settled by diplomacy if the hotheads can be made to back off."

"Of course you realize that we'll be perceived as pacifists," Sorel said dryly. "As limp-wristed fellows with lilies, who want to turn the other cheek and let the Spaniards shoot it off."

"Hearst himself has said so," Toby remarked sardonically. "Lord, how I dislike that man! Our task is to convince the public, which is howling for a nice, patriotic war and a little flag-waving to take their minds off the recession, that they are being diddled by Hearst. He doesn't give a damn about the poor Cuban insurrecto, writhing under the Spanish heel, any more than he does about the jobless Americans in his own backyard. He wants to sell newspapers and be a hero—someone else to tote the guns, of course."

"Bravo, Mr. Holt!" Sorel said. "An oratorical gift to match your convictions. That's why we hired you. That and a name that no one can question for courage. When preaching peace, it helps to be a man who has already taken his lumps in a war." He cast a sly look of amusement at Crampton Cullen, the fourth man at the table. "On whatever side."

Cullen had fought in the last war, too, for the Confederacy. The Southerners might have lost and been foolish to get into the war in the first place, but no one could question their courage. Toby and Cullen were to be a team in their lobbying and speech making. Toby was glad to have Cullen and relieved that, so far as they knew, neither of them had ever shot the other one's relatives.

The war they were trying to stop now had been brewing for over two years, but it was not, in Toby's opinion, America's war. Mere geographical proximity did not, he maintained, give the United States the right to run neighboring countries' internal affairs for them, not even under the guise of protecting American citizens— and particularly when those American citizens had played an active part in starting the fight. He knew what meddlesome American sugar planters had done in Hawaii under the name of reforming the government. They had, in his opinion, re-formed most of it right into their own wallets, to the detriment of the native population. And they had given the United States a bad name in the process.

When Cuban insurgents had revolted against Spanish rule in early 1895, they had been liberally supplied with money by American sugar planters on that island. Toby doubted that the planters had any real sympathy for the Cubans, to whom they had paid slave wages and were now paying a form of protection money—to avoid having their fields burned. Toby considered the sugar planters to have much the same motive as their counterparts in Hawaii: eventual American domination of the government. Neither group employed tactics he was willing to support, any more than he could give his sympathies to Spain. That country, want-ing to quell the revolution quickly, sent in General Weyler, who lost no time in acquiring the nick-name of "Butcher."

Weyler rounded up Cuban civilians and sent them to concentration camps while Spanish sol-diers pursued the guerrillas. Camp conditions were appalling, and as the Cuban captives there began to die, American sympathies, nearly always on the side of the underdog, began to demand that America step in. But step in and do what? No one knew exactly—just step in and support the insurrectos, the "freedom fighters." No one had a plan for what to do afterward. Hearst and Pulitzer certainly didn't seem to feel that they needed one. Then president Cleveland appealed to American citizens to stay out of the mess and refrain from sending aid to the insurrectos. But Hearst and Pulitzer had waved the flag so broadly that anyone who spoke for moderation and diplomacy ran the risk of being branded a moral coward, and an un-American one to boot. Hadn't we fought our own revolution? Didn't that mean we should support the Cubans'? Yes and yes! said Hearst and Pulitzer triumphantly.

In 1896 Congress favored granting belligerent status to the revolutionaries and, as a sop to diplomacy, offered its services as arbiter to Spain to arbitrate independence for Cuba. Understandably, Spain rejected the offer, and Congress appropriated $50,000 in relief for U.S. citizens in Cuba. By 1897 the sensational press was having a field day reporting atrocities that were never committed and engagements that were never fought. The newspaper descriptions were far above and beyond the inevitable horrors of war that were actually occurring on both sides.

Secretary of State John Sherman complained to Spain of General Weyler's brutality and a week later signed a treaty of annexation with the Hawaiian government. Congress had yet to ratify it, but it probably would. So America, looking forward to Hawaii's becoming an official American territory, was expanding its influence and its geographical holdings. It was also ready to take charge of the world and tell it how to manage itself. Never mind, Toby thought grumpily, that it couldn't manage its own domestic affairs well enough to prevent bloody labor wars and a shifting population of homeless men, drifting by the thousands in search of work that didn't exist. Everyone always knew how to manage someone else's business.

Now, just this month, Spain had inaugurated a moderate premier, Sagasta, in Madrid. Rumor had it that he intended to recall General Weyler and put an end to the concentration camps, possibly even to offer home rule to Cuba. An honorable settlement was still possible, Toby thought optimistically. Tim, still on the Continent with Elizabeth on their honeymoon, had cabled an editorial to the Clarion offices in San Francisco. His stance favored an honorable settlement with Spain, which put him in the thick of the mess and at odds with Hearst, Pulitzer, and most of the West Coast newspapers as well. Tim had written to Toby to report irately that Pulitzer, abandoning even common-sense pacifism, was rumored to have remarked that he rather liked the idea of a war—not a big one—but one that would arouse interest and give him a chance to gauge the reflex in circulation figures.

"Pulitzer is an opportunistic scoundrel," Tim had signed off furiously, "and a disgrace to journalism. Confusion to the enemy, and best wishes from Paris. Going soon to Vienna. Keep 'em flying, Dad."

Toby intended to do whatever possible to stave off the war. Even his friend Theodore Roosevelt

was becoming the worst of the warmongers, bur-
bling constantly about what a great thing it would
be "for us to take action on behalf of the Cubans.
And a splendid thing for the navy, too."

That depended on your definition of splendid.
The Foundation for International Relations had
another definition entirely, and with Cullen's
help, Toby was planning to present it to the public
in a speech in two days' time. He supposed he
would get tomatoes thrown at him, figurative if
not literal, but eventually he and those who shared
his views would make some headway—if Congress could temporarily be restrained from passing out the rifles.

Toby wondered with a certain amusement if he
was becoming a radical in his old age. He had always considered himself something of a conser-
vative, at least in comparison to his older children;
but looking back on his life, he thought now that
maybe he had been a radical after all, just under
the skin. Certainly he had annoyed all his con-
servative constituency half to death while he had
been in the Senate, a fact that had everything to
do with why he hadn't been reelected. There had
always been a streak of the troublemaker in the
Holts. The older he got, the more inclined Toby
felt toward taking that reputation for his own. His
father had called it living by his conscience, but
a lot of other people had called it less flattering
things, even when Whip was solving their problems for them.

The introductory meeting at the foundation

didn't last long. These men were inclined toward getting things done with a minimum of discussion. Sorel, Leverage, and Cullen faded away toward their own offices in the stone house that sprawled on the edge of the university in Georgetown. Toby collected his files and walked down the hall to his own. He settled at his desk with a sense of purpose. An honorable settlement was possible, and surely it could be achieved, now that Sagasta had been installed in Madrid. Toby opened his files and adjusted his spectacles. It felt good, very good, to have real work to do again.

XIII

"I'm sure Alex can think of a wonderful idea for the decorations. She's always so clever. Artistic talent seems to run in the Holt family." Lucinda Hoffman beamed at Alexandra while the other ladies sipped their tea.

"Mrs. Blake is my sister-in-law," Alexandra said, feeling stubborn. "I'm not a blood relation."

"Yes, but you're soooo good with flowers," the other ladies chorused.

Alexandra, rubbing her temples, wondered if the women were as bored as she was with planning this charity event and would do anything to get out of watching florists stick flowers in vases for it. Whatever she designed, Alexandra knew that the florists would pay no attention and do whatever they had planned anyway—probably while snickering behind her back about the "artistic" pretensions of political hostesses.

The party was a subscription ball to raise money for the Children's Fresh Air Fund—or maybe it was the Red Cross. For a moment, Alexandra found that she couldn't remember. Or maybe she just didn't care. No matter how worthy the cause, the affair was always dull and indistinguishable from all others.

"An Oriental theme," Lucinda Hoffman added. "Right up your alley, Alex."

"I know!" Rosanna Lucas chirped. "Let's make it a costume ball—the court of the mikado. We can wear wonderful clothes and make all the men wear kimonos." She giggled. "Can't you just picture Herbert in a kimono!"

The other women tittered, too. Herbert Lucas was nearly spherical. In a kimono he would look like a Christmas tree ornament with a bow around its middle. The ladies were not particularly clear on the differences between masculine and feminine costume in Japan. But they knew that all their husbands would look, and feel, ridiculous playing dress up. Alexandra wondered if they were taking vengeance for being forced to lead silly lives.

"Oh, yes, let's," Lucinda Hoffman said, a gleam in her eyes. "I don't believe it's ever been done, and anything Oriental is terribly fashionable just now. Alex, what a pity your Mr. Nakamura has been recalled."

"Yes," Alexandra murmured. She didn't mention that she wouldn't dream of asking Mr.

Nakamura to help produce a Gilbert and Sullivan parody of his country. Lucinda and Rosanna weren't interested in authenticity anyway, just in the chance to wear something exotic and expensive that would never be worn again. She thought of suggesting that they just all give their clothing allowance to the Fresh Air Fund or the Red Cross, or whatever, and skip the party. Instead, she poured herself another cup of tea. Such magnanimity would be unheard of, and certainly wouldn't be reported in the society pages of the Washington Post. Newspaper coverage of their extravagances inspired them to try to outdo every other charitable committee.

"Oh, famous!" Rosanna said. "I have a length of the most wonderful brocade that Herbert brought me from China. I've been dying to do something with it, and I haven't quite had the nerve to have a gown made up out of it."

"Oh!" May Prilliman bounced excitedly in her chair. "I know a fabulous little upholsterer who does wonderful things with Chinese silks. The rest of us could get our yard goods from him."

"Oh, we could!" They looked as if the idea of buying their dress material from an upholsterer, of all people, was quite bohemian and wicked.

"Of course, Alex surely has something on hand, too," May said with a sly grin.

They all laughed gently and looked knowing. Alexandra's friendship with Mr. Nakamura was, to them, a little scandalous.

"Alex, you haven't said anything," Lucinda

Hoffman remarked. "Don't you think it's a famous idea?"

"Oh, certainly," Alexandra said. "I'm sorry, Lucinda, I'm afraid I just can't keep my mind on it." She rubbed her temples again. Lucinda's parlor was hot and stuffy. The fashionable accessories of wax flowers, china shepherdesses, ivory pagodas, seashell vases, fringed Spanish shawls, and all the other clutter that two full-time maids kept dusted seemed to fill the room to the ceiling. She felt as if it were all closing in on her. "I don't know what's the matter with me lately. I feel so tired all the time, but I haven't been doing anything."

The others nodded sympathetically. "I feel like that sometimes," Rosanna agreed.

"She needs a little pick-me-up." May winked at Lucinda.

"I've been wondering if I ought to see a doctor," Alexandra confessed.

"I've found the most wonderful tonic." Lucinda winked back at May. "You try it, dear, and see if you don't feel better. We'll all have some."

"Oh, yes, let's."

"All right," Alexandra agreed.

The other ladies scooted their chairs closer to the tea table while Lucinda unlocked a drawer in her curio cabinet and took out a little cloisonné box with a hinged lid. Alexandra watched with passive curiosity as Lucinda opened it and set it on the table. It was filled with something that looked like bath salts.

"My special powders," Lucinda explained. "They make me feel like a new woman."

"What is it?"

"Peruvian coca. But you don't have to drink it—not like that disgusting wine the druggists sell. I can't abide the taste of that."

"You just inhale a pinch," Rosanna said. She seemed to be familiar with it. "Like Sherlock Holmes." There were assorted nods and murmurs from the other women.

"Well, he uses a needle," said May, who was a devotee of Doyle. "But we don't do anything so horrid."

"Oh, cocaine." Alexandra had heard of it. Innumerable patent medicines, easily obtained, perfectly legal, contained coca leaf. Using the pure drug seemed harmless. The other ladies were taking small pinches of the powder and holding them delicately to their nostrils. Maybe it would do her some good.

She put a pinch from the cloisonné box on the back of her hand and inhaled it, the way May showed her.

It was amazing how it lifted her mood. Before she had finished her cup of tea, she couldn't understand how she could have been so depressed. She felt a little odd but wonderfully energetic. In mere minutes Alexandra felt that she had gained a whole new outlook. She felt confident, happy, ready to tackle anything. She felt the way she used to feel, back in Portland, when the children were small.

"Isn't that delicious?" Lucinda asked happily. "I can't tell you what it does for me. Sometimes I just don't think I'd get through the day without my special powders."

Alexandra smiled, bemused. "Yes, I believe you're right."

"And it's perfectly safe," Lucinda assured her. "I buy it from the nicest doctor. He personally makes each packet up for me. He's not my regular physician; he's a nerve specialist. I'll give you his address if you like."

"Maybe I should consult him," Alex replied. She had been considering medical attention. Lucinda's interior design looked bright to her now, elegant and interesting. Alexandra began to realize what fun working with Lucinda on this party would be—already she was beginning to get clever ideas for the decorations. "It's just amazing," she mused. "I must just have been needing a tonic. I never thought it could make such a difference."

"I know people who swear by it," May told her. "A preacher who is a particular friend of mine— he's simply riveting in the pulpit—told me that it never fails him when he's feeling dragged out. It's such a burden to work for the parish all week and then try to be brilliant on Sunday morning. I asked him how he did it, and he told me he often relies on coca to pick him up."

"He recommended my doctor," Lucinda said. "And you know it can't be wrong if a preacher feels it's beneficial."

"Certainly not," May said. "It makes you feel so energetic, it must be good for you."

"And there's not a drop of alcohol in it," Rosanna said triumphantly. "Not like those tonics that—well, you know."

Many patent cures were heavily laced with alcohol. Nice ladies didn't drink—certainly not in secret. The ladies who took these cures chose not to discuss them—but if they did talk about the tonics, it was with disapproval. Coca was happily free of alcohol, and that made its use quite respectable. Uneasy, Alexandra remembered other stories she had read about cocaine. They didn't seem congruent with the lift she was enjoying. "I've read," she said hesitantly, "that a great many people have become addicted to—"

"Oh, pooh," Lucinda said. "This isn't the slums. We aren't dope fiends, for goodness sake!" She gave a silvery laugh, and the other ladies laughed, too.

"We don't inject it!" Rosanna said, horrified.

"This is quite different," Lucinda assured her.

"If doctors and preachers are recommending it, I for one don't propose to be concerned," May said. "It's a harmless diversion, and Lord knows we need something to get us through the social season."

"We certainly do!" Alexandra smiled, happy to be convinced. Nothing in Lucinda's pretty house could connect the goings-on with the desperation of poor women driven to take drugs such as laudanum or to overuse even beneficial ones like co-

281

caine. Of course it was beneficial. She felt better than she had in years. She rubbed her palms together, eager to conquer the task at hand. "Let's get this train back on the track! We have a party to plan! We can't let the Fresh Air Fund down."

Of course it was the Fresh Air Fund! How could she have forgotten?

When Alexandra left Lucinda's house, she still felt energetic, ready to take on anything. By the time the carriage reached home, however, the mood had faded.

What happened? she wondered, dismayed. Somehow it had just slipped through her fingers. She tried to catch it back, to be gay and happy and energetic. Surely she could do it. She tried singing: "A wand'ring minstrel I, a thing of shred and patches, of ballads, songs and snatches. . . ." She waltzed dreamily across the front hall; but the mood didn't come back.

The housekeeper caught her dancing and stood expressionless until Alexandra tottered to a stop. "Mrs. Holt, Mr. Holt called. He's going to be late at the office, said he'd eat downtown."

On his first day? "Thank you. Then I guess it will just be Sally and me. We'll have something light, please." Alexandra, waving the housekeeper away, felt cold and unaccountably ready to cry. She felt as if her body was fighting against some ailment, but she knew it wasn't that.

The cook came in, wiping hands on a voluminous starched apron, tied over a gingham everyday dress. "Miz Jenkins say you want something light for supper." Her tone was mildly accusatory. Cook and housekeeper vied constantly for position in the household pecking order and addressed each other formally.

"Why, uh, yes," Alexandra confessed. "If you could manage." She knew she stood convicted of giving dinner orders through the wrong channel.

Cook was half-mollified. "Well, I got a nice bit of tongue I could slice."

"Anything," Alexandra said vaguely. She hated tongue. "Anything."

Three days later, Alexandra sat and stared down at sliced tongue again, while Sally made the face she saved for dishes she didn't like. Alexandra made a mental note to tell the cook to stop buying the stuff. Nobody liked it.

And where was Toby? He was supposed to be home that night. He had made a speech the night before, with Crampton Cullen. It hadn't been well received, but it had gotten into all the newspapers. Sometimes Alexandra thought that if it weren't for the newspapers she wouldn't know what was going on with her husband. Toby was too consumed with his job and the rapidly changing political situation to talk about anything that was already over. Whenever she asked him anything, he looked either preoccupied or annoyed.

"This is horrid," said Sally now, stabbing the meat with her fork. "Who wants to eat something's tongue?"

"You like livers," Alexandra pointed out.

"I can't see livers." Sally stuck her own tongue out and, cross-eyed, looked down at it. "You have to tell her what to fix. If you don't tell her something specific, she always fixes tongue."

"I expect she's trying to train me," Alexandra said absently. "Well, at least your father won't mind having missed dinner."

"Is he making another speech?" Sally moaned.

"I don't think so, dear. Not tonight. Why?"

"I was just the laughingstock of the entire school, that's all," Sally said.

"You mean that some of the students disagreed with your father's opinions," Alexandra said. She was used to translating Sally, who had a flair for the dramatic.

"Senator Lorton said he ought to be horsewhipped," Sally said. "Priscilla Lorton told me so at lunch, and everyone heard her."

"And what did you do?" her mother inquired.

"I told Priscilla I'd pull her ears off if she said anything bad about Dad. Everybody in Washington says he's a coward!"

They heard the front door open and close, then the sound of footsteps.

"Be quiet!" Alexandra said. "I won't have you saying things like that in front of your father."

"I'm not saying them," Sally said rebelliously. "All the girls at school are saying them. How would you like it if people were going around calling your father a Spanish sympathizer?"

"A what?" Toby came in and sat down heavily

at the table. "Tongue? Good Lord, Alex, you know I hate—"

"I know. I'll tell her not to buy it anymore." Alexandra waved a hand wearily at the offending dish.

Toby bent his gaze on his daughter. "Sally, would you care to repeat what you were saying?"

"I wasn't saying it," Sally said. "Everybody at school was saying it. I don't see why you can't support the insurrectos like everybody else."

"First of all, I don't not support the insurrectos," Toby explained. "I don't support either side."

"Well, what does that mean?"

"That I support peaceful means to a resolution."

"So you don't want to fight, right?" Sally said.

"Correct."

"Well, everyone at school thinks that's cowardly."

"Everyone?" Toby looked at her closely, over the top of his spectacles.

"Well, everyone I care about. Priscilla Lorton, Mary Margaret Ethridge, Milly Hoffman . . ."

"Lucinda Hoffman is a friend of mine," Alexandra said. "If she doesn't take exception to your father's politics, Milly has no business doing so."

"That's just grown-ups," Sally said scornfully. "They can go around being friends with people even if they don't agree with them."

"That is a trait we had hoped you might eventually acquire," Toby said.

"Well, it's not fair!" Sally said. "All my special friends—"

"You mean the most popular girls," Toby interjected.

Sally ignored him. "They all think we ought to go over there and show those Spanish—"

"You mean their fathers think so," Toby said. "Let me explain something to you. It is not their fathers, or me, either, who would be over there showing the Spanish whatever we might show—them. It is the young men—boys Michael's age."

"Michael couldn't go. He has a bad heart." Sally sounded as if she felt her brother would be missing something grand.

"Tim would almost inevitably go as a correspondent. The chances of any individual's coming home alive and unhurt would not be good. War is not a lot of patriotic flag-waving at someone else's expense, while that someone else does the fighting. War is a last resort, to be avoided whenever possible. We are nowhere near exhausting the opportunities for peace. You tell that to your 'special friends.' "

Sally sniffed and prodded the tongue with her fork again.

"And don't eat that if you don't like it. Go ask Cook to give you an apple." Toby put his own fork down. He stood up and kissed Alexandra on the cheek. "I'm afraid I have work to do tonight—so I might further embarrass Sally." He grinned at his daughter and chucked her under the chin, a gesture for which she considered herself far too old. "I'll be in my study if you need me, dear," he said cheerfully.

Soon Alexandra found herself alone at the table and staring at the plate of tongue. She supposed she might as well go to bed. There didn't seem to be anything else to do. She would like to talk to Toby, she thought, but she would never be able to stay awake until he came to bed.

In the morning Alexandra dragged herself from under the covers and looked at the business card that Lucinda Hoffman had given her. Sally had already left for school and Toby for his new office. Alexandra sat down at the upstairs telephone, lifted the receiver, and gave the operator the number off the card.

"I would like to see Dr. Nagel, please. For a consultation."

"Well, my dear, you are simply run down." Dr. Nagel had a kindly smile and a sleek goatee. His eyes shone with sympathetic interest. He patted Alexandra's hand after examining her in his consulting room. She hadn't asked him to come to the house, although she was not sure why. For reasons she couldn't put her finger on, she did not want to tell Toby—she didn't want to worry him.

"I really do feel dreadfully dragged out. Lucinda Hoffman told me how much good you did her," Alexandra said hopefully.

"Ah, yes." Dr. Nagel smiled, and his eyes twinkled at her. "A charming lady. Did you try the remedy I gave her?"

"Well, yes," Alexandra admitted. "I know one isn't supposed to take other people's medicine, but she said it was harmless."

"Oh, definitely. Cocaine is a derivative of the coca plant, quite natural. It's a true wonder drug when used properly, beneficial for a number of ailments as well as a superlative tonic and nerve restorer. I rely on it myself."

"It did make me feel better." Alexandra couldn't quite bring herself to ask for the same prescription. It was a drug, of course, and for its use to be all right a doctor had to make the decision. But of course it wasn't a drug—not that kind of drug—or she wouldn't consider using it.

"Well, now, I think it would do you a great deal of good," Dr. Nagel said. "I'll have some made up and sent around to you, and we'll see how you do with it. When a lady is as debilitated as you appear to be, it is essential to restore bodily strength as well as the nerve tone. Cocaine is an excellent remedy. I have known patients who, when taking this prescription, accomplished double the amount of work of which they were previously capable and with no fatigue afterward. I'm certain that you'll be your old self again in no time."

"That's exactly what I want," Alexandra said, encouraged. "I just want to be my old self."

Dr. Nagel smiled, avuncular and jolly. "I can practically guarantee it."

It seemed to take forever for the packet he had promised her to be delivered. Alexandra answered the door herself, and after she had tipped the messenger boy, she took the parcel up to her bedroom. She unwrapped the brown paper and looked with hope at the tin of white powder. Would it work the same magic? All I want is to feel like myself. She sat down at her dressing table and set the tin among the perfume bottles. She took a pinch and inhaled, then leaned back in her chair and waited.

In a few minutes the same feeling of being on top of the world overcame her. Oh, life was so much better with this tonic. She was careful to think of it as tonic. Cocaine sounded so . . . well, so like a drug. She had heard that it was used to wean people from morphine addiction. But in the powdered form it surely was different.

Goodness, she thought, there was so much to do! Alexandra got out her "party" book, the blank volume in which she recorded the plans and menus for all her entertaining, with careful notes regarding what people had liked and what they hadn't, the competence of caterers and florists, diagrams of all the decorations and seating arrangements, and ideas for the next event. When she had first begun to give parties in Washington, the process had been fascinating, right to the last-minute detail. Her parties had always been well attended, then lavishly written up in the newspaper society pages. Now she was a "noted" hostess —that was what the columnists called her.

Alexandra turned to a blank page and wrote carefully: The Court of the Mikado. The concept might be frivolous, but they were raising money for a good cause. And she did know a lot about Japan. She began to scribble ideas. The florists would have to be carefully watched so that they did not overstuff the vases in European fashion. Alexandra felt capable of handling the most recalcitrant florist now; she would simply be firm. It was going to be splendid!

She tucked the book under her arm. Feeling excited, she got out her sketch pad and took it to the dining room table, where there was room to spread out. She was just sitting down when she remembered that she had left the tin of powder on her dressing table. It wouldn't do to leave it sitting out, although she was reluctant to consider just why. She ran back upstairs, looked around for someplace to keep it, and unlocked the drawer of her dressing table where she kept her good jewelry. Unlike many fashionable wives, Alexandra still shared a bedroom with her husband; but Toby never went in her jewelry drawer, so he would not come upon it there. She wouldn't want Toby to worry about her health and drag her off to some other doctor besides Dr. Nagel—Dr. Amos, for example, who was such a stuffed shirt. Dr. Nagel knew just what she needed.

She tucked the tin at the back, behind the padded velvet box that held her sapphire necklace and the emerald choker Toby had given her for their twentieth anniversary.

Alexandra trotted back downstairs, singing a little song to herself, then opened her sketch pad. She was still working hard, diagramming a giant painted fan to use as a backdrop for the musicians, when Toby came home unexpectedly, in time for tea.

"Look!" she said gaily. "See what you think of this. One can't dance to Japanese music, of course, but I thought we might have a flute player for the intervals."

"Flute player?" Toby peered over her shoulder.

"Yes, of course. I swear I am going to squelch Lucinda's silliness and make this event as authentic as I can."

"What event? Alex, what are we doing that I don't know about?"

"Not us, silly. The Fresh Air Fund Ball! Didn't I tell you about it? Well, I'm designing it, and it's going to be such fun. And look!" She pulled out another sheet of paper. "Here are my designs for our costumes. What do you think? It's a samurai warrior. I got it out of a book that Mr. Nakamura gave me."

"I think if you want me to wear that, you'll have to get me drunk first," Toby said, regarding a lop-sided sketch of a costumed figure.

"Oh, pooh, you know I can't draw," Alexandra said. "It will be splendid when it's made up. And quite dashing." She gave him a sly smile. "And it will suit you perfectly. You have a much better body than all those old political potbellies. You'll look very fierce and dashing, and I'll be the envy of every woman there." She turned in her chair and reached an arm around his waist. "You are a handsome devil."

"I'm glad to see you so cheerful." He bent down and kissed her with growing interest as she snuggled up next to him.

"I don't suppose you're going to be home tonight?" she whispered.

"I'm sorry, darling. I have to go out again, and I'll be in late."

"Oh. Oh, well." Alexandra returned cheerily to her sketch pad.

Toby had been going to suggest that she wait up for him, but she was already drawing again, humming to herself. "Where's Sally?" he asked.

"At her piano lesson." Alexandra uncapped a bottle of colored ink and began drawing flowers on the fan. "As soon as I finish this, I'm going to run out and look at fabrics."

"But it's nearly five o'clock."

"Already? Oh, dear. Well, I suppose I'll have to wait until tomorrow. I know! I can work on the menu. I want to try things out in the kitchen and see if I can come up with something Japanese that Americans will actually eat."

"Little raw squids on crackers?" Toby suggested.

Alexandra laughed. "No, no squid," she said cheerfully.

Alex was busily drawing, so Toby left her to it. Because she didn't seem interested in tea, he went into the parlor and ate sandwiches and cake by himself. Tea seemed to him a silly meal, but it was de rigueur in Washington, and he probably wasn't going to get dinner if he stayed late at the office. He was eager to get back to work; Crampton Cullen had arranged a meeting with a deputy from the State Department.

A fleeting feeling of guilt that he ought to be home more was easily shed. Alexandra was deep in plans for yet another party. Maybe that was all she had needed to cheer her up. She had seemed to Toby to be listless lately, but obviously he was mistaken. That was a relief. With a sandwich in his hand, he went into his study and took down an atlas from which he intended to extract a territorial argument against intervention in Cuba. He bit into his sandwich and buried himself in the atlas.

Alexandra put down her brush. A wave of fatigue was washing over her, dimming the colors that had glowed so brightly on her fan. She sat back and shook her head to clear it. I want to finish this tonight, she thought fretfully. She picked up her brush again with determination, but the new work looked smudgy and awkward. Maybe she needed a little more tonic. She glanced over her shoulder at the door to Toby's study. It was still shut.

Alexandra slipped up the stairs to her bedroom and unlocked the dressing-table drawer. The tonic made her feel wonderful, but the effect just didn't last. Maybe she was supposed to keep taking it until she was cured? Dr. Nagel's instructions said "Take as needed." If she shouldn't take more than one dose a day, wouldn't he have said so? Of course he would.

She felt shaky and cross. She couldn't face feeling like this tonight. She took a pinch out of the tin and held it to her nose. She wouldn't take any more than just this.

There. Now she'd feel better. Not wanting to trouble Dr. Nagel, she decided to ask Lucinda about the dosage tomorrow.

The bedroom door opened suddenly, and she jumped.

"I'm going back to the office," Toby said. He looked at her. "Are you all right?"

"I'm fine. Fine and dandy." She kissed him quickly and turned him back toward the stairs. "I was just . . . freshening up."

After he had gone, she flew to the dressing table and stuffed the tin back in the drawer. Should she tell him about the tonic and how much good it was doing her? Alexandra wondered as she relocked the drawer. No, there wasn't any need to.

Alexandra called on Lucinda again the next day to discuss plans for the ball. They both had a little of Lucinda's powder to get them going and giggled over it. Alexandra discovered that Lucinda hadn't told her husband, either. It was their little secret pick-me-up. Men, who all drank whiskey and smoked cigars, could be so stuffy over anything that women took for their nerves.

Lucinda said that she only took it once every day or so, but if one was feeling really dragged out, then surely there wasn't anything wrong with taking more. Reassured, Alexandra went home and had a little at bedtime because Toby wasn't home again and she was bored. . . .

After a few weeks, Alexandra found that her supply had run out, but Dr. Nagel obligingly sent her a refill. He didn't seem to think that she was taking too much. Gradually, though, Alexandra realized that she was taking more and more. After its effects wore off, she seemed to suffer greater fatigue than ever; but then she took a little more powder and within minutes was all right. Tales of people becoming addicted haunted her, but she dismissed the doubts by thinking of Lucinda. Just fancy Lucinda Hoffman a drug addict! And of course she herself could stop taking the tonic at any time. People who were addicted couldn't do that.

The only trouble was that she didn't mention anything about it to Toby, and sometimes he simply wouldn't leave her alone so that she could take her tonic. He would sit on the bed and chattily discuss that infernal revolution, while she was trying to pull herself together for dinner.

"So Leverage has a date to dine with the Spanish ambassador—"

"Yes, dear. I'll be down in a minute." Alexandra's eyes flicked toward the dressing table. She just needed to settle her nerves.

"I'll keep you company while you dress. I feel bad about being gone so much."

"That's all right," Alexandra assured him. "I don't mind. I mean, I do mind; but I understand how important your work is. We'll talk at dinner." She picked up her hairbrush and swiped it distractedly through her unpinned hair.

"I'll wait," Toby said maddeningly. "So anyway, we have high hopes for Leverage working his famous tact on the ambassador, and if we can just get a commitment out of him to some reasonable gesture—"

Alexandra coiled her long hair into a knot and tried to put the pins in it, thinking, Oh, for goodness sake, I don't care about the Spanish ambassador!

"—and Crampton has presented a very decent proposal to my former colleagues in the Senate."

"That's nice, dear." Alexandra dropped a hairpin. Her hands shook. "You really don't need to wait for me. I thought you needed to work on something before dinner. Toby, I simply can't do my hair with your watching me. You know I can't!" The chignon slipped to one side, and she began pulling pins out of it.

Toby looked at her with surprise. "All right, I'll be downstairs." His tone was genial, but he cast her a curious glance as he left.

After he had gone, she snatched the drawer open.

A few minutes later her hair was perfectly done, and she came down to join Toby and Sally for dinner. "I'm sorry I was so cross, darling," she said, eyes bright, as she sat down across from her husband.

"You're working too hard on this ball," Toby said, helping himself to roasted goose. "It's not good for you to get so frantic."

"Oh, I'm all right." Alexandra looked at her plate without interest and took a tiny bite.

Toby talked around a mouthful. "The cooking has improved enormously. You're obviously paying more attention to the menus."

"Oh. Thank you." She smiled. "No more tongue." She pushed the food around on her plate.

"Aren't you hungry?" Toby asked.

"No, I'm trying to lose just a little weight before the party." She wasn't a bit hungry. "My costume has so many layers, I don't want to look like one of those round dolls with all the other little dolls inside them."

"Well, don't overdo it," Toby said absently. "You look fine to me."

"You should see my costume," Sally said importantly. "And we're going to paint our faces, just like the Japanese ladies!"

"Are you allowed to go to this?" Toby inquired.

"For just an hour," Alexandra said. She looked at his raised eyebrows. "She talked me into it," she added, throwing up her hands and laughing. "And I don't really see any harm."

In fact, Sally had thrown a temper tantrum that would have done a two-year-old proud, and

297

Alexandra hadn't had the strength to argue with her.

"Well," said Toby, "if your mother thinks so. . . ."

"All the girls at school will be jealous," Sally said. She cast a dark glance at her father. "That'll fix them." She obviously felt that if she couldn't have a father with the correct political views, at least she could have the advantage over her detractors socially.

"That's not the best reason for wanting to do something," Toby said mildly.

"Toby, it's important to her," Alexandra said. Raising the children, particularly a girl, was her province. "Let's just forget about it, shall we?"

"Certainly."

After dinner, Sally departed, reluctantly, to do her schoolwork, and Alexandra fled upstairs to the bedroom to get there before Toby could. But when she took the tin out of her dressing table, she sat looking at the powder for a long moment and felt troubled. She seemed to need to take the cocaine more and more often. It wasn't really curing her; she was becoming dependent on it just to feel passable. What if she couldn't stop? Of course she could stop! she told herself. She'd stop tonight, just to prove it. With a gesture of determination, she put the unopened tin back in the drawer.

Alexandra sat for a long while staring at that drawer. She really should throw the powder away. But when she proved she could stop taking it, then there wouldn't be any need to throw it away. She could just use it on those occasions when she felt overworked. She could keep the powder if she promised herself to use it only once in a while.

She bargained with herself for a few minutes more, then relocked the drawer to show her determination. Her urge to open it again panicked her. I'll just leave it there. There was nothing in that drawer that she would need in the next few days, so she wouldn't be tempted to open it.

She tried to concentrate on something else, but nothing was much fun to think about. Finally she undressed and got into bed. I just need sleep. It was only nine o'clock.

When she woke in the morning, Alexandra felt flat, dull, weighted down with a dreadful sensation of futility. There didn't seem to be any point to anything. Toby had already gone to his office and Sally to school.

Feeling very alone, Alexandra sat at her dressing table. Unstoppable tears slipped down her cheeks. She had given nearly all her time to being Toby's wife and somebody's mother—her stepchildren and her own babies. Mike, Alexandra's first child, whom she had nursed through rheumatic fever and a sickly childhood, was married and gone. Tim and Janessa were long gone. Sally was almost grown-up, more interested in spending time with her friends than with her mother. Even her horses were on the ranch in Oregon. When she married Toby, she had thought she would live on the Madrona, raise her horses and her babies, and Tim and Janessa. But that was not how life had unfolded for her. But why was she crying over that now? She looked at the locked drawer of the dressing table and knew what would make her feel better. No!

Alexandra got up and dressed. She would stay away from it for just three days. Well, maybe for two days. She made deals with herself, arguing with herself the way Sally battled with her when she wanted something—wheedling, promising: two days, just to prove she could.

Alexandra went down to breakfast and found that Cook had cleared away the table. She looked forlornly around the breakfast room.

"Mrs. Holt, you want to eat?" Juanita, her dark eyes concerned and penetrating, too penetrating, stood in the doorway.

Alexandra shied away from what she was sure was Juanita's suspicion. "No, I think I'll just wait for lunch." The words came out sounding strange to her, forced and lying.

Juanita put her hands on her hips. "Mrs. Holt, what's the matter with you lately? You are not acting right. I know."

"I'm just fine, Juanita. Go away." Her voice rose and cracked on the last words.

Juanita shook her head. "Something's wrong."

Alexandra fled from the room and shut herself in Toby's study. She needed something to get herself through this. She opened a cabinet where she knew he kept a bottle of whiskey for visitors.

Maybe that would settle her nerves. She drank some. Her stomach heaved, and she bent over the spittoon, also kept for visitors, and her empty stomach sent the whiskey back up. Weeping, she sank down in the leather armchair.

Eventually she managed to get up and order the carriage brought around. She had to get away from Juanita. Juanita knew. She got her cloak and went outside.

"Where you want to go, Mrs. Holt?" The driver stood beside the carriage door and waited for orders.

"Just—just around the Mall. Just a nice drive." She climbed in before he could see her start crying again.

By the time Toby came home, she was in bed again, resting. They had tickets to the theater that night, but she really didn't think she could go after all. As she told him so, she made her voice relax. Did he look suspicious? She did not know for certain. He left her alone.

Somehow she made it until the end of the following day. But by then Toby had gone out again, while the locked drawer and the tin of cocaine were still there.

She didn't try to stop herself from taking it. Life was easier, floating once more in the arms of the drug rather than fighting against it. Everything felt all right now. Of course she could stop if she wanted to. She had already done it once. Hadn't she?

XIV

New York, 1897

Charley was coming home! Janessa's face lit up as she read his letter—loving, eager, and missing her, just like Charley. He'd be home in a month.

> I am under attack by homesickness (wifesickness). The lure of alien microbes (not to mention Israel Richardson's cook— her culinary skills) has given way to be re-united with you and the children. I miss you, and I've booked a ticket on the Campania in a cabin sans corpse, I hope.

Janessa read the letter a second time, then folded it and stuck it into her pocket. Lord, how she missed him! If anything could get her through the next few weeks, it was the prospect of Charley's coming home. His letter was the one bright spot in her embattled days.

The conflict that had begun with Araminta Haggerty's desire to have no more babies had escalated until combatants had begun to voice not only their philosophical differences on the issue of contraception, but their personal ones, flinging accusations like grenades in the hallways. Adam Sells and Horace White were no longer speaking to her except to threaten to resign. Only their genuine dedication to the hospital kept them on staff. Head Nurse Anna Williams was tight-lipped and condemnatory and spoke to Janessa over patients' bedsides with clipped professionalism. The junior nurses were on either side of the battle and quarreled with one another in the nurses' lounge.

Dr. Sergei Antohin, the fourth of the hospital's resident physicians, had been out of the city when the first skirmishes had been fought. Having returned to find full-scale war raging, he had taken a position in support of Janessa as a matter of political principle; but he was, after all, a socialist and a Russian, said Horace White and the righteous among the nurses. What could you expect from someone like that?

Even Sergei declined to make his views public. There were bigger wars to be fought, he said. What could you expect from a man? asked the nurses in Janessa's corner. Only Reuben French, the hospital's administrator, maintained an iron-clad neutrality. His job was to keep the foundation's facility operational, but it was becoming harder daily.

French poked his head inside Janessa's office now as she put Charley's letter away. He bore the expression of a wary cat, but he appeared determined to give her news of the latest sally. "Dr. Lawrence," he said with no preamble, "Mrs. McLeod and Mrs. Meigs have been to see me. They are threatening to withdraw their financial support. You do want this hospital to stay afloat?"

"Of course." Janessa tried not to sound irate.

"The painters were not quite finished covering the vandalism by the time the ladies had arrived," French said.

Janessa groaned. Coming to work early, she had found "Whores" scrawled in whitewash across the hospital doors and ordered them scrubbed and repainted. "We need a night watchman," she said now.

"We need an end to the necessity for one."

"I am not going to crawl in a hole because of a little vandalism."

French sighed. "Mrs. Meigs is on the foundation board, which meets at the end of this month. Your activities are going to be the main item on the agenda."

"You wish me to stop speaking in public?" Janessa asked with forced sweetness. "I thought that education was among the purposes of the foundation."

"Advocating contraception does not come under the heading of education in most people's minds," French said. "Immorality and blasphemy were a couple of the terms they suggested."

"Then obviously they need to be educated."

The administrator tried another tack. "Are you aware that doctors have been arrested for merely selling feminine syringes?" he inquired.

Janessa stiffened. "Feminine syringes may be purchased in any drugstore for the purposes of hygiene. What else a woman with them is her own business."

"This hospital is just getting its feet on the ground. It cannot afford controversy. It cannot afford this!" French slapped that morning's edition of the New York World on her desk. A column on the editorial page had been circled with red ink. "You are jeopardizing everything you've worked for."

Janessa picked up the paper and flinched. "I know," she said dismally.

"This hospital is your creation," French said. "But let me give you a word of warning, Dr. Lawrence. You have a very strong standing here, but you are not sacred."

After Reuben French had gone, Janessa read the editorial and gritted her teeth. It accused her of being an affront to common decency, a corrupter of moral values, an insult to the purity of womankind, and a danger to the social fabric of New York City.

Stung, Janessa blinked back tears. She knew the whitewash on the front doors was her fault. She balanced that against the memory of desperate women, given a choice between not having physical relations with their husbands and having sickly babies they could not afford to feed. She could find no answer to satisfy everyone. Having come to a new and passionate conviction in midlife, she could not and would not let it go. But what was she going to do? And how was Charley going to react when he came home?

Her indecision was interrupted by a commotion in the hallway. Nurses' voices rose, and a man was shouting. Running footsteps went past her door. Janessa flung it open. The uproar was coming from the waiting room. Two orderlies wheeling a bed ran past her. In an instant she was at their heels.

A woman had collapsed on the waiting-room floor, and the admitting nurse was bent over her. The woman's face was flushed and hot to the touch, and when Janessa knelt to lift one lid, the eye stared blankly. Blood was pooling between her legs, flowing fast enough to soak through her skirts and trickle across the floor.

"She's hemorrhaging!" The nurse snatched the shabby skirts back.

Anna Williams materialized with a handful of bandages, which Janessa desperately packed between the woman's legs. The stench of well-advanced infection assailed her nostrils. Standing above the women, the man continued to rage incomprehensibly. The orderlies fought with him to keep him back.

"Whores! Harlots! Bloodsuckers!"

"Get him out of here!" Janessa didn't look up.

He writhed in the orderlies' grip. "Keep your filthy hands away! I am her husband! I say! God knows! God punish her! God punish you!" By this time, nearly the whole hospital staff had gathered. They dragged the man, still screaming, down another hall.

"Get her on the bed!" Janessa ordered.

Anna Williams and Janessa lifted her and followed the bed at a trot as it was wheeled away.

The husband's screaming sounded in the distance.

"What is it?" Adam Sells, businesslike now, appeared at Janessa's elbow.

"Miscarriage or a botched abortion," Anna Williams answered as Janessa ran for the sink in the operating room, to scrub.

Sergei Antohin came after her, then shouldered her aside. "Stay out of it," he told her. "That fellow out there has got the notion that it's your doing."

"Go to hell," Janessa snapped.

"He's out there calling you a murderess."

"I never saw her before. And I don't do abortions." Janessa pushed her way to the sink and picked up the bottle of carbolic acid.

By the time she got to the table, Adam Sells was already working on cutting away the woman's heavy, blood-soaked skirt. "Jesus Christ," he murmured. Blood, thick and evil smelling, pooled around his hands. "Butchers!" He bit the word off between his teeth.

They could all see by now that it was an abortion, self-induced with a coat hanger or else hideously performed with an implement equally primitive.

The doctors worked quickly, desperately, silently, except for an occasional muttered curse or a request to the nurses, their quarrel shelved in the urgency. The woman had lost a dangerous amount of blood, and she was in shock from the infection, which had plainly been festering for days. Her uterus had been torn to shreds.

Dr. Sells looked at Janessa across the table.

Janessa nodded. "Ether. Put her under."

They proceeded to take out the uterus. There was nothing left to salvage except perhaps her life—if the anesthetic didn't kill her. If she survived, she might even be grateful, Janessa thought grimly. It was obvious that she had already borne numerous children.

After they were through, Janessa found Sergei propped against the wall, arms folded, waiting for her in the hall. "So?"

"She may live," Janessa said tiredly. "We didn't kill her on the operating table. Where's her husband?"

"We sedated him," Sergei said. "He wanted to come after you."

"I want to go after him," Janessa retorted. "How could he have waited so long to bring her in?"

"He didn't know. She didn't tell till she thought she was dying. And you stay away from him. You already operated without his permission—that is going to make trouble. If he sees you, he'll go for the police."

"Sergei," Janessa said wearily, "I never saw that woman before. Surely he can't think I did that to her."

"He knows about you," Sergei said darkly. "You make yourself famous."

"I advocate contraception, not abortion!" Janessa said, exasperated.

"People don't make a distinction," he said. "Come. I take you somewhere."

"I still have rounds to make."

"Pah! What you make is trouble. Leave that to old revolutionaries like me and just make medicine."

"Maybe if you old revolutionaries would take a stand with me on this, there wouldn't be so many oppressed workers. Maybe there'd be enough jobs to go around."

"A fine capitalist plan. Keep the workers from having babies, so they stay outnumbered and can't fight for their rights."

"Oh, quit it. I'm not going to argue politics with you."

"If you think this isn't politics, you don't have both oars in the water," Sergei commented. It was an American phrase he liked. "You make rounds, then I show you."

"Oh, all right." Sergei was as stubborn as a mule. She knew that he would keep after her until she went with him wherever it was.

Sergei Antohin had made his way to America at fourteen and worked his way through public school and then medical school. He had founded a street-corner clinic where workers could be inoculated simultaneously against smallpox and capitalist oppression and had signed on with the Brentwood Foundation only when he could no longer scrape together the funds to keep his clinic open. Although Horace White and he occupied opposite ends of the political spectrum, Sergei the atheist was as idealistic in his own way as was Horace the preacher's son. Janessa went to make her rounds, knowing that Sergei would wait for her.

The woman whose uterus they had removed was still sleeping. A nurse sat at the bedside, reading. Janessa gazed down at the patient's face, her skin stretched like a too small piece of parchment over the bones. She had scarcely glanced at the woman's face until now. She picked up the chart. The woman was twenty-nine, although she looked forty-five. Her name was Mary Brooks.

"Is her husband still here?"

"He went home," the nurse said uncomfortably. "He wanted to call the police and make us let him take her with him, but Dr. Sells threatened to charge him with assault. I think maybe he was really afraid of the police. He doesn't have a job."

And no telling what he's been doing to put food on the table. Adam Sells used blackmail, Janessa thought, troubled. "I want to talk to her when she wakes up."

"So does Dr. Sells," the nurse said. "He wants to find out who did it. Mr. Brooks said she went to somebody."

"I want to find out, too." Janessa and Adam Sells were in agreement on that. "I'll be back later tonight."

The nurse nodded. "I don't want Dr. Sells to be angry with me," she whispered, "but I think you are right. It shouldn't have come to this for the poor thing." She looked pityingly at the woman, then entreatingly at Janessa. "But don't tell him I said so."

"No, I won't." The nurses who had taken sides in her battle were in a more precarious position than the doctors. Janessa didn't blame this one for wanting to stay safe.

Sergei, apparently to prevent any last-minute escape, was waiting for her in her office. Janessa put on her coat and hat while he watched. He led her out to Cherry Street, where they caught a trolley headed uptown. Janessa was curious to know where he was taking her. She was mildly surprised when Sergei alighted in front of an imposing gray stone church.

She raised her eyebrows at him. "Getting religion, Sasha?" she asked, using his nickname now that they were out of the hospital environs.

"No," he said amiably. "You are getting education. It is a good thing that you have not had your picture in these newspapers."

As Janessa followed him inside, she craned her neck to read the notice board that listed the services. The Wednesday evening sermon topic was "Family Purity in God's Eyes," preached by the Reverend Windrow Walker. Janessa glared with suspicion at her escort.

"Be quiet and say your prayers," Sergei said as they knelt in a pew at the back. He bent his head with ostentatious piety.

The service began. The church was not Janessa's denomination, but she managed to follow along reasonably well in the prayer book and glanced now and again at her friend to see what he was doing. He was reading the Service for the

Burial of the Dead at the back of the book with what she thought was a supercilious expression. Occasionally he chuckled.

Janessa poked him. "If you're going to be in church, be respectful."

Sergei was unrepentant. "You wait," he said.

They sang a hymn, then the congregation settled into the pews to hear the sermon. The Reverend Windrow Walker had not gotten very far in his lesson before Janessa's cheeks were flushed red.

"And what is God's command to woman? Brothers and sisters, it is written that woman's highest duty—nay, her noblest calling—is that of wife and mother, to raise up her children to the glory of God. What more blessed role could any among us ask? And what of the woman who would shirk that duty? What of the man who would aid her to make a travesty of the marital union for the selfish pleasures of the flesh? Both she and he stand degraded, no better than the common harlot who defames our streets! Brothers and sisters, there is in our city an institution, a hospital, where wives are lured to damnation—I say damnation! —and openly given the means to shirk their duties and depart from God's ways! It is God's command that we unite against this pernicious evil and the unnatural woman who encourages it!"

Furious, Janessa sat stiffly. Her white-knuckled hands shook on the covers of her prayer book. Her throat felt constricted. She wanted to get up and flee but knew that she had better not.

Sergei reached over and clenched her hand. "You need to hear," he whispered. "You need to know what you're causing."

The service was finally over. Janessa marched out, cheeks flaming, anonymous but accused, in the midst of the congregation of the righteous. Murmuring their indignation as they went, they spilled through the church doors.

"You needed to hear," Sergei said again when they were a short distance from the church. "Pretty soon it will be your own minister calling you names in the pulpit."

"He wouldn't!" Janessa said indignantly. But had his behavior toward her been odd lately? She knew it had. And the churchwomen's guild had not invited her to the last sewing circle. Of course she rarely went, but this time they hadn't even asked her. She felt outcast, shunned.

"These people will close the hospital if you go on," Sergei predicted. "You are tearing down their ideas of morality. They won't stand for it."

"I'm not immoral," Janessa protested.

"Not to me," he allowed. "But I'm an atheist. You frighten people. You frighten even me a little. Contraception for everyone would change the way men and women are with each other. What would keep women virtuous?"

"I don't see any advantage to being virtuous out of fear," Janessa said.

"It is better than not being virtuous at all," he said.

"And virtue isn't the point, Sasha! That poor

313

woman we operated on this afternoon is the point. If she had been able to keep herself from conceiving in the first place, she wouldn't have been desperate enough to abort."

"You aren't going to get away from the question of virtue," Sergei said. "It is bad enough that men philander. Do you want women to, also? Then what holds the family together?"

"I thought you agreed with me!" Janessa said indignantly.

He shrugged. "I do. But I know when you aren't going to win."

"Women have as much right as men! Not to philander, but to enjoy marital relations without fear," she finished primly.

"To enjoy sex," Sasha said, under no euphemistic constraints. "You are more revolutionary even than me."

"Maybe I am," Janessa muttered.

"Maybe you get crucified, too," Sergei said.

Feeling troubled and rebellious, Janessa left Sergei at the hospital door and went inside to see Mary Brooks again. The woman was awake now, and the nurse reported that her fever had dropped. She clung precariously but tenaciously to life.

Janessa motioned for the nurse to leave, then sat down by the edge of the bed. "I'm Dr. Lawrence. I operated on you today."

"I know about you." Her voice was a thready whisper.

"That's why I made him bring me here."

"Your husband?"

Mary nodded. "He didn't want to. He doesn't hold with doctors looking at women's parts. But I reckon maybe he didn't want me to die after all. He didn't take on like that until he saw it was your hospital we'd come to."

"Why?" Janessa had checked the records to be sure. Mary had never consulted any of the doctors at this hospital or its clinic.

"He blames you for putting ideas in women's heads." She smiled weakly and with faint irony. "I already had ideas. I bought one of those sponges and tried to use it—a woman friend told me how. But he found out and threw it away. And then he held me down and—and did it to me for spite."

"Dear God," Janessa whispered, appalled beyond professional objectivity.

"I've had six already," Mary said. "Four that lived. I couldn't face it no more. I'd rather die."

"You nearly did. I have to ask who did this to you."

"I already told the other doctor," Mary said despairingly.

"All right then. You won't have to talk about it anymore. Did Dr. Sells tell you why we had to operate?"

Mary nodded. "He said you took my womb out." Tears trickled down her cheeks. "I reckon now he won't want me no more. Now I'm not— not a woman."

"You are a woman! Your uterus is not you." Janessa knew she wasn't going to convince Mary, much less her husband, of that. She wondered indignantly how Mary Brooks could want a man like that; but it wasn't entirely a matter of wanting. With four children, where would Mary go? "At least you won't have more children," she said, trying to offer some practical comfort.

"Maybe he won't be at me all the time," Mary agreed. She blinked her tears away. "When I'm . . . in the family way, he goes with bad women. I always hated knowing that. I reckon now he'll start again. But I can't help feeling like I'd rather he did, if he'll leave me alone." She turned her head away. "I can't stand to think about it anymore."

The husband would go to prostitutes, who used contraceptives, and there was the link to morality that made the whole issue such a swamp. Everyone knew that prostitutes kept themselves from getting pregnant; therefore, any woman who did the same must also be a bad woman. Why else would a woman fear pregnancy if she wasn't up to something immoral? Never mind the fear of death in childbirth, or childbed fever, or more babies than she could afford to feed.

It was the moral issue that people—from Anna Williams to the Reverend Windrow Walker to Mary Brooks's husband—thought of first. Contraceptives were "obscene" materials because the notion of unregulated sex was obscene. A woman was not supposed to have intercourse with her husband without the church and the government leaning over the bed to make sure she did it properly. Janessa felt a growing outrage. And women like Mary Brooks were left in such a situation that they preferred that their husbands go to prostitutes rather than make love to them. She doubted that what Mary Brooks's husband subjected her to could be called making love at all, and it occurred to her that she was singularly blessed in Charley.

I've led a sheltered life, Janessa thought, mildly startled by the idea. I have no idea what goes on with other people. The more she thought about Mary Brooks and Charley and the Reverend Windrow Walker, the more she could see no clear solutions.

Janessa looked at Mary's chart. There was one thing she could do for Mary, given Mary's mental state at the moment. "Has Dr. Sells examined you tonight?"

Mary shook her head fearfully. "Does he have to?" she asked.

"Somebody has to," Janessa said gently. "I thought you might rather it was me." It was bad enough to have a man see your private parts while you were unconscious, but when you were awake . . .

"Oh, yes, please."

Janessa took out a thermometer and stuck it in Mary's mouth. "Just hold that under your tongue, and we'll get your temperature while I have a look."

Mary flinched when Janessa touched her. The incision looked reasonably decent, considering the hurry they'd been in, Janessa thought. She could see no further signs of hemorrhage. With the source of infection removed, Mary stood a fair chance of pulling through. Janessa changed the dressings as gently as possible, then pulled the sheet back up. She read the thermometer—still a fever, but lower.

"Are you in pain?"

"You'd be in pain if somebody had cut you open," Mary said with an unexpected burst of spirit.

Janessa grinned. "Sorry. Doctors get a little tactless sometimes." She tucked the sheet around Mary as she talked. "We get taught this idiotic series of questions at medical school, you see. Some professor's idea of proper bedside manner." She poured a glass of water from the pitcher by the bed and held it to Mary's lips. "It's a rule: We aren't supposed to assume anything on our own, even that a patient who's just had an abdominal incision is going to hurt. Silly, really. Of course it hurts. We can do something about that." She set the glass down and wiped Mary's mouth with a cloth. "I'll send a nurse with some morphine for you. You're going to have to stay with us for at least a week, maybe two."

Mary clutched Janessa's hand. "Dr. Lawrence, I got to thank you for what you done. I know there's people who don't like what you say, but

318

I think you're the best person I ever met. God bless you."

"I'm just a doctor," Janessa said uncomfortably. If I was everything you think I am, you wouldn't be in this fix. "The morphine will help you rest. I'll see you again tomorrow."

She updated Mary's chart and stopped at the nurses' desk to order the morphine and tell them that she had checked the patient so Dr. Sells wouldn't need to. She hoped he wouldn't be aggravated by that—he probably would be—but the fewer men who Mary saw right now, the better.

It was late when Janessa got home. The twins and Kathleen were in bed. Kathleen had left a plate of pork chops and applesauce for her in the kitchen. With no one to watch her and be horrified, Janessa picked a chop up with her fingers and gnawed it while she poured herself a glass of milk. She drank that standing at the kitchen counter. After she had finished, she walked down the darkened hall and munched a second chop.

She looked in on the twins. Brandon was burrowed under his covers like a caterpillar, asleep on his stomach with his bottom stuck up. Lally had, as usual, kicked off all her covers and lay sprawled on her back like a starfish, crosswise in her bed with one foot hanging off the edge. Janessa turned the blanket sideways and draped it over her, thinking about Mary Brooks and her four babies. I'm blessed, she thought again, no matter what that preacher thought.

But she began to realize that Sergei Antohin was right, too. She was treading on thin ice. If there were many more sermons and newspaper editorials, the foundation board would push her, founder or no, out of Brentwood Hospital. They would have to; the hospital couldn't risk open scandal. And if she found herself arrested under the Comstock Law, she could never go back. The hospital was her channel to help women like Mary Brooks. How could she jeopardize that?

Oddly enough, the thought of being arrested didn't trouble her much. If Tim's wife, Elizabeth, could get arrested for what she believed in, so too could Janessa. In fact, it was almost tempting; but without the backing of the hospital, it would be a singularly futile gesture.

Janessa tiptoed out of the babies' room. As she threw her chop bones in the garbage, she wondered if Tim and Elizabeth were going to have babies. She was certain that Elizabeth knew exactly how to avoid pregnancy if she wanted to and would not hesitate to do so. What did Elizabeth think of Janessa's activities, she wondered. The women's movement encouraged voluntary motherhood, but judging from Anna Williams's reaction, it disapproved of artificial means. It all came back to the question of protecting women. Would easy contraception simply give men another way to shirk their responsibilities and cause them to think of their wives as whores? Anna believed it would. Janessa washed her hands at the sink, trying to wash away doubt and scrub certainty to the surface. It didn't work.

In the morning Reuben French, girded for battle, was in her office again. Grasped in his hand was another frothing article in the *World*, which had given Janessa nearly as much space as the fighting in Cuba.

Janessa forestalled him. "I have reached a decision, Mr. French." She hung her coat on the hook behind her door and set her hat on the skull that decorated her office shelves—a habit she knew French considered eccentric.

The administrator looked wary. "I devoutly hope it includes retracting your statements on the subject of contraception. An inspector from the police department was here this morning. Dr. Antohin managed to persuade him to wait; but one more public statement from you will do it, I fear."

"I am sure it would," Janessa agreed. "So you'll be happy to know that for the time being, I am not going to make any more."

Mr. French was not soothed by "for the time being." "Ever, if you please, Dr. Lawrence. The obscenity laws are enforced at the discretion of the police, but even for a foundation with prominent backers, they cannot ignore a public scandal."

"Public seems to be the operative word," Janessa murmured. "Odd, since I consider the whole question to be a matter for private decision."

"I'll prepare a statement of retraction for you to issue to the press," French said.

"I didn't say retraction," Janessa responded quickly. "Mr. French, I thought about this all night, and the only conclusion I could come to that my conscience would allow is to tread water, so to speak. I plan to take a leave of absence for several months. I have family in Washington, D.C., and there is an established and successful women's hospital there. I'd like to study its methods. I'll provide you with regular written reports of their operation, which you may find useful."

"Having you out of town will be useful," French retorted.

"Exactly. Two or three months should allow the moral avengers in New York time to simmer down. I'll refrain from public speaking on the subject after I return. I will, however, continue to research the most efficient methods of contraception for use by women whose physical health prohibits further pregnancies. I may perhaps use some of my patients as test subjects." She held up her hand as French opened his mouth. "Take it or leave it."

"Take it," a voice behind her advised, and she turned to find Dr. Antohin in the doorway.

"Don't you knock?" French asked irritably.

"Take it, or she will do something foolish and go to jail. And then the old ladies with the pearls and the checkbooks will not give us any more money. Also Dr. Lawrence is a good doctor who is willing to work for the pittance the foundation

322

can pay. And she has a fine reputation when she is not making immoral speeches."

"That is a particularly backhanded testimonial," French commented, suppressing a laugh. "I'll need to consult with Dr. Sells and Dr. White. Dr. White is extremely upset over—"

"I will talk to him," Sergei offered.

"No, you won't," French and Janessa said together.

"You talk to Adam Sells," Janessa suggested. "But leave Horace alone. Mr. French can talk to Horace. You don't speak his language."

"My English is perfect."

"It's not, and I'm not talking about your English."

"I am in better smell than you at the moment."

"Hah! Better odor," Janessa corrected. "Horace is a good doctor, and the supply of physicians who aren't interested in getting rich is limited. We can't afford to lose him, either. It's one of the reasons I've decided to do this."

"You decide because I talked sense into you," Sergei said.

"If I had sense," Reuben French said moodily, "I'd go into another line of work. Dr. Lawrence, I will expect you to stay in Washington for three months, minimum. Provided that you do not get yourself arrested there, I'll accept your offer." He glared at the bookcase. "And don't put your hat on that thing! It makes the old ladies nervous."

"All flesh is grass," Sergei said happily.

"But in our profession, we don't care to remind people of it," French retorted.

The Russian lifted his bony shoulders in an eloquent shrug. "See where our troubles come from? You speak reality. Everyone wants morals instead."

XV

"So you got run out of town, eh?" Mike Holt asked. Janessa was making a list for Kathleen of items to pack, while Eden played with the twins.

"I did not get run out of town," Janessa said with dignity. "I am taking a leave of absence to study the operations of the Washington Women's Infirmary."

"By popular demand," Mike teased. "Do you smell something burning?"

"Oh, Lord!" Janessa flew into the kitchen. Mike ambled after her. She opened the oven door and found that the fish she was baking was just beginning to blacken. "I'm surprised you even know what this brouhaha is all about," she said, snatching the pan out of the oven. Mike read the entertainment trade papers front to back but was known to let his subscription to the *Journal* stack up until Eden finally threw the papers out. "This is the first time you've even mentioned it to me."

"I know when something's on fire besides your fish," Mike said. "I didn't see any point in mentioning it, though. It's your business. I'm inclined to think you're right on principle, but I did wonder if I was going to have to bake you a cake with a file in it."

Janessa set the pan with the fish on top of the stove and regarded it pessimistically. It was Kathleen's half day off. "Do you suppose we can eat this?"

"We're capable of it," Mike said. "But are we willing?"

"Oh, be quiet. I think it's only burned on the edges."

"Fish are nearly all edges," Mike pointed out, but he took a fork and flaked away the black parts. "I think we called the engine company in time. Whip up a little dill sauce, and we can still fool the public." He began to set the kitchen table.

Eden came in, carrying one twin and leading the other by the hand. She hefted them into their high chairs. "Well, I think you're right, and I don't think you should back down," she told Janessa.

"Bless your immoral little heart," Janessa said.

"Eden moves in very bohemian circles since she took up with me," Mike explained. "She's thoroughly corrupted."

They sat down to fish, masked in dill sauce, and salad and rice, Janessa's staples on Kathleen's days off. Janessa could cook if she had to—if she could keep her mind on it—but she rarely had time and felt too rusty to tackle anything complicated. With Charley gone, she ate uncomplainingly whatever Kathleen produced—corned beef and cabbage and potatoes more often than not.

There was a bright spot: "I'm looking forward to Dad and Alex's cook," Janessa said.

"High off the hog," Mike agreed. "Maybe you'd like for us to come along?"

Janessa knew he wasn't serious. Mike was in the middle of directing a new moving picture. The vaudeville theaters had proved a good market for the novelty, and there were even a few theaters opening that showed nothing but moving pictures. Eventually, she thought, Mike would make very good money at it. For now Mike and Eden lived simply, happy just to be together and to swim in the fascinating waters of the theatrical world. Eden had inherited money, but they were saving it, they said, in case they started to starve. Mike and Janessa were both aware that Eden quietly wrote checks to artists and actors down on their luck. She did it so self-effacingly that hardly anyone else noticed; but there were people in New York who would cheerfully have died for her.

"What does Dad think of what you've been up to?" Mike inquired of his sister.

"I haven't said anything to him about it," Janessa said. "I was sort of saving it. I hope my ill repute hasn't traveled that far."

"He reads the New York papers," Mike said. "He knows."

"Then I assume he approves," Janessa said placidly. "Dad usually speaks his mind when he doesn't."

The three of them grinned at one another. Toby had spoken his mind to Mike about moving pictures versus gainful employment but was gradually changing it.

"In any case, he isn't a tyrant like Uncle Henry," Eden said. She still hadn't forgiven Henry for the way he had treated her beloved Mike. "I know what Uncle Henry would think of what you've been up to, Janessa."

Janessa held a forkful of fish out to Brandon. "Has anyone heard from Uncle Henry? Or Aunt Cindy?"

"Haven't heard any good," Mike answered. "Mama wrote that Uncle Henry was going up to the Madrona to try to make Aunt Cindy come home, but Mama didn't know what would come of it. I had a letter from Peter, too. He sounded pessimistic about it."

Janessa sighed. "They were so in love with each other, from the time they were children. Everyone was so ecstatic when they got back together after their first marriages. Things finally worked out between them. That was the year after you were born, Mike. I was at their wedding. They looked like two people who'd been through hell and finally found heaven. I hate to see this happen to them."

Eden put her chin in her hand. "How do you make love last?"

"Lord knows," Janessa said.

"I always thought it just stayed the same forever," Eden continued, "but it doesn't seem to."

"Charley and I have had our ups and downs, and we've gotten through them. You will, too," she added, in case Eden was unnerved. "I think maybe we're all more flexible than Uncle Henry."

"Uncle Henry's about as flexible as a brick," Mike said. "Thank goodness for Mama and Dad." He smiled at Eden. "We'll just steer by their star."

You couldn't find a better star to set your sights on, Janessa thought, hugging Toby and Alexandra, then Sally, on the train platform in Washington. It was wonderful to be home with them. Janessa had not grown up in the Washington house, but home was anywhere her father and Alexandra were.

"You've been bad," Toby said, chuckling, folding her into his overcoat in a bear hug. "Don't think I don't know about it."

"I'm not penitent," Janessa said.

"Good." He released her, and she hugged Alexandra again and then Sally. Alexandra felt thin to her, but her eyes were bright, and her face was animated. They all bundled Janessa, with Kathleen and the babies, into the big carriage. Alexandra put Lally on her lap and cuddled her.

"You're a scandal," she informed Janessa, then laughed. "No wonder I don't have more grand-babies."

"I gave you two at once," Janessa said. "Stop complaining."

They drove Janessa home to the big house on Connecticut Avenue and took her up to the guest room that was always hers.

"I put something special for you in here," Sally said, pointing proudly at the wall.

It was a framed sampler, knots of climbing roses outlining the alphabet and a text from the Rubaiyat:

Look to the Rose that blows us—"Lo,
Laughing," she says, "into the World I blow:
At once the silken Tassel of my Purse
Tear, and its Treasure on the Garden throw."

The colors were jewellike, bending imperceptibly from stitch to stitch, glowing like the roses. The last sampler she had seen Sally working at, and grumbling at the chore, had been a scrawl of wayward stitches, smudged with dirt and spotted with blood from pricked, recalcitrant fingers.

"It's beautiful!" Janessa said. "Heavens above, what happened?"

"I got the hang of it," Sally answered. "I liked the way I could make the roses twine and the way the Rubaiyat makes them sound."

"She's a hedonist," Alexandra explained. "But now she does beautiful needlework."

Sally looked embarrassed. "It's just a baby thing," she said. "I'm too old for samplers now."

"Oh," Janessa said. "Well, I wish you'd do me one for Christmas. It's far better than anything I ever managed. I think you have your mother's talent."

Sally didn't answer. There was suddenly something odd about the moment, something awkward.

"We'll leave you to unpack now," Alexandra murmured.

They faded away, seemingly without cohesion, leaving Janessa alone. Her mood of homecoming dissipated.

Janessa passed a hand over her forehead, thinking that it was her own uncertainty and unsettled spirit that had done it. If she felt herself an interloper, it was an insecurity she had brought with her. Her family hadn't changed. Perhaps she had sounded condescending—Sally was older, of course.

Depressed, Janessa unpacked and changed into a fresh dress. That afternoon she would go to the Washington Women's Infirmary and begin what she intended to do. Gradually the warmth of the family circle would take her in and make her feel secure, not battered and accused. Security was the other thing she had come there for.

At the infirmary she was a visiting dignitary. Almost audible murmurs of recognition and curiosity—and, perhaps, disapproval—followed her down the hallways. Laura Fisher, the doctor assigned to escort her, bent an angry, dark-browed gaze on a trio of nurses whispering at their desk. They fell into silence.

"This is Dr. Lawrence from New York," Dr. Fisher said. "She is here to make a study of the infirmary, so I expect her to be given every consideration."

"Certainly, Doctor." The eldest nurse shook Janessa's hand smoothly. "We're honored to have you."

"Thank you," Janessa said gravely. "I know you will have many valuable things to teach me."

They went on, conducting introductions and exchanging platitudes. Janessa wasn't sure what Dr. Fisher thought of her. Laura Fisher was businesslike, with spectacles on her nose and graying black hair knotted into a firm bun. Her dark brows nearly met across her forehead, giving her the air of a hanging judge, and her stout figure was encased in a carapace of whalebone as impenetrable as a turtle shell. But her nose, through some genetic irreverence, was tip tilted and delicate, as if her birth nose had been lost and a chorus girl's grafted on to hold her spectacles.

"We have three operating rooms," Dr. Fisher said, "with the latest equipment." She threw open the doors to one of them and displayed gleaming enameled cabinets against tiled walls. The floor was tiled as well, with a drain at the center. The operating table was spotless, its pad encased in a stiffly starched sheet stretched so tightly, it might have been a coat of whitewash. Anesthesia apparatus rested in its own case, and basins and instrument stands were positioned precisely about the table.

Janessa was impressed and said so.

"You're young," Dr. Fisher told her. "When I

331

think of what an operating room looked like only fifty years ago—well, it doesn't bear thinking about. Someone's parlor as often as not, and no aseptic techniques. I remember watching my father operate in a Prince Albert coat and stick the suture threads through his lapel to keep them handy. He and his assistant gave the patient half a bottle of whiskey, and then two farmhands held him down. I was terrified, and I got a whipping afterward for watching. I don't know which was worse—the whipping or seeing that man being restrained. Now we use ether and chloroform, and cocaine for topical use. I'm not sure my nerves would stand what my father had to do."

"I'm not as young as all that," Janessa murmured. "There have been amazing changes since I was in medical school—I suppose not the least of which is some acceptance of women in the profession. Did your father object to your taking up medicine?" Dr. Fisher appeared to have been a woman of determination at an early age.

"He said I'd never marry if I went into medicine." Dr. Fisher's mouth twitched in a sardonic smile. "He was quite right about that. Come along, and I'll show you our pride and joy." She swept Janessa out of the operating room and down a hall to another room, which contained a bed and a seat with a reclining back and neck support, like a dentist's chair. Opposite it was an electrical cabinet with a long heavy tube protruding from it.

"Roentgen's apparatus," Dr. Fisher announced

proudly. "We have been fortunate in obtaining the services of a trained radiologist."

"I want one," Janessa said yearningly. "I have been after our administrator for months to set up a radiology laboratory. He persuaded me to hold off because the equipment keeps improving." She chuckled and stroked the wooden cabinet lovingly. "But I want one now."

"Well, we held off, too," Dr. Fisher said. "The earliest ones required too long an exposure, and their operators developed cutaneous lesions. And of course the machine was seized on by every quack in the country, who claimed to cure everything with it, from warts to spinal deformity. This model, however, shortens the exposure time somewhat, and it has proved an invaluable diagnostic tool. So many of our elderly patients suffer from advanced bone disease. Perhaps our radiologist can give you some ammunition to recite to your administrator. Yours is a foundation hospital, is it not? You need an elderly patron with osteoporosis; that's what you need."

"I'm afraid our elderly patrons are not speaking to me at the moment," Janessa murmured.

"We've heard of your—activities," Dr. Fisher said.

Janessa sighed. At least Dr. Fisher hadn't thrown her out. "I hope my presence won't make trouble for the infirmary. I assure you, my only purpose here is to study your institution."

"I assured our staff of that when you made application to us," Dr. Fisher said crisply.

"Do you disapprove?"

Dr. Fisher, brows knit, contemplated the X-ray machines. "In theory I do, but I'm not married. I can't in conscience speak to the situation of a married woman."

"Innumerable men have felt that they could," Janessa commented.

"Precisely." Dr. Fisher pursed her lips. "I do not wish to commit the same error."

"Oh."

"I've seen too many of my gender die from the simple fact of having had too many babies. From my point of view, there is a simple solution to that. It requires no means except self-restraint. But apparently that is harder than it sounds. I don't know. I've never had to practice it."

"It's complicated," Janessa said. "I suppose it depends upon whether one treats sexual relations as a vice, like drunkenness."

"I believe I was brought up to regard it more as a medicine, to be taken only for a purpose," Dr. Fisher said thoughtfully. "I know that my mother regarded it as unpalatable. She felt it a duty. I can't say I was disappointed not to marry."

"I should think not," Janessa said, and then felt that she might have been untactful.

Dr. Fisher appeared to be contemplating the question. "As you say, very complicated. It is ignorance that troubles me, you see, not immorality. I've been accused of that myself, for taking up medicine. It makes me cautious of appearing immoral in any further way." She gave Janessa a direct look. "I trust you will bear that in mind while you are with us."

"Certainly," Janessa agreed.

"I've been given very clear instructions to keep my dreadful opinions to myself," Janessa informed her father at dinner.

"What opinions?" Sally looked interested.

Janessa took a moment to compose her response. "About women being able to choose how many babies they want to have."

"Oh, that," Sally said scornfully. "I read about that in the newspaper. Some preacher in New York made a speech about you. At least I think that was what he was talking about. The article wasn't very clear."

"No," Toby said. "Thank God."

Janessa thought that Toby was with her in principle, but that he felt uncomfortable anyway. He appeared to find a change of subject in order.

"Alex," he said, "when is this shindig of yours? Janessa's going to need a costume for it, isn't she?"

Alexandra looked up from her plate, as if startled. "Yes, of course." She turned to her stepdaughter. "I've already ordered it, dear. You'll just need a fitting."

Janessa had her fitting the next day, and her sense of isolation within the family was only accentuated by seeing herself in the mirror, robed in brocade, an enormous stiff obi pinned about her middle, her hair stuck through with ivory pins.

335

Little bells and silk wisteria blossoms dangled from the ends.

Alexandra's gown was a copy of the one she wore in a painted portrait that hung in the parlor. Mr. Nakamura had given the painting to her for her birthday one year. It had been painted on silk in Japan, from a photograph. The Japanese artist had dispensed with her Western costume and clothed her to his liking in Oriental splendor. It had made everyone in the family nearly fall down laughing, but Alex loved it. Sally had a similar dress. On the night of the ball, Toby emerged reluctantly from his dressing room. He was resplendent in a deep green hakama, loose, skirtlike trousers underneath a kimono in shades of green and russet on cream-colored silk, depicting cranes and willow trees. He refused to look in a mirror.

The family climbed into the carriage, settling in with some care so that Toby's swords didn't poke anyone. These were thrust through his sash in approved samurai fashion, but he was finding them unwieldy.

"At least you're prepared to fight if anyone laughs at you," Janessa pointed out.

"I take comfort in the fact that everyone else will look as silly," Toby retorted.

Sillier, Janessa decided when they arrived at the Ebbitt House ballroom. Herbert Lucas, with Rosanna firmly on his arm, had swords, too, and was carrying a fan.

The ballroom was a wonderful profusion of chrysanthemums in Oriental vases, with a giant painted fan of Alex's design serving as a backdrop for the musicians. Janessa, holding her trailing skirts with one hand, wandered through the crowd, navigating carefully in raised clogs that made her feel like a horse with unaccustomed shoes. She wore tabi with them, white cotton socks that fastened at the ankle and had a divided toe for the clogs. With the gentlemen deprived of their usual formal black and white, the ballroom flowed with color and fluttering bright silks. Because it was a costume party, the ladies had acquired theatrical makeup kits and had a fine time with them. Nice American ladies did not paint their faces, but everyone knew that Japanese ladies did. The effect in some cases was extraordinary. May Prilliman had powdered her face parchment white and looked, in Janessa's estimation, like something that might haunt a graveyard.

Clutching her skirts, trying to perfect a graceful sway in her walk, Janessa angled through the gathering and looked for people she knew. Alex's friends fluttered around her, exclaiming over her costume, pretending politely not to have read the newspapers. But curiosity gleamed in their eyes.

"So delighted to have you with us. Dear Alex has done wonders, don't you think?"

"You must let me introduce you to my daughter and son-in-law. And do you know the Benders? Senator Bender is from Oregon. Of course you do."

"Ho, ho!" Ephraim Bender clapped her on the

shoulder. "Mrs. Lawrence. You look elegant. Just like a picture."

Janessa smiled sweetly at Ephraim Bender, whom she loathed. The man had beaten Toby out for his Senate seat in the most recent election. Even in kimono and hakama Bender looked like a con artist. Janessa had a long memory—longer, obviously, than the idiot who had decided to present him to her. She saw Alexandra looking daggers at him. Of course, because this was a charity ball, rivalries were set aside for the greater good—in the form of the extraordinary amount of money Bender had paid for his ticket.

Janessa sidled away before he could ask her to dance. He had a way of pretending that unpleasantnesses had never happened. The Holts were still powerful, in Washington as well as Portland. Janessa edged toward the refreshments table and let a waiter in a stiff white jacket and black trousers, the only normal clothes in the room, hand her a cup of champagne punch. The table was laden with bowls of fried prawns and vegetables cut into peculiar shapes. There would be a full dinner served at midnight, but an unwritten rule stated that there must be a constant supply of food both before dinner and after. Janessa wondered how many of the Fresh Air Fund children and their families could have been fed from that night's offerings—and what they would do with the prawns or the radishes shaped like sunbursts.

Janessa ate a prawn and concentrated on not dribbling the dipping sauce on her obi. It was pale blue silk, with a design of shells and fish, and she suspected that it would spot horribly.

A gentleman held a napkin out to her. "Fearfully messy fare, isn't it?"

"Horribly. And I have no idea what to do with these sleeves." Janessa raised an arm, trailing deep pocket sleeves. Gold carp swam across them, rippling in the folds. She met the gentleman's eyes and blinked suddenly. He blinked back. He hadn't expected it to be her, either, she could tell. Janessa took a deep breath and managed to say, "How are you, Brice?"

"Very well, thank you." Dr. Brice Amos looked dubiously at her, no avenue of escape in sight.

Janessa found herself with no emotional reaction at all to the man who had once jilted her. Well, she thought, surprised, that's nice. She had known he was in Washington, of course. In fact, he was Alex's doctor. Naturally he would be at the ball. "You look quite interesting," Janessa said with a fixed smile.

Brice Amos let out a breath of relief, as if he had been braced for much worse. Certainly he had gotten much worse the last time they met. "Darn silly costume," he grumbled. "I feel like a nun or something in all these skirts."

"I'm wondering how we're supposed to dance," Janessa said. She wriggled a clog-shod foot. "If I take these off, my skirts will drag across the floor; but if I don't, I'm sure to break my neck."

Janessa decided to take a leaf from Ephraim Bender's book and pretend that no unpleasantness had transpired between them. It was quite relaxing to discover that she could do it. She looked at Brice carefully. He was still very handsome. He had a cleft chin and curling gold ringlets that were only just starting to go gray. But her heart did no pitpats over him. "I suppose Alex will know what to do about these skirts," she said. "She wouldn't miss out on dancing."

"How is your stepmother?" Brice inquired.

Janessa cocked her head at him. "I was about to ask you that. She seems not quite right to me. She's lively enough, but she's thin." This was the way to be with Brice, she realized suddenly. Doctor to doctor, comfortably discussing other people's health.

"She hasn't consulted me," he said. "I wouldn't ordinarily say anything—but since you're a physician . . . it's been some time since she has had a visit. Your father seems to be under the impression that she's seen me quite recently. You might want to—well . . ."

"Push her a little?" Janessa asked. "I will. Alex thinks she's still young—she's not so much older than I am, and years younger than my dad; but, well, we're all getting on."

"Aren't we?" Brice smiled with practiced charm. That smile was his stock-in-trade. He slipped easily into the notion that they were merely old friends. Or was there something uneasy in his smile? Janessa liked the thought that she might be making him nervous.

"How is your practice getting on? I hear you

have founded a women's hospital. Most impressive." He clearly wasn't going to bring up any other activities.

Janessa decided she wouldn't, either. She'd bet she knew what Brice thought about them, anyway. "I'm here to study the Washington Women's Infirmary," she said, leaving it at that. "And how is your practice?" Brice made an excellent living off Washington wives' dyspepsia. Janessa told herself firmly that she wasn't to sneer at that. His social conscience wasn't her business. Brice was an excellent doctor. Janessa was the one who had recommended him to Alex.

"It's going reasonably well," Brice said. "Although the vacuity level seems to be running fairly high among my patients just now."

Ah-ha. Maybe at midlife the shallowness of the stream Brice swam in was actually beginning to get to him. Quit it. You aren't a social reformer. That's already got you in trouble. She nodded sympathetically and refrained from making a comment, which was no easy task.

"I suppose these women are simply bored," Brice muttered. "Half of them call me in with nothing really wrong with them."

Janessa chuckled. "You're still too good-looking."

Brice eyed her warily. "I doubt that it's that. They simply haven't anything to do and are too featherbrained to think of something."

Janessa grinned at him. "Perhaps for women to go into the professions is not such a foolish notion, then." Brice's previous opinion of women as doctors had not been flattering.

"It's possible for women to find useful work that doesn't take them out of their proper sphere," Brice said unencouragingly. His opinion didn't seem to have changed so much after all. "Of course I wouldn't presume to criticize your own choices." There was the hint of a smile on his lips. "That has never been a particularly safe thing to do. And you seem well adjusted. You're married and have children."

"Yes," Janessa murmured. She slid her tabi-clad feet out of their clogs. The thong was giving her a blister; she could feel it. "I take it that having children is your notion of 'well adjusted'?"

"You haven't taken up peculiar religions or spiritualism, or become addicted to 'nerve tonics,' " Brice said with disgust.

"Nerve tonics?"

"Among the rich and bored there's a fashion for cocaine lately. You haven't encountered it?"

"I don't work with the rich and bored," Janessa told him. "I've encountered cocaine use. But I wouldn't have thought that in your circles—"

"It's quite fashionable," Brice growled. "It's considered very Continental. I've seen three otherwise respectable wives and mothers who've made themselves dependent on it. Worse yet, several men of my own profession are addicted. I blame that man Conan Doyle. And the patent medicine industry. And irresponsible quacks—I won't dignify them by calling them physicians—

342

who'd rather make a fast dollar treating symptoms and not cause." His nostrils flared, and he dusted his hands as if shaking away some taint. For all his shallowness, Janessa had never met anyone as rigidly upright in some respects as Brice.

"I've seen addicts, of course," Janessa said. "There's a great deal of concern over cocaine use among slum women. The, er—" She searched for a euphemism. "The unfortunate ones." The prostitutes. What a silly phrase, as if any woman who lived in a tenement wasn't unfortunate.

Brice obviously knew what she meant. It was a common politeness. People spoke of the social evil, not of prostitution. He snorted, then made a derisive motion, smoothing the deep blue folds of his kimono, which he wore with the air of a man who has unaccountably found himself in public in his smoking jacket.

"Here, there has been a great to-do over the use of cocaine by the Negroes," Brice informed her. "The citizens are convinced that they'll all be murdered in their beds by drug-crazed fiends. They conveniently make no connection with the snake oil they buy to make themselves feel peppy. I'm utterly disgusted with the members of my profession who pander to it."

Janessa smiled, a little slyly. "Why, Brice, how refreshing to see you actually worked up about something."

"I'm as capable of getting 'worked up' as the next man," Brice said stiffly. "I think that infernal flute player has finished his piece. It sounds like teakettles whistling to me. Do you want to dance?"

The flute player had bowed, dipping a head full of dark, artistic curls, and the orchestra was tuning up. Janessa bunched her skirts into her obi until they were ankle length—it seemed the only way—and gave her arm to Brice. They circled among the other waltzers, who were having the same difficulties. The edge of the floor was littered with discarded clogs and rice-straw sandals. Herbert Lucas lumbered by, stepping on his hakama, but Rosanna had been unsuccessful into bullying him into clogs and tabi. He wore black patent dancing pumps, and Janessa noted that he had ditched his fan. His swords stuck out behind him to the danger of other guests.

Brice was an excellent dancer. Janessa noticed other women eyeing her enviously. How ridiculous at this stage in their lives! And how gratifying to notice that it no longer made her feel smug.

She danced twice with him, though, because when the orchestra played the cakewalk, he unexpectedly knew how to do it. What they all looked like, wearing Japanese clothes and doing the cakewalk, Janessa couldn't imagine. She saw Alexandra dancing with Toby, strutting happily. Alex's costume suited her perfectly. Sally was dancing with a young attaché from the British embassy and looked sixteen at least. Janessa suspected that the attaché thought she was. It must be nearly time for Sally to go home.

Janessa danced with her father and with several

of her father's friends and Crampton Cullen from the Foundation for International Relations. Cullen was gallant and Southern in an antebellum way; but he talked politics with her as if he naturally expected women to take an interest, which was gratifying. Perhaps women took more interest than men in proposals for peace.

When supper was served at midnight, Janessa discovered that Sally was still there, eating oysters with the British attaché. Alexandra must have forgotten all about her. Janessa called for their carriage, swooped down upon Sally as diplomatically as possible, and detached her from her dinner partner.

In the cloakroom Sally turned to Janessa. "I want to stay!" She was furious. "I was having fun!"

"You're too young," Janessa said. She pulled Sally toward the door, wondering if she was actually going to have to drag her.

Sally's expression was outraged. "Mama didn't say I had to leave!"

"Mama forgot," Janessa said shortly. "Behave yourself, or I'll find Dad." She bundled Sally into the carriage while Sally protested that she had never been so humiliated.

"You just want to keep me a baby all my life!"

"You're lucky you got to go at all. You didn't see Milly Hoffman here. And Milly's mother looked quite shocked to see you," Janessa said grimly.

"It's not fair!"

"Give over, Miss Sally," the coachman said. He

had worked for the Holts long enough to feel privileged. "You ain't no ways old enough." He whipped up the team while Sally pounded the upholstery in fury.

Janessa went back inside. Her head was aching. When she went to hang her own wrap back up, she found Alexandra in the cloakroom. Alexandra jumped.

"I sent Sally home," Janessa said.

"Oh! Oh, goodness, I forgot all about her, what with . . . everything." Alexandra waved a hand vaguely, and her voice trailed off. "Thank you." She hurried out of the cloakroom.

Janessa went back to the supper room to make her apologies to Crampton Cullen, her own dinner partner. Puzzled, she watched Alexandra as she ate. It wasn't like Alex to neglect Sally. If Alexandra didn't watch out, Sally was going to grow up to be a monster. And why wasn't Toby paying any attention? Janessa found herself reluctant to get involved. She had already made enough trouble. But something was wrong.

XVI

"It was a huge success. I'd like to see anyone top that." May Prilliman waved the society page from the *Washington Post. The Post* had sent an artist as well as its most prominent society columnist, and a drawing of the Ebbitt House ballroom, afloat with exotic dancing figures, graced the page. That proved it.

"The prawns were cold."

"Not till the end. Someone allowed the chafing dish to go out."

"Everyone who's anyone was there. Just everyone."

Janessa lounged in Lucinda Hoffman's Turkish corner and listened to the committee rehash the ball. It was pleasant to curl up on the overstuffed sofa and listen to women with nothing more to worry about than the prawns' being cold. She sipped her coffee and ate another macaroon while the chatter went on around her.

"I'm utterly exhausted, though." Rosanna Lucas put her feet up on a fat ottoman and balanced her coffee cup in her lap.

"Now, girls, we can't slack off. We have Christmas to think of." May set down the Post. "And there's certainly plenty to do."

"We have to have something no one's done. I refuse to make those silly angels again."

"What about candy in sea-grass baskets?"

Janessa found her eyes closing as the women argued about whether or not sea-grass baskets had been done.

Verity Blanchard, who wore a practically un-adorned shirtwaist and a hairdo that was severe by Washington standards, asked timidly if the committee mightn't just take up a subscription to pay for distributing Christmas baskets, thereby alleviating the need to sell anyone anything.

Oh, noooo, said the ladies. That wasn't how it

347

was done. Rosanna Lucas lifted an eyebrow at Lucinda Hoffman. Really, her expression said, Verity was such a country girl.

"Verity, why don't you just scribble out a plan for it, and we'll think about it?" Lucinda suggested. "Rosanna, you and May and Alex come and help me fetch our books from last Christmas." The other three jumped up. "Verity can keep Mrs. Lawrence company."

Mrs. Lawrence was falling asleep. Verity began to make dutiful notes on her pad. She was totting up columns of figures when Janessa forced herself to open her eyes.

"Oh, dear," Janessa murmured, stifling a yawn. "Please forgive me."

Verity smiled at her. "It must be tedious for you to listen to all of this."

"Not at all," Janessa said, aware that she had behaved very much as if it were. "This sofa is just much too comfortable. And it was a very late night last night. Perhaps you could tell me where Mrs. Hoffman's bathroom is."

"Of course. Straight through the parlor, and it's the door on the right."

Janessa wove her way through the elegant clutter of Lucinda's parlor and found two doors on the right. They looked identical, so she tried the first and found instead a workroom with a sewing machine and filing cabinets. Lucinda, Alex, May, and Rosanna sat around the sewing table, and their heads were bent over a cloisonné box of white powder.

"Janessa!" Alex's hand jerked convulsively, and the box went flying.

"Oh, dear," Lucinda said, watching the white powder drift to the floor.

May giggled, while Rosanna explained, "We're just having some of Lucinda's marvelous tonic. Such an exhausting time last night."

Alex made frantic shushing motions with her hands.

"You're such a sleepyhead this morning," Lucinda said, smiling hospitably at Janessa. "Perhaps you'd like to try some?"

"No, thank you," Janessa said. She stared at Alex, but Alex had closed her eyes. "I was just looking for the bathroom. But please, let me help you clean it up."

"That's not necessary," Alex told her, but Janessa bent and lifted the box onto the table. In so doing, she purposely got some of the powder on her fingertips.

"Really, we'll sweep up," Lucinda said. "I'll sweep up. Verity will be waiting for us. Why don't you girls keep her company?" She gave a silvery laugh. "Verity's such a stick-in-the-mud."

Janessa slipped into the bathroom—behind the other door—as the ladies bustled out. She rubbed the pinch of powder she had abstracted onto her gums. It tasted dreadful and made her gums numb. She knew exactly what it was.

After Janessa returned to the group, conversation was forced. Alex looked like a penned deer. They stayed only long enough to vote against

Verity's plan on the unarguable grounds that it was too simple; one had to do something, something elegant, if one wanted any recognition for one's efforts. If charities didn't sell pretty things, who would be interested in them?

"We all sell them to one another, anyway," Alex murmured.

The minute the carriage pulled up under the portico back at the Holts' house, Alex jumped from it with an incomprehensible excuse and fled upstairs. Janessa, fire in her eyes, followed her stepmother.

As Janessa appeared in the doorway, Alex whirled around from her dressing table and slammed the top drawer closed.

Janessa advanced on her. "Give me that."

"Give you what?" Alexandra leaned against the drawer.

"I think you've lost your mind." Janessa pushed her out of the way and snatched open the drawer.

"Those are my private things!"

Janessa pulled out the box from Dr. Nagel. "Good God, Alex! How long have you been using this?"

"That's none of your business. And it's just a tonic."

Janessa marched over to the window, forced up the sash, and emptied the box.

"No!"

Janessa threw the box across the room. "Tonic, my foot!" she screamed at Alexandra. "That's cocaine! We use it for an anesthetic. It's not some harmless curative! Who's this Dr. Nagel?"

Alexandra grabbed the bedpost and took a deep, steadying breath. She stood tall, dignified. "It doesn't do any harm." She forced an airy note into her voice. "And when did you get so prissy, miss? You weren't raised that way."

Janessa exploded. "Is this what you do at your little soirées? Take drugs? Does Dad know?"

Alexandra stamped her foot. "It's not a drug! How dare you accuse me of—of I can stop anytime I want to!"

Janessa folded her arms. "Can you, Alex? You don't look like it to me. Would you and your friends like to come with me and call on some other women who use cocaine? The women who sell their bodies on street corners? They can quit any time they want to, too, but they never want to badly enough. Sometimes they die of heart failure. Sometimes they have seven-month babies who die of convulsions. Tell that to your society friends!"

"How dare you!" Alex's face was flushed, two bright crimson spots burning on her cheeks. "How dare you! Barging into my room and behaving like a self-righteous prig! What I do is none of your business! You've embarrassed this family half to death, and now you think you can pry into my life?"

"Your life! This is my family! What about Sally? Running around at that ball till all hours because you were so full of your—tonic that you forgot about her. Look at her, Alex! She's a monster. She'll be totally uncontrollable in another year if you don't pay attention to her."

Janessa was shouting, and Alex was shouting back. Each vaguely realized that the servants would hear them, but both women were too far gone in their anger to care.

"Sally's spoiled, with nothing on her mind but indulging herself!" Janessa yelled. "And you're no better—taking drugs and planning parties to get your name in the newspaper."

"Who's indulging herself?" Alex screamed back. "You've made us all a scandal, getting yourself talked about and preachers preaching sermons about you."

"At least I have the courage of my convictions. And you think I'm right anyway—you said so. Am I supposed to ignore people in need?"

"I don't care what you do, as long as you leave me alone!" Alex began to cry. "You don't know anything about it. You don't care who you hurt as long as you can tell yourself how right you are!"

"I asked you before—does Dad know about this? Does he know why this whole family's falling apart?"

"I doubt he even cares," Alex spat back. "Of course it's all my fault. It couldn't possibly be your father's. You don't even love me!" Alex flung herself, wailing, across the bed.

Janessa rubbed her aching head. "I love you when you're rational. I love you enough not to tell Dad if you promise to tell him."

"I don't want to tell him," Alexandra said, her face muffled in the pillow. "I'll stop. I promise. Now just go away and leave me alone."

"You bet your boots you'll stop," Janessa said. "Because I'm going to see to it."

Alexandra sat up again, eyes blazing, her auburn hair coming out of its pins. "I said get out of my room!"

Toby was home for dinner, but that was because Janessa had telephoned him and asked him to be there.

Janessa, looking grim and hard, took her place at the table with nothing more than a lift of her eyebrows at Toby.

He raised his shoulders at her in an unspoken query. "I ought to be at the office," he muttered.

Alexandra's eyes and nose were red, and she appeared to be coming down with a cold. She looked as if she devoutly wished her husband were at work.

Sally, still sulking over being packed home from the ball, pointedly didn't speak to her sister. It was possibly the most unpleasant family dinner they had had in years.

"Well, Pudd'n, what did you do today?" Toby, attempting joviality, inquired of Sally. Under lowered brows, he shot another glance at Janessa, silently asking why the hell she had dragged him home.

"I went home after school with Mary Margaret Ethridge," Sally answered. "School was horrid, but Mary Margaret was green when she found out I went to the Mikado's Ball." She gave Janessa a dark look.

"Am I to assume that Mary Margaret Ethridge is now speaking to you despite my deplorable politics?" Toby asked.

"I suppose," Sally allowed. "But it's still embarrassing. Anyway, everything is horrid. We wanted to go skating tomorrow, and they've closed the park for some kind of stupid repairs. Now we don't have anything to do." She poked fretfully at her fish. "I hate fish."

Alexandra, looking past Janessa, made an effort to focus her attention on Sally. "Isn't there another rink across town, dear? Couldn't you and Mary Margaret go there? Juanita would take you."

"Motherrrr. Nobody goes there."

"Why not? I've heard it's a perfectly nice rink."

"We don't go there," Sally said flatly. "The people who go there wear funny clothes."

"Sally . . ." Toby looked at her closely. He obviously did not like what he was hearing.

"Some of them have accents," Sally continued. "And they don't wear nice things. We don't like them."

"Sally! That is not—" Toby broke off.

Alexandra had pushed her chair back, a tic working beside her mouth and tears starting to flow. She put her hands to her face, and then she stumbled out of the chair and fled. They heard her footsteps running up the stairs and the bedroom door slamming.

Toby looked at Janessa blankly and then at Sally. "Sally," he said, "that is deplorable. People are not to be judged by their clothes or accents. You may take your dinner into the kitchen and finish it there."

Sally's face crumpled. "I didn't do anything!" she wailed.

"All the same, I want you to eat in the kitchen," Toby said carefully. "I need to talk to your sister."

"I hate you!" Sally howled. "I hate everything about this stupid family, and I hate that skating rink!" She picked up her plate and stomped out with it.

Toby looked down the table at Janessa. "What in the hell is going on?"

Janessa listened to the sobs emanating from the kitchen and Juanita's worried voice. "Don't you think you were a little hard on her?" Janessa asked. "She didn't—"

"Probably," Toby admitted. "But I'll worry about her later. I'm more concerned about Alex at the moment. Tell me why you called me to come home from the office."

Janessa looked at her plate. She felt rather like the Reverend Windrow Walker. "Have you noticed anything that's happened in the last year?" she inquired, wondering how he could have been so blind. "You might at least have noticed Sally. She's turning into a vapid little snob, like Mary Margaret Ethridge, I daresay. And you and Alexandra haven't done spit about it."

355

"I'm sure Alex can take her in hand," Toby said, disconcerted.

"Alex is upstairs having a nervous breakdown or something very close to it," Janessa said flatly. "Alex is upstairs trying to scrabble up a few grains of the cocaine I threw out the window this afternoon."

"What?"

"Cocaine. A derivative of the coca leaf." Janessa slipped into her medical lecture voice. "A stimulant and also an excellent local anesthetic. An unfortunate ingredient in many patent medicines. Alexandra's been using it straight."

Toby goggled at her.

"Maybe I ought to think about why she's felt the need for it," Janessa said. She had had the afternoon for her self-righteousness to fade. Now she felt rotten. "I'm afraid I didn't consider that. I just chewed her out for it. I'm going upstairs and try to make amends."

She left him, still openmouthed, at the table and went to tap on Alexandra's door.

"Go away," Alexandra said in a miserable, muffled voice.

Janessa went in anyway. Alexandra was facedown on the bed, sobbing into the pillows. Janessa sat down beside her and laid a hand on her shoulder. Alexandra flinched. "Alex," she said softly, "I'm sorry. I wasn't very kind."

"You were hateful," Alexandra said into the pillow. "But you were right about Sally. I've been an awful mother." She shook convulsively, and

Janessa stroked her back, trying to still the twitching muscles. "It's this awful city, Janessa. No one cares about anything but surface things here. The men are all busy running the world, and the women don't have anything for themselves. I don't really talk to your father for weeks on end."

"Alex, couldn't you have brought your horses out here? You aren't cut out for this life."

"My horses!" Alex wailed. "I want my horses. But there's no place here for them. They need land, and we can't afford to buy a farm here or in Virginia or Maryland and keep up the Madrona, too." She spoke into the pillows, her voice barely intelligible. "Times are bad. The recession has hurt us."

"You aren't nearly as bad off as a lot of people," Janessa said severely, then wished she had kept quiet. That didn't make Alexandra's situation any better. Actually, Janessa thought wryly, a dose of being poor might do Sally some good. "If I had to spend my time at things like that committee meeting this morning, I think I'd take drugs, too," she said frankly. "You have to find something better to do."

"What?" Alex demanded. "Toby loves Washington. I can't ask him to leave." Burrowing deeper into the pillows, she put her hands over her head and laced her fingers together in her tangled hair.

"Have you talked to him about it? Alex dear, I wish you'd turn over and look at me."

"No."

"Alex, you're craving the drug. You're going to feel like this for a while, until your body gives it up."

"I need some," Alex said, weeping. "Just a little."

"Do you really want that?"

"No, but I don't want to feel this way, either."

"Alex, sit up."

"I don't want to. You're ashamed of me."

"I'm not," Janessa soothed. "I'm sorry I was so mean. But I'm going to make an appointment for you with Brice Amos. You're not even eating."

Panic filled her voice. "No! I don't want to see him! I don't want to tell him!"

"Well . . ." Janessa thought about her conversation with Brice at the ball and reconsidered. Brice wouldn't be kind. "Well, if you won't see Brice, then you'll have to see me."

Alexandra sat up at that. Her eyes flashed with a semblance of their old spirit. "Janessa, I am not going to have my own stepdaughter treating me like some drunk who can't be trusted to stay out of the whiskey bottle." Her reddened face was swollen and slick with tears, but for a moment she even sounded more like her old self.

"And who helped to deliver your babies?" Janessa asked.

"I wasn't ashamed of having babies," Alexandra muttered.

Janessa looked down at her hands, doctor's hands, scrubbed red with carbolic acid, nails neatly trimmed. How was she supposed to be a doctor and a daughter at the same time? "You'll do better if you decide you're not going to be ashamed of this, either," she said slowly. "I couldn't count up the times I've done something stupid. If I had to be ashamed of them, too, I'd never get anything done."

"I don't know how I'm going to do it," Alexandra whispered. "I'm scared."

Janessa looked up. "Can Dad come in?" She could see his shadow in the hall, waiting.

"You didn't tell him!" Alexandra looked horror-stricken.

"I thought it would be easier on you if I did," Janessa admitted, "so you wouldn't have to. I didn't tell Sally," she added hastily as she saw them both at the door.

Sally's face was as red as her mother's, and she clung to Toby's hand. She looked frightened and very, very young. She sniffled audibly. Alexandra, half-scared, half-defiant, stared at Toby.

He came and, tugging Sally with him, sat on the bed. Janessa got up to make room for them.

"I don't know what I did," Sally mumbled, bewildered.

Alex made a visible effort to compose herself. "You didn't do anything. I'll talk to you later about the way you and Mary Margaret feel about that skating rink. But my being so upset didn't really have to do with you."

"Dad already talked to me," Sally said morosely.

"Well, then." Alexandra tried to put a bright note in her voice. She looked warily at Toby.

Toby reached out an arm and pulled her to him hard. He looked nearly as stricken as she did. Janessa faded into a corner, wondering if she should stay or leave. After having stirred things up, she felt the outsider again. She wished Charley were there. Just two more weeks . . .

Toby was holding Alexandra tightly, rocking her, cradling her, and Alex was sobbing into his shoulder. Blindly Alex reached out and pulled Sally toward them, too.

"I'm going to resign from the foundation," he said into her hair.

Alexandra jerked back. "You can't do that!"

"Why not?" he asked heavily. "I've been beating my head against a wall anyway. If we're going to get into a war, we'll do it. I no longer have the luxury of flattering myself that my presence in Washington is going to make an iota of difference."

"But you haven't thought it out!"

"I thought about it all the way up the stairs," Toby said. "That was all it took."

"I couldn't bear it if you left Washington for my sake."

"Why not? I stayed for your sake. I thought you liked it here."

"I did like it here," Alex said mournfully. "At first. But it got . . ."

"I know." He kissed her disheveled hair.

"And you wanted to stay," Alex said accusingly.

"I did. But you're more important to me, and I'd appreciate it if you wouldn't feel guilty about that. That's the way it's supposed to be. Sally's more important to me, too. We're going back to the Madrona. We're going to have a life where you get up in the morning and plant a garden or train a horse."

Sally glowered but didn't say anything. At the moment she appeared frightened enough to acquiesce.

Alex looked from one to the other of them. She buried her face in Toby's coat again and cried. "Thank you! Oh, Toby, thank you!"

Toby seemed startled at the intensity of her gratitude. As Alex continued to cling to him, Janessa slipped out of the room.

It took two weeks to shut the house down. Alexandra stayed in bed all the first day, alternating between sleeping and crying. But the next day she got up, teeth clenched, and helped pack. At the end of the two weeks, Janessa put them on the train, promised to see that everything was properly shipped, and hugged Alex one last time. Alex looked brittle, but she was eating again. Janessa thought she had gained a little weight. Janessa and Toby had been very careful to keep an eye on her all week and pretend that they weren't; but Janessa thought Alex realized it anyway. One evening, while Janessa watched grimly, Alex had defiantly drunk three shots of whiskey because she couldn't sleep; but other than that one lapse, Alex had toughed it out. Soon, with something to do, with a life with some substance to it, Alex would be all right. Janessa felt confident about that.

Sally's resignation hadn't lasted as long. "I suppose I can find something to do in the sticks," she said with martyred disgust as a porter held the car door for her.

Janessa chuckled. Sally needed the Madrona as desperately as Alex did. The "sticks" would improve Sally no end. Janessa waited until the train was out of sight, then went to see about arranging for the freight.

With everything properly dispatched, she took a hack back to the house. She assumed that Kathleen had already eaten with the twins, put them to bed, and closed herself in her room. Janessa was prepared for a solitary dinner under depressing circumstances—what little furniture the house still contained was draped in sheets. Juanita had gone home with the family; the Washington servants had been paid off with a bonus that would more than carry them until they found other places.

Her bleak mood did not last long. She found Charley in the driveway, paying off his own cabbie. He broke into a smile when he saw her, and she hurled herself into his arms.

"I'm so glad to see you! What on earth are you doing here?"

"We docked a day earlier than we expected. I heard from Mike that you'd taken it on the lam down here, and I thought you might want some moral supportor immoral support." He nuzzled her neck and ears, knocking her hat askew. "Lord, I missed you."

Janessa would have snuggled closer if she hadn't already been plastered to him. "I missed you, too," she breathed. "It's been awful. I have about two hours' worth of grisly things to tell you, but first come inside and see the twins."

"By all means." Charley looked slightly unnerved. "I can't go anywhere if you don't let go of me. Not that I want you to, you understand, but it might be more private in the house."

Janessa backed off about half an inch. "I can't bear to let go of you. It really has been awful. I think things are all right now, but—"

"I knew something was up when I saw the house," Charley said. "Let's go inside."

She went with him gratefully, holding his hand, staring up at his face, just enjoying looking at him, the curve of his neck and the endearing way his ears stuck out. A world with Charley in it felt much more solid to her.

Kathleen had not put the babies to bed. He hugged them, and they shrieked with delight and clung to him in even more limpetlike fashion than Janessa had done. After Kathleen had detached them and taken them off to bed, Janessa and Charley dined by candlelight on the scullery table that was one of the few sticks of furniture left in the house. Finally they went upstairs and made love on a hideous horsehair settee, then slept on it quite blissfully, entangled in each other's arms.

The next day they left the rented house on Connecticut Avenue. The place was bare of all but the furnishings it had contained when the Holts had moved in almost nine years before.

Janessa dropped the key through the mail slot for the landlord. It made a hollow thunk on the floor inside. A hack was waiting for her under the portico. Kathleen and Charley and the babies had already settled inside it. There was nothing left to do now but go home with Charley. She couldn't even go back to the hospital until the end of the year—she had promised. But Charley was home. Thank God for Charley.

Janessa climbed in, and the hack rolled down the cobbles, trunks strapped on behind.

XVII

Portland, Oregon, October 1897

Henry Blake was courting his wife—or trying to. Cindy and he seemed to have reached an impasse, Eulalia thought, that neither one could or would break through.

Eulalia, mother to Cindy and stepmother to Henry, went from one to the other, trying to push, to shove, to fit them into place. They were unfailingly kind to her and stone-faced to each other. In between, she mothered Midge, who had been delighted to see her father arrive at the Madrona. Now the child was growing more and more frantic because no resolution had been found.

Midge had taken to spending her days in the barn, letting the ranch hands teach her to plait a lariat or watching, with a certain horrified fascination, as they castrated a colt. She played with Mai and White Elk's children—taffy-colored, almond-eyed youngsters with caps of black hair as thick and straight as a horse's mane. She wished aloud that she looked like them, and Mai laughed and predicted that Midge was going to be a beauty and that ducks shouldn't wish to be chickens. Midge peered into Mai's ivory-frame mirror and felt dissatisfied. Since Frank went away, no one had told her she was pretty.

"Here, look." Mai lifted Midge's sandy brown hair and fluffed it into a pouf over her forehead. She slipped a pair of silver eardrops shaped like bells onto Midge's ears. "That's what you will look like when you are grown. Very beautiful, very elegant. Besides, Finney Williams thinks you're pretty. He told me so."

"He did?" Midge looked startled.

"He did indeed. He was very impressed," Mai said knowledgeably.

Finney Williams was a ranch hand, aged sixteen. He was a wanderer, a thin-boned, towheaded boy who had arrived at the Madrona in the summer and said that Coot Williams, one of Toby's permanent hands, was his father. Coot had scratched his head and counted on his fingers and said, well, he supposed the boy could be. So Finney had stayed.

Midge looked in the mirror again and shook her head a little. The bells tinkled.

"You see how pretty you are?" Mai asked. She knew that Cindy Blake would hardly consider Finney Williams a suitable match for her daughter. Telling Mai that he thought Midge was pretty was probably the longest sentence he had spoken to anyone. But Midge was only twelve or thirteen, Mai thought. There was no harm in letting her feel courted. She wished wistfully that she possessed the power to fix the thing that truly troubled Midge, but Mai knew that she didn't. White Elk, who had grown up on the Madrona, said that Colonel and Mrs. Blake were too much alike; when they fought, they were like the birds that attacked themselves in the window glass every spring at mating season.

"Can I stay and help you fix supper?" Midge asked. Mai and White Elk's house fascinated her. It was full of Indian blankets and Chinese silk cushions and smelled faintly of the incense that Mai burned to her heathen gods—that was what Abby Givens, Eulalia's cook, called them. The children romped on the buffalo-hide rug, speaking English and Chinese alternately. And Midge never knew what interesting foodstuffs she might find in the kitchen.

"If it's all right with your mother."

"Gran won't mind," Midge said, and Mai didn't remind her that she had said her mother,

366

not her grandmother. Cindy would second any permission that Eulalia gave. Cindy's concentration was given almost entirely now to bending her husband to her will and letting him know that she would not be bent to his. Secure in the knowledge that Midge would come to no harm on the Madrona, Cindy let her roam as she would. Mai let Midge keep the eardrops on.

The woman and girl went into the kitchen. "I am making spring rolls," Mai said. "Will you chop cabbage?"

Midge took the small kitchen cleaver and began to sliver the cabbage as finely as thread. On the table was half a boiled chicken to be picked apart and a stack of spring-roll wrappers, paper-thin squares of dough kept moist under a damp cloth.

The kitchen smelled of strange spices and more incense from the brass burner in the kitchen god's niche. Mai explained that every New Year's Day he went up to heaven to tell the jade emperor how his family was doing and if they were paying proper respect to their ancestors. There were other wonderful things in the kitchen: dried turtles and mushrooms and glass noodles that Mai bought in Portland's Chinatown.

When she married White Elk, who was used to American food, she had learned to cook it for him. But gradually she had won him over to more exotic fare—at least some of the time. They had a ham at Easter and a turkey at Thanksgiving and a goose at Christmas, and rare roasted beef as often as Mai could stand to look at it. But White

Elk liked spring rolls very much. Midge did, too—and dumplings and egg-flower soup and other exotic dishes, the contents of which the girl was never quite sure. The foreman's cottage was like the door into a whole different world, in which she could live and pretend sometimes that she belonged, eldest sister to Mai's children. Sometimes, guiltily, she pretended for a moment that Mai and White Elk were her parents, lovingly united.

White Elk came in and hung his big peaked Stetson on the peg by the kitchen door. He sniffed the air. Mai was heating a pot of oil to fry the spring rolls. "I may have to take mine to the barn," he said. "That red mare's getting ready to foal." He ruffled Midge's hair. "Hello, assistant cook."

"Jezebel?" Mai asked. The red mare, one of Alexandra's show beasts, had a long, fancy show name, but the ranch hands knew her as Jezebel because of her attitude.

"Coot says it's too early. But he doesn't know what he's talking about." White Elk snagged a piece of cooked chicken off the carcass, and Mai slapped his hand away.

"And how do you know?"

"She bit me," White Elk explained, munching. He grinned. "Coot doesn't understand a refined lady's temperament." The horses that the Madrona bred and sold were mostly cow ponies and cavalry remounts. Alexandra's show horses were an unusual sideline. Without Alexandra there to train them, their breeding program had been nearly stopped; but the red mare had taken matters under her own control. No one knew what sort of foal she was about to produce, because no one knew how she had gotten pregnant in the first place. She had simply developed a sly look and started getting bigger.

Midge began to shred the chicken. She resisted the temptation to munch on it, too, and they finished preparing the spring rolls. Mai dropped them one by one into the boiling oil while Midge shooed the children away from the pot. As soon as the rolls were ready, White Elk wrapped five in a napkin and went back to the barn. Midge ate hers, then headed reluctantly home, across the yard. The big house loomed homey and inviting in the quickly darkening dusk—brick and clapboard walls punctuated by the saffron glow of lit windows, white gingerbread under a rising moon—but Midge walked slowly, her feet dragging. The happy family of her childhood would not be inside. Instead, her father and mother would be sitting on opposite sides of the parlor fire, the emotional chill between them nearly stifling the flames. And her grandmother would be unhappily serving as a buffer to keep them civil.

Midge let herself in through the kitchen door, where Abby was washing dishes, and walked to the front hall, where she gathered her schoolbooks. She took them into the parlor and curled up in front of the fire while Henry and Cindy glared at each other over her head. A cat was asleep on the hearth, and Midge, stroking its hot fur, elicited a drowsy purr. She opened her history book and stared at Abraham Lincoln. She had always thought that he looked nice—rough and craggy.

Midge liked the Portland school, liked it much better than the exclusive girls' school she had been sent to in Washington. There were all kinds of interesting people in the Portland school: farmers' children and bankers' children, and the children of the cannery and sawmill workers downtown. It would be nice to live there always, to grow up on the Madrona—if only her parents could do it, too. But her father was going to have to go back to Washington; he'd said so.

"Well, Midge." Henry looked at her open book. "You're studying Mr. Lincoln, I see. Aren't you a bit late tonight starting your homework?"

"I'm really finished," Midge said. "This is for next week. I just wanted to read some more." Midge never had trouble with her schoolwork. She was always ahead in her classes. "We're doing the Civil War. It's strange to read about an actual war that your family was in." There had been no wars, not for America, since then. Midge had never known what it was like.

"It's much more pleasant at thirty years' distance," Cindy said. "I remember being scared to death that your uncle Toby would be killed."

"We were all on the right side, weren't we?" Midge asked.

Eulalia, who had been born in South Carolina, made a noise of amusement. "The war wasn't the same for us way out here as it was for the people farther east. We had to worry about our men—Toby and Grandpa Lee and your grandfather Whip—but no troops fought on our fields or burned down our houses."

"Are we going to fight the Spanish?" Midge asked. Somehow reading about the Civil War made the possibility of that seem more real.

"Probably," Henry said. He glanced at Cindy and away again. His difference with Toby over that subject was another bone of contention.

Midge took note and changed the subject. "White Elk says Jezebel is going to foal tonight," she announced.

Henry stood up. "I believe I'll just stroll out to the barn and see how she's doing."

Midge sighed. Her attempt to lessen tension had failed. She picked up her books. "I'm tired, Mama. I think I'll just go to bed."

Cindy and Eulalia looked after them in silence. Finally, Eulalia said, "Dear, you are making that child very unhappy."

"I know," Cindy said, miserable. "But I don't know what to do about it. Bringing her out here was the best thing I could think of to do."

"I thought you came here trying to track Frank," Eulalia said.

"Oh, Mother, I don't know. I think I just came home to hide."

Eulalia picked up her knitting from the basket by her chair and moved the needles slowly. Her fingers were growing arthritic. "Dear, it breaks my heart to see you and Henry like this. You know he loves you, or he wouldn't be here."

"I'm not sure that matters anymore," Cindy said. "We've been married a long time. Love . . . wears off, maybe."

"After what you went through to marry him in the first place? You've been in love with Henry since you were children."

"It didn't make much difference, though, did it? He married someone else."

"That's water under the bridge, dear," Eulalia said. The needles clicked a few more times. "I was bitterly angry at him over that, but I've always felt that that woman trapped him."

"Maybe he trapped himself. Maybe that's what Henry does. Just like he's done over Frank."

"Would it bring Frank home if Henry changed his mind?" Eulalia asked softly.

"No," Cindy said. "That's why I can't forgive him."

"Maybe if you forgave him, he'd change his mind."

"It's too late for it to matter," Cindy said tiredly.

Eulalia looked at her middle-aged daughter's set lips and the crow's-feet etched around her eyes. "Are you going to divorce him?"

"Certainly not!" Cindy said. "Mother, how can you even suggest such a thing? I have Midge to think of."

"We've never had a divorce in the family," Eulalia said. "I don't approve of it, but people do do it nowadays."

"Well, I won't," Cindy said, aware that she had only the previous year supported a friend through a divorce, with every sympathy for her. Her husband had had a mistress, which seemed to Cindy a lesser matter than Henry's sins. Of course a court wouldn't think so. Browbeating your wife and children isn't grounds. "I haven't anything to charge him with."

"I don't know whether or not to be relieved," Eulalia murmured.

"Mother, don't tell me you're taking his side!"

"No, dear, I think he's wrong. But what I think makes no difference; you're the one who married him. I remember thinking when Henry came back that it was a good thing that Reed was dead. You never loved Reed the way you did Henry."

"I loved Reed enough," Cindy said rebelliously. "I might have been better off if he hadn't died. Then I well, people ought to watch out what they wish for. They're liable to get it."

"You certainly wanted Henry," Eulalia remarked.

Cindy's eyes filled with tears. "I want Henry the way he used to be. We were so—joyful. I don't know what happened to us."

Eulalia sighed. "I don't, either." She stuffed her knitting back in its basket, then pulled the lid down firmly to protect her efforts from the cat. "Dear, I'm going to bed, too. I can't stand any more of this."

"I'm sorry, Mother," Cindy whispered.

"So am I," Eulalia said. "I suppose it will all work out some way."

Alone in the parlor, Cindy paced the room until the cat, annoyed by her restlessness, got up and left, too. Was this what she was going to do with the rest of her life? Live on the Madrona with her mother? Portland was a big city now. She could close her gallery in Washington and open one there. Midge and she could travel. That would be broadening for the child. And Cindy could start drawing again. She hadn't done any work of her own since Frank left. She could set up a studio on the ranch, in one of the outbuildings. Some semblance of a life began to take shape in her thoughts, but she couldn't quite make it coalesce around the gaping holes left by Frank and Henry.

Cindy paced to the window. In the distance someone hurried by with a lantern. She supposed the red mare was foaling after all. She picked up Eulalia's discarded shawl, wrapped it around her shoulders, and went out on the porch. Leaves scudded by on a quick wind. It was almost Halloween.

"Cindy."

She turned to find Henry sitting and smoking a cigar in an old wicker chair on the porch, his feet on the railing. "Will you come and talk to me?"

"I was just thinking," Cindy said, "about the time you and I put the Givenses' goat in the privy."

"Why on earth were you thinking about that?"

"It's nearly Halloween." She didn't join him. She leaned against her own section of the railing.

"We'll have to set a couple of the hands to watch the property, or we'll have brats knocking down the mailbox," Henry said.

"You get more stiff-necked every year." Cindy glared at him through the darkness. "Maybe you should go and steal a goat. It might liven you up."

"I'm not particularly proud of that now," Henry said. "Although you seem to be."

"I'm not totally ossified, either!" Cindy snapped. "I'm not trying to pretend I wasn't ever young."

"Is that why you're so set on defending Frank?" Henry demanded. "You want to be an adolescent again? You're a wife and mother."

"That doesn't mean I have to be a martinet like you. We aren't a pair of bookends."

"I used to think we were," Henry said sadly. His anger faded into bafflement. "I want you to come home with me."

"I can't. I can't leave Frank."

"Frank isn't here!"

"He's closer to me here than in Washington. He won't ever come back to Washington unless you give him some sign that he's welcome."

"He isn't welcome," Henry said flatly, "until he accepts his responsibilities."

"He's nineteen now, Henry. He'll have changed. You won't be able to push him into your mold anymore."

"He's still my son, and he still must fulfill certain expectations."

"God give me strength, Henry. You aren't King George." Cindy smacked her fist on the porch railing. "I want my son."

"You've done everything you can to find him," Henry said.

"Then I'll stay here until he comes to me."

"What about me? I'm your husband. You know I came here to take you and Midge home with me."

Cindy stared at him, trying to see through the darkness not only of the moment but of the last years, trying to peel the years from Henry's face, trying to find the man who had been her heart's love. Wasn't he in there somewhere?

"I can't go back with you, Henry, not like this." Where have you gone? Was love just youth and passion? Wasn't it also enduring companionship? How could someone change so drastically? Had he metamorphosed the night when he fought with Frank? Or had he been changing all those years, and she had been too blind or too unwilling to see it?

"What about Midge?" Henry demanded.

"Midge likes it here," Cindy said. "She likes it better than in Washington."

"She's my daughter!"

"And what happens when she grows up and you don't like her politics or her husband, or the way she does her hair? How will you treat her then? Or doesn't a daughter matter as much as a son?"

Henry sat up, furious, and flung his cigar over the railing.

"You'll start a fire," Cindy said. She went down the porch steps to stamp out the cigar.

"Midge is everything to me!" Henry shouted. "She's everything I hoped her mother would be!"

"Oh, wonderful," Cindy said. "She can probably hear you, you know. That ought to make her feel just wonderful."

"I have every hope for Midge," Henry said, lowering his voice with difficulty. "I'm not going to allow you to separate me from her."

"Maybe that's just what I ought to do," Cindy threatened. "Or you'll keep her in a tighter box than you tried to keep Frank."

"Frank brought this on himself."

Cindy came back up the steps. She held the cigar between thumb and forefinger and dropped it disdainfully into the spittoon by the railing. "It may have escaped your attention," she said icily, "that both of Toby's sons went their own way, against their father's wishes, and that he now enjoys an excellent relationship with each of them. Because he had enough sense to see he had to let them find their own way."

"Don't quote Toby at me," Henry said. "I thought his behavior was very ill-advised."

"Yes—he was so ill-advised that his sons still speak to him."

"Neither one is here running the Madrona where he ought to be."

"Ought to be? Don't you ever get tired of thinking you're right?"

"Not when I am right," Henry said simply.

"Then I can't see any point in talking to you
at all." Cindy started for the door.

Henry got up out of his chair and caught her
by the wrist.

"Let me go!"

"Not until we settle this."

"It's settled, Henry! Let me go!" She twisted
her arm, but he held on.

The tendons stood out on the back of his hand.
"I've given up work I ought to be doing," he said,
breathing hard. "Important government work.
And you've kept me here for weeks."

"I haven't kept you," Cindy retorted. "I told
you to go away."

"I'm not leaving without you. You're coming
home with me." He jerked at her wrist, trying to
pull her toward him.

Cindy stared into his face. "Why, Henry? Why
do you want me?"

"You're my wife."

Cindy looked away from him at that, out at the
yard and the drive with its twin rows of Madrona
trees. They looked depressing and unpleasant in
the late fall. The leaves made a dry, sad whisper.

"I'm your wife," she muttered sadly. "Is that
all?"

"You want me to say I love you?" Henry demanded. "Is that it? All right, I love you."

"Then let go of my wrist."

"No. I love you, but I don't like you very much just now—not the way you've been behaving. And I don't think anyone else would, either."

"You always know what everyone else is going to think or ought to think. Well, I don't like you!" Cindy jerked on her wrist again, and his fingers opened.

"I don't know what's the matter with you lately. You've become totally unstable. I think you ought to consult a doctor. Even your mother thinks you're out of control."

"She never said any such thing!" Cindy said, outraged.

"She said it to me," Henry said blandly. "She said she thinks you're overwrought."

"Of course I'm overwrought! That's not the same thing."

"You're at an age when women get hysterical. I've been reading books about it, trying to understand you."

"How dare you!" Cindy glared at him, resisting the sudden overwhelming urge to hit him. She balled her hands into fists.

"I think you need help," Henry said. "I want you to come back to Washington with me and see a specialist."

"I wouldn't go to a dogfight with you!" Cindy shrieked. "You want me to be crazy so you can be right. You always have to be right!" She turned on her heels and stopped abruptly when she saw White Elk on the path.

White Elk looked as if he had been about to

retreat. But now that she had seen him, he stopped, too. He took off his hat and scratched his head dubiously. "I didn't mean to intrude, but I thought—I thought you might like to see something funny in the barn. But, uh, well, maybe another time."

"On the contrary," Cindy said sweetly. "I should love to see something funny right now." She swept down the steps and gave White Elk her arm—she was wearing good slippers, not the best for traction. She heard the oyster shells crunch on the path behind them, out of cadence with their footsteps, so she knew that Henry was following. Fine. Henry could do what he pleased.

"Did the red mare have her foal?" she asked, voice conversational and carefree—too carefree. She sounded hysterical to herself now. Damn Henry.

White Elk chuckled. "Yep."

When he didn't explain, Cindy glanced up at his face, sharp angled and amused in the moonlight. He was saving the joke, whatever it was. She had known White Elk since he was a child, had helped to raise him. He seemed more familiar to her now than Henry.

There were lanterns lit in the red mare's barn, and the light spilled through the open door. Alexandra's thoroughbreds had their own barn, separate from the "riffraff's," on a small hill. Several of them poked their noses over loose-box doors to snort at Cindy. Coot, Finney Williams, and Howie Janks, another longtime hand, were gathered around the red mare's box, shaking their heads and grinning.

"Dangedest thing I ever seed," Howie said.

"Females." Coot pushed his hat onto the back of his head. "There just ain't no telling."

White Elk led Cindy to the loose-box door and stood aside, chortling, waiting for her reaction.

Jezebel lay smugly in fresh straw, licking her foal. Its coat, the same copper-penny color as its dam's, was still wet, and the foal rested atop a tangle of spidery legs. From the top of its head protruded a pair of ears like semaphores.

"Oh, my Lord, it's a mule!" Cindy burst into laughter.

"And we ain't even got a jack on the place!" Coot slapped his thigh with his hat.

Cindy held her sides, laughing. The red mare looked at her haughtily. Cindy laughed harder, letting the laughter wash through her, over her.

"We figure it must have been Givenses' donkey," White Elk said. "But how she did it—"

"She knows," Howie said. "Look at her. Lord God, I never saw anything so funny. I ain't gonna be the one to tell Miz Holt, though."

"You suppose Givens is gonna want a stud fee?" Coot asked, and they howled and doubled over with laughter.

Cindy, her sides shaking, held on to the loose-box door. She heard Henry come in, but she didn't care.

Henry stood a little behind them, away from the spluttering ranch hands.

"This has to be the best-pedigreed mule in the history of Portland," White Elk said, trying to draw him in to the camaraderie.

"I expect so," Henry agreed. But he didn't seem interested in the joke. He looked at his wife. "Cindy . . ." He spoke from beyond the circle, as if to pull her out.

Cindy looked at him over her shoulder. There didn't seem any point to her anger. She searched for some other feeling but couldn't find it. Whatever had been there was gone, just gone. He might have been a visitor standing beyond the light, an intruder in her home. She turned her head away from Henry without speaking.

The next morning Henry packed his bags. Midge clung to him on the porch steps while Howie Janks waited with the buggy. Eulalia kissed Henry on the cheek. "Your father has work to do now," she said, to comfort Midge. "He'll be back to see you."

Cindy watched from an upstairs window as Henry climbed heavily into the buggy. After it had rolled away, she went downstairs to try to tell Midge all the wonderful plans she had made, to help her understand that it would all work out . . . somehow.

As Cindy, Eulalia, and Midge watched, a telegraph boy on a bicycle passed the buggy in his approach to the house.

"I hope that's not for Henry," Eulalia said. "It's bound to be, and it's just missed him."

Midge brightened. "If it's for Daddy, we can send someone after him. He can come back for a while."

Cindy looked down into her daughter's hopeful face but said nothing.

The boy stopped his bicycle at the steps and tipped his cap. "Mrs. Blake?" Eulalia and Cindy each held out a hand. "Mrs. Leland Blake?"

Eulalia took it and tore it open. Telegrams never boded any good. . . . Her face brightened. "It's from Toby! Oh, Cindy, Toby and Alex are coming home!"

"To stay?"

"That's what it says!" Eulalia's eyes shone. "Midge dear, go and tell White Elk for me. We'll have a lot of getting ready to do!" She looked at Cindy as Midge trudged away. "Now we'll be a family again. They'll be here for Thanksgiving. And for Christmas! And Midge will have Sally to play with. We'll all have something to make us feel better."

"I suppose so," Cindy said dully.

Eulalia put her arms around her. "My darling girl, nothing is ever done with. Just give Henry some time. He may come around."

Cindy sighed. "I don't know if I'll want him if he does. That's the trouble."

Midge found White Elk in the barn, inspecting Jezebel's woods colt.

"Ha!" he said at the news. He smacked the red mare's flank and said to her, "Your mother's coming home, Jezebel. You'd better have a good explanation ready." Taking note of the tear trickling down Midge's cheek, White Elk closed the stall door and said, "Everybody but the ones you want, right?" he asked her.

Midge nodded silently. White Elk sat down on a tack box and pulled her onto his lap. Today she didn't seem too old for that. "Everything comes back someday. Everything's a circle, if you can hold on long enough."

"I don't think Daddy and Frank know that," Midge said sadly.

Henry climbed down from the train in Washington in a cold November downpour. Everything looked so bleak, Henry could easily believe there would never be another spring. He had had four days to think, four days to conclude that he wasn't willing to lose his daughter. How he was to manage it, he didn't know; but Cindy was not going to be allowed to steal Midge from him in revenge for Frank. He was baffled that she should want to separate herself from him, too. He was certain now that something, possibly something physical, was wrong with her, to make her behave this way.

For the first time, though, he felt desperate enough to consider compromise. Toby had always been able to exert older-sibling influence on Cindy. If making peace with Toby was what it took, ignoring Toby's wrongheaded politics and his refusal to hold Mike to account, then Henry would do it. He felt proud of his willingness to bend for his wife's sake. She had said that he always thought he was right. Well, he was willing to ignore the fact that he was right. That would prove her wrong.

He hailed a cab and gave the hackman Toby's address. He would go there first, even before he went home. They would see that he was the reasonable one by how far he was willing to compromise.

But the house on Connecticut Avenue was blank faced, its windows shuttered. Henry stared at the front door, tried the lock, then pounded on the door.

"They gone, boss." A gardener pushing a lawnmower came around the side of the house. "They gone, move out. I just here cleanin' up for the owner. Place up for rent now."

Gone?

The rain, which had let up, started to pour again in a wet sheet, soaking his hat and overcoat. "Where did they go?" he managed.

The gardener, who had already turned away, shrugged. "Back west, I hear," he called over his shoulder.

Henry's teeth clenched. They hadn't even bothered to tell him. It was plain that Toby had taken Cindy's side before even hearing the facts. They would all be together on the Madrona, united in a closed family circle that did not include him. Well, the hell with them then, he thought. The hell with them all.

He got back in the cab. They would find out

how wrong they were about Cindy. Cindy would find out how wrong she was when it all blew up in her face. He wasn't sure he could ever forgive her, but she would find out. He'd have that satisfaction.

XVIII

Dawson City, Yukon Territory, November 1897

Frank Blake woke in icy darkness and staggered out of bed, a blanket wrapped around his shoulders and over his long underwear. The dogs complained sleepily as he jostled them, feeling for his boots. His socks felt as if they would freeze solid on the floor. It was unbelievably cold outside, but he had to urinate; certain things didn't take account of the temperature. Some of the less fastidious sourdoughs just used a corner of the cabin because everything froze solid anyway; but Frank figured they'd be mighty sorry for it in the springtime.

Shivering, he stumbled to the door and fiddled the latch open. Red and green flickers of light lit the northern sky, and entranced, he stopped to watch, in spite of the cold. He didn't stop long, though. He had been cold even in bed, with four Hudson's Bay blankets, a caribou skin, and two dogs for covers. Outside, the creek had frozen. Winter had shut the Yukon down till thaw. On a clear day, he could still get around on snowshoes or a dogsled, but he didn't much want to.

Frank hadn't been to town since the Old Man Winter party. That had lasted three days by the time everyone had finally sobered up. Jake had woken severely depressed to find that he had not been the top bidder for Lulie and had proceeded to order more champagne until he passed out again. The curly-haired boy who had wanted her had disappeared with his dog team into the night. Frank had spent the next couple of days with Peggy, but she'd been too distraught about Lulie and too busy with her mountains of laundry to give him much attention.

Frank presumed that Peggy was doing fine, what with the business the townsfolk would bring her over the winter, but he missed her. It was lonely as hell out there. He inspected his make-shift thermometer; the whiskey was frozen, but the bottle of pain killer wasn't. Since it was still liquid, he took a swig and climbed back in bed, letting the fiery current of alcohol run out to his fingers and toes. It was probably eating his guts out, he thought. The dogs snuggled back up, twitching and dreaming dog dreams.

Frank dozed another three hours until the dog breakfast alarm went off. They stuck wet noses into his collarbone to tell him it was time to get up. Frank pulled on flannel-lined blue jeans, a flannel shirt, and a heavy sweater over that. He put some wood on the embers of the fire, hacked an icicle off the wall for coffee water, and a chunk of frozen caribou off the haunch that hung from the ceiling. The dogs bounded out the door, ran in circles, barking, and came back in to sit salivating by the fire. Frank had spent the days he couldn't stand to work outdoors adding a few refinements to the cabin, including making a table and chairs of green wood. The hole in the creek bank was deeper, and the pile of dirt outside his door was higher; but he still didn't know if he had any gold.

It was enough of a satisfaction for him just to survive up there; he wasn't at all sure what he would do with money if he got rich. He couldn't see himself buying champagne and diamond stickpins and parading around Dawson in a plug hat. As far as he could tell, none of the miners knew what to do with their money after they got it. The few family men among them returned home, but the rest stayed in Dawson, dribbling their newfound riches through their fingers. The saloonkeepers and land speculators got rich, and one saloon girl had done so well by the generosity of her clients, she retired to San Francisco to open her own parlor house. The man they had seen dragging a grindstone up Chilkoot Pass proved to be as perspicacious as the man with the cats. He had made a fortune sharpening picks blunted by the icy ground. Peggy was probably getting rich, too. Again, Frank thought about how much he missed her.

He flipped the steaming chunk of frozen caribou into the skillet. "You boys want to go to town?" he asked the dogs.

After they had eaten, he hitched the dogs to the sled, and they bounded happily over the frozen snow. A cloud of fresh powder boiled up like seafoam around them. It took the better part of the day just to get to Dawson, while the brief winter sun came and went. Dawson glowed magically in the distance; lantern light reflected like diamonds off the snow.

Up close the illusion dissolved into rutted streets black with smoke and mud and the slops that its denizens tipped cheerfully from any handy window. It bustled with people, and a light shone invitingly from Peggy's window. The thought of enough warm water to bathe in was nearly as enticing as Peggy herself.

When he pounded on the door she opened it and peered out, her red hair tied up in a kerchief and a work apron over her dress. "Is that you under there?" she asked.

Frank pulled off his fur hat and earmuffs, then unwound the muffler from his face. Rime sparkled in the collar of his sheepskin coat and on the back of his mittens. He whistled the dogs into the warmth of her cabin, then sighed with contentment.

Peggy smiled at him. "How'd you know I wanted you to come?"

Frank's eyes lit up. "Pure instinct. I missed you, too." He reached for her and gave her a long kiss. She was steamy warm and smelled of soap.

"I want you to take me out to see how Lulie's getting on," Peggy said as he let go of her. "I haven't heard a word from her."

"And here I thought it was me you yearned for," Frank said, aggrieved.

"Well, I do," Peggy admitted. "But I want you to take me to Lulie. I'm that worried."

Frank shucked off his coat, blew his nose loudly, in a huge red handkerchief, then spread his arms to the warmth of the stove. "You don't figure that no news is good news?"

"I do not," Peggy said.

It was a long way out to Dahl's cabin; otherwise, the man wouldn't have bothered to hire a wife for the winter. "It'll take a good two days just to get there."

"Frank Blake, I'm not even going to give you dinner, if you treat me this way."

Frank lifted his hands in surrender. "All right, all right. But the trip's going to cost some. My dogs can't pull that big a load."

"Fine," Peggy said. "I got money."

Frank turned around to warm his backside. "Don't you think it's time that you gave up trying to keep track of that noodle brain?"

"Not now," Peggy said stubbornly. "She's out there all by herself, and I don't like it. I didn't like that Dahl, either."

Frank grinned. "Just because he wouldn't be your choice, seeing as how I'm a lot handsomer—" He noted Peggy's expression and realized that this wasn't the time to tease her. "Okay, sweetie, I'll take you out there. The silly tart's been on my conscience, too, I guess."

"Don't you call her that!" Peggy said. "She's not a tart."

Frank raised his eyebrows. "If it walks like a duck, and it quacks like a duck . . . Give up, Peg. Lulie likes being a tart."

"Only because she hasn't gotten it through her head that it's dangerous," Peggy said.

"Who do you think is going to explain it to her? Dahl?"

"I hope not," Peggy said grimly.

Frank nodded. "We'll head out there tomorrow. She'd probably like some company. I expect Dahl's out at his diggings all day. Now do I get supper?"

"Chicken and dumplings," Peggy said cheerfully. "Dried apple tart."

Frank snickered.

"Pie."

He bathed behind the partition while she got the food ready. He could hear her whistling over the stove. When he came out, clean in the spare clothes he always kept at Peggy's, he saw that she had changed, too, out of her old calico and into the emerald silk. There were candles on the table. Frank blinked.

"I thought we might make it like a party," she said, lighting them.

"Sure thing." He looked around the room, paying more attention now. "You've made it real nice here." There were calico curtains on the windows now, and real glass, not old bottles, behind them. A braided rug covered the floor, and she had decorated the walls with pictures he remembered from her house in Sierra—a beribboned kitten in a basket of roses and a Hawaiian scene depicting a kneeling maiden in some type of sarong on the slopes of a volcano.

"You lugged that stuff all the way up here?" Frank asked, incredulous.

"Those have important sentimental attachment to me," Peggy said.

"Sure, honey," Frank said. She had brought the rose-flowered teacup, too. It sat proudly next to a heart-shaped candy box, atop a newly whittled shelf, on curlicued brackets.

Peggy lowered the kerosene lantern wick. Its flame glowed blue, then went out. The candles leaped up in golden circles of light. "I even got a bottle of champagne," Peggy said. "If you ain't sworn off it, after that three-day drunk."

"I've had plenty of time to recover," Frank said. He looked at her suspiciously. "How did you know I was coming?"

"I figured you'd be here sooner or later," Peggy said. "I been saving it."

Frank twisted the wire off the bottle neck, then working the cork out with his thumbs, popped it. It shot jubilantly across the room, and he filled their glasses—real champagne glasses, he noted, probably bought or borrowed from one of the saloons. Peggy was setting up housekeeping.

After they had eaten, Frank held his hand out, palm up, across the table. "Hey, Madame Blavatsky, tell my fortune."

Peggy traced the lines and calluses. "I don't think I'm up to it," she said finally. "I don't think you know what you're likely to do next."

Frank turned his hand over and took hers. He got up and came around the table. "I know what I'd like to do right now," he suggested. They could hear music faintly from the Daybreak Saloon down the street. He waltzed her around the room, holding her close. She might have awful taste in art, he thought affectionately, but she had saved a bottle of champagne especially for whenever he might show up.

In the morning Peggy hung a Closed sign on the door and locked the bathhouse and cabin with a brass key in brand-new locks. It wasn't even light yet, dawn and nightfall being relative terms in this country. Peggy and Frank rented two more dogs from a kennel. "I never heard of a livery stable for dogs," Peggy said, laughing. "Ain't this an amazing country?"

She introduced them carefully to Frank's pair. The rented dogs, old hands, took no guff from Frank's puppies. They settled in to the lead traces, and Frank's dogs bounded obligingly in their tracks. Peggy was bundled in a buffalo robe on the sled, and Frank stood behind her.

"First time I rode on a sled!" Peggy shouted back to him through the wind.

"I hope you still like it by tonight, after you've frozen your ears off!" Frank shouted back.

Peggy knew a sourdough with diggings south on Eldorado Creek, about halfway to Dahl's claim. They could stop there for the night. Everyone liked Peggy. She would be made welcome anywhere. Besides, it was no weather for sleeping in the open. Gradually, near midday, the sun came up and bled with pinkish light over the snow. The ice in the trees glowed rosily, and Peggy clapped mittened hands together. "It's beautiful!"

Frank peered over the folds of his muffler. It was beautiful, he admitted, an enchanted kingdom, stark and vicious but lovely. When the sun vanished again, a full moon lit the landscape and made it shine silver bright. The moon had been up for hours when they reached Ratty's cabin. Frank had no idea what Ratty's real name was. In the Yukon, newcomers learned early not to ask personal questions. Stiff with cold, Frank and Peggy pounded on the door until Ratty opened it. His dogs barked and hurled themselves at the visitors.

Ratty beat the dogs back with his hands, ham-like appendages that could swat a dog halfway across the room. "Get away, you dang fools!" He peered at Frank and Peggy. "Well, I be danged, Peggy! You found somebody crazy enough to bring you out here. Already told her I wouldn't do it," he informed Frank. "I don't want no truck with that Dahl. He keeps to himself." He shook his head, capped with a verminous wool hat. "Not like some folks. Dahl ain't going to like your coming to his place."

"We're just going visiting," Peggy replied. "Don't be a stinker, Ratty. Anyway, I brought you a pie."

"Well, hell." Ratty beamed at her. "If you don't come back, I reckon I can send the Mounties after you. They come through every three, four months."

Peggy and Frank set out again in the morning for the half-day run to Dahl's cabin. She was eager; he was reluctant. He wanted to stay and talk to Ratty, who had a sluice box that, he claimed, beat all other designs hands down.

"Will you come on?" Peggy asked impatiently. "You can look at that old sluice box on the way back. It won't be warm enough to use one for another six months anyhow."

Resigned, Frank climbed on the back of the sled, and they moved out again into the nearly perpetual darkness. Neither one had ever been this far out on Eldorado, but they had directions from the freight carrier who had taken Lulie's things out. "Turn east at the forked tree," Peggy said.

"Yeah, right." Frank peered at his compass. "Maybe that's it." He didn't want to scare Peggy —there wasn't much point in it now—but it wouldn't be fun if they got lost. It would kill them, probably.

They found it, though, just as the sun was making its brief showing—a log cabin chinked with mud. It appeared desolate under a stand of naked birches. Smoke rose from a tilted chimney pipe. A lean-to barn beside the cabin suggested that Dahl was prosperous enough to own a horse, but there was no other indication of human comfort.

"Lord God, that's the ugliest place I ever saw," Peggy said, staring at it.

Frank shrugged. "Looks like my place."

"Yeah, and no woman would live at your place, either," Peggy muttered. "Well, come on."

Frank, feeling a sense of foreboding, urged the dogs forward again. He would have thought Lulie would have put a plant in the window, at least. She liked things nice.

"Lulie?" Peggy called.

There was no answer.

"Lulie?"

Peggy was climbing out from under her fur robes to knock on the door when it opened. "Lulie, it's me, Peggy!"

Dahl emerged with a shotgun. He nearly filled the doorway. A wool cap was pulled down over his bronze-colored hair. The ends stuck out beneath it. "What the hell do you want?"

"I want to see Lulie," Peggy said indignantly. "I'm a friend of hers. I come visiting."

Dahl stared at her. "Get out of here."

"I want to see Lulie," Peggy said. "I come all the way from Dawson."

"Then get back to Dawson."

"Now just a minute!" Peggy said. She stuck her chin out. "We—"

"Peg," Frank warned quietly.

"This ain't a hotel," Dahl said. "Get outta here before I shoot you."

"I want to see Lulie. Lulie!" Peggy shouted.

"Shut up, Peg!" Frank turned the team around as Dahl leveled the shotgun. "Mush!"

"Frank!" Peggy swiveled around in the sled, bracing herself against the sides. "We got to stay and—"

"Like hell we do," Frank said. He shouted at the dogs again, and they lengthened their stride, bellies to the snow. They heard the crack of the shotgun behind them.

"Jesus and Mary!" Peggy cowered in the sled.

"Still want to go back?" Frank shouted. He thought they were out of range, but he didn't let the dogs slack off. Dahl probably had a rifle, too. Finally, after half a mile, he slowed them.

Peggy stuck her head up. "What about Lulie? I got to know what's happened to her."

"I don't know what we can do," Frank said. "She may be fine. And we aren't any match for that bastard. I'm not going to get in a gunfight with him."

They limped back to Ratty's, Frank blessing the fact that Dahl's cabin was only a half-day run. If they'd had to spend the night in the open . . .

"Hell, no, I ain't going back there with you," Ratty told them. "Man's within his rights. Folks don't trespass out here. I heard he don't like visitors."

"But what about Lulie?" Peggy said.

Ratty scratched his chin. "I don't know. Guess she better be glad she ain't married to him permanent."

"You could've let her come in, Bill," Lulie said. She looked up at Dahl and rubbed her arm. She would probably have welts where he had grabbed it.

"Ain't got no business out here. You took on to be my wife. My wife ain't got no time for tea parties."

"You could've let me talk to her!"

Dahl didn't answer. He just picked up his shotgun and went back outside. He took that shotgun everywhere.

Lulie sat at the table and picked with a fingernail at its grimy surface. There was no way she was ever going to get it clean, not after the way he'd let it go. She pulled her shawl around her tighter. It was cold in the cabin, but Dahl got after her if she burned too much wood. The place was depressing. Everything was covered with a layer of hardened grease and lamp smoke. The bed was just a straw mattress and a pile of blankets on the floor. How could a man who had money live like this? she wondered. The only thing in the place that looked nice was his dogs—Dahl fed the dogs better than he did her. She had tried to fix the place up, but he just stomped in with his boots covered with frozen mud, then thawed them in front of the stove. He wouldn't even let her sew curtains or fix a pretty arrangement of pine boughs for over the door. He said he didn't want her wasting her time.

Lulie massaged her smarting arm again, then rubbed her hands across her eyes. When Peggy had driven up, he had grabbed Lulie hard by her arm, till she felt like his fingers were going to poke right through, and told her to sit down and keep her mouth shut. She wished now that she hadn't, but she had to admit that he scared her a little. He didn't think anything of shoving her around if he didn't like how dinner tasted, and he was big and heavy, and sex was painful. Maybe Peg had been right. Maybe she shouldn't have done it. But now she had seven thousand dollars in the lining of her trunk. For reassurance Lulie stroked the top of the trunk. She reckoned she would just have to stick it out.

Lulie got up and put a pot of water on the stove to make stew for supper, then took a bucket of feed out to the shed for the horse. Dahl had gone off hunting with the sled. Maybe he'd be gone overnight. Sometimes he was.

She pushed the shed door open and poured the grain into the feed box. The horse was a wiry little mustang, winter shaggy. Lulie rubbed its withers while it ate. She wasn't allowed to pet the sled dogs; Dahl didn't want them to get spoiled.

He came home that night after all. Lulie had supper ready—she knew she'd better, just in case. But he was empty-handed and in a bad mood.

"Well, cheer up. You'll get something next time

out," Lulie said brightly. She kept trying to treat him the way she had always treated men—women were supposed to jolly them along and keep them cheerful.

"I didn't ask you," Dahl growled.

"I was just tryin'—"

"Just shut your trap!" Dahl pushed her out of the way, and she stumbled against the wall. "I'd a done fine if your fancy-pants friends from Dawson hadn't showed up and scared off the game."

"You scared them off yourself, firin' that shotgun," Lulie said. She knew as soon as she closed her mouth that she shouldn't have opened it in the first place. Dahl came at her with his hand raised and slapped her across the face.

"I told you to shut up. It's your fault we ain't got nothin' to eat, yammerin' at me all the time. I got no use for a woman who keeps yammerin'." He hit her again.

"Owww! Don't!" Lulie put her hands across her face. "You got no right to hit me!"

"Man can beat his wife if she needs it," Dahl said, panting. "Teach her to shut up." He drove his fist into her shoulder, knocking her down. He hit her in the face again.

Lulie, whimpering, rolled over on the floor, trying to keep her back to him. His booted foot crashed into her ribs.

"Now get up and get me supper," he said.

Lulie moaned, clutching her ribs, feeling the blood run hot and salty from her nose. "I can't," she cried.

"You better," Dahl said. "That's what you're for." He jerked a chair out from the table and sat down in it, waiting.

Lulie got up slowly and dipped a cloth in the water she had put on for coffee. She washed her face. Her ribs felt as if they were on fire. Every time she took a breath, pain shot clear through her. She managed to put the coffee on to boil and spoon out a plate of stew for Dahl. He wouldn't care whether or not she ate. While he was eating, she went outside and vomited in the snow. Crouched on hands and knees, she cleaned her face again with snow while her fingers went numb.

When she was too cold to stay outside any longer, she went back in. Dahl had finished eating and was cleaning his shotgun. Lulie took the dirty plate off the table and washed it. She didn't know what he was likely to do. Finally she lay down on the bed, pulled the blankets over her head, and hoped that he would leave her alone.

Her ribs hurt so much she couldn't sleep. She lay with her face to the wall and listened while Dahl fed the sled dogs. They settled into their place in front of the stove with a brief flurry of yaps and snarls. Dahl aimed a booted foot into their midst, and they subsided. He lay down heavily beside her and rolled her over.

"I can't," Lulie whimpered. "You hurt me."

"I paid for you," Dahl grunted. "And I'm going to get my money's worth." He yanked her skirts up.

In the morning he was gone. Lulie got up slowly. He never told her where he was going. Maybe he'd gone hunting again, or maybe he was working the new diggings down the creek. He had finished last night's stew for breakfast but hadn't put more wood in the stove. The cabin was icy. Shivering, she built the fire up some and crouched in front of it.

She sat that way a long time, just thinking. Then she pulled the mirror out of her trunk and looked at her face. It was swollen, purplish black and red, worse even than the last time he had struck her. Miserable, she stared at her reflection until she couldn't bear to look anymore.

As she put the mirror back, her hand brushed the bump in the lining where she had hidden the seven thousand dollars. Weeping, Lulie pulled it out and set it on the table. She took five hundred back and stuffed it down the front of her dress. She had hardly been there a month, but she figured she had earned that much.

Terrified that Dahl might come back, Lulie hurriedly packed her jewelry and as many clothes as she could get into her carpetbag and abandoned her trunk. She pulled on her coat, mittens, and boots, wrapped her shawl around her head and shoulders, then went out to saddle the horse.

The mustang whickered at Lulie as she heaved the saddle onto its back. It hadn't been out of the shed in days. The snow was too deep, but Lulie didn't care; the risk was worth the taking. She tied the carpetbag to the back of the saddle and climbed up, then clung to the saddle horn as the horse lurched out of the yard. It stumbled in the drifted snow, but Lulie could see the trail that Peggy's sled had left the day before. She would follow that. Dahl's trail went in the opposite direction. She looked fearfully over her shoulder and kept going.

The snow was packed solid under a light powder. Every so often the horse's hooves broke through, but it gamely lumbered out again and kept on. Everything was white and shining in the moonlight. Lulie felt as exposed as a target at a shooting gallery. She took to the edge of the trees, trying to follow the sled trail with her eyes. She had never known she could be so cold. The horse stumbled on, and she clung to the saddle.

Hours passed. The sun came out, and the temperature rose briefly. As the abbreviated winter's day was plunged again into darkness, the air became even more frigid. Even her mind seemed numbed by the cold. Lulie turned the floundering horse onto the sled trail again because she couldn't see it otherwise. The traveling in the tracks was easier for the animal. Lulie wept when she saw the track turn toward a distant cabin. She yearned for the fire that sent smoke up the squat chimney. But, she wondered, what if Dahl was there, looking for her?

The mustang tried to head for the cabin, but she yanked its head around and skirted away. Beyond the cabin she saw the sled trail again; it forked. Lulie had no notion of how to read tracks, but she guessed that Peggy must have come one way, then gone back another. To Frank's, maybe? Peggy must have had Frank with her. She wouldn't have gone out alone. And Dahl had yelled about her "friends" from Dawson. It must have been Frank. His cabin was off Caribou Creek, not so far as Dawson. Lulie tried to get her bearings, then took the track that she thought looked as if it crossed over the other, that appeared to point toward Caribou.

She was cold, so cold. It seemed easier just to lie down in the snow and die. The cuts on her face stung, and her ribs ached like fire—the only parts of her that weren't numb. The horse struggled on. I'm likely to kill this nice horse, too, she thought. Lulie put her head down on the animal's neck and cried. The tears froze and stuck to her lashes.

She didn't know how long she had been out there. She knew she must be hungry, so she ate cold biscuits out of her carpetbag and gave the horse a feed of grain, leaning down to let it mouth the oats from her hand. She was afraid to get down for fear she couldn't get back up. After the horse had eaten, she drummed her heels against its flanks to make it move again.

They stumbled on through an endless icy dream scape, and Lulie went to sleep . . . passed out. She woke as the horse whickered weakly and jerked at the reins. There was another cabin in front of them. Its windows were dark. This time the mustang wasn't going to be turned away.

Lulie knew she had to go in, no matter who was there. But the sled tracks went to the door. She stopped, terrified now that she had followed someone else's tracks. Oh, Lord, please not Bill's! she prayed. But she had to go in, or she'd die. The horse was nearly gone, too.

Numbly Lulie slid from the saddle and rattled the cabin door. No answer. She rattled the door again, then pounded on it, but no one came. Crying, she shoved her weight against it, and it opened.

Lulie stumbled in and saw the faint glow of a banked fire. On a table, a lantern sat with matches carefully beside it. The lantern flowered into light, and she saw with huge relief that this was Frank's cabin. She recognized his trunks and the books of poetry on a rough-hewn shelf.

Lulie lurched back out and grabbed the mustang's reins, leading it past the strange mountains of frozen dirt beside the door. The horse balked at the doorway, and she smacked it on the behind.

"Get in there! Get in there where it's warm!" The animal snorted and went through the doorway.

Lulie laid more wood on the fire. She pulled the mustang's saddle off, took the bit from its mouth, then crawled into Frank's bed.

Frank had bypassed Ratty's and gone straight back to his own diggings. His cabin was between Dahl's and Dawson, and Peggy and the dogs were just about bushed. Then he had brought Peggy into Dawson the next morning, returned the dogs to the kennel, spent the night, and finally headed home.

Now he stopped and stared. Smoke was coming from his chimney, and what appeared to be hoofprints marked up his yard. He knew that any desperate traveler might have taken refuge there. Miners left their doors unlocked for just that reason. They hid their gold and didn't own anything else worth stealing: Any man who went out in this weather took his dogs and his gun with him.

Frank unhitched the dogs and drew his pistol just in case. The dogs were snuffling at the door. Frank pushed it open and blinked. Someone was asleep in his bed. What's more, there was a horse in his cabin. It was standing by the stove and licking bacon grease out of his skillet.

Feeling ridiculously like one of the Three Bears, Frank raised the pistol and asked, "Who are you?"

Lulie sat up, shrieking.

"Oh, my God." Frank put the pistol down. "Lulie!" He looked at her bruised face and was appalled.

"I run off," Lulie said, shivering in his blankets. "I thought you was him." She burst into tears.

"Dahl?"

Lulie nodded, tears running down her face.

"He did that to you? We've got to get you to Dawson to a doctor. Did you come all the way on that?" He gestured at the horse. The dogs were staring at it. This was their cabin . . . but the animal was large.

"It's Bill's," Lulie said. "Mr. Dahl's." She made a stab at what she knew were proper manners. "I'm sorry about the mess. I'll clean up. But the poor thing was so cold. I was afraid I'd killed him."

"You're lucky you didn't kill yourself," Frank said. "Didn't you hear Peggy calling you?"

"Bill told me to keep quiet," Lulie said. "And I was scared of him."

"I'm not surprised," Frank said grimly, looking at her face. "I'm taking you to Peggy. And a doctor." By now he could probably go to Dawson and back in his sleep. "We can't leave till morning, though." He looked at the horse again. "I suppose he might as well stay here. I don't have a barn."

He set about fixing supper, and when Lulie tried to help, he shooed her back to bed. "You may have a broken rib, damn it. You don't have to be my wife."

She lay back down, grateful. Meanwhile, Frank took the horse outside for a walk and was gratified when it decided to relieve itself in the yard instead of by the stove again. In the morning he bundled Lulie into the sled and tied the mustang on behind. His dogs would have to pull him and Lulie without help; there was no alternative. In the shape Lulie was in, she probably couldn't manage the dogs while he rode the horse. Because Frank felt guilty for having left Lulie with Dahl, he spent the drive into Dawson trying to figure out what he could have done instead. He couldn't come up with an answer, but Peggy was sure to think it was all his fault.

She did. She chewed him out up one side and down the other, while she undressed Lulie and inspected her bruises. She shouted at Frank to go and get the doctor, as if he hadn't already been planning to.

Relieved, Frank escaped to round up the doctor, who also served as a dentist and veterinarian. Frank was unsure in which specialty Dr. Jones had actually acquired his training, and he was absolutely certain that Jones wasn't his real name. Frank thought he'd have the man look at the horse, too.

He and the doctor were halfway back to Peggy's, just passing some miners outside the Daybreak Saloon, when a dogsled came flying down the street. Dahl leaped from it. His infuriated bellowing perked up the miners. It was a mild day for the Yukon, and there was a fair-sized crowd of them.

Dahl spotted Frank. "You! She's with you!"

"Who?" Frank said, grabbing the doctor's arm to keep him quiet.

"My wife! My wife I bought. You give her back."

"I don't have your wife," Frank said, and Dahl reached into the sled for his shotgun.

Heartache Johnson bustled out of the saloon. "Now just a minute. We ain't going to have no shooting."

"We are if I don't get my wife," Dahl threatened. "I paid money for her, and I'll shoot somebody sure as you're standing there."

XIX

"Now look here." Heartache, blanching, steeled his nerves and stepped forward between Frank and Dahl. Dawson had no real system of government, but Heartache functioned as a kind of unofficial mayor. No one had ever wanted to shoot him for it, though. "Now, Mr. Dahl," Heartache said as placatingly as possible, "are you saying that Lulie ran off with young Blake here?"

The miners looked interested.

"Yes!"

"Are you talking about a romantic triangle?" Heartache asked him.

"He is not!" Frank erupted.

"Him and that redhead woman was out to my place earlier. Next thing I know, she's stole my horse and gone." Dahl looked around at the assembled men. "They put her up to it. Horse thieving's serious." He jabbed a finger at Frank. "Where's my horse, Blake? You ain't going to get away with stealing my horse."

"I didn't steal your horse," Frank said, goaded. "I don't want your horse. You are beholden to me that you even have a horse. I lugged it into town from my place for you, instead of letting it wander around as some wolf's dinner."

"Where'd you get my horse?" Dahl said menacingly.

"Lulie rode it to my cabin," Frank said. "After you gave her a black eye and kicked her ribs in."

"I didn't but shove her around a little to teach her how to do things my way," Dahl said.

"That why she run off?" one of the loungers asked.

"Hell, I figure a man's got a right to straighten out his wife," a sourdough said.

"That's right." Another nodded sagely. "And whores get a lot of fancy ideas."

"You haven't seen what she looks like!" Frank informed them.

"You better get her out here," Dahl said ominously.

"Where is she?" Heartache asked. "At Peggy's?"

"Yeah." Frank knew that there wasn't much point in pretending she wasn't. Peggy's would be the first place they'd look. "I came out to get Dr. Jones here for her, so maybe you better listen to what he has to say."

"Always glad to offer a medical opinion," Jones said. He looked at Dahl. "Domestic difficulties are not my line."

Dahl started down the street toward the laundry. Frank and the doctor ran to catch up with him, while Heartache Johnson and the Daybreak Saloon boys followed in a kind of parade.

Dahl jerked the door open, and Frank shoved the doctor through it under Dahl's arm. Frank wedged himself in front of Dahl. "You aren't invited in."

"Then she's coming out," Dahl said. "Lulie, you get out here."

"No." Lulie looked at the crowd behind him and felt safer. "No! I ain't gonna. You hit me, and that wasn't in the bargain."

"I paid for you."

"I gave most of it back," Lulie said. "You know I did. I left it on the table. I didn't take but five hundred, for the time I been there."

"You made a bargain. I got rights." Dahl looked at the men crowding behind him. "Legal rights."

"Well, now," Heartache said, "he may have a point. Matter of contract law."

"You aren't no lawyer!" Peggy said indignantly.

"Well, you ain't, either," Heartache said. "You may be guilty of aidin' and abettin'."

Peggy stood up and put her fists on her hips. "You get out of my place so Doc Jones can see to Lulie. She gave Dahl back his money, and she's not going anywhere!"

Heartache looked uneasily at Dahl. He still had the shotgun in his hands. "Looks like we got an impasse," he muttered.

"Citizens' court!" somebody behind him yelled.

Shouts of encouragement echoed through the crowd. "That's the ticket!"

Heartache brightened. "We'll settle this legal, Mr. Dahl."

"You got no legal standing," Dahl growled.

"We got as much as you do." Heartache stood his ground. "And there's more of us."

A chorus of agreement rose behind them. A citizens' court always livened things up.

Dahl hesitated, and Heartache chose to accept that as acquiescence. He counted out twelve men from the miners behind him. "You all are the jury. I'll be the judge." He looked at Lulie and Dahl. "Either of you folks got lawyers?"

"Of course they don't," Peggy snapped. She gave Frank a baleful look. "You be Lulie's lawyer. You did a good enough job as auctioneer."

"I'm not a lawyer," Frank protested.

"And Heartache's not a judge," Peggy retorted. "At least you been educated."

"Who's gonna represent Mr. Dahl?" a juror asked.

"I'll find somebody," Heartache said. "That's not your department. Now you all scram and let Miss Lulie confer with her attorney."

Citizens' court was an impromptu affair, held next door to the Daybreak Saloon in the Dawson meeting hall, a frame cabin with a tent extension to hold onlookers. The witness stand was a chair and a fruit crate. As an unofficial legal system, it worked fairly well. Its edicts were enforced by public pressure and an occasional vigilante committee. So far it had dealt with disputed land claims, the theft of a dog team, and a fatal shooting on the upper floor of the Monte Carlo Saloon. The dog thief had been hanged. The murderer had got five years in prison, on the grounds that the accused had been too drunk to know what he was doing, and no one knew the victim anyway.

The courtroom, lit with kerosene lanterns, was packed for Lulie's divorce trial—that was what Heartache Johnson had decided they should call it. He reasoned that Lulie's arrangement with Dahl was a marriage contract, even if a limited one. If she wanted out of it, she had to get a divorce.

The jurors filed in, wearing the cleanest clothes they could find, an indication that they took their duties seriously. Heartache wore a saloon girl's black silk evening cloak with full sleeves and looked suitably judicial in it. He had acquired a lawyer for Dahl, who had protested he didn't need a lawyer but was shouted down. The lawyer was a miner who also protested on the grounds that he had been disbarred in the States; but those were better qualifications than anyone else had, so he was also shouted down. He looked at Dahl apprehensively and appeared to be wondering what would happen if he lost.

"All right," Heartache said, pounding a claw hammer on the bench, a table removed temporarily from the saloon. "You all are supposed to stand up when I come in."

Everyone stood up and sat back down again.

"That's better. All right, counsel for the plaintiff will go first." He nodded at Frank.

"She's not the plaintiff; we are," Dahl's lawyer pointed out.

"She wants the divorce," Heartache said. "That makes her the plaintiff. What the hell does it matter anyway?"

Dahl muttered something to his lawyer, who was named Smith—or said he was. "It's a matter of principle, Your Honor," Smith said.

"I'll make a note of it," Heartache said. "Mr. Blake, get on with it."

Frank, who had no notion of the proper proceedings except what he had gleaned from novels and theatrical productions, put Lulie on the witness stand.

"Raise your right hand," Heartache said. "What's your last name?"

"Murchins," Lulie whispered.

"Miss Lulie Murchins, do you solemnly swear you're gonna tell the truth?"

Lulie looked indignant. "Of course I am."

"Say, 'I so swear,' " Frank said.

"I so swear."

Frank had no clean clothes left in Dawson, so Peggy had appropriated one of her customers' frock coats for him. It was too tight across the shoulders.

He paced to the front of the room, hands behind his back.

"You're going to wreck that coat," Peggy said in an audible whisper.

Frank hooked his thumbs in his belt instead.

"Your Honor, we intend to prove—"

"You're supposed to do that before you call your witness," Heartache said. "And I don't want to hear what you intend to prove. Just go on and prove it."

Dahl's lawyer put his head in his hands.

Frank glared at Heartache. "Miss Murchins, would you just tell us in your own words why you left Mr. Dahl?"

"You can see why I left," Lulie said. She turned her face to the jury. "He beat the tar out of me. I got bandages all around my middle, too, but I can't show you that."

"Aw, go ahead," a spectator urged.

"I need someone to keep order in here," Heartache said. He pointed at a hefty logger in the audience. "You do it. You're the bailiff."

The logger swung around and took the other man by the collar. "Pipe down, or I'll throw you out."

"And was this attack unprovoked?" Frank asked Lulie. "Did you do anything to make him hit you?"

"He didn't like me talking," Lulie said. "And he wouldn't let me see my friends."

"And how did you leave?"

"I waited till he was gone, and I lit out on his horse," Lulie said.

"And did you give back the horse?"

"You gave it back," Lulie said. "Frank, you know all that."

"The jury doesn't," Frank said. "And did you give back the money Mr. Dahl paid you for living with him until spring?"

"I left it on the table for him. All but five hundred. I figure I earned that much."

"All right. Thank you. Dr. Jones?"

"Wait a minute," Smith said. "I'm supposed to cross-examine her."

"Oh."

"Miss Murchins," Smith said, "are you married to Mr. Dahl?"

"Well, sorta," Lulie answered.

"By the terms of your contract, are you married to Mr. Dahl?"

"Yeah, I guess so."

"And has Mr. Dahl deserted you?"

"I'm tryin' to desert him," Lulie said. She looked at Smith as though she thought he might be feebleminded.

"Precisely," Smith said. "And has Mr. Dahl been unfaithful to you? Has he dallied with other women?"

"No."

"Is he a convicted felon? Has he been committed to an insane asylum?"

"No. Well, he might have been."

" 'Might have been' does not count, Miss Murchins. Thank you."

Lulie got down and went to sit with Peggy again. Peggy put an arm around her.

"Now can I call Dr. Jones?" Frank asked.

Dr. Jones testified that the plaintiff had indeed been beaten by somebody and had sustained a bruised rib cage, a split lip, a black eye, and various lacerations and contusions. He added that the horse was not in good shape, either. Pressed by Mr. Smith, the doctor had to admit that he couldn't say for certain who had administered Lulie's beatings.

Peggy testified that she had gone with Frank to Dahl's cabin and that Dahl had run them off with a shotgun. Under cross-examination she had to agree that Dahl had a right to be antisocial if he wanted to. She also agreed that she had been in attendance when Lulie agreed to be Dahl's wife for the winter.

Frank had no more witnesses to call. Smith began calling a list of people who had also witnessed Lulie's contract with Dahl. Heartache finally said in exasperation that that part of it wasn't in dispute.

"Yes, it is," Frank said, struck by this thought. "It's not legal for people to get married on a short-term basis. No offense intended to Miss Murchins, but that amounts to prostitution. And since prostitution is not legal, I submit that the contract between them can't be legal, either, and ought to be thrown out."

Heartache leaned over the bench. "This whole trial isn't legal if you want to get right down to it—not if we were in the States. But we're not in the States or even any civilized part of Canada; we're off in the godforsaken hinterland, and therefore we're as legal as you're going to get out here. And therefore I am not going to entertain that notion."

"Motion," Smith correction.

"I'll call it what I want to," Heartache said. "I'm the judge."

Smith put Dahl on the stand. The big man explained that he had only shoved her around some. She talked at him all the time, he said, and that made him lose his temper. If she'd behaved, none of it would have happened.

"I feed her right," he said. "I give her a roof over her head. I gave her seven thousand dollars. I haven't broke my part of the bargain."

"You beat her up!" Peggy yelled indignantly.

There was a mutter of agreement from a knot of saloon girls at the back of the room.

"One more outburst, and I shall have you summarily removed," Heartache said. He looked pleased at having got the chance to say that. "You gentlemen can sum up now. We haven't got all day. Saloons are going to be filling up, and I got business to attend to." In Dawson the saloons filled up at noon. The jurors looked thirsty and checked their watches.

"Your Honor and gentlemen of the jury," Frank began. He thought he sounded pompous, but he thought maybe that was good. "I submit to you, with no aspersions cast on my client's character—"

"You called her a whore," Peggy said indignantly.

"I didn't," Frank said. "Will you shut up, Peg? Gentlemen, I submit to you that this marriage was not legal in the first place and so requires no divorce because they aren't married anyway. Miss Murchins is free to go where she chooses, seeing that she has returned the better part of Mr. Dahl's

418

money and is willing to return the remaining five hundred as well."

There was a yelp from Lulie, and Peggy shushed her. "It's worth it, you ninny," she hissed.

"Moreover," Frank said, "I submit to you that my client was so desperate to escape Mr. Dahl's brutality that she undertook a thirty-mile ride in the foulest weather at risk of life and limb. You've seen what he did to her. Is there a man of conscience here who could force a helpless woman back to suffer further brutality from a man like that? And furthermore," he added as an afterthought, "she has returned Mr. Dahl's horse, so I don't want to hear any more about the blasted animal. Thank you." He sat down, feeling that somehow he hadn't put that as well as he might. He wasn't a lawyer, blast it. Why did Peggy keep getting him into things like this?

Smith stood up. He harrumphed portentously and patted his watch chain. The manner seemed to be coming back to him. "Your Honor. Gentlemen of the jury. There are certain actions recognized by law as sufficient grounds to separate those whom God has joined together—"

"God didn't do any joining!" Frank protested.

Heartache whapped the bench with his hammer. "Counsel for the plaintiff is out of order."

"Certain grounds are prescribed by law as sufficient to grant a divorce," Smith said. "Adultery. Desertion. Insanity. Imprisonment. The jury will note that domestic dispute is not among them. Now, Miss Murchins has admitted that Mr. Dahl has been faithful to her, has not deserted her, and is neither insane nor in jail. In the best-regulated households, quarrels may occur. A man may lose his temper. Most certainly he regrets it afterward, as my client does." He glanced at Dahl, who nodded hastily. Smith looked at the jury and spoke confidentially. "Now, gentlemen, violence is always regrettable, but—man to man—haven't we all lost our tempers once in a while? And doesn't a wife have a responsibility not to provoke her husband unreasonably? It takes two to make a quarrel. The husband is, after all, head of his household and must discipline and instruct his family for their education and betterment. If wives could get divorced every time they had a spat, there'd be no marriage at all in our society. We'd be degenerating to primitive ways. In other words, gentlemen, I am asking you to support the sanctity of marriage—even marriage in the short term. My client wants to patch things up with his wife. Let's give him the same respect—the same rights, gentlemen—that we'd want for ourselves. Thank you." Smith sat down.

Heartache said, "The jury will go next door and consider its verdict. And stay out of my booze!"

The jury filed out with uneasy glances at Dahl and Lulie. Everyone else settled in to wait. The audience, having had its opinions bottled up during the trial, let them loose.

"A man's got a right to smack his wife if she don't behave," a planer from the sawmill said. "Stands to reason."

420

"Well, I guess he got the right, but he hadn't ought to—not that hard."

"What else you expect him to do? And whoever heard of a female getting divorced over it?"

"I'd divorce you," a saloon girl said indignantly, "if you did me like that."

"Well, hell, that's why we got laws. You can't just let females run around getting divorces whenever they feel like it."

"Hmmmph. It's no wonder you ain't married," the saloon girl retorted.

The planer turned around in his chair. "I ain't married because there ain't no women up here, exceptin' you tarts."

"Don't you call me a tart!" She leaned forward and took a swing at him.

The planer ducked and came up with his fist raised.

"That's enough!" Heartache pounded his hammer on the bench. "You folks aren't the jury. If you start brawling, I'll throw you all out."

The combatants' companions hauled them back into their chairs. No one wanted to miss the verdict.

The jury wasn't gone very long. They filed back in, listing enough to make Heartache narrow his eyes at them suspiciously. "I ought to smell your breath," he muttered. "Have you reached a decision, or have you just been over there drinking my liquor?"

"We just had a sip to think by," the foreman said with dignity. "We reached a verdict, all right."

"And would you care to tell us what it is?" Heartache waited with elaborate patience. "Or do we have to guess?"

"Well, we chewed it over some, and it seems to us, Your Honor, that a man smacking his wife some ain't exactly unheard of. And we never heard of no wives leavin' on account of it. So we think she ought to go back with him."

Lulie wailed in distress.

"But we think he ought to promise he ain't going to hit her no more, too," the foreman added.

Heartache pounded his hammer down before anyone could start arguing again. "The court finds for the defendant," he announced. He gave Dahl a stern look. "Furthermore, the court orders the defendant not to belt the plaintiff again. It's the court's opinion that you overdid it. Women take a light touch." Heartache adopted an air of judicial instruction. "Marriage is an exercise in mutual responsibility. You understand, Mr. Dahl?"

"Yes, Your Honor," Dahl said, expressionless.

Heartache addressed Lulie. "Now you go on back and put a steak on that eye. You're going to be fine." He brought the hammer down again. "Court dismissed."

Lulie got up slowly. Smith poked Dahl, and Dahl rose and held his hand out to her.

"There now," the foreman said, pleased.

Dahl led Lulie out of the tent.

Peggy gripped Frank's hand, nearly breaking his fingers.

"I'm sorry, Peg," he told her. "I did my best."

Peggy's shoulders slumped. "She brought it on herself. But I just can't rest, knowing she's out there by herself with him."

"The jury's decided. There's not much else we can do," Frank said. "She got a court order he's not to hit her again."

"How much good do you think that's going to do, out there on Eldorado?"

"Maybe some. If he does it again, she can make them turn her loose. Dahl won't want that."

"The jury was afraid he'd come back and shoot them," Peggy said derisively. "Bunch of weasels. I saw them looking at him." She glared after their retreating backs. "And they better hope they can find another female to wash their dirty shirts!"

Peggy and Frank walked in dispirited silence back to the laundry. She pushed the door open and looked inside. "It's almost Thanksgiving. I thawed a turkey I was saving, but now I don't know if I've got the heart to cook it."

"Sure you do," Frank said. He took her hands. "Lulie's going to do fine. People can stand anything that's finite. I know. I found that out. And she'll still have her seven thousand dollars. That'll cheer her up. Let's cook your turkey. I used to help my mother make a good corn-bread stuffing. I'll bet I can still remember how."

"You'll stay in town?" Peggy asked.

"Sure. I haven't got anything waiting for me but a hole in the ground. That'll keep."

They unwrapped the butcher's paper around the turkey, then plucked it.

They would eat the turkey with canned beans, and cranberry sauce, and the stuffing gleaned from Frank's childhood memories.

"Lulie ought to be here," Peggy said fretfully.

Frank watched as she stuffed the turkey. Her starched white laundry apron was tied over her dress. He thought of his mother. The memory was almost indelible: Cindy, with one arm stuck up inside a turkey, cornmeal on her forehead where she had brushed the hair from her face with the other, glasses on the tip of her nose—they always slid down. She would push them back up, and then there would be cornmeal on her nose. He wondered if she was thinking of him now, too. He wondered what his father was doing, then angrily shoved that question away. Every so often it came to him, like a slap in the face, how angry he still was at his father.

"You look like a dog with rabies," Peggy said. "What's the matter with you?"

Frank shook his head, grinned, and put his arms around her, squeezing her soft warm breasts while she had her hands in the turkey and couldn't swat him. "Nothing, sweetheart. Not a thing."

The next day they went out, cut a Christmas tree, loaded it on the sled, and tramped alongside on snowshoes. The brief winter light sparkled on the ice in the branches, and Frank wondered if he ought to marry Peggy. Maybe it was just thinking of his mother that had made him take that notion. Peggy didn't seem to want it; at least she had never mentioned it. And what with Lulie and all, it didn't seem the right time to ask.

They set the tree up in Peggy's cabin and hung it with tin stars, which Frank had cut from can lids. Peggy popped corn to string in garlands. It was early for a Christmas tree, but Peggy liked it. It was, she said, a cheer to have around. Frank guessed that she had wanted to put up the tree with him.

"I'm making you a present," Peggy said. "But you can't see it till Christmas."

What was he going to give her? Frank thought about it as he snipped stars. He couldn't decide. He snipped a can up the side, unrolled it, and hammered it flat, then cut an angel from it for the top, its arms bent inward to hold a candle. He climbed on a chair and set it up, its curling, feathered wings curved in benediction over the popcorn garlands. The tin stars glimmered in the lantern light.

On December first he went back to his diggings but promised to come back to celebrate Christmas with Peggy. His tenuous thoughts of marriage had been left unspoken. Whether Peggy had perceived them, he couldn't say. Winter in this country did strange things to people's notions of what they wanted. It crystallized them or made them pop up unexpectedly, like frost heaves. They might, he told himself, look different in the spring.

Lulie sat at the table in the cabin on Eldorado Creek and waited uneasily for Dahl to come back. The little tree she had cut looked out of place in its corner, as if it, too, would rather be elsewhere. But it was almost Christmas; folks ought to have some trimmings, she thought. She had made sprays to hang over the windows and a wreath for the door. Dahl would see it when he got in. I ain't gonna take it down, she thought defiantly.

There was no telling if he would want her to. He'd hardly spoken a word to her in the nearly four weeks since they'd gotten back from Dawson, but he had never said much to her anyway. He hadn't hit her since; she had to give him that. Maybe he really did care something about her. It was easier to hold on to that supposition than to be scared all the time. Maybe he really was sorry, in his own, mean way. Maybe nobody had ever done anything nice for him. Maybe he would like the wreath and the sprays.

Lulie looked dubiously at the sprays. They seemed naked over the uncurtained windows, as if they needed something else. She got up and searched in her trunk. She had a red silk shawl. She could always buy another, couldn't she? She took out her scissors and began to cut up the shawl.

She made bows for the center of the sprays so the pine boughs hung out on either side. Another bow was set on the top of the tree, to go with the pinecones she had tied on with red thread. One

426

last bow with long, trailing ends would be tied at the top of the door's wreath. She cut it carefully, all the way across, so it had fringe on each end.

Lulie went outside and, singing, tied it on. " 'God rest ye, merry gentlemen. Let nothing you dismay.' " That did look better, merry and bright. She went back inside and scanned the cabin for anything else she could use. She felt better.

Lulie rummaged in the open shelves. " 'Remember Christ our Saviour was born on Christmas Day, to save us all from Satan's power when we were gone astray.' " Behind the whiskey bottles, she found a jar of feathers she had almost forgotten. She wished she could get rid of the whiskey bottles—Dahl drank too much and even took whiskey with him to his diggings—but she didn't dare pour it out. She took her feathers to the table and sorted them. She had found a handful of white owl feathers; a cluster of spotted ones had been part of a little pile of bones and debris beside the shed—some fox's lunch or maybe a wolf's. She didn't like to think of wolves that close to the cabin, but she had seen their tracks in the snow. Anyway, they were afraid of people, Dahl had said.

Lulie fanned out the clump of speckled feathers and snipped a tiny red bow to hang it with. She put it on the tree and hung the white owl feathers one by one around the branches.

The door banged open, and Dahl came in, the dogs surging around him. Their sleek white ruffs

427

were beaded with snow. Dahl's blunt face and wide, thin mouth were truculent. "That's a god-damn waste of time," he said, glaring at the tree. "I knew you'd been up to something soon's I saw the door."

Lulie stood her ground. "I already got your supper ready," she said. "I got all my chores done, and I had extra time. There's nothing else to do out here."

"You can mend my clothes." Dahl grabbed the whiskey bottle off the shelf and took a swig from it.

"I did," Lulie said. She hesitated. "I even made you a Christmas present." A cravat, painstakingly stitched.

Dahl snorted. "Well, you won't get one from me. You already been paid." He took another drink. The dogs sniffed the tree. One of them hiked its leg against the lower branches. Dahl guffawed.

Lulie stood forlornly in the center of the room. "I just wanted to make it nice."

"Dogs know what to do with your goddamn tree," Dahl said. He tilted the bottle up again. Lulie thought he was half-drunk already. "I'll get your supper," she offered.

"And after that you can get the goddamned tree out of here."

Dahl shoveled stew into his mouth and did not look at her. But she watched him, her own plate in her hands.

"I want to keep the tree," she said. "It ain't hurting you none. And you shouldn't swear that way about it. It's sacrilegious."

Dahl wiped his mouth with his hands. "I've had enough outta you." He emptied the whiskey bottle down his throat and went to sit in the far corner. He took his knife out and began punching holes in a piece of harness.

Lulie washed the dishes in silence. Maybe he would forget about the tree if he got drunk enough. The dogs whined for their supper. "You want me to feed them?" she asked. She wasn't allowed to, without asking.

Dahl reached for a fresh bottle of whiskey. He opened it without answering and went on with what he was doing, stabbing holes through the leather. Lulie fed the dogs. When she was finished, she sat down beside the tree and watched the snow fall outside the cabin windows. After a while she began to whistle softly to herself.

It was coming down hard when Dahl looked up and seemed to hear her for the first time. He lurched out of his chair. A nearly empty bottle sat on the floor. "I've had enough of you. I told you to get that tree out."

"It's not doing harm," Lulie said. "I worked hard on it. I used my red shawl and my owl feathers and—"

Dahl swung his arm wide and sent her sprawling into the tree. "I told you to get rid of it!"

Lulie scrambled out of his way. "You ain't supposed to hit me!"

"You do what I tell you! I got no use for your

trash! You're gonna learn to mind me!" He hit her again, not an openhanded slap but with a hard-fisted punch.

"No! Stop!"

He hit her again and again while she cowered against the tree, until finally she fell into its branches and the tree came down, bucket and wet dirt heaped on the floor. Dahl pinned her in the branches and pounded her with his fists. His breath in her face reeked of whiskey.

Lulie sobbing, tried to roll away. "Don't! Please!"

Dahl stood up and kicked her, driving her body farther into the branches of the Christmas tree. The light swam in her eyes, and she ceased pleading and began to moan. Dahl aimed a final kick at her back. "Next time you mind me, or I'll kill you." He staggered away toward his bottle.

Lulie lay still in the wreckage of her tree. She felt as if she was dying. After a while she heard Dahl's snores from the bed. He would have a terrible hangover. Tears slid silently from her eyes into the mud on the floor. Despairingly Lulie crawled out of the tree. She would never get away from him before he caught up to her. She stood and slowly tried to straighten, whimpering with pain.

She saw Dahl's shotgun propped against the wall. Slowly she hobbled toward it. She lifted it, heavy and cold, and turned toward the bed. Dahl lay sprawled facedown. Lulie aimed the shotgun and pulled back the bolt. Dahl didn't move. She fired it into his head.

XX

Lulie didn't want to see what was on the bed. The dogs had looked curiously at the body once, then retreated to wedge themselves under the fallen Christmas tree.

Keeping her eyes averted, Lulie packed her trunk and the carpetbag. She sneaked one look at Dahl, and her stomach heaved. She began to sing resolutely: " 'Let nothing you dismay, remember Christ our Saviour . . .' "

She felt for the money in the trunk, took it out, but put it back in again. Her first impulse was to leave it there, but she figured she would need it. After she had the trunk packed, she dragged it outside. Whimpering with pain, she got it into Dahl's sled by gritting her teeth against the pain. She hurt so bad she wanted to scream, wanted to go back inside, where it was warm, and lie down. But she couldn't, not with his corpse in there.

She remembered the mustang in its shed and limped over to pull the door open. Snow was still coming down, blanketing everything. She knew she couldn't take the horse. "You'll do all right, I reckon," she told the animal as she left it with plenty of food. "You'll have to."

Next she had to take care of the dogs. Inside the cabin, she stood in front of the tree and tried to coax them out. They looked at her, wolfish eyes

431

deep in the branches. "I had to," she explained. "I didn't have no choice." She got some lumps of meat and held the offering in an extended palm. "Come on now, boys. You don't know it, but you're better off without him, too." They pricked their ears, whining. She sang "God Rest Ye Merry Gentlemen" for them again. They seemed to respond to it. "'To save us all from Satan's power . . .' Come on, now."

They came out slowly, sniffing the meat. She had never been allowed to feed them by hand. They took the meat at last, licking her fingers while she scratched their soft ears. They looked at the body again and whined. Lulie followed out of the cabin.

Lulie hitched them up as she had seen Dahl do, and they waved their tails, comforted by familiar duty. Lulie took one last look at the cabin. Her red scarf bow on the door hung dismally, the fringes frozen stiff.

Frank was asleep when his dogs began to bark. They hurled themselves off the bed and clawed at the door. "Shut up, damn it," he muttered. They didn't, so he sat up and lit a lantern. Nobody would travel in this cold; but if a caribou was out there foraging for feed, he didn't want to let opportunity pass him by. In this weather he could shoot it, then go back to bed and dress it out in the morning . . . as long as he was willing to do it with a hacksaw. He got his rifle and, swatting at the dogs, unbarred the door.

The dim shape of a sled came toward him, drawn by four pale dogs. It might have been the ghost of some prospector moving silently under the moon. Whoever was riding the back of the sled was hunched over, unmoving and unrecognizable. The hair began to prickle on Frank's neck.

The sled neared his yard, and the dogs were real enough. The driver didn't move. Frank trotted through the snow and shook a bundled figure by the shoulders. The head tipped back, and a cold, bloody face looked up at him, almost unseeing.

"Oh, my God!" Frank picked Lulie up and ran for the cabin. He laid her on his bed and felt frantically for a pulse. It was there, thin and thready, and her skin felt as cold as a corpse to him. He unhitched the dogs, let them in, and began throwing wood on the fire. Lulie moaned, and he turned back to her, grabbing the whiskey bottle as he went.

"Here. Swallow." He managed to get some of it down her, then whistled his own dogs back to the bed and put Lulie between them while he peeled off her frozen clothes. She had purple bruises all down her ribs and buttocks. Frank stripped off his own clothes and got in bed with her, pulling dogs and covers around them, letting his body heat warm her. Lulie moaned and clung to him. He didn't think she was even half-conscious.

That son of a bitch, that son of a bitch, that

433

son . . . He said it over and over in his head, a furious litany. Lulie felt like ice in his arms; but after a while she began to warm, and he didn't think she was going to die on him. He got up, shivering as the icy air hit him, put more wood on the fire, then got back in the bed with her.

Despite his best intentions, he fell asleep. He woke in the morning—morning being by dog time and clock time, not by daylight—and found her breathing evenly, her cheeks pink again under the cuts and bruises. His dogs and Lulie's—that is, Dahl's he guessed—were huddled uncertainly by the stove. Frank slipped out of bed and pulled on his long underwear and his clothes. He got some more dry clothes and put them by the bed, then felt her pulse. It was better, steady now. Lulie was tougher than he would have imagined.

Her eyelids fluttered.

"It's Frank," he whispered. "You're okay."

Her eyes opened all the way.

"What happened, honey?" he asked gently.

"I killed him," she rasped, then closed her eyes again.

Peggy opened her door and stared at the apparition looming out of the snowstorm at her.

"Let me in," Frank said.

Peggy pulled him inside. "What are you doing out in this weather? Are you crazy? Christmas isn't for two days. You could've waited."

"I need you," he told her. "You've got to tend to Lulie till it lightens up some. Then I think maybe I can get her out of here downriver to Forty Mile."

"You aren't making sense," Peggy said. "You're frozen and crazy."

"Give me some coffee." While she made it, he told her about Dahl and watched the color drain out of her face.

"Dead?"

"She blew off his head with a shotgun."

"Jesus, Mary, and Joseph."

"I left her at my place and told her not to open the door to anybody. She had the sense to bring the money with her, thank God. I bought four new dogs with some of it. With my two, I think they can haul us both and her trunk. If we can get to Forty Mile, I can take her over the border into the States." He shook his head wonderingly. "Funny to be running from the law into the States."

"But he beat her again!" Peggy said indignantly as she handed him a cup of coffee. "Drink this and start thinking straight. Nobody would convict her of defending herself."

"I am thinking straight, Peg. She waited till he passed out, on his belly in the bed, and she fired a shotgun into the back of his head." He grimaced. "His brain's going to be all over the cabin."

Peggy blanched. "Frank . . ."

"She shot him in the back, Peg. I doubt a jury would hang her, but do you want to chance her going to prison? And for all I know, the damn fools

435

might hang her—she stole his dogs. Got all the way to my place with them." He stared down into his coffee. "God knows how she did it."

"If you've got Dahl's dogs," Peggy said practically, "why did you need a new team?"

"If we get caught with Dahl's dogs, a jury will hang her," Frank answered, "and probably me, too. I'm not going to rest easy until I get those dogs off my place. Nobody had much use for Dahl. If we get a good start, maybe no one will chase her. But if she gets caught with those dogs . . ."

Peggy looked incredulous. "Are you telling me that dogs are worth more than a man's life?"

"Out here they are," Frank said. "Give me more coffee."

"Oh, God, Frank," Peggy whispered, her eyes wide. "I hate this place."

Lulie was waiting for them. She was wearing Frank's long underwear and jeans, and a flannel shirt that came past her knees. Her dress was drying by the fire. She was sitting on the floor, playing with Dahl's dogs.

"I been layin' plans," she said while Peggy stared at her battered forehead. "If I can hide out across the border till spring, I'm goin' up to Nome. If I keep these clothes on, maybe no one will know I'm a girl."

Frank started to say like hell they wouldn't, but he stopped himself. Something had happened to Lulie, besides being beaten half to death. She was thin, a slip of a thing, with nothing like Peggy's buxom, robust figure. She all but disappeared into his shirt. And the unique quality about her, which had seemed unknowingly to communicate strong erotic appeal, had vanished.

"Do you know what you're doing?" Peggy asked, wrestling with the same realization. "I told you you'd get in trouble, and now you have. And if you think anyone's going to think you're not a girl—" She stopped and chewed her lip thoughtfully. "Oh, hell. You'll have to cut your hair."

"I know," Lulie said sorrowfully. "But it'll grow back."

Frank looked uneasily at the dogs. The room seemed particularly full of dogs—ten of them: the four he'd bought, plus Dahl's dogs and his own. "I don't know what to do with these blasted dogs. I'd like to sneak Dahl's back to his place, but I can't just turn them loose. And I don't want anybody finding the body till I've gotten Lulie away from here. I guess they're just going to have to stay."

"I'm leaving tomorrow," Lulie said. "Then you can take them back."

"You aren't in any condition to travel," Peggy said.

"And I'm going with you," Frank said.

"I can make it by myself." Lulie went on scratching a dog's ears. She seemed unperturbed, dazed, maybe.

"No, you can't. It's a good fifty miles. You about killed yourself getting here."

Lulie smiled dreamily. "You know what I'd like? I'd like a Christmas tree. You ought to have a Christmas tree, Frank."

Frank and Peggy looked at each other. "You go on and sleep some more, honey," Peggy suggested gently. "We can cut a tree if you like." She took Frank by the arm and drew him away. "She's not right in the head," she whispered. "If we give her what she wants, maybe it'll keep her from fretting."

Lulie got up and lay down on the bed among the dogs. When she awoke, the tree was in the corner. There were bows on it. Lulie smiled and sat looking at it while she took Frank's scissors and cut her hair.

They slept three to the bed that night, there being only one. When Peggy awoke, she snuggled dreamily against Frank's warm body in the dark. But there was nobody on her other side. Peggy sat up and frantically patted the sheets in the darkness.

"Frank! She's gone!"

He jerked awake. Peggy fumbled with the lantern. Its light flowed across the room, defining the Christmas tree, the dress hanging by the fire, and Frank's dogs yawning on the bed. Dahl's team was curled by the stone oven. The new team was gone. Peggy, with Frank at her heels, ran to the window. There was nothing to be seen through the glass, distorted roundels of old bottles that bent the darkness and flung it back at them. Frank jerked open the door.

Dahl's sled was gone, with its load of Lulie's trunk and carpetbag. A note was pinned with a kitchen knife to the door. "Good-bye and thank you. I took your compass."

They stared at the dwindling tracks. The snow had stopped, and the sky was clear. It was Christmas Eve.

"Can we catch up to her?" Peggy asked.

Frank laid a hand on her red flannel sleeve. Someone else was coming, but not from the way Lulie had gone. They waited, and Jake hove into full view in the moonlight, driving an empty sled. Frank snatched the note off the door and stuffed it in his long underwear.

"You hear the news?" Jake shouted.

"No," Frank called before Peggy could say anything.

"Some feller found that Dahl's horse running loose," Jake said. His brows beetled furiously above a crimson nose. He appeared to be quite sober, however. "If he's hurt that little lady again, I'm gonna bust his face in."

Apparently Jake had heard about Lulie's first escape. How he had gotten wind of the horse so fast, there was no telling. The sourdoughs' grapevine worked even in winter by its own ways. A visit here, a man met hunting there . . .

"I'm headed out that way," Jake said, pulling up to the door. "Enough's enough, by God. You come with me, Blake."

Frank's fingers bit into Peggy's arm. "I'll follow in a little while," he said, surprised at how even

439

he could keep his voice. "But I have to dress, and I haven't fed my dogs yet."

"Don't you dally," Jake said. "I'm liable to haul off and shoot the bastard." He turned his dog team around. "Mush!"

Frank went back in the cabin and towed Peggy with him. "I've got to get out there before he finds out somebody already took care of that for him. Feed the dogs, will you, Peg?"

"What about Lulie?" Peggy asked. "Aren't you going to look for her?"

"Can't. Not now. I've got to be fast. Besides, she's got my compass." Frank thanked God that Lulie had managed to take off in a full moon again. Maybe Dahl went crazy every full moon, he thought. That wouldn't surprise him. He pulled on his pants and shrugged into the rest of his clothes.

He hitched his dogs and Dahl's all in a string to his sled. "I hope to hell nobody sees me," he muttered. He turned around and grabbed Peggy by the shoulders. "You sit tight. Stay here. So help me, Peg, if you take off after Lulie, I'll skin you alive if the wolves don't do it."

"You aren't leaving me anything to go on," Peggy said.

"Good." Frank climbed on the sled and headed the dogs out, keeping as close to the trees as possible. He would have to double back some, then swing wide if he was going to pass Jake without being seen. Momentarily he begrudged Lulie his compass. If he got lost . . .

With six dogs, he fairly flew, sailing over the layer of fine powder, raising a spray all around them. Dahl's dogs were well trained. Frank wondered if he had trained them the way he tried to train Lulie.

It took all day to make his way to Eldorado Creek. He looked over his shoulder the whole time, but he came wide around the back of Dahl's cabin with no sign of Jake or any other interlopers. Whoever had found the horse was probably looking for Lulie, not checking on Dahl.

Frank quickly unhitched Dahl's dogs from their makeshift harness and shoved them through the door of the cabin. He took one look at Dahl and gagged.

"You make purty good time," Jake said behind him. Frank jumped. " 'Specially with two dogs."

"I found these fellows wandering loose outside," Frank said. "Just now." The dogs had retreated under the fallen Christmas tree.

Jake lifted his lantern. Their coats were frosted with snow. "Uh-huh," he said noncommittally. "Just got here myself. You do that?" He jerked a thumb at Dahl's corpse.

"He's frozen stiff," Frank said. "Use your head."

"Maybe we both ought to," Jake told him pointedly. "Where's his sled?"

Frank jerked his head up. I've forgotten the sled. His fingers clenched in his mittens. "The dogs were half frozen. God knows how long they've

441

been running loose. I busted it up and burned it to warm them up some."

"Uh-huh," Jake said again. He paused, considering. "Well, I reckon maybe I helped you." He glanced at Dahl but didn't let his gaze linger. "I reckon he was getting ready to go out in it when he got shot. That sound right reasonable to me. It sound reasonable to you?"

"Very reasonable," Frank said. He flicked a glance at Jake to be sure he wasn't misunderstanding the old man.

"I reckon she had her reasons," Jake said. "Poor little thing, I hope she makes it." Some commotion outside made him turn his head. "Posse's comin' "

Half a dozen teams of men and dogs were converging on the cabin. Frank stood aside to let them in. They stamped the snow from their boots and stared.

"Jesus Miracle-Workin' Christ."

"Blowed his head clean off."

"You suppose that's even him?"

"You could turn him over and see."

"Oh, Lord, I suppose we got to."

Eventually it occurred to someone to ask if they ought to chase after Lulie. No one seemed to have any doubt about who the murderer was. Her trunk was gone, and the toppled tree offered mute evidence of another battle.

"Don't see much point in it," Jake said. "Poor little thing's probably et by wolves, what with the horse runnin' loose."

"There wasn't no saddle on the horse," one man said.

"And Dahl's dogs are here," said another.

"Reckon she'd bedded down for the night when they got her," Jake offered, undeterred.

"Murder's serious, Jake!" the first man protested.

"So's beating a woman half to death!" Frank snapped suddenly. "And you were on the jury that sent her back to him. How's that sit in your stomach?"

An uncomfortable silence enveloped them.

"I heard since," another man said slowly, "he killed a woman out on Chistochina last year."

The juror blanched.

"If you ask me," Jake said solemnly, "the devil's got our friend Dahl. And if he ain't got Lulie Murchins by now, he'll get her sometime, so maybe we ought to just let the devil sort it out. Unless you boys think you know more than old scratch?"

No one answered.

"In the meantime, while you're jawing, you might consider our Christian duty to take his earthly remains back to Dawson till the ground thaws enough to dig a hole." Jake pulled a blanket from under Dahl and to everyone's relief tossed it over the body.

"Move!" Jake said. "Git! You got any arguin' to do, you can do it in Dawson."

They loaded Dahl, mercifully concealed in the blanket, onto a sled, then hitched Dahl's dogs behind another. The Mounties would impound them, Frank supposed, when one eventually showed up.

"I still don't like it," the juror grumbled. "I admit she's on my conscience, but it don't feel legal to me."

"It's not legal!" Frank snarled, goaded. "If we had a sheriff in Dawson instead of a half-baked kangaroo court, we might make out better!"

"Heartache's called a town meeting," Peggy said.

Frank looked up from the gift box in his lap. Peggy had knitted him socks, good heavy ones for winter. She was ever the practical woman. He'd had no idea she knew how to knit. "What's on Heartache's mind?" he asked. "Not the shooting. . . ." It was a trifle late for that. Frank and Peggy had limped back to Dawson to celebrate a belated Christmas two days before New Year's Eve.

"No." Lulie would be long gone, if she'd made it to the States. Peggy looked toward the door, as if she could see her friend in the distance. She did that frequently. "Seems the boys took what you said to heart about having a sheriff. Heartache wants to elect one."

"Fine idea. Are you going to open your present or not?"

Peggy lifted the lid of her own box. "Aw, Frank!" It was a little Nativity scene, laboriously carved from pine. Frank had sprinkled the angels'

444

wings and the baby's halo with gold dust and glue. "Aw," she said again. She looked at it from all sides, tracing with one fingertip the curly coat of a shepherd's lamb. "I never had anything so pretty." She cradled it in her lap and smiled at him across the warm stove.

The crèche, which had looked so primitive to Frank's critical eye as he had packed it, seemed suddenly to look a lot better. He took off his boots and began to put on the new socks. "Maybe I'll stay in for the town meeting," he said.

Peggy put the crèche on her shelf with the rose-flowered cup. The window caught her eye again, and she lifted the curtains. Frank wished she would quit doing that.

"You think she made it?"

"Honey, there's no way to tell." Frank got up and drew her away from the window.

"Word's got round you bought four new dogs," Peggy said.

"Word's also got round I sold them again to a man from Chistochina," Frank said. It had been news to him, too. "I think maybe Jake thought of that." He grinned. "That old man has a head for detail."

"When he's sober," Peggy agreed. "You think Jake knows?"

"I know Jake knows. He's been chewing himself up because he passed out and let Dahl buy her. Jake's all right."

"Yeah," Peggy said. She thought about Jake. "Maybe this isn't such a bad country after all."

"It's just new," Frank said. "Pretty soon we'll be so civilized, we'll be unrecognizable."

"Look," Peggy said from the window. "Heartache's putting up a sign." She squinted. "Elect a Sheriff. Bring Law to Dawson."

"This meeting will come to order. That means shut up." Heartache had brought his hammer with him, and he whacked it three times until the audience paid attention.

"Now it's been proposed that we elect ourselves a sheriff here, so we got some guidelines, so to speak, and a legal way to lock up miscreants and riffraff."

"You lock up the riffraff, you ain't going to have no citizens!" someone shouted.

"If the population doesn't come to order, I will eject it," Heartache said. "Now Frank Blake originated this idea, so I'm going to have him tell you why it's a good one."

Frank stood up. He hadn't expected to participate to this extent, but Heartache had collared him just before the meeting. As a man possibly suspected of dog stealing, Frank decided not to make waves. He surveyed the many faces, which appeared either expectant or hung over. "You all know what happened over Christmas. It's a sad thing when matters come to a pass like that on the Lord's day, and we might not have had this happen if we'd had real law in Dawson. We did our best with a citizens' court; but citizens aren't lawmen, and that's a heavy burden to lay on folks.

And it turns out those folks made the wrong decision."

The former jurors shuffled in their chairs.

"I'm not going to lay blame at anybody's door," Frank said. "The men did what they thought was best. We'll still have need of the institution of a jury trial. But a jury's decisions have to be followed up. If we'd had a lawman here, he could have done that. He'd have had the right to go out to Dahl's cabin and a right to see how things were going there. Then we might not have one corpse laid out at the undertaker's and most likely another one out in the woods somewhere without even a Christian burial."

Everyone nodded in solemn agreement, aware of having done their duty by the book but still plagued by holes in the procedure—holes best plugged by a lawman, Frank assured them. Frank was beginning to get into the spirit of it.

"We need to elect one man and give him the right and the responsibility to see that folks play fair with one another out here—someone to protect us from one another if need be, someone to whom a citizen can go for help." Frank began to put his back into it. "Someone with grit and perseverance, to jail the miscreant and aid the distraught."

"Hear, hear!" Someone shouted.

"That's right! We need a sheriff!"

"Hallelujah!" The last interjection was slightly slurred, and someone else muttered, "Shut up, you dumb cluck. You ain't in church."

"We need a man of integrity! A man of courage!

A strong man with nerves of steel!" Step right up and see the reptile show!

"All in favor vote aye," Heartache said.

"Aye!"

"Now who's going to run for sheriff?"

An utter silence fell. And the people looked around with anticipation.

"We can't elect a sheriff if nobody runs for office," Heartache said. "You goons have got to nominate somebody."

"I nominate you!"

"You can't nominate me. I'm conducting the meeting."

"What's that got to do with it?"

"I nominate Bill Smith!"

"Well, I don't accept, and I nominate you."

"Blake! Let's nominate Blake!"

"Oh, no, you don't," Frank said. Maybe he'd been a little too eloquent. He began to regret his talent for oratory.

"Do you all mean to tell me that not one man in this town is willing to do his civic duty and be the sheriff?" Heartache demanded.

"I didn't notice you volunteering!"

"How are we going to have an election if nobody'll run?"

"Hold it anyway. The man that gets the most votes has to take the job."

Heartache scratched his head. He looked at Smith. "Is that legal?"

"I guess it's legal if we vote that it is," Smith replied.

"But what if the winner doesn't accept?" Frank asked.

"The winner has to accept. That's what we all vote on now. We all vote that if any one of us wins the election, he'll take the job. Otherwise, we aren't going to get a sheriff. Now which do you want? Law and order or anarchy?"

The people all looked at one another again. There were a lot of citizens in Dawson. The odds of someone other than themselves winning were pretty good. "Law and order!"

"Does everyone here agree to accept the position of sheriff of Dawson City should he be chosen by the will of the people?"

"Aye!"

The election was set for late February, to give the outlying miners a chance to hear the news and come in to vote. There was some protest over that on the grounds that anyone who didn't have to run the risk of winning shouldn't get to vote; but the majority felt that the more voters, the better odds of losing. They thus agreed to count votes from all comers.

Frank went back to his diggings, even though Heartache protested that if he wasn't in the public eye, no one would remember to vote for him. That's exactly what I have in mind, Frank thought, hitching up his dogs.

The citizens of Dawson set about proving their own personal irresponsibility and ineligibility, and campaigning after their fashion—for one another. Posters went up advising citizens to Vote For Bill

Smith—A Man With Legal Training. Bill Smith snatched them down and pasted up his own, Heartache Johnson, A Proven Leader. Finally Heartache had to call another meeting to prohibit the defacing of election posters. After that they proliferated until every available surface was covered. Unable to take their own posters down, reluctant candidates concentrated on putting up as many other names as they could. The town's only printing press ran overtime, and Peggy wondered uneasily if Frank ought to have taken off like that. There were a lot of Vote For Blake posters.

Frank looked at them, aghast, on election eve. Out of sight had not proved to be out of mind.

"You can't take them down," Peggy warned. "They made a rule."

Frank went out and commissioned three dozen posters for Heartache Johnson and another two dozen for Bill Smith. Bill seemed to have the edge, due to Heartache's ability to pay his printing bills with free drinks in the Daybreak. It seemed only fair to even things up.

Judging by the crowd in Dawson City, every outlying sourdough had gotten the word of the election. Whether or not they much wanted a sheriff, any gathering was a break in the winter doldrums and not to be passed up. In the Yukon, winter desperation might drive men to any lengths for the sight of a human face. Even strangers from as far away as Forty Mile made the trip just to see the fun. Trappers whom no one had laid eyes on in months suddenly popped up, snowshoeing in to stare at the lights of Dawson and mutter that it was becoming a danged metropolis.

"Are we going to let them vote?" the candidates wondered uneasily, and Heartache, who was getting worried about his possible success, said absolutely: one man, one vote. In fact, as the candidate in favor of progress, he insisted on it. Trappers hated progress, he confided to his bartender. That ought to sour them on him.

"If you ask me, you got a real loose cannon here," the bartender said, mopping the counter top. He didn't care; nobody had put up posters for him. Still, a sheriff's saloon might improve customers' manners some. The bartender was tired of breaking up fistfights. "Maybe you'll win," he said with hope.

"Go to hell," Heartache muttered.

Voters lined up at the polls early the next morning and filed through the lantern-lit meeting hall to cast their ballots. When Lawyer Smith spotted a rival candidate who, he claimed, had been through once already, he got an indelible pen and began marking palms with it.

"Are you accusing honest citizens of cheating?" the candidate demanded.

"Not if I don't see any more black X's," Smith said. "Now get out of here. You've voted enough."

Frank, who had managed to vote twice before anyone took notice, went back to Peggy's to await the results. He felt reasonably sure of a landslide for Heartache Johnson, on the basis of a straw poll he had taken at the door.

"Well, nobody who was going to vote for you would tell you," Peggy said.

"Maybe I should have just stuck with Heartache," Frank muttered. "I may have diluted the vote with Smith."

"I might have mentioned that if you'd asked me first," Peggy remarked, grinning. "But seeing you didn't even bother to let women vote, I guess you figure we can't add." She didn't seem particularly offended.

"What makes you so cheerful?"

"I've got a secret," Peggy said. "Look here." She pulled a tattered envelope from her apron pocket. "Fellow from down toward Forty Mile came looking for me while you were out. Said some young kid had paid him good to bring me this. Then he just took off again."

"Young kid?" Frank pulled the single sheet of smudged paper from the envelope, and suddenly he grinned, too. "Lulie!"

Dear Peg,
Me and the dogs made it to Forty Mile, tomorrow we're going to get across the border where there is a camp I hear, and sit tight til spring. Nobody knows I got the m. or I am a g. so I will be alright. You are a true friend, you and Frank, thank you for the Christmas tree. Best regards from your friend, L.

"I've been thinking she was dead somewhere,"

452

Peggy said. "I've been saying Hail Marys for her. I can't tell you what a load off my mind this is."

"I wouldn't stop the Hail Marys just yet," Frank said. "She's got a long way to go."

"She's tougher than I knew," Peggy said. "I still can't imagine it. It's like there was a whole other person down under there, and it finally just busted loose. People are a mystery."

"Life's a mystery," Frank said. He slid his hands around Peggy's waist. She seemed to have shed the shell of absentminded distraction she had worn since Lulie took off. "Certain aspects of it require constant investigation," he murmured in her ear. She snuggled against him, and relief over Lulie translated itself in a quick, sparked moment of need for each other. She didn't even tell him to shut the dogs in the bathhouse. Frank tumbled her into bed, pulling the blankets over them to shut out the roar from the meeting hall up the street. Those yahoos would be at it all night.

It was four in the morning when the yahoos pounded on the door. Peggy, just drifting into sleep, poked Frank with a finger. Frank put the pillow over his head.

"Blake!"

Peggy tried subterfuge. "Go away! He's not here."

"He is, too! Blake!"

"They'll knock the door down." Peggy got up and put her wool wrapper on.

"Oh, God." Frank climbed out of bed and put

on his underwear. He shoved the dogs away from the door.

"Open up! We got news!"

Frank dragged the door open and found a torchlit crowd milling outside. More shouting voices could be heard in the distance.

"Do you know what time it is?"

"We got news!" Jake's ceremonial top hat bobbed above the crowd. He waved a tattered newspaper.

"Being as you're our new sheriff, we thought you ought to know." Heartache gave him a wicked grin.

"Congratulations." Bill Smith pumped his hand.

Dawson's only preacher coughed portentously. He eyed Frank's underwear and Peggy's wrapper. "As a man of the law, your duty now is to lead an upright life."

Hands reached out and hauled the preacher away before Frank could seize on a chance to disqualify himself.

"I want a recount!" Frank demanded.

"You aren't going to get one now. Everybody's too riled up. Listen to this!" Heartache grabbed Jake's newspaper and held it up to the torchlight. "The damned Spanish have gone and blown up one of our battleships! Right in Havana Harbor!"

"What?" Frank grabbed the paper from Heartache.

"I expect we're at war by now. As an American citizen, Blake, it's your duty to stand up for law

454

and justice against the oppressor. Just put your hand on this Bible."

"We don't have any Spaniards up here," Frank protested.

"You never know when we're going to get some. Anyway, you are duly elected, and you aren't going to weasel out of it." Heartache grabbed Frank's hand and stuck it on the Bible.

"You want me to hold him down?" someone asked helpfully.

Frank stared at the newspaper. War. It seemed very far away, almost impossibly far. The thought spun across his mind that his father would be in it. Then Jake took the newspaper back, and the torchlit crowd came sharply into focus, with Peggy's red hair and red plaid wrapper blazing like competing bonfires at the perimeter. She slipped a hand through his arm, and Cuba and the country of his childhood receded farther, spinning out into the night until he could hardly see them through the wheel of the northern stars. Frank rested his hand on the Bible.

"Repeat after me," Heartache said. "I, Frank Blake . . ."

Author's Note

For inspiration and some great stories, I am indebted to my brother-in-law, Edward Peatow of Guerneville, California, who once ran away with the circus.

For the reader interested in the beginnings of the birth-control movement in this country, I recommend Women's Body, Woman's Right by Linda Gordon and From Private Vice to Public Virtue by James Reed.

Much of the information on cocaine use—no new problem, it would seem—came from Cocaine by John C. Flynn and The American Disease by David F. Musto, M.D.

The saga of Charley, the guinea pigs, and the corpse is borrowed from the true-life adventures of Dr. Victor Heiser, who was assigned to the Marine Hospital Service at the turn of the century. He recorded his memoirs in An American Doctor's Odyssey.

Thanks also to my editorial support staff at Book Creations Inc.: Laurie Rosin, senior project editor; Marjie Weber, copyeditor, and Donna Marsh, keyboardist.